Dawn of a New Day

James Preston Hardison

authorHOUSE®

AuthorHouse™
1663 Liberty Drive
Bloomington, IN 47403
www.authorhouse.com
Phone: 1 (800) 839-8640

Published by AuthorHouse

ISBN: 978-1-5462-6746-1 (sc)
ISBN: 978-1-5462-6745-4 (e)

Library of Congress Control Number: 2018913281

Print information available on the last page.

This book is printed on acid-free paper.

Contents

DEDICATION

This novel is dedicated to my wife, Ann.
My children
Grandchildren
Great-grandchildren
Sister Ruby

To the people that have read my novels and told me how much they enjoyed reading
my work, thank you all!
James Preston Hardison

Chapter 1

The chapel at Braden's Funeral Home was filled to capacity as friends, relatives, customers and acquaintances came to pay their last respect to John Miller. Before his untimely death, John owned and operated a neighborhood grocery store. It was four nights ago at closing time that he was robbed and killed by a lone gunman wearing a ski mask.

It was an emotional time for all present as they observed twelve-year old Danny Miller standing in front of his father's casket with tears streaming down his face. His face was pale, him looking at the lifeless body of his father.

A short time later Beth Miller, Henry and Delores Miller, Danny's grandparents walked quietly to where Danny was standing. Henry placed his hand on Danny's right shoulder and whispered, "Son, your father's funeral is about to start, I think we should go back to our seats and sit with your grandmother."

Tearfully, Danny turned toward his grandfather and whispered, "Grandpa, it's not right that my daddy is dead! Why would someone want to shoot my daddy?"

"Son, I have no idea why the robber wanted to hurt your daddy. The law is trying to determine who killed him."

Danny turned and gently placed his hand against his father's face. Leaning over the casket, he whispered softly, "Daddy, I love you more than I can even say. I will always keep you in my memory! Danny wiped his watery eyes, "I promise you right here and now--------one way or other, I'll find out who your killer is. I'll kill the no-good rascal!" Henry took Danny's hand and they returned to their front row seats.

Trembling and in tears, Beth stayed in front of her husband's casket for one last look at the man that she had loved since she was in the ninth grade at Bellevue High School. She placed her hand gently against her husband's face, expressing her unyielding love and devotion. Sensing that his daughter was about to faint, George Eason hurried to assist Beth back to her seat.

All was quite as Reverend Jake Stryker walked up to the podium. For several seconds he looked downward as though he was searching for the proper words to speak. He looked up and said, "This is a very sad time for John Miller's family, relatives, neighbors and his friends that are gathered here today. However, I want to remind everyone here that John was a man of God. That being said, he is in Heaven this very day with Jesus Christ our Lord. He was a hard working family man that seemed to like everyone that he came in contact with. He always had a smile when he talked with anyone. Many of you sitting here today were helped by him in one way or another. I don't remember one single Sunday in eleven years that he failed to attend church services at Grayson Baptist Church. That's how long I've been preaching there. We often ask ourselves why God allows certain things to happen to us or our loved ones, but we never seem to come up with an appropriate answer. Only God himself knows the answer to that question. Let's all bow our heads and go to our Lord in prayer. Lord, you more than anyone know that John Miller was a man of God. Please bless his heart-broken family. Allow peace and tranquility to infiltrate their lives. Lord, give them the strength and courage to carry on as time passes by. Please assure his wife and son Danny that they have an opportunity to rejoin their loved one after their lives have ended here on earth. For the others sitting here today, let John Miller's life be a role model for them to follow. Lord, bless his young son that always thought of his father as the greatest man on earth, his buddy and his best friend. Amen."

After Reverend Stryker took his seat, Lora Gaskins, a close friend of John and Beth sang two songs, 'Lord I'm Coming Home' and 'Amazing Grace'.

In tears herself, Beth placed her arms around Danny as he tried hard to sniff back his tears. Henry placed his hand on Danny's shoulder when Reverend Jake Stryker asked everyone to stand at the completion of the service.

Twenty-five minutes later, all was quiet at Cedar Oaks Cemetery as family members of John Miller took their seats underneath the spacious canopy that hovered above the gravesite. Before taking his seat, Danny laid a pretty red rose on his father's coffin. Tearfully, he stared toward his father's coffin as though the world had ended for him. After taking his seat next to his mother, she whispered, "I love you very, very much."

At the close of the service, Henry Miller could no longer hold back the sadness that he felt for his son. Tears flowed freely from his eyes. His wife, Delores passed him a tissue to dry his eyes. George Eason, Danny's other grandfather placed his hand on Henry's back. "Henry, we all loved your son more than I can possibly describe. Please let Dora and me know if there is anything I can do for you or John's family."

Henry wiped his watery eyes. "I appreciate those kind words, George. You and Dora have always been there for John's family whenever you were needed. Anyway, I appreciate you saying those kind words at this difficult time."

Later that day, several cars were parked in Beth Miller's yard. Some of the people were close friends and neighbors of John and Beth, others included both sets of Danny's grandparents. There was an abundant amount of food on Beth's dinner table, donated by family and friends.

While everyone else was talking or listening to others inside the house, Danny walked quietly into the family garage. He placed his hand on the fifteen foot bass boat that he and his father had used many times on their fishing trips. He opened his father's tackle box and took out a special, top-water fishing bait. He remembered the time his father caught a nine-pound, four-ounce bass using that bait. After meticulously placing the bait back into the tackle box, Danny dropped to his knees in tears. From inside the kitchen his mother heard him crying. She hurried into the garage; she placed her arms around her son. His mother whispered, "Danny, it hurts me greatly when you cry!"

"Mother, it's not fair that Daddy is dead! How will we manage with him gone? I tell you one thing right now------ you're not going to operate that store and get yourself killed!"

"No, son, I'm not going to keep the store. I'll put it up for sale as soon as possible. I have a good job with Madison Electronics and I make enough money to pay our bills and put food on our table. Please come inside and talk with your grandparents and our other friends and relatives. Your Grandfather Henry would be more than happy to take you golfing or sight-seeing whenever you care to go."

"I didn't see Grandmother Delores crying at the funeral or the cemetery," remarked Danny, curiously. "Mother, it was her son that lay dead in that coffin."

"Make no mistake about it; Mrs. Miller's grievances were kept inside of her. Quite often it's difficult for older individuals to cry out loud like younger people do. She loved John very, very much. In fact, John's parents were devastated when they heard that he had been killed during that robbery."

"Mother, what was the very last thing Daddy said to you before he was killed?" Danny asked, inquisitively.

"He said that he loved me very, very much."

"What was the last thing he said about me?"

"His exact words were that you were the finest son that any father could ever have hoped for. Danny, your father loved you more than I could ever explain! His only regret was that we couldn't have another child just like you."

"Doggone, Mother, now you're crying!"

"I'll be alright," Beth answered. "Let's you and I go inside and have some of that food our neighbors brought over."

"I'm not very hungry."

"I believe I could smile a little, if you were to eat something," Beth commented.

"In that case-----I'll try to eat something."

John Miller's death happened during the second week of Danny's summer vacation from Clarkson Middle School. Danny was promoted with top honors from Mrs. Alice Keller's sixth grade class. All during the school year he was looking forward to fishing and having a grand time with his father.

Beth Miller was given two weeks leave from Madison Electronics to take care of personal business and to get her life back to some degree of normalcy. Two days after her husband was buried, Beth contracted with a local real estate agency to have her business property appraised. The appraisal would include four acres of land, grocery store, stock and equipment.

Before his death, John had three employees; two-part time and one full time employee that worked at his store. The full time employee was Jason Edwards. Jason was experienced in all aspects of the grocery business. Whenever John was off with his son somewhere, Jason operated the grocery store as if it was his own. Jason was home with the flu the night that John was gunned down. Percy Johnson and Dell Carter were part time workers at John's grocery store. Their primary jobs were to keep the store shelves stocked with incoming products. Working at the store was a secondary job for each of them.

Detective Randy Johnson rang Beth Miller's doorbell on the third day following her husband's funeral. Danny answered the door. "Son, is your mother home?" The detective asked.

"Yes sir, she's in the laundry room."

"My name is Randy Johnson. I'm with the sheriff's department."

"I remember you, Mr. Johnson. Your daughter is named Shelia. Remember, she introduced me to you at school one day when you were there. My name is Danny. Shelia and I are in the same grade."

"Yes, I do remember now. Son, I'm very sorry about what happened to your father."

"I appreciate that. I hope you get that murdering scoundrel that shot my Daddy. I'll go get my mother." He hurried toward the laundry room. "Mother, Detective Randy Johnson is at our front door! He works for Sheriff Alan Hicks!"

"Is he wearing a sheriff's uniform?" Beth asked.

"No ma'am, he doesn't have on a uniform."

Danny followed his mother to their front door. Detective Johnson was looking toward the front yard as Beth opened her door. "Danny informed me that you're some kind of law officer," said Beth.

"That's true, Mrs. Miller. My name is Randy Johnson. I'm a detective with the County Sheriff's office." He took out his wallet and showed her his identification and his detective badge.

"When Danny told me that you work for Sheriff Alan Hicks I was curious why you weren't wearing a sheriff's uniform."

"Sheriff Detectives are not required to wear uniforms all the time while they're on duty," the detective answered. "Mrs. Miller, if I may I would like to go inside your house and ask you a few questions concerning your husband's death."

Beth motioned for him to come inside. She and Danny lead him into their living room. "Before you start asking me questions, would you care for something to drink?" Beth asked. "I've got ice tea in the refrigerator and a fresh pot of coffee."

"Ma'am, you're very kind. If it's not too much trouble I will have a cup of coffee."

"How do you like your coffee?"

"Just the coffee----please, I don't use sweeteners or cream."

"Mother, I can get him a cup of coffee," said Danny. "I'll bring you a cup, too. I already know you want one pack of sweetener in your coffee." Danny walked quietly toward the kitchen.

"Mrs. Miller, you have a mighty nice son."

"Thank you for saying so. I don't think Danny will ever get over the death of his father. John and my son were extremely close to each other."

"Mrs. Miller, Danny may never get over the death of his father, but time heals all wounds. There will come a time of acceptance for you, as well as Danny to move on with your lives. According to all the good things I've heard about your husband, I'm sure he would want nothing but total happiness for you and his son."

"Well, here's the coffee," said Danny. He handed his mother her cup, and then he handed the detective his cup.

"Mrs. Miller, I'll get right to the point as to why I'm here," Detective Johnson remarked.

"Well for one thing-----the robber was well camouflaged and wearing a hood over his face. Two things the perpetrator did that don't make any sense at all. The robber did take cash out of the register, but he didn't take any money that was lying on the counter within three feet of the cash register. I guess your husband had aid a stack of bills there at closing time while he was counting his receipts for the day. Unless the robber just happened to overlook the money, he should have seen it lying on the counter. There was about three hundred dollars in that stack. By the way, that money will be returned to you in a few days. Have you been back into your grocery store since your husband was killed?"

"No, John's father locked the store for me following my husband's death, but neither he nor I have gone back inside it. I might never go into that store again. I told Jason Edwards, one of our employees to keep the store closed for now. As quickly as I can, I'm putting it up for sale through a local realtor."

"Mrs. Miller, everyone in the neighborhood knew how much your husband loved you and his son. Do you know someone named Mr. Joe Goodman?"

"Yes, Mr. Goodman is one of our customers and a good friend of my entire family. Why do you ask if I know Mr. Goodman?"

"According to your store's surveillance camera, Mr. Goodman was the last customer in your store before a robber came in and killed your husband. Mr. Goodman swears that the family portrait of you, Danny and John was hanging on the wall that night he left your store. Providing that's true, why on earth would a robber be interested in taking your family portrait with him?"

"Are you certain that it's gone?" Beth asked, surprised.

"I'm very certain! At first, after talking to Mr. Goodman, I thought it might have fallen to the floor or something during the robbery, but that didn't happen."

"I don't understand!" Beth remarked. "I have no idea why someone would take that portrait. Does it make any sense to you?"

"Mrs. Miller, we don't have a clue to that question. In fact, the whole scenario of that robbery doesn't seem just right," Detective Johnson responded. "As a general rule, robbers don't leave any money behind that is noticeable to the naked eye. Danny, will you do me a great big favor and go outside for a few minutes. I would like to ask your mother a few personal questions."

"Its' okay, son," said Beth, "how about going outside and watering my flowers for me, especially those beside the utility barn." Danny left the house. "What kind of personal questions are you going to ask me?"

"Mrs. Miller, we don't think for a moment that you had anything to do with your husband's murder. What I'm trying to determine is whether you've noticed anyone that may have shown some interest in you at any given time."

"Detective, I've loved my husband from the first day I laid eyes on him. That love has never faded since we've been married. I've never shown any interest in any man other than my husband."

"Mrs. Miller, I wholeheartedly believe you, but that doesn't mean that someone is not interested in you. In fact, I don't even know if the robber even knows who you are. Perhaps we'll never know why the robber took the portrait off the wall. All I wanted to ask you is this, has any man been overly nice to you in the last few weeks or months that may be perceived as flirting with you? If my hunch is correct, there's a killer out there that was willing to kill your husband to get him out of the way. That being said, sooner or later a man will try to befriend you and your son. Mrs. Miller, I hope my theory is wrong, but if true-----your life and that of your son could be in danger if that person determines that he can't ever become a part of your life."

"Detective, why would anyone kill my husband because they might like me somehow?"

"Mrs. Miller, I do hope you take what I'm about to say in the right way, but you're an incredibly beautiful woman. Men have been known to kill for far less beauty than yours. I just want you to know that my office and I will do everything possible to solve your husband's murder. I want you to do me a big favor."

"What's that?" Beth asked.

"Let me know if someone starts showing a great deal of interest in you over the next few days or weeks. Mrs. Miller, will you do that for me?"

"Yes, Detective, I'll do that." The detective handed Beth a card with his name and telephone number on it in case she ever needed to call him.

"Mrs. Miller, I appreciated you not becoming irate when I asked you those personal questions," remarked Detective Johnson. "I told Sheriff Hicks that you would probably run me out of your house when I started asking you that line of questions."

"More than anything, I want my husband's murder solved. I honestly believe that if Danny knew who killed his father he would wind up in big trouble."

"Why do you say that?"

"At my husband's funeral, I heard my son vow that he would kill the man that shot his father. Officer, I feel certain that Danny wouldn't hesitate to do just that!"

"Mrs. Miller, do you have guns in your house?"

"Yes, my husband owned a gun cabinet full of guns. Some of them are pistols and others are shotguns and rifles. John used to take Danny to the woods so they could do some target shooting. Danny knows how to shoot all of them."

"Is the gun cabinet locked?"

"Yes, my husband always kept it locked when he wasn't cleaning or using the guns. The sheriff's dept returned his keys, personal effects and wallet to me a couple days ago."

"My advice to you is this-----don't let Danny get his hands on the gun-cabinet keys. I'll keep you posted on any progress we make concerning your husband's murder."

Danny hurried inside the house after Detective Johnson drove out of the driveway. Beth was sitting on the couch when he came into the living room. "Mother, what did the detective want to talk about?" Danny asked. "You look like you're worried about something!"

"I'm not worried. I was just thinking about your father."

"You still haven't told me what the detective wanted to know."

"The detective just wanted to ask me a few personal questions."

"Mother, why did that murdering scoundrel take our family portrait from the store?"

"The detective asked me the same thing. I have no idea why anyone would want to do that! Anyway, the detective told me that was kind of unusual for a robber to do something like that."

"Mother, you're crying again. It makes me real sad to see you cry."

Beth wiped her watery eyes with a tissue. "I miss your father so much!"

Danny placed his arms around his mother and tearfully responded, "You've still got me."

A big smile came across Beth Miller's face as she hugged her son. "That's true, and I'm eternally grateful that I do have you with me. I don't think I could take being by myself at a time like this."

"What's going to happen to Daddy's three employees since his store is closed?" Danny asked.

"The two part-time workers still have their primary jobs. They won't be hurt too badly from losing their jobs with the grocery store. However, Mr. Jason Edwards doesn't have another job. While he's finding another job, I'm going to pay him a full month's salary. I'll give the part-time workers a week's pay. I'm hoping whoever buys the grocery store will retain all three of them in their employment. However, there's no guarantee of that. I wish I could do more for them, but I'm not financially able to keep paying them with the store closed."

"I feel sorry for them," Danny commented. "Mr. Edwards has a son about my age."

"I'm sure everything will work out for them in the end," Beth remarked.

"Mother, do you know what I would like to do?"

"No, what would you like to do?"

"I would like to go to granddaddy's farm tomorrow morning. I would like to spend the entire day with Grandpa George and Grandma Dora."

"That sounds like a fantastic idea, but why don't you ever want to go visit with John's parents?"

"Mother, I love granddaddy Henry and Grandma Delores as well, but they live in the city. Your mother and father, Grandpa George and Grandma Dora owns a big farm. They have lots of animals for me to see. Do you understand what I'm saying, Mother?'

"Yes, Danny-------I suppose I do."

Chapter 2

George Eason was gathering eggs from his hen nests when Beth and Danny drove into his yard at 9:00 the next morning. Seeing his granddaddy inside the chicken pen, Danny ran to him.

"Grandpa, we've come to stay the whole day with you and grandma!" Danny said, excitedly.

"That's wonderful, son. We'll have a great time doing things together while you're here. Take this basket of eggs to your grandmother while I go feed old Betsy and her two calves."

"I thought old Betsy just had one calf."

"That's true, but I had another cow to die after she gave birth to a pretty red calf. I thought I might lose that cow's calf too, but old Betsy took to that little calf just like it was her own. Now scoot along with those eggs; I'll let you feed my three horses when you get back."

"Oh boy, I'll be right back!" Danny voiced, excitedly.

Beth was talking with her mother when Danny came in carrying the basket of eggs. His grandmother gave him a big hug. "Mother, Grandpa is going to let me feed his horses!" He headed for the door.

"Danny, tell your grandfather not to be too long," said Dora, "tell him that breakfast will be done in fifteen minutes."

"Okay, Grandma, I'll tell him." Danny closed the door behind him, and then he started running toward the horse stable.

"Mother, aren't you cooking breakfast a little later than usual?" Beth asked.

"I suppose I am," Dora answered. "Since Henry is semi-retired we seem to sleep a little later. I want you and Danny to have breakfast with us this morning."

"I'm not very hungry. I had a small bowl of corn flakes about five o'clock this morning."

"Five o'clock this morning! Why were you up at that time of the morning?" Dora asked, curiously.

"Since John was murdered I can't get enough sleep. Last night I had a terrible nightmare."

"What kind of nightmare?" Dora inquired.

"I dreamed that I walked into our grocery store and saw someone pointing a gun toward John as he lay on the floor. I screamed, and that's when the hooded individual turned toward me with his gun pointed toward my head. Suddenly, my husband made a moaning sound. The murderer quickly turned in John's direction as he lay on the floor bleeding. I ran out of the store as fast as I could. I thought I was going to be shot at any second. The next thing I knew my son was yelling, 'Mother!

Mother, please wake up!' Oh God, I don't know if I will make it or not with John gone!" Tears slid down Beth's face.

"Beth, you're crying------now look what I've caused!"

"It's not your fault, quite often I have these crying spells. Do you think I'll ever get over my husband's death?"

"Yes, I'm sure you will. John was our son-in-law and we thought the world of him. I, too, have the same kind of crying spells, but I really don't see how my crying solves anything. No matter how much I cry, your husband will still be dead. At sometime in the future, whether you like it or not, you'll have to go on with your life."

"Mother, what do you mean?".

"It's too soon to even talk about it now, but someday you'll find yourself a decent man to share the rest of your life with."

"Mother, the last thing in the world I'm interested in right now is a man!"

"And it should be the last thing on your mind right now, but time heals all wounds."

"What about wounds?" George asked, coming into the kitchen.

"Oh, nothing," remarked Dora. "Beth and I were just talking girl talk among ourselves."

"Grandma, I fed the horses all by myself," said Danny, smiling.

"Dora, I believe I'll teach Danny how to become a farmer."

"George Eason, you'll do no such thing! Danny is going to a wonderful college after he finishes high school. Farming is not as profitable as it used to be."

"Why is that?" Beth asked.

"The answer is very simple. Fertilizer, seeds, poisons, gas and farm equipment is much more expensive now. For example, chicken feed that used to be four or five dollars for a fifty pound bag is now twelve to fifteen dollars, depending on which kind is bought. The list goes on and on for other farm products."

"No wonder so many farmers are going out of business," Beth commented.

"I'll soon have a fine breakfast for all of us. George, take Danny out back and show him your new bass boat while I finish cooking breakfast."

"Grandpa, I didn't know you had a new bass boat!"

"I bought it about nine days ago. In fact, I haven't been fishing on it yet. How would you like to go with me to Borden's Lake one day next week?"

"I would love to do that!" They walked back inside of the house.

"Beth, are you alright?" George asked. "You look as though you've been crying."

"I'll be okay. I've got so many things on my mind right now since my husband was klled."

"What are you going to do about your grocery business?"

"Well, there's one thing for sure, Mother------I'm not about to operate it! I'm going to try to sell it. I've already turned it over to a realtor."

9

"What about the three individuals that worked with John?" Dora asked. "Do you suppose they'll be able to find another job?"

"Two of those employees were temporary workers. They already had full-time jobs working somewhere else. They were mostly hired to stock shelves. However, I am very concerned for our full time employee. His name is Jason Edwards. Daddy, do you know Mr. Edwards?"

"Yes, I certainly do know Jason. In fact, he has a son about Danny's age. You need not be concerned any longer about Jason Edwards being out of work."

"Why is that?" Beth asked, curiously.

"Jason Edwards is already employed at Smith Brothers Grocery near your home town. Garland Smith, co-owner of Smith Brothers Grocery, hired Jason Edwards to be the assistant manager of that big store."

"Don't those brothers own other stores in different towns?" Beth asked.

"Yes, as a matter of fact they do. I believe the Smith brothers own nine other grocery stores."

"Beth, you'll do just fine taking care of your monthly bills and anything else that happens to come along," Dora commented. "Danny, you're a growing boy; how many fried eggs should I cook for you?"

"Just two, Grandma. Mother, Grandpa is taking me fishing next week on his new boat!"

"He is?"

"Beth, why not bring Danny here sometime Sunday and let him stay with us to the following Sunday?" George asked.

"Is that what you want to do, Danny?"

"Yes, I sure would like to do that, provided its' okay with you!" He answered, smiling.

"That will be fine with me. Just make sure you don't fall out of daddy's boat."

"You know that I'm a good swimmer!"

"Danny, a lot of people are good swimmers, but some of them still drown in the water for various reasons," Beth commented.

"Your mother is absolutely right, Danny. One can never be too careful when they're in or around water."

"I know that, Grandpa. Have you ever known me to be careless when I was around water?"

"Danny, you're putting me in a bind when you ask me a question like that. Just tell your mother that you'll always be careful when you're in the water or out of the water."

"Grandpa, I thought you were my buddy."

"Danny, I am your buddy, but you wouldn't want me to tell an outright lie, would you?"

"Okay, Mother------I promise to be very careful from now on when I'm near the water, in the water or on the water, okay."

"I'm glad to hear you say that. Mother, you sure have cooked up a big breakfast," Beth commented.

"It might seem that way, but George and I have never been what you call light eaters. I want you and Danny to sit down and enjoy this food. After breakfast you and I will go into the living room so

I can show you what I bought for myself about two weeks ago. George wanted a boat, so I decided to get something for myself. George and Danny can go do whatever they want to."

"Danny, how would you like for us to ride my horses today?"

"Grandpa, I would love to do that! Will you let me ride the white one?" He asked, eagerly.

"Of course I will. You can even pretend that you're the Lone Ranger while you're riding Silver."

"Do you really have a horse named Silver?' Beth asked.

"Yes, I certainly do! I've got three horses, and they're named Silver, Lady and Gertrude."

"Gertrude!" Beth commented, smiling. "Why on earth did you name a horse Gertrude?"

"In many ways that horse reminds me of my seventh grade school teacher. Her name was Miss Gertrude Walls."

"Are you kidding me?"

"No, Beth----- I'm not kidding. That horse walks just like Miss Walls did, like she was sneaking up on you." Everyone at the table started laughing.

After breakfast, George motioned for Danny to follow him outside. When they got into the yard, Danny asked, "Grandpa, where are we going?"

"I'm going to saddle up Lady and Silver so we can go for a ride. Do you still want to ride the horses?"

"Yes sir, I sure do!" Danny answered with a big grin.

Henry saddled up the horses they were going to ride. Danny was a little nervous as he straddled his horse, but very excited that he was going to ride Silver. "Where are we headed this morning, Grandpa?"

"I thought we might ride down by my pond and see if Gretchen is still down there with her babies."

"Grandpa, you've got a name for just about everything! Who in tar nation is Gretchen?" Danny asked, with a puzzled look.

"Gretchen is my Mallard duck. She's got nine little baby chicks that follow her wherever she goes. She had twelve baby ducks when I first saw her in my pond."

"What happened to the other three?"

"I don't know whether a snake, turtle, hawk, or maybe a fox got them."

They arrived at Mr. Miller's pond about ten minutes later. They observed Gretchen in the middle of the pond, surrounded by her nine baby ducks. Suddenly, a big splash occurred in the water. "Grandpa, did you see that?"

"I sure did."

"Now there's only eight little ducks! What made that big splash?" Danny asked, curiously.

"That was a big bass that grabbed one of Gretchen's babies. I had no idea that bass were taking those little ducks."

"That was awful, Grandpa. Why don't that mother duck get her little ones out of that pond?"

11

"There are several reasons for that. First of all, ninety percent of their food is inside the pond. Secondly, those little ducks wouldn't last a day if they were to get out of the water."

"Why is that?"

"Because they would be in danger from foxes, hawks, opossums, owls, hawks, snakes, dogs, and cats"

"Grandpa, I know one thing!"

"What's that, Danny?"

"I sure wouldn't want to be a duck!" Danny answered, him shuddering.

"How would you like to ride over to the old George Wellington house? People say that old house is haunted. I didn't believe in ghosts, but one day I was riding by there and I heard a funny sound coming from that house."

"What do you suppose the sound was?" Danny asked.

"I have no idea what was making that sound, but it sure got my attention. Would you like to ride over there?"

"I sure would! How far is that old house from here?"

"It's a little over a mile from here. It will be a nice ride; we can ride across my farm and then across Mr. Jesse Week's farm until we get to the narrow road leading up to that old house."

They commenced riding across Mr. Miller's field. "Grandpa, why do people think that old house is haunted?"

"The story of this house goes back a long time ago. Anyway, from what I've heard, George Wellington was picking huckleberries in Vine Swamp on a Saturday morning. He was alone at the time, and Vine Swamp is a very big place. Sometime that day, Mr. Wellington was bitten by a rabid animal. No one knows whether it was a fox, raccoon or some other animal that bit him. He, apparently, got lost and became disoriented after being bitten; he remained in the swamp until he was rabid himself. No one knows how he got out of the swamp. Mr. Wellington came home and killed his entire family while they were sleeping."

"My God, Grandpa, what did he kill them with?"

"He used a hatchet; the same hatchet that he had taken with him to Vine Swamp. He killed his wife, two young sons, a thirteen year old daughter and his aging mother."

"How terrible, Grandpa! Why would he do such a thing to his own family?"

"Mr. Wellington was insane when he killed his family. What happened inside that house wasn't discovered until four days later. Judy Jones, a relative of Bertha Wellington opened the front door of the Wellington house. She screamed out loud, seeing the blood-soaked body lying on living room floor. She notified the law."

"Grandpa, how did Mr. Wellington die?"

"No one really knows, but rabies is probably what killed him. Now, do you still want to ride by the George Wellington house?"

"I don't think so! I think I'll stay away from that house as far as I can get! In fact, if I were to hear a weird sound coming from the Wellington house today it would unhinge my joints!" Danny commented, him shivering.

Three days later, Beth Miller's phone rang in the early afternoon. Beth picked up the phone; she was surprised to hear Mrs. Karen Roberson, her real estate agent's voice. "Mrs. Miller, I've got some great news for you! Your grocery store and surrounding property is being sold to a large grocery chain at the exact amount that you and I agreed on! They want to triple the size of the store! Isn't that great news?"

"That is wonderful news, Mrs. Roberson! That will be one less thing that I'll have to worry about. We've got a lot of perishable inventory in our store. How long before they can do something with those foods?"

"Mrs. Miller, the whole transfer process is being handled expeditiously. In fact, I have a certified check in my hand right now for the full amount that you and I agreed on. I assure you that the check is authentic. Do I have your permission that the company can remove your perishable goods to one of their other locations while we're completing the ownership process?"

"Yes, Mrs. Robinson that will be fine with me. When will they start expanding their new property?"

"I was informed that the store expansion would start shortly after the acquisition of your property. They'll have to remove everything inside your store before they can start the expansion process. Mrs. Miller, I'm deeply saddened by your husband's death. I hope they find that awful person that killed him."

"I appreciate you saying that, Mrs. Roberson. Please give me a call when it's time for you and me to meet at the lawyer's office."

"I'll be glad to."

"Who was that on the phone?" Danny asked, curiously.

"It was my real estate agent. They've sold our grocery store. It's hard to believe that they sold it so quickly."

"How much money will we get?"

"Well, we're selling more than the store. We're selling several acres of land that the store is sitting on and everything inside the store."

"I still don't know how much money we'll be getting," Danny responded.

"Three hundred and forty-seven thousand dollars after the real estate agency gets their percentage."

"Gosh, that sounds like a lot of money! How come we're getting so much?"

"Our store is located in a prime location, according to Mrs. Roberson."

"Mother, are we still going to Grandpa George's house Sunday?"

"Yes, I promised you that I would take you."

"There's just one thing," Danny remarked.

"What's that?"

"I hate to leave you home by yourself."

"That's sweet of you to say that, but I'll be just fine. Are you still having those bad dreams like you were telling me earlier?'

"Yes, sometimes two during the same week. Mother, at times I'm so sad that I don't know what to do. It's like I have emptiness inside my body. I know it's because my father is dead. Do you think I'll ever be happy like I used to be?"

Beth placed her arms around her son. "Of course you will. Your father's death bothers me a great deal as well. However, your grandmother tells me that time will heal that wound for each of us. Let's just be thankful that we have each other. Danny, I love you more than anything. When you go to your granddaddy's house I want you to be careful around all his equipment, and especially around his livestock. Do you know that he's got a big bull in a pen by himself?"

"Yes, Mother, I know about Big Brutus."

"You're telling me that the bull's name is Big Brutus?"

"Grandpa did say old Brutus is a little on the mean side," Danny answered, smiling.

"Well, there's one thing for certain------you had better stay away from that rascal!" Beth demanded.

Beth took her son to his grandparent's house on Sunday as she had promised him. She packed enough clothes in his suit case to last him until the following Sunday. She told her mother that she could only stay a few minutes that morning. "Beth, I hate to see you leave so soon after driving twenty minutes from your house!" Dora remarked. "Why are you in such a hurry this morning?"

"I don't want to miss going to church today."

"Grayson Baptist Church is a sizeable church," said George. "They might not even miss you this morning."

"That's true, but I know someone who would surely miss me if I were not in church this morning?'

"Who might that be?" Her father asked.

"God would know for sure! John and I enjoyed attending church on Sundays. I believe with all my heart and soul that he is in Heaven right now or at least his spirit is."

"Beth, before you go, I want you to take a container of brownies with you. I baked them last night while your father watched that fake wrestling match. Besides, when you were a little girl you simply loved my freshly baked brownies."

"Grandma, may I have a brownie?" Danny asked.

"You surely can. I'll pour you some fresh milk to have with your brownie. George got the milk from one of our cows this morning." Dora handed Beth her container of brownies.

"I want you to enjoy your visit with your grandparents, but I want you to be exceptionally careful around your granddaddy's farm equipment. I, especially, want you to steer clear of daddy's mean bull!" Beth leaned over and gave her son a loving hug. Afterwards, she hugged her mother and father.

"I love you, Mother," him placing his arms around her waist.

"I love you as well." Beth turned toward her father. "Daddy, I hope you and Danny have a swell time together."

"You can count on that. We're going to have a busy week, riding horses, going fishing, and driving my go-kart."

"Daddy, don't tell me that you've got a go-kart!"

"Beth, Henry drives around in that go-kart just like he was thirteen years old," said Dora.

"Mother, do you want me to catch you some fish?" Danny asked, smiling.

"Of course I do-------providing, you can catch some fish that don't require scaling, skinning, or cutting them open with a knife," she smiled.

"Beth, it's good to see you smile again."

"Daddy, I appreciate you saying that. Well, I've got to go or I won't have time to get ready for church." Beth waved farewell as she drove her car out of the driveway.

A few minutes later, Danny and his grandparents were sitting in the living room. "What are you thinking about?" George asked. "You act as though you're about to cry."

"I was thinking about a fishing trip that my daddy and I were on."

"Why don't you tell your grandmother and me about that trip?"

"Daddy and I got up early that morning because he planned to take me to Sheffield's Lake as he had promised me. My daddy always did what he promised someone. Before we left that morning, Daddy cooked us some eggs, rice and smoked sausage. Mother was still in bed when we left for the lake that morning."

"I guess about this time you were getting very excited about your fishing trip," Dora remarked.

"I sure was excited. It was one of the happiest days of my life being with my daddy, and heading toward Sheffield's Lake. It took about an hour for us to get to that big lake. We quickly launched his boat into the water. Afterwards, Daddy parked his van and trailer where he was supposed to. We got into his boat and then headed toward an island that's inside the lake. Near that island is where we started fishing. Grandpa, I caught the first two fish."

"What kind were they?" Henry asked.

"One was a bass and the other one was a catfish. The bass was too little to keep, but the catfish went into our cooler. It was about an hour later that Daddy caught that big bass that you've seen mounted on our wall." Danny lowered his head in despair. "My daddy will never be able to take me fishing again." Tears came into Danny's eyes.

George handed Danny a tissue to dry his eyes. Dora and I are saddened by your father's death more than you could ever know. Crying or grieving often helps to relieve sorrow or sadness in the living, but it won't ever bring back the dead. Your father left you with the same thing he did us----- precious memories. As often as you can, remember those times when your father was with you and the love you and he had for each other."

"It makes me so sad that he got killed the way he did! I know this might not sound right, but I would like to shoot the man that killed my daddy!"

"Son, you wouldn't want to shoot anyone, would you?" George asked, deeply concerned about his grandson's remark.

"Just as sure as my name is Danny Miller, I would kill him and not regret it one bit! That man took away half of all the happiness that I will ever have!"

"Danny, I'm surprised to hear you talk like this?" Dora remarked. "What if your mother ever heard you say something like this?"

"I've already told her the same thing more than once! I hate the man that killed my daddy!"

"Danny, try not to think about how he got killed," Dora advised. "Only think about the good times you had with your father like your grandfather just told you. You came here this week to have a good time, didn't you?"

"Yes." Danny answered.

"George, why don't you take Danny fishing tomorrow, instead of Tuesday? There's no rain in the forecast for the next several days."

"I guess I could do that. How about it, son? Would you like to go fishing tomorrow?"

Danny wiped his watery eyes and answered, "I sure would, Grandpa!"

By 7:20 the following morning, George and Danny were on their way to Borden's Lake. George noticed that Danny seemed to be in serious thought about something. "You seem to have something on your mind, Danny. Is it something that you would like to share with your old grandpa?"

"I was wondering why you and grandma only had one daughter. It seems that parents would always have an extra son or daughter just in case something happened to one of their children."

"I don't believe I thoroughly understand your question." George answered.

"Well, it seems to me that if parents had an extra child or two, it wouldn't hurt as bad if one of them got killed or died."

"That's not true, Danny. It would hurt parents just as bad if one of their children died or got killed, no matter how many children they had. Now, I have a question for you."

"What is the question?"

"Which one of us will catch the largest fish?"

"That would be me, Grandpa!"

"I have one additional question. Who will catch the most fish?"

"That would be me, as well!" Danny answered, him smiling.

George and Danny arrived at Borden's Lake at 9:20 that morning. Danny assisted his grandpa in launching the boat into the water. They and their fishing equipment were in the boat fifteen minutes later. Danny started baiting his hooks as his grandpa steered the boat toward a small island in the middle of the lake.

When they stopped near the island fifteen minutes later, Danny was the first one to start fishing.

"Are you using a cricket or worm?" Henry asked.

"I put a big night crawler worm on my hook. I'm after a big one, Grandpa."

"Well, I've got a little advice for you, young man."

"What's that?" Danny asked, him looking toward his grandfather.

"Look for your cork," said Henry, smiling.

"Where is my cork?" Danny asked, excitedly.

"The last time I saw it------it was going down. My suggestion to you is to pull on your line."

Excitedly, Danny stood up. "Grandpa, I've got something big! Look at my fishing pole!" His fishing rod was bent almost double.

"I believe you do have something big. Keep your line tight." They couldn't believe their eyes when a giant bass surfaced the water. "My goodness, Danny-----that's a ten pound fish for sure! Don't give him any slack!"

"Grandpa, he's reeling off some of my line!"

"That's no problem; you've got plenty of line. Just don't let your line become slack."

"Do you want to reel him in? I'm afraid I might lose this big fish."

"No, I'm not going to reel your fish in." George answered. "If I reeled him in-----then you couldn't say you caught the fish. You're doing fine. Just take your time while I get our fish net ready. That's it; bring that big boy close to the boat."

"Grandpa, I've never had a fish to bend a fishing pole like this one is!"

"That's because you've never hooked a fish this big. That's it, just a little closer and I'll slide my fish net underneath your fish. Okay, I'm bringing him up. My goodness, Danny------this fish is a lot bigger than my record one! This bass will weight ten pounds for sure!"

"Grandpa, wouldn't it be nice if we had a camera now? I would be able to show my mother me holding this big fish."

"Danny boy it so happens that I do have a camera inside my fish well. Soon as I get this hook out of your fish's mouth-----I'll weight your fish with my portable scales. After that I'll get my camera. Your mother will be so excited when she sees a picture of you holding this big bass. I can take this fish to a taxidermist for you."

"Grandpa, I just want my picture taken with me holding this fish. After that, I'm going to put my fish back into the water. Is that okay with you?"

"Of course it's okay, but we better get this fish into the water hurriedly after that. Henry weighed the bass, and then he took a picture with Danny holding the almost eleven pound bass. Danny was pleased when his fish started swimming downward and away from the boat. A loving smile appeared on George face, noticing the smile on his grandson's face.

Chapter 3

Beth was up early the following morning. She wanted to do some laundry and some much-needed house cleaning. While sitting in her favorite chair holding a cup of coffee, she happened to look out her living room window. Her neighbor, Mr. Harry Spears was standing on his front porch looking toward her house. For several minutes, Beth observed him gazing toward her house. Mr. Spears had always been nice and friendly to her and her family. She determined that he must have something on his mind, but she didn't know what it might be.

A few minutes later, Mr. Spears was still looking toward Beth's house when she decided to do some laundry and house cleaning.

Beth decided to check her mail about noon time that day. She opened her front door and was surprised to see twelve long-stemmed roses neatly displayed on top of a cardboard box. Beth looked around to see who might have placed them there, but she saw no one. When she picked up the bundle of roses she noticed a small white card that was attached. The card only contained four words which were 'To a beautiful lady'. Beth happened to look up and saw Mr. Spears standing on his porch. He was looking in her direction. Still holding the flowers, she hurried inside her house. Beth looked out her window to see if Mr. Spear's was still standing on his porch. She determined quickly that he must have gone back inside his house. All at once, Beth became angered that Mr. Spears or any other man would send her roses so soon after her husband's death. Beth burst into tears; she angrily threw the roses into the trash can, and then she hurried into her bedroom. She picked up a picture of her husband as she sat down on the edge of her bed, holding the picture tightly against her chest. Tears flowed freely down her face, her wondering why any decent man would send her flowers while she was still mourning the death of her husband.

A few minutes later, Beth picked up the telephone and called the sheriff's office. She asked if Detective Randy Johnson was in the office. She was told that he was out at the minute, but if she left her phone number they would have him call her. After Beth hung up the phone, she looked out her living room window to see if Mr. Spears was back on his porch. There he was, as bold as ever, looking straight toward Beth's house. She sat down in a chair and observed him as he paced back and forth on his porch as though something was bothering him.

Beth was startled a few minutes later when her phone rang. Upon answering her phone she heard Detective Johnson's voice. "Is this you, Mrs. Miller?"

"Yes, it is. I hated to call you, but I'm confused about something. I was wondering if you could come to my house when it's convenient for you to do so."

"That won't be a problem," Detective Johnson responded. "I've got to take care of a small errand, but I can be there in about forty-five minutes."

"That will be just fine."

Thirty minutes later, Beth heard someone walk onto her porch. Her doorbell rang a few seconds later. Satisfied that it must be the detective, she opened her front door. She was startled when she saw Mr. Spears standing in front of her door. "Mrs. Miller, if you have a few minutes, I would like to talk with you?"

"Mr. Spears, I'm expecting Detective Randy Johnson here any minute. What do you want to talk with me about? I told you that someone from the sheriff's office was on their way here. In fact, here comes the detective now." Mr. Spears turned around; he saw a car turning into her driveway." He hurried off her porch. "Mrs. Miller, I'll talk with you later!"

Beth was still standing on her porch when Detective Johnson walked up her steps.

"That man seems to be in a hurry," the detective remarked.

"That man is partly the reason I wanted you to come to my house. Let's go inside and I'll tell you why I asked you come."

The detective followed Beth into her living room. "I don't know if I should have called you or not," said Beth. "Would you care for some coffee or tea?"

"I appreciate the offer, Mrs. Miller, but I don't care for anything to drink. Something must be bothering you, is that why you asked me here?"

"Mr. Spears, my neighbor, the man you saw a few minutes ago has acted rather strange today," Beth remarked.

"In what way has he acted strange?"

"He's been on his porch several times today. Each time he was looking straight toward my house."

"Well, Mrs. Miller, it's not against the law for someone to look towards another person's house," Detective Johnson commented.

"Until today, I have never seen him stare toward this house! There's something else, someone placed twelve long-stemmed red roses on my porch either last night or sometime this morning. A rational man wouldn't dare place a bouquet of roses on a woman's porch so shortly after her husband was murdered."

"Mrs. Miller, you do have a point in what you just said. Was there a note attached to the flowers?"

"Yes, there certainly was. The note read, 'To a beautiful lady'. I threw the roses and that blasted note into my trash can!"

"You don't have any idea who put those flowers on your porch."

"No, I certainly don't!"

"Do you suppose Mr. Spears placed the flowers on your porch?"

"I've been wondering about that," Beth answered.

"Why was he here a little while ago?"

"He never told me what he wanted, except that he needed to talk with me. He was eager to leave my house after I told him that you were due here any minute."

"Did Mr. Spears ever show any romantic interest in you before your husband was killed?"

"I was never aware of it if he did," Beth answered. "Quite often, when my husband was home he would come over for brief visits."

"Is he married?" The detective asked.

"Not now, his wife died about two years ago. Detective, do you think my imagination is playing tricks on me?"

"No, I don't think that all, Mrs. Miller. Two facts are certain; someone left twelve long-stem roses neatly wrapped on your porch, and Mr. Spears doesn't seem to be himself all of a sudden. The first fact signifies that someone is romantically interested in you. Who knows, that might well be your husband's killer. The killer did leave your husband's grocery store with a picture of you in his hands. I don't have just cause to search your neighbor's house for any possible clues concerning his behavior, but I would surely like to do just that."

"Detective Johnson, do you think I'm in any kind of danger? Mr. Spears has always been very nice and friendly to my family."

"I'm not sure, Mrs. Miller. It's difficult to predict what some of this country's nut cases are prone to do. If anything else occurs causing you to feel uncomfortable or uneasy, I want you to call me right away. I would be very interested in knowing who placed those roses and note on your porch. Mrs. Miller, my advice to you is to keep your doors and windows locked at all times. Please call me whenever the need arises."

"Detective, you're very kind. Thank you for coming."

Beth Miller was fast asleep at twelve o'clock that night. A few minutes later she awoke, hearing someone walking outside her bedroom window. Frightened and to the point of panic, she sat up in bed; she listened attentively as someone tried to push her window up. She quietly opened her top dresser drawer and took out her late husband's .38 Smith and Wesson. All at once the noise stopped. She heard footsteps as the would-be-intruder walked away from her window. Still holding the pistol, Beth eased herself off the bed; she walked quietly down the unlighted hallway. She felt her way along until she was standing inside her living room. Beth became numb with fear, hearing someone walking on her front porch. She nearly dropped her pistol when she heard someone doing something to her doorknob. Realizing that someone was about to break into her house, she raised her pistol toward the top of the doorway and fired. She heard someone run off her porch. Beth hurried to her living room window to see if she could see the person, but she didn't see anyone. Almost scared out of her wits, Beth turned on the room light. She laid her pistol on the couch and then dialed 911. "May I help you?" The 911 operator asked.

"Yes! Someone tried to break into my house! I'm all alone! Please send someone here!" Beth cried.

"When did the attempted break-in occur?" The operator asked.

"It happened just before I dialed 911? My name is Beth Miller! I live at 356 Candlewood Drive! Please hurry!"

"Mrs. Miller, someone will be there shortly."

Beth wiped tears from her eyes with a nearby tissue as she waited impatiently for the law to arrive.

Within several minutes, two sheriff's cars came into her yard. Beth heard their sirens blasting before they got to her house. She turned on her porch light, and then she opened her front door. It was two deputies from the sheriff's office. "Are you the one that called 911?" Officer Brad Wheeler asked.

"Yes! Someone tried to get into my house! I scared off whoever it was by firing a shot toward the doorway."

"Where's the gun now?" Officer Wheeler asked.

"It's lying on my couch."

"Brad, you need to call Detective Randy Johnson," said his partner, Dale Hendrix. "Take a good look at the porch, near the doorway. Do you see what I see?"

"Yes, it's drops of blood from the doorway to the end of the porch."

"Do you mean I may have shot someone?" Beth asked.

"It seems that way, Mrs. Miller."

"That had to be a tall person," said Beth.

"Why do you say that?" Officer Wheeler asked.

"I only wanted to scare whoever it was. I thought I held my gun high enough that I wouldn't hit whoever it was."

"Brad, Mrs. Miller is right about the person being tall. Look up here at the door. The exit hole from the bullet is higher than my head. I'm six-foot tall."

"I'll call Randy Johnson right now," said Officer Wheeler. "Mrs. Miller, we're going to check the grounds for any kind of evidence. Why don't you get comfortable in a nice chair?"

"Officer Wheeler, I could make us a fresh pot of coffee."

"That would be nice, Mrs. Miller."

Beth and the two deputies were sitting in the living room when Detective Randy Johnson came into the house. "Mrs. Miller, Brad told me that you've had a very frightful night."

"Someone tried to get into my house. At first, the person tried to get my window open. Since that attempt was unsuccessful someone came to my front door. I was scared silly, so I got my husband's pistol and quietly walked to the living room. That's when I heard someone tinkering with my doorknob. I thought someone was about to come into my house, so I fired my gun toward the doorway. I held the gun high enough that I thought the person wouldn't get hit. I just wanted to scare the person off."

"Officer Wheeler, I want to see the blood stains that you told me about," said Detective Johnson." The officers went outside. "I see the exit hole that you told me about. It surely weren't a short man that tried to break into her house. Have you men checked the yard for evidence?"

"We found an empty shoe on the other side of her shrubby," said Officer Wheeler. "It's a size thirteen shoe and it has two spots of blood on it."

"Place the shoe in a plastic bag," said Detective Johnson. "The lab will be able to determine the blood type from the blood on that shoe. Brad, I want you to contact the hospital to determine if anyone has checked in with a bullet wound. Dale, I want you to take this shoe back to our office for safe keeping. I'll remain here until daybreak so Mrs. Miller can go back to bed. I believe someone is hell bent on harming her somehow."

Beth was drinking a cup of coffee when Detective Johnson came into the living room. He took a seat opposite from hers. "Did you find anything in my yard?" Beth asked.

"We found a blood-stained shoe, size thirteen. Mrs. Miller, I really didn't notice yesterday, but how tall would you say Mr. Spears is?"

"I really don't know, but he was taller than my husband."

"How tall was your husband?"

"He was almost six feet."

"Mrs. Miller, why don't you go back to bed? I'm going to stay here until daylight so I can do some further checking."

"Detective, I couldn't sleep a wink right now."

"Do you have any more coffee in your pot?" Detective Johnson asked.

"Yes, I would be happy to get you a cup." Beth fell asleep on her couch about an hour later.

Detective Randy Johnson drove away from Beth Miller's house at daybreak. He thought he had enough justifiable cause to get a search warrant to search Harry Spears property. Judge Allen Blakely issued a search warrant for Mr. Spears' property at 9:15 that morning.

Beth looked out her bedroom window at 10:30 that morning. She saw Detective Johnson knocking on Mr. Spears' front door. Two more deputies waited a few feet from his porch. She noticed that the detective was holding some papers in his hand. Beth watched, curiously, as Mr. Spears front door opened up. "Yes, officer, what seems to be the trouble?"

"Is your name Harry Spears?"

"Yes, that's my name."

"Mr. Spears, how tall are you?" Detective Johnson asked.

"I'm six foot, four inches tall."

"What size shoe do you wear?"

"I wear a size 13 shoe. What in the hell is this? Why are you asking me these stupid questions?"

"I have a legal order to search your house?"

"Let me see that blasted paper!" After reading the warrant, Mr. Spears asked Detective Johnson what they were looking for. The detective assured him that he would know the answer to that question, if they found what they were looking for.

"Mr. Spears, is something wrong with your hand?" Detective Johnson asked.

"Yes, I cut my hand last night while cutting a steak."

"I want you to stay on your porch while we search your house," said Detective Johnson.

The three officers searched Mr. Spears' house for fifteen minutes before they discovered something interesting. On the top shelf of his closet was the missing portrait from John Miller's store. The detectives didn't let on to Mr. Spears that they had found something that would tie him to John's murder. A few minutes later, Detective Johnson found a ski mask under the edge of Mr. Spears' back porch. It was identical to the one used by John Miller's murderer. Detective Johnson had enough evidence now to charge Harry Spears with murder and robbery.

The three officers walked from behind the house to Mr. Spears' front porch. He was sitting in a wooden chair, his face lowered.

"Mr. Spears, place your hands behind your back. You're under arrest for robbery and murder," said Detective Johnson. "Do you recognize the family portrait of Beth Miller and her family that Deputy Lonnie Fields is holding? Also, do you recognize the ski mask that Deputy Gaskins is holding?"

"No, I do not know anything about that ski mask the deputy is holding!" Mr. Spears voiced.

"We found it underneath your back porch, Mr. Spears!" Detective Johnson yelled out.

"I don't care where you found it! I've never seen that thing until now!"

"I suppose you didn't take the portrait out of Mr. Miller's store after you shot him dead!"

"Detective Johnson, I swear to God that I haven't killed anyone! I swear I didn't kill Mr. Miller!" He voiced, tearfully.

"Mr. Spears, that portrait didn't get on your closet shelf by itself."

"You're right about that, Detective Johnson. I hid that portrait until I could talk with Mrs. Miller next door."

"I'll bet you're the one that was tampering with her window and her front door knob about midnight."

"Detective, that's not true! I never went outside of my house last night! I'm telling you the absolute truth!"

"Tell me this, why were you at Beth Miller's house yesterday?' Detective Johnson asked.

"I wanted to tell her about her portrait."

"What were you going to tell her concerning the portrait?"

"I was going to tell her that the morning after her husband was killed that someone left that portrait on my front porch. I wanted to explain to her that I had nothing to do with her husband's murder. I was afraid to carry the portrait to her without explaining how I wound up with it. Detective Johnson, someone has done a very good job making it look like I killed Mr. Miller."

"Mr. Spears, we found one of your bloodied shoes over by the hedging in Mrs. Miller's yard. You'll spend years in jail if blood on that shoe matches your blood."

"I tell you I didn't go to Mrs. Miller's house last night! You've got to believe me! I'm being framed for something I didn't do!" Mr. Spears yelled out, tearfully.

"I've heard enough. Lonnie, read Mr. Spears his Miranda rights. After that you and Gene take him to the courthouse for booking. I need to stop by Mrs. Miller's house for a few minutes."

Beth was looking out her window when the deputies helped Mr. Spears into the backseat of their patrol car. She noticed that Detective Johnson was walking across the yard toward her house. Beth was eager to hear what just transpired at Mr. Spears' house. She opened her front door as Detective Johnson walked onto her porch.

"Mrs. Miller, I think we just arrested your husband's murderer. In fact, we found your family's portrait, and a ski mask at his house like the one the murderer was wearing the night your husband was killed. We don't know if Mr. Spears was the one trying to get into your house last night, but we'll be checking on that."

"I don't understand! Mr. Spears has always been a very nice, humble man. He's been a friend of ours since we moved here. He doesn't look like the type that would kill someone," Beth remarked.

"Mrs. Miller, murderers never do look like you might picture them to be. Anyway, I don't think you'll have to worry about someone trying to break into your house since we've got Mr. Spears locked up."

"Detective, did Mr. Spears say why he took the portrait off the store wall?'

"No, Mrs. Miller, he didn't say anything about that. He swore up and down that he was innocent of your husband's murder."

"Do you believe he's telling the truth?" Beth asked.

"If he's innocent, someone has gone to a lot of trouble to make him appear guilty. Mrs. Miller, I hope things will be much better for you now. Please-----if ever you need me again, don't hesitate to call me."

Chapter 4

It was Wednesday morning; Danny was sitting at the breakfast table with his grandparents. "George, how excited was Danny when he caught that big fish?" Dora asked.

"He was very excited. At one point he wanted me to reel in his fish, but I wouldn't do that. I wanted him to have the experience of hauling in that big bass."

"Grandma, my fish was bigger than the one grandpa has hanging on his wall," said Danny, smiling.

"How many fish did your grandfather catch?" Dora asked.

"He caught ten and I caught seven. I beat on the most weight caught, but he beat me on the number of fish caught. We had a lot of fun, didn't we Grandpa?"

"Yes, we sure did."

"What would you like to do today?"

"Grandpa, could I feed your horses?"

"Sure you can. Just make sure you don't give them more feed than what I've already shown you. How would you like to feed old Brutus?"

"George, that might not be a good idea," said Dora, "that old bull is meaner than a provoked wildcat."

"Grandma, that bull won't hurt me. I don't have to go inside his pen to feed him."

"Son, I rather you not even go around that Brahma bull."

"He'll be alright," George responded, "Brutus can't be any danger to Danny unless he goes inside his wired fence."

Danny was in the horse barn a few minutes later. He had already given hay and some grain to two of the horses. When he dumped a measured can of grain into Silver's feed box he heard loud noises coming from Brutus's pen. He hurried around the barn; there he saw a large dog fighting with a much smaller dog. It looked to Danny as if the larger dog was going to kill the small dog. Without regard to his own safety, he grabbed up a short piece of board. He, hurriedly, crawled underneath the bull pen; holding the board in his right hand, Danny raced toward the fighting dogs. He hit the big dog twice with the board before the larger dog quit biting the smaller one. Expecting Danny to hit him again, the larger dog ran off. The small dog lay helpless on the ground; blood oozed from his neck and body. As if it was his own dog, Danny picked up the injured animal and cuddled him in

25

his arms. Still holding the dog, Danny turned around; he saw Brutus pawing at the ground, reading himself for a charge. Danny looked horrified at the sight of the bull standing forty yards away.

Almost hysterical, his grandfather yelled out, "Run, Danny----run!" "Get the hell out of there!" When Danny started running, so did the bull. Still holding the dog, he ran for all his might until he got to the edge of the fence. He dropped to the ground, and then he rolled underneath the fence just in time before the bull got to him. "My God, Son! My God, I told you as plain as I could to not go inside Brutus's pen! Why did you disobey me? For heavens' sake------what in the world is wrong with Mrs. Penn's registered dog?"

"Grandpa, I'm sorry for not doing what you asked me to do, but a large dog was killing this little fellow," Danny answered, tearfully. "I had to do something to help him. I was so excited when I saw them fighting that I forgot all about your bull."

"Danny, I nearly had a heart attack when I saw Brutus looking toward you inside his pen. When he started pawing at the ground, I knew right then and there that he was going to charge after you. Do you realize how close you came to being killed?"

"I'm sorry, I won't ever go into Brutus's pen again----I promise! What are we going to do about this dog?"

"We'll take this poor critter to Mrs. Sarah Penn's house right now. I'll bet anything that she doesn't know where Frisky is. This is the first time I've seen Frisky out of her yard."

"The dog's name is Frisky?"

"Yes, and I bet Mrs. Penn is very upset not knowing where her dog is."

"Where does Mrs. Penn live, Grandpa?"

"She lives across the road from me in that large brick house. Frisky is bleeding pretty badly; we better get her to Mrs. Penn's house right away."

George and Danny were parked in Mrs. Penn's yard a few minutes later. They walked onto her porch; George rang her doorbell. Mrs. Penn opened her front door. She looked horrified when she saw her bloodied dog in Danny's arms. "George Eason, what in the world happened to my dog?" Mrs. Penn asked, tearfully. "I've been looking for Frisky for the last hour! Please------you and your grandson come inside while I call the veterinarian." George and Danny took a seat on her living room sofa while Mrs. Penn dialed the veterinarian's number. She came back into the living room a few minutes later. "My husband is on his way here. He'll take him to the doctor soon as he gets here. Son, why is your arm bleeding?"

"Mrs. Penn, I sent Danny out to feed my horses. He heard two dogs fighting while he was in the horse barn. When he walked around my barn he saw a large dog attacking your dog. Without a moment's thought, he grabbed a stick to fight off the larger dog. In order to do that, he had to go inside my bull pen. I'm afraid Frisky would have been killed if my grandson hadn't gone into Brutus's pen."

"Are you telling me that this young boy went inside that mean old bull's pen to save my poor little Frisky?"

"Yes, Mrs. Penn, that's about it. The bull chased Danny to the other side of my fence. He barely escaped with his life. Until you said something, I didn't realize that he came in contact with the barbed wire."

Mrs. Penn was doctoring Danny's arm when her husband came into the room. "George, your grandson is growing up."

"Yes he is. Danny, I want you to meet a very important man. Standing before you is state Senator Joe Penn."

"Son, don't let your granddaddy fool you. I'm no more important than anyone else."

Danny shook his hand. "I'm pleased to meet you, sir."

"Joe, this young boy saved our dog from being killed by a much larger dog," said Mrs. Penn. "In fact, he went inside Brutus's pen to save Frisky."

"Son, you're a lot braver than me. There's no way I would have gone in that mean old bull's pen!"

"Joe, what are you saying?" Mrs. Penn asked, a frown on her face. "You wouldn't have done it for Frisky? I guess you wouldn't have gone in there to save me, either!"

"I guess I would have weighed my options," he remarked, winking at Henry.

"Joe, before I get any more upset, I want you to take Frisky to Dr. Randall. Tell him that I want my dog well cared for."

Joe picked up the dog. "George, you and Danny come see us any time. I'm going to the doctor's office now before I further aggravate my charming wife." Joe hurried outside.

"Danny, I want you to do me a great big favor."

"I will if I can, Mrs. Penn."

"I want you to take this hundred dollar bill for saving my precious dog. Before you say anything------I know already that you don't charge anything for your heroic action. However, I would be grateful if you will accept this money."

"Grandpa------!"

"Its' okay, Danny-----take the money from Mrs. Penn," said George. "She wants you to have the money for saving her dog."

"Thank you, Mrs. Penn. I really appreciate you giving me this money."

"You're more than welcome. George, you've got a mighty fine grandson!"

"You're right about that, Mrs. Penn. Danny is one of a kind!"

It was Thursday morning, three days since Harry Spears was arrested for robbery and murder. Beth had just sat down on her couch when the phone rang. She picked up the receiver. "Mrs. Miller, I'm Karen Roberson, your Real Estate Agent. Would it be convenient for you to meet me at my attorney's off at two o'clock today? We need you to sign some papers so we can give you a certified check for your grocery store and its' surrounding property."

"Two o'clock will be just fine, Miss Roberson. I believe you told me one time that your agency uses Mr. Gordon White as your attorney."

"That's correct, Mrs. Miller. I look forward to seeing you at two o'clock today."

After talking with Miss Roberson, Beth dialed her parents. Her mother picked up her phone. "Hello, Beth, I'm very glad you called."

"Mother, is something wrong?"

"No, my dear, I just wanted to tell you what a swell time Danny has had with us this week. Gorge has spent a good part of each day entertaining Danny. That boy has been fishing, boat riding in Briars Creek, golfing, frog gigging, and horseback riding. I think George has had the time of his life being with Danny since he's been here. Danny saved Mrs. Sarah Penn's dog from being killed by a much larger dog. She gave Danny a hundred dollar bill for him saving her dog."

"It's hard to believe that Mrs. Penn would let her expensive dog out of her house," Beth commented.

"Actually, she didn't let Frisky out of her house," Dora responded. "She found out a little later that her maid, Verna Sutton was responsible for allowing Frisky to sneak by her when she opened the back door to go out. How have you been since I saw you last Sunday?"

"It's been a very eventful week for me. I'll tell you all about it when I come Sunday morning to pick up Danny. By the way, where is Danny today?"

"He's helping his granddaddy pick tomatoes from our garden. Beth, he's the smartest young fellow I know of. Sunday, I'll have some vegetables ready for you to take home with you. I do hope you'll let Danny come back again during his summer vacation."

"I will, indeed, mother. Danny loves to visit with you and daddy." Well, I'll see you early Sunday morning. Bye."

Beth's doorbell rang a few minutes later. Before opening the door, she looked through the peep hole to see who it was. She recognized Detective Johnson right away. She opened her front door. "Detective Johnson, you must have some news for me."

"Yes, I certainly do. May I come inside?"

"I'm sorry, of course you can," said Beth. The detective followed her into the living room. "Would you care for something to drink?"

"No thank you, but I do appreciate you asking. Mrs. Miller, I've got some rather bad news for you. Mr. Harry Spears is not the one that tried to break into your house."

"He isn't?" Beth asked, extremely concerned.

"His blood type didn't match the blood we found on your porch or the blood stains on that shoe we found in your yard."

"Is Mr. Spears still in jail?"

"Yes, he's still in jail because we've got him charged with your husband's murder. Mrs. Miller, it's not customary that we do what I'm about to ask you to do, but it may help us determine his guilt or innocence."

"Detective Johnson, what would you have me to do?"

"Mr. Spears is begging and pleading with us to let him talk with you concerning his charge. I'll guarantee your safety if you decide to talk with him."

"It would be a terrible thing if Mr. Spears wasn't guilty of his charges," Beth commented.

"Yes, it would be terrible, but there's a great deal of evidence that he did kill your husband. He's tall like the man on the store video camera. He had your family portrait on the top shelf of his closet and he had a ski mask under his porch. That ski mask is identical to the one the murderer wore during the robbery. You said yourself that he acted rather unusual the day you called me to your house."

"Detective, when would you want me to talk with Mr. Spears? I can't do it this afternoon because I've got to be at a lawyer's office. Tomorrow is Friday; I could go to the court house sometime during the day."

"That would be fine, Mrs. Miller. Had you rather do it in the morning or the afternoon?"

"Would eleven o'clock tomorrow morning be okay?" Beth asked.

"That would be perfect. You'll have nothing to fear because you and Mr. Spears will be separated by a bullet proof, glass petition. Just come into the Sheriff's office tomorrow morning and I'll escort you to a special room where you and Mr. Spears can talk. Mrs. Miller, as I said when I first got here, Mr. Spears is not the one that tried to break into your house. This means the perpetrator is still out there somewhere. I'm not trying to scare you, but I would keep your pistol nearby when you go to bed."

"Do you think he might come back some night?" Beth asked.

"It's hard to say whether he'll come back or not, but now he knows you're armed and that you will shoot, if provoked. In case you lost my card, I'm going to give you another one. Keep it handy in case you need to call me. Mrs. Miller, where is that fine looking boy of yours?"

"He's staying with his grandparents until Sunday."

"My daughter introduced me to Danny about a month ago while I was at their school. Shelia and Danny are in the same grade."

"How many children do you and your wife have? Beth asked.

"I only have one child. Shelia was only five years old when Doris was killed by a drunk driver."

"Oh, my God, that's terrible!" Beth voiced, loudly. "Without your wife, how in the world did you manage for the next seven years?"

"It was very difficult, Mrs. Miller, very difficult, indeed. In addition to my work, I've spent the last seven years taking care of my daughter. Well, we both seemed to have lost the person we loved the most. Mrs. Miller, please call if you ever need me."

"Thank you very much for telling me about Mr. Spears. I'll be at the courthouse at eleven tomorrow."

Beth signed away her grocery store and its surrounding property that evening. Attorney Gordon White handed her a certified check for three hundred and forty-seven thousand dollars.

"Mrs. Miller, that's an awful lot of money," said Mr. White. "I do hope you have a good Certified Public Accountant to advise you on your money."

"Yes, I do have one. Do you know Mr. Cecil Borden?"

"As a matter of fact I do know Mr. Borden. As a C.P.A., he's as good as they come. He'll be able to give you some great advice for your money."

With a great deal of apprehension, Beth walked slowly down the hallway of the Courthouse the next morning. She arrived at the sheriff's office at 10:48. With his door opened, she saw Sheriff Alan Hicks and Detective Randy Johnson sitting at the sheriff's desk. They both got up when Beth walked inside. "Mrs. Miller, please have a seat," Detective Johnson commented. Beth took a seat near the detective. "Sheriff Hicks and I have been discussing your near break-in at your house. We've come up with two scenarios. One, it was a randomly selected house for someone to steal whatever they could. The other situation is far more complicated, and it depends on whether Harry Spears is telling us the truth, that he didn't kill your husband."

"Detective Johnson, what are you saying?" Beth asked, curiously.

"Mrs. Miller, if Mr. Spears is innocent that means there's a killer somewhere that has a great deal of interest in you. Why else would he remove that portrait of you and your family from your grocery store? If Mr. Spears is being framed, someone has done a lot of planning prior to the robbery and murder. He selected someone about his same height, someone living next to you, left your photograph on Mr. Spears' porch and placed a ski mask underneath his porch. In all probability, it's someone that you may know or have known. That being said, whoever it is will most likely try to contact you somehow or force his way into your home."

"Wouldn't he be afraid to come back now since I shot through my door?"

"Not necessary, the person could very well be some kind of psychopath that has a strong attraction to you," Sheriff Hicks commented. "For the next couple weeks I'm having one of my deputy's cruise by your house two or three times each night."

"I appreciate that. Does that mean that you think Mr. Spears is telling the truth?" Beth asked.

"Mrs. Miller, he could be telling the truth or he could be lying," Sheriff Hicks spoke. "We're hoping your talking to him today will help us decide which it is. Mr. Spears will think that you and he are talking privately, but the conversation in the room will be recorded. Detective Johnson, take Mrs. Miller to the visiting room. Mr. Spears will already be there."

When they got inside the visiting room, Beth noticed Mr. Spears sitting behind a glass wall; his head was lowered. "Mrs. Miller, please take a seat in front of Mr. Spears. Pick up your phone when you're ready to talk. He'll do the same with his phone. I'm going outside the room to give you both some privacy." Detective Johnson left the room.

Beth picked up the phone. Tearfully, Mr. Spears did the same. "Mr. Spears, I understand you wanted to talk with me."

"Mrs. Miller, I prayed that you would talk with me. No matter what happens to me, I want you to know that I didn't rob your grocery store, and I certainly didn't kill your husband. Mrs. Miller, I'm telling you the honest truth!"

"Mr. Spears, why did you act so irrational the day you came to my house. You said you needed to talk with me. However, you left abruptly when Detective Johnson showed up. Also, I saw you that day standing on your porch. You kept looking toward my house, why was that?"

"I wanted to return that family portrait, but I was afraid to."

"Why were you afraid to do that?"

"For several reasons. First of all, I didn't know if you would believe me or not that it was left on my porch. When I was on my porch I kept asking myself if I should take that family portrait to you. While shopping at your husband's grocery store, I've seen that portrait many times hanging on the store wall."

"You could have turned the portrait over to the law."

"I could have, but the news media kept saying that the killer was a tall man. The morning after the robbery I was shocked to see that portrait on my porch. Mrs. Miller, do you really think the law would have believed that a murderer just happened to leave that portrait on my porch?"

"Mr. Spears, what about the ski mask they found underneath your porch?" Beth asked.

"I swear to God that I was shocked when they found that thing underneath my porch! I had no idea that the murderer, whoever he was, had left two incriminating items at my house!" Mr. Spears wiped away tears from his eyes.

"Detective Johnson said that you told him that you never left your house the night my husband was killed."

"That's the absolute truth, Mrs. Miller. I wish to God that I could prove that fact! Wait at minute! Wait a minute! Oh, my goodness! I forgot all about it!" Mr. Spears stood up, him smiling.

"Mr. Spears, what is it?" Beth asked.

"About the same time the robbery took place I heard a knock on my door. I opened my door and saw a man standing there. He said his car was about a half block from my house and it was out of gas. He wanted to know if I would sell him some gas. I told him that I had about two gallons of gas in a can on the back of my porch. I told him he could have the gas and the can because I had two more gas cans in my utility barn."

"Did he ever say what his name was?" Beth asked.

"Yes, he certainly did. Let me think------oh yes, his name was Frank Howard, and he worked at Simpson's Lumber Company. I wish I had thought about that when I was being interrogated. Mrs. Miller, I want you to tell them what I just said."

"I'll do just that. Mr. Spears, right after my husband was killed, did you place a bundle of red roses on my porch?"

"I surely did not, Mrs. Miller. What kind of man would do that while you were in mourning over your husband's death?"

"Mr. Spears, I'll tell the sheriff what you said upon my leaving this room. Is there anything else that you would like to say or ask me?"

"Yes, there is something that I want you to do. More than anything, I want you to believe that I'm innocent. You and your husband have been very kind to me over the years. Mrs. Miller, since the death of my wife I have been a very lonely man. Even though you're a very beautiful lady------not once have I said anything or done anything inappropriate toward you."

"No you haven't, Mr. Spears."

"Please tell the sheriff about Frank Howard coming to my house! Thank you for coming here today. Mrs. Miller, no matter what------I hope you'll always be a friend of mine!"

Beth waved bye as she headed out of the room. A deputy came to Mr. Spears and escorted him back to his cell.

Sheriff Hicks and Detective Johnson were waiting outside of the family meeting room when Beth came out. "Mrs. Miller, you did exactly what we wanted you to do inside that room," said Sheriff Hicks. "At the official time of the robbery and murder, we didn't have a clue that Mr. Spears was home, perhaps giving his gas can and some gas to a total stranger. Detective Johnson and I will drive to Simpson's Lumber Company this afternoon and we'll talk with Mr. Frank Howard. We'll let you know the outcome of that conversation."

"Thank you very much. I would be very interested in knowing whether Mr. Spears was telling the truth or not. I, sincerely, believe that he was telling the truth."

After having a late lunch that day, Sheriff Hicks and Detective Johnson drove to Simpson's Lumber Company. They made their way to the front office. Sheriff Hicks asked the receptionist how he could get up with Mr. Frank Howard. "Sheriff, what a coincidence, he just walked into the office. That's him with the blue shirt on."

"Thank you very much," said Sheriff Hicks. They walked up to the man wearing the blue shirt. "Pardon me, is your name Frank Howard?"

"That's right, Sheriff Hicks, how may I help you?"

"Mr. Howard, is there somewhere we could talk in private?"

"Sure. We can go into the conference room down the hall."

Frank closed the conference room door, and they all sat down. "Sheriff, how can I help you?"

"Mister Howard, I'm hoping you can help us solve a matter that we are investigating."

"I don't know how I can do that, but I'll certainly tell you anything I know. What's on your mind?"

"Some time over the last two or three weeks, did your car run out of gas anywhere?" Sheriff Hicks asked.

Looking puzzled for a moment, he answered, "Yes, I did run out of gas about two weeks ago."

"Did you run out of gas in the country or somewhere in town?" Detective Johnson asked.

"It happened in town."

"Do you remember what street it was that your car ran out of gas?" Sheriff Hicks asked.

"My memory is not always the best, but the street name had the word Candle in it. Oh, now I remember, it was Candlewood Drive. I remember it clearly now because it was a very eventful night."

"How do you mean, eventful?" Sheriff Hicks asked.

"Well, I'll start from the beginning," said Mr. Howard. "When I ran out of gas there were no gas stations in sight. I didn't know what I was going to do until I saw this house with the porch light on. Reluctantly, I walked to the house and knocked on the front door. A man came to the door; he was dressed like he was about to go to bed. I asked him if he would sell me a can of gas. I was kind of shocked when he said he wouldn't sell me any gas, but he would give me about two gallons, as well as the gas can. He told me that he had gas in two or three more gas cans. I'll never forget that man! He was very nice!"

"Mr. Howard, you mentioned something about that being a very eventful evening," Sheriff Hicks commented.

"It surely was. Anyway, I poured the gas into my car, and then I headed for the nearest gas station. I don't normally turn on my radio much, but this time I did. The local news happened to be on. A news flash came on my radio saying that Miller's Grocery Store was robbed about ten minutes ago, and that the owner had been shot and killed."

"I have one more request for you?" Sheriff Hicks remarked.

"Just tell me what it is," answered Mr. Howard, smiling.

"I have photographs of four different men in my hand. I want you to see if you recognize any of them." The sheriff spread the photographs on the conference table.

Mr. Howard picked up one and then quickly laid it down. He did the same thing with the second one. When he picked up the third one he commenced smiling. "I can't remember his name, but this is the man that gave me his can of gas."

"Mr. Howard, you've been an immense help to us," said Sheriff Hicks.

"Well, I don't know what this is all about, but I'm glad I did a little something to help the law."

"You've done a great deal more than that, Mr. Howard," Detective Johnson remarked. "You just gave a man his life back!"

Chapter 5

At 9:45 the next morning, Harry Spears was taken to Sheriff Hicks' office. Immense sadness was prevalent on his face as he stood before the county sheriff. "Mr. Spears, do you have any idea why so many people are in my office this morning?

"No, Sheriff, I do not know why they're here." He lowered his head in despair.

The sheriff stood up; he raised his voice, "I'll tell you exactly why they're all here! We're going to celebrate your freedom!"

Mr. Spears seemed confused, momentarily, as he looked across the room at everyone clapping their hands and smiling. "Sheriff, are you saying that I'm free of the charges against me?" He asked, bewildered.

"That's exactly what I'm saying! You're a free man, Mr. Spears! You can walk out of here this very minute, but I hope you won't. These officers, including myself, want to share that large cake sitting on the corner table with you. It's our token of respect for a man wrongfully accused of a crime he didn't commit. Mr. Spears, you were arrested on the evidence that we had at the time of your arrest. We had no other alternative, but to charge you with robbery and murder. We've positively concluded that you had nothing to do with the crimes that you were charged with. I hope you'll be a good sport and have coffee and cake with us."

"Sheriff Hicks, I would be delighted to have some cake and coffee with you and your personnel," he said with a broad smile. "There is just one little thing."

"What is that?" The sheriff asked.

"How will I get home?" Everyone burst into laughter.

Detective Johnson walked up to Mr. Spears and said, "I'll drive you home after we indulge in some cake eating. I need to stop by and tell your neighbor the good news."

Detective Johnson drove into Mr. Spears' yard about an hour later. "Mr. Spears, I don't know any other way to say it, but I'm very sorry for what we've put you through. There was a lot of evidence against you."

"I know that, Detective Johnson. Had I been in your shoes, I would have done the same thing. I've got no hard feelings toward you or Sheriff Hicks. All I want to do now is call my ailing mother to tell her that I'm no longer a suspect in Mr. Miller's death."

Detective Johnson extended his hand to Mr. Spears. They shook hands, and then Mr. Spears exited the patrol car. He waved bye to the detective, and then he hurried toward his house to call his mother.

Beth was standing on her porch when Detective Johnson pulled into her driveway. He exited his car and started walking toward Beth's porch. "Am I seeing things, or was that Mr. Spears that just got out of your car?"

"You're not seeing things, Mrs. Miller. Mr. Spears has been cleared of all charges against him. He's a very happy man."

"That's wonderful news," said Beth, smiling. "I know his mother will be very pleased."

"Do you know his mother?"

"Yes, I've talked with Mrs. Edna Spears on several occasions during the last few years. In fact, I talked with her last night on the phone. From what I've been told, she doesn't have very long to live."

"Mrs. Miller, what's wrong with Mr. Spears' mother?"

"She's got an incurable cancer on her brain. She said her last wish would be for her son to be found innocent of his charges. I guess now that poor woman can die in peace."

"Mrs. Miller, there's still one thing that we can't forget," said Detective Johnson. "Your husband's killer is still out there somewhere. In all probability he's the same one that tried to break into your house. He's the same one that tried to frame your neighbor for your husband's murder. I still say that the killer is someone that you might recognize if you were to see him. He's the one that placed those roses on your porch. It seems that he's deeply infatuated with you to the point of murder."

"Detective Johnson, what am I supposed to do?" Beth asked, extremely concerned.

"As Sheriff Hicks said before, deputies will be driving by your house at night for the next two or three weeks to keep the would-be-intruder at bay."

"Thank you for being such a good friend during this trying time," said Beth. "I'll be glad to have my son back home."

"Danny is a fine boy, Mrs. Miller. I know you're very, very proud of him."

"Yes, I certainly am."

Detective Johnson left Beth's house a few minutes later. Afterwards, Beth looked out her window toward Mr. Spears' house. She could only imagine how excited he was to be free once again. Beth decided that she would do the neighborly thing and walk over to his house and welcome him back home. She pressed his doorbell a few minutes later. He opened his door.

"Mr. Spears, I just had to come over and tell you how thankful I am that you're no longer in jail."

"That's very kind of you to say that, Mrs. Miller. I just got off the phone with my mother. She just told me something that made me very happy, but before our conversation ended she told me something that made me very sad."

"What was that, Mr. Spears?"

"She said she was very happy to hear that all charges had been dropped against me. After that, she told me that she was ready to die." Tears came into Mr. Spears' eyes. "Mrs. Miller, can you imagine what it would be like to have lots of money, but no relatives at all, except for an ailing mother that wishes to die?"

"I talked with your mother last night, Mr. Spears. She is very, very proud of you. She told me that you've always been there for her when she needed anything. She told me something else, but I'm not sure I should mention it to you."

"I would really like to know what she said, Mrs. Miller."

"Okay, I'll tell you what she said. She said she had made peace with her Lord. She realized that her time on this earth was going to be very short. Her last wish in this world would be for you to find a good woman to spend the rest of your life with. Mr. Spears, you're a very handsome man; there's no reason that you can't find someone to share your life with. Well, I've been standing on your porch long enough. I just wanted to come over and welcome you back into our neighborhood."

"Thank you kindly, Mrs. Miller. It's very reassuring to know that I have a good friend living next door to me."

Beth Miller drove out of her driveway at eight o'clock Sunday morning. She was on her way to her parent's house to bring her son home. She had been on the road only minutes before her mind shifted to her late husband, and the way he died. She used a nearby tissue to wipe away her tears. She tried very hard to think about something else, but the thought of her husband being killed was heartbreaking for her. Her tears finally dried up after focusing her mind on her son. She realized that a great deal of her future happiness would be spending time with him.

Beth pulled into her parents' driveway twenty-three minutes later. Danny was looking at his grandfather's horses when his mother stepped out of her car. He raced toward her as fast as he could go. "Mother, I'm real glad to see you!" Danny sounded. He placed his arms around her waist.

"I'm glad to see you, too. Where are your grandparents?"

"Grandpa went to town to get something. Grandmother is in the house. Come on, we'll go see what she's doing," said Danny. "Have you missed me since I've been gone?"

"More than you'll ever know," Beth answered. "My goodness, Danny----how did you come by those scratch marks on your arms?"

"Mother, it's a long story. Do I have to tell you?"

"I'm your mother! Those look like they were deep scratches at one time! Now, how did you get them?"

"If you must know-----please wait until Grandpa comes home."

"Okay, but I won't forget to ask daddy about your scratches," Beth vowed.

Dora Miller was washing dishes when Danny and Beth walked into the kitchen.

"Mother, I see you're busy as ever."

"I'm just washing a few dishes"

"Grandma, do you still have any more of those good-tasting biscuits left?" Danny asked.

"I surely do. They're in that covered dish on the kitchen table. Beth, that son of yours has got a big appetite."

"Yes, I know I'm surprised he doesn't put on a great deal more weight than he does."

"Grandma, don't I have a pretty mother?"

"Don't I have a beautiful daughter?" Dora answered, smiling.

"It's sweet of you both to say that." Beth responded, smiling.

"Beth, I want you to sit down at the breakfast table while I cook you a couple eggs. There's already some cooked ham, sausage, and my special made biscuits already cooked. I can hardly wait until you try some of Henry's honey spread on one of my flaky biscuits."

"Mother, I declare------you're always trying to do something for others."

"To tell you the truth, I wouldn't have it any other way," said Dora, smiling. She broke two eggs into a frying pan as Beth took a seat at the breakfast table.

"Where does daddy keep his bee hives now?"

"He keeps them at the edge of our woods. We've got a lot of flowering plants and bushes planted near the hives."

"Mother, Grandpa can walk right up to the hives without getting stung."

"Well, that's partly true, Danny, but he has to wear protective gear when he removes honey from his hives. Okay, Beth, here's your eggs the way you like them." Beth took the plate and sat it in front of her.

"Danny, would you care for some more fried eggs?"

"No, Grandma, I'm going to have a couple biscuits with some of Grandpa's honey smeared all over them."

About a half hour later, George, Dora, Beth and Danny were sitting in the living room.

George looked toward Beth and asked, "Has the law found out who killed your husband?"

"No, not yet. My next door neighbor, Mr. Harry Spears was arrested for John's murder for a few days, but it was determined that he had nothing to do with the robbery or murder."

"I've known Harry Spears for years," George commented. "He's a very good man that wouldn't hurt a fly! Why in the world was he arrested in the first place?"

"Someone planted incriminating evidence at his house concerning the robbery and murder," Beth answered.

"They what----!"

"Someone placed a ski mask underneath his porch. It was one like the murderer was wearing, according to the law. The portrait of me and my family was also found at his house. It was the one that use to hang in the grocery store."

"Why did Mr. Spears have that portrait?" Dora asked.

"Apparently, the murderer left it on his porch to incriminate him. Someone tried to break into my house a few nights ago."

"My Lord, Beth-----what did you do?" Dora asked, shocked to hear such news.

"At first the person tried to come through my bedroom window, but whoever it was couldn't raise the window. I heard him walk away from my window, but I was fearful that he might try to unlock my front door. When I walked quietly into my living room, I had John's pistol in my hand. I listened carefully as someone was messing with my door handle or the door lock. I felt as though the door would open any second. I did the only thing any red-bloodied American would have done."

"What!" Dora asked, as she leaned forward, with bulging eyes.

"I fired the pistol toward the doorway."

"Mother, did you shoot the sneaking scoundrel?" Danny asked, angrily.

"Well, to make a long story short, the law came and they determined from the blood drops on my porch that the person was, indeed, wounded. However, the person did flee from my house, leaving a blood spattered shoe across from my hedging. Detective Johnson from the sheriff's office believes that the murderer of my husband is the same man that tried to get into my house. Daddy, what kind of man would leave a dozen long stem roses on a widow's porch within days of her husband's death?"

"Only a lunatic or a real nut case would do something like that."

"I asked Danny how he got those scratches on his arm, but for some reason he wanted you to tell me how he got them."

"Beth, your son went into Brutus' pen to save a little dog from being killed by a much larger dog. He realized very quickly after running the larger dog off that his own life was now in danger. Danny ran fast as he could to get out of the bull's pen as Brutus came charging toward him. I know he did a very unwise thing, but he did save Mrs. Sarah Penn's dog from being viciously killed. For his heroic action, Mrs. Penn gave Danny a hundred dollar bill."

"Danny, you knew better than to go into that bull pen!"

"Mother, when I saw that big old dog holding that little dog in his mouth I couldn't help myself. I grabbed up a stick and I hurried inside that fence to get the big dog off the little one. At that particular time I didn't even realize that I was even in the bull pen. What was I suppose to do------let the big dog tear the little one to pieces?"

"Okay, Danny------it's over with and you're safe," Beth commented. "We'll just leave it there. How bad was Mrs. Penn's dog hurt?"

"To tell you the truth------Frisky was in a bad way when Danny got her out of the bull pen." George answered. "Since Frisky went to the vet's office, she's recuperating very well. I know what Danny did was reckless and somewhat foolish, but what a brave boy you've got! I couldn't be more proud of my grandson."

"Grandpa, show Mother the picture of my fish," said Danny, enthusiastically.

"Dora, will you get me the picture of Danny holding his nearly eleven pound bass? It's on our mantle." She handed it to her husband. "Look at your son, Beth; he's holding that big bass that he caught all by himself. In fact, that's the largest bass I've ever seen."

"My goodness-------that is a big fish! Danny, what did you do with your fish?"

"Mother, I put it back into the water."

"Why didn't you keep the fish?"

"I thought that old fish deserved another chance to be free and roam around in that big lake. Mother, when we get home I'll make darn sure that no one harms you!"

"Speaking of home------Danny and I need to be heading that way. I've got a lot to do today. I start back to work tomorrow morning."

"Grandma and Grandpa have got a big surprise for you," said Danny, smiling.

"They do---!"

"Yes, Beth, we've got a big ice cooler full of fresh-picked vegetables already processed and packaged for you to place inside your freezer," said Dora. "We've, also, got you a basket of vine ripened tomatoes, cucumbers, and some freshly-picked okra."

"Grandma, you forgot to tell mother about the two watermelons that Grandpa brought home for us."

"Yes, I certainly did. George picked two of his nicest watermelons for you and Danny. The name of the watermelons are called Congo. Henry plants a variety of watermelons each year, but Congo watermelons are his favorite."

"Mother, I really appreciate the vegetables and watermelons. Have you filled up your freezer from your garden?"

"We've filled up two large freezers, and we've shared our garden with our neighbors. I hate to see produce go to waste."

"Well, Danny, I'll go outside and unlock the trunk of my car," said Beth. "We should be able to put the cooler and watermelons into it. We'll put your dirty clothes that you brought into the backseat of the car."

George and Danny loaded the ice cooler and watermelons into Beth's car. Afterwards, Danny hugged his grandparents for his enjoyable stay, and so did Beth. They waved bye as they headed out of the driveway. Beth and Danny both remained quiet for several minutes. Finally, Danny spoke, "I'm mad as I can be!"

"Son, why are you mad?"

"It makes me mad as a bothered hornet to know that someone tried to break into our house! Mother, I shouldn't have left you alone for a whole week!"

"Danny, I'm just fine. I would have been even more afraid if you had been home the night of the attempted break-in. It was only right that you spend some time with your grandparents. What was the most fun thing you did while you were there?"

"I had fun each and every day."

"I realize that, but there must have been that one funny moment that you burst into laughter."

"Well, since you put it that way-----there was one time during the week that I laughed so hard that I was crying and laughing all at the same time."

"Tell me about it.".

"Well, Grandpa and I walked down to one of his irrigation ponds to do a little fishing. One side of the pond had been mowed, but the other side had grown up with tall grass, weeds and vines. After fishing for about thirty minutes, Grandpa said the fishing was better on the weeded side. I told him that my better judgment was causing me to stay on the cleared side. I wasn't about to walk over there, afraid I would step on a snake. Well, Grandpa was determined to go fish in his favorite fishing spot which was on the weeded side of the pond."

"What happened when he got to the over side?"

"Grandpa had only been over there about five minutes when I heard him holler out, 'My God- it's a big water moccasin!' Grandpa turned to run away, but his foot got caught in some vines. He tripped and fell face forward into the grass. Well, I only laughed a little bit then, but he got up quickly and started off again. Same as before, he tripped again from the vines. When he got up this time he yelled out, 'Dam, Sam something has got my feet'!"

"Danny, what in the world did your grandpa do then?" Beth asked, extremely concerned.

"I don't know."

"What do you mean-----I don't know?"

"I was on the ground laughing and crying at the same time! It was the funniest thing I've ever seen."

"I'll bet your grandfather didn't think it was funny. What did he say to you when he finally got back to where you were?"

"He only said four words," Danny answered.

"What were the four words?"

"Some friend you are!" They both burst into laughter.

A few minutes later, Danny turned toward his mother and said, "I wish you would do me a favor."

"What is the favor?"

"I would like for you to stop by Cedar Oaks Cemetery. I would like to visit my daddy's grave."

"Son, I'll be glad to. Last week I placed some new flowers in his vase. While I was at the cemetery, guess who I saw."

"Mother, I have no idea who you saw."

"I saw Mr. George Boone standing by your father's tombstone."

"Who is Mr. George Boone?"

"Son, that elderly man was your father's high school principal."

"What did he say about Daddy?"

"He said he was the best at everything while he attended Bellevue High School. Your father was the captain of the school's basket ball team. He was an honor student, outstanding base ball pitcher and he was chosen as the President of his junior and senior class. Mr. Boone said one other thing that I didn't know. He said that one time your father saved an eleven year old girl from drowning in Miles Lake. Mr. Boone said your father was never one to brag, but he did a lot of good for other people." Tears came into Beth's eyes.

Danny handed her a tissue. "Mother, please don't cry. I've told you before that it makes me very sad when you cry."

"I'm sorry, Danny, sometimes I can't help myself. Oh my goodness!"

"Mother, what's wrong?"

"I just remembered something!" Beth voiced, a bit startled.

"What did you remember?" Danny asked, him leaning toward his mother.

"John bought two things for you the day before he was killed. He asked me to give them to you the next day, but hearing the bad news concerning his death I forgot all about it until now."

"What did he buy for me?" Danny asked, inquisitively.

"He bought you a sterling silver necklace and a sterling silver bracelet. Each piece has an inscription engraved on it."

"What does the inscription say?"

"Let me think----oh yes, its' like this, the sterling silver pendant for your necklace is inscribed with four words that read, 'My Mother Loves Me'. Your bracelet has similar inscription which reads, 'My Father Loves Me'. Danny held his head downward as tears raced down his cheeks. He placed his hands over his eyes so his mother couldn't see his face. Beth didn't say a word as she sniffed back her own tears.

Beth and Danny stood in front of John Miller's tombstone for thirty minutes. Each of them was trying to find peace in their heart concerning what had happened to their love one. "Mother, do you think Daddy is with Jesus Christ this very moment?"

"Yes, I certainly do, Danny."

"Will Jesus punish the man that shot and killed Daddy?"

"You've asked me something that I can't answer. Only God would be able to answer that question."

"I hate the man that killed my Daddy! I would like to shoot him right between his eyes!"

"My goodness, Danny-------you shouldn't be saying things like that! What in the world has come over you talking like that beside your father's grave?"

"Mother, I can't help myself! I've got so much hate for that man that I don't know what to do! He ruined our lives forever!" Danny remarked, tearfully.

"Son, that's not true. We've got each other and our fond memories of your father. I want you to listen to me-----and listen well! Your father wouldn't want you to have hate in your heart. I knew your father a lot better than you did. John would want us to have happiness in our lives, not hate or total sadness! Danny, as much as you and I loved your father----he no longer exists, except in our hearts. Please believe me-----you won't always be sad and unhappy as you are now. Before you even realize it one day you'll be married and have your own family to love and take care of."

"I understand that, Mother------but what about you? How will you ever have happiness in your heart with Daddy gone?"

"Danny, I'm a Christian lady. I'm sure God will find a way for me to be happy once again."

Chapter 6

The following Saturday morning, Beth and Danny were eating breakfast. Danny nodded his head back and forth. "Why are you doing that?" Beth asked.

"Doing what?"

"You've been moving your head back and forth as though you've got something on your mind."

"I was just thinking about Mr. Harry Spears. He seems so unhappy whenever I'm around him."

"Danny, he's got a right to be unhappy; his mother has incurable cancer. His wife is dead, and he doesn't have to work like most men. He sits alone in that big house all day and that's enough to drive a normal person insane."

"Why doesn't he have a job?" Danny asked.

"He doesn't need the money. After graduating from college his primary goal for the next twenty years was to make money, lots of money. Mr. Spears had the good fortune of making the right investments during those years. I don't know how much money he has, but I've been told that he is a multi-millionaire."

"He don't act like a man with a millions of dollars." Danny remarked.

"No, he certainly doesn't. He's just a nice, lonely man with lots of money."

"His two-story house is very big, but he doesn't live in a mansion. I thought all millionaires lived in mansions."

"Not always, Danny. Mr. Spears has no desire to live in a mansion."

"You should see what he's got stored inside that three-car garage of his," Danny remarked, excitedly.

"You've been in his garage?"

"I was at his house yesterday. He asked me if I would like to see something pretty. Well, you know what my answer was concerning that question. Anyway, he took me inside his garage and I've never seen so much stuff! He had a new looking bass boat, a Harley Davidson motorcycle, three bicycles, a canoe, fishing equipment, kayak, two sets of golf clubs, two sets of bow and arrow equipment, and an old timey car that looked like it was new. The Harley Davidson

Motorcycle had less than a hundred miles on the mileage indicator."

"Danny, always remember this one thing during your lifetime--------money alone never makes anyone happy. Mr. Spears has all those things you mentioned, but he doesn't have anyone to share them with. He bought those things to bring some pleasure and happiness into his life. Without a wife or close friend, purchasing those things didn't help him very much."

"We're his friends."

"That's true, but we still aren't what you would call very close friends with Mr. Spears."

"Why is that?"

"I don't know if I can explain it to you or not, but I'll try. Mr. Spears is somewhat anti-social. That means he's not what you would call a people person."

"You're right, you're not explaining it so I can understand it," said Danny.

"I'll try again," said Beth. "Mr. Spears is a bashful sort of individual that doesn't like to mingle with other people very often. In fact, he's close to being a recluse."

"What's a recluse?"

"Danny, you're making this very difficult for me. My last word on the subject is this; a recluse is a person that avoids most people and lives a more solitary life."

Moving his head back and forth, Danny remarked, "No wonder Mr. Spears is so unhappy. Who in the world would want to live like a recluse?"

"I see you're still wearing your necklace and bracelet."

"Mother, I don't think I'll ever take off the last gift that my daddy ever bought me. Oh, by the way, did you see the way that blonde headed guy was looking at you at the mall yesterday? I wanted to go kick him in his-------!"

"Danny, that's no way for you to talk! You can't kick someone every time they do something you don't like! I do like most women do when something like that happens."

"What's that?"

"We ignore obnoxious men like that!"

"Mother, do you think you'll ever get married again?"

"My goodness son, why would you ask a question like that?"

"Well, for one reason-------you're still a beautiful woman."

"It's much too soon to even discuss my marrying again, but I do appreciate your nice compliment concerning me. Do you realize that you'll be a teenager on your next birthday?"

"Mother, my birthday is a long ways off."

"I know how excited I was when I became a teenager."

"How did you feel when you became a teenager?"

"Oh, it was a wonderful feeling. The feeling of greater maturity made me see the world in a different light. It was then that I put away a great deal of my childish ways. Becoming a teen is when your body starts experiencing a rash of changes that's hard to explain."

"Mother, I'm only twelve, but I'm not six years old. I know what changes you're talking about."

"Oh!" Beth mumbled. "What would you like for your birthday?"

"I'm not sure what I want, but I do know who I want invited to my birthday party."

"Besides your grandparents, who could that be?"

"I want you to invite Shelia Johnson to my birthday party."

"Is there any particular reason why you would invite her and not some of the other girls you know?"

"I can think of four reasons right off the bat. She's beautiful, got a great personality, extremely intelligent, and I like her a great deal."

"My goodness, it sounds like you've got yourself a girlfriend," said Beth, smiling.

"Mother, let's go to the city park this afternoon. We haven't been to the park at all this summer. We could stop at a fast food place and take some food with us to the park.

You know you would like to see those different colored fish swim around and around in the park's pond."

"Okay, you talked me into it," said Beth. "Is there anything else that you would like for me to do?"

"Well, as a matter of fact there is something else I would like for you to do."

"Out with it, what would you like for me to do?"

"Invite Shelia Johnson to go with us," Danny answered, him grinning.

"You want me to pick up my phone and call Detective Randy Johnson and ask him if his daughter can go to the park with us! Is that what you want me to do?"

"Yes Mother, it's as simple as that," Danny answered, smiling.

"If it's so simple I'll let you call Mr. Johnson to see if Shelia can go to the park with you and your mother."

"All of a sudden it don't seem so simple," Danny remarked. "Okay, I'll call Mr. Johnson and I'll ask him myself! Look up his number for me and then I'll make the call. I'll need to know what time we can pick Shelia up from her house, that is------if she can go with us to the park."

"Tell Mr. Johnson that we'll be at his house at two o'clock, provided Shelia can go with us."

Beth looked up Randy Johnson's phone number from her phone directory. She wrote the number on a small piece of paper and then she handed to Danny. He sat down in a chair near their house phone. With some reservation, he picked up the receiver; he just sat there with the phone in his hand."

"Danny, what are you doing?" Beth asked.

"I'm thinking."

"What are you thinking about?" His mother asked.

"I was thinking about Mr. Johnson, and how mad he might get when I ask him if Shelia can go to the park with me. He does carry a gun with him whenever he leaves his house."

"Danny, you know very well that Mr. Johnson is not going to shoot you for asking his daughter to go on a picnic with us," said Beth. "You've got his number, now dial it!"

With a great deal of apprehension, Danny dialed the number that his mother gave him. A man answered the phone. "Is this Mr. Randy Johnson?" Danny asked.

A stern sounding voice replied, "Yes, may I help you?"

"Mr. Johnson, this is Danny Miller. Remember me, my mother's name is Beth Miller."

"Yes Danny, I remember you and your mother," Mr. Johnson replied. "How are things going with you and your mother?"

"Everything is fine, Mr. Johnson. Sir, my mother and I are going to the city park this afternoon and have ourselves an old timey picnic. I would like for Shelia to go with us, if you wouldn't mind."

"Hold on for a minute," said Mr. Johnson, "I'll go ask her if she would like to go." He came back to the phone about a minute letter and said, 'Shelia said she would love to go on a picnic with you and your mother. What time should she be ready?"

"Mother and I will be at your house at two o'clock today to get Shelia."

"That will be fine, Danny. Tell your mother that I said hello."

"I will Mr. Johnson. Thank you for letting Shelia go with us."

"You're welcome, Danny. I'm sure she will have a great time at the park with you and your mother."

Beth and Danny arrived at Randy Johnson's house at 1:52 that afternoon. Randy and Shelia walked onto their porch. Danny exited his car quickly so he could open a car door for Shelia. Randy walked out to the driver's side of Beth's car. Shelia got into the backseat, and then Danny sat down next to her. "Mrs. Miller, I hope you're doing well these days."

"Mr. Johnson, I've gotten to the point that I'm not as fearful about someone trying to break into my house."

"That's very good," Randy remarked. "Boy, you've got some food in that container that smells very good. My nose tells me you got some good old fried chicken in there somewhere."

"Mr. Johnson, we're going to the park to eat some of this good smelling food. Why don't you go with us?"

"Danny, I really do appreciate the offer, but perhaps later would be a better time for me do something like that, especially since the situation is like it is. I believe your mother understands what I'm trying to say. Mrs. Miller, I hope you and these kids have a wonderful time at the park."

"Thank you," Beth replied.

Danny and Shelia were all smiles as Beth drove her car toward the park. "Mother, Shelia has her birthday about a month after I have mine," said Danny.

"Shelia, do you help your father with the housework, such as cooking, washing dishes and doing the laundry?"

"Yes, Mrs. Miller, I often do those things you just mentioned. My father has taught me how to do nearly everything a housewife would normally do as far as work is concerned."

"You must love your father a great deal."

"I do. I love him more than I could ever say. My father has had a very difficult time accepting my mother's death. Quite often I wish that he would meet a nice lady to spend the rest of his life with, but I'm not sure that will ever happen. Mrs. Miller, I've heard my father say that you were a very nice lady."

"Well, that was nice of your father to say that," Beth commented. "Well, we're at the park. I'll drive over to that vacant shelter with the nice benches underneath it so we can enjoy our food."

"Mrs. Miller, you sure did bring a lot of food for our picnic," Shelia commented.

"I want you and Danny to eat all you care to eat, and then I want you and him to enjoy your day in the park."

Following their meal, Beth observed Danny and Shelia having a great time on the playground equipment. She was very glad that her son was finally smiling and having a good time instead of being tormented by his father's death.

About an hour later, Beth noticed a man sitting alone under one of the park shelters on the other side of the park. At first she paid no attention to him, but when she looked again he was gone.

Beth walked to where the fish pond was located, which was about a hundred yards from where she had parked her car. A few minutes later, she happened to see that same man sitting on a bench near where her car was parked. He was wearing sunglasses and a hat. She wondered why a man would be wearing a hat underneath a shaded oak tree.

At 5:30 that afternoon Beth told Danny and Shelia that it was time for them to go.

"Mother, we've had a great time today!" Danny sounded. "Didn't we, Shelia?"

"We sure did, Mrs. Miller. I'm very glad I was invited on your picnic."

Danny and Shelia got into the backseat. Beth opened her door on the driver's seat. On the floor board of her car was a sealed envelope. She stood there wondering how that envelope got into her car. She picked up the envelope, and then she sat down. Beth started to open the envelope, but decided to wait until she got home to open it.

Randy Johnson was sitting in his porch swing when Beth pulled into his driveway. He walked to Beth's car as Danny opened Shelia's car door for her. "Mrs. Miller, how did your afternoon go?" Randy asked.

"We had a wonderful time. I think your daughter thoroughly enjoyed herself. I know my son had a great time."

"Were there very many people at the park?" Randy asked.

"Not at all, which was surprising to me," Beth answered.

"There were several women and children in the park, but I only saw one grown man. By the way, he acted a little on the weird side."

"What do you mean----weird?"

"Well, for one thing he kept looking toward me while he moved from one park bench to another. The last time I saw him he was on a bench next to my car. Wait a minute------maybe that's why I had that sealed envelope on my floor mat. I'll bet that man may have placed it in my car."

"Mrs. Miller, don't touch that envelope again until I get a pair of latex gloves from my vehicle." Randy walked hurriedly toward his car.

Randy came back to Beth's car; he offered the gloves to her. "Mr. Johnson, if you don't mind, will you open the envelope? I've got a bad feeling about its' contents." He carefully unsealed the envelope and withdrew a single sheet of paper. Beth observed Randy's expression change as he read the paper's contents. "Mr. Johnson, what does it say?"

"Shelia, why don't you take Danny inside and show him your talking bird," Randy suggested.

"I've never seen a talking bird!" Danny commented, excitedly. The kids exited Beth's car; they hurried inside Randy's house.

Randy handed the letter to Beth for her to read. It read, 'Titter tatter, your head I'm going to splatter. You don't remember me, but I've always remembered you! That's why I took that picture and frame from your grocery store. I've had you on my mind for years. Until you shot my ear off I wanted you for myself, but that's all changed now. I'm going to shoot your ear off just like you did mine. After I get through with you, I'll put a bullet into your back just like I did that husband of yours. I nearly bled to death that night you shot me on your porch. That was a sneaky, underhanded thing you did by shooting through your door. I wasn't expecting you to do that. If you knew my name, you might know who it is that's going to kill you. I'll give you a tiny clue as to who I am. My name could be George, Ralph, or even Sam, but you could care less and you wouldn't give a damn. On second thought, I don't think I'll tell you who I am. It might be days, weeks, months or even years before you see my face and my one ear. Make no mistake about it------I'm going to kill you and your son for shooting off my ear! When you least expect it, that's when it will happen!'

Tears came into Beth's eyes. She handed a latex glove to Randy so he could take the letter. What am I going to do?"

"Mrs. Miller, how did the man look? Was he short, tall, fat or thin?"

"Mr. Johnson, he was wearing sun glasses and a hat; he was too far away from me to describe him in detail. I know one thing------he was a tall, slender man."

"Do you think you could recognize him if you saw him again?" Randy asked.

"I don't think so. How am I going to protect myself and my son from this lunatic?"

"There's no question about him being a lunatic. Also, he's your husband's killer and the same man that attempted to break into your house. I'm going to talk with the sheriff and see what the best way would be for his office to give you some protection. From now on, don't open your door to anyone that you don't know or trust. Always have your pistol available to protect yourself. Without question, keep it away from Danny. Mrs. Miller, I'm sorry to say this, but you've got a real problem on your hand."

"Do you suppose there are any hidden cameras at the park?" Beth asked.

"That's a good point," Randy remarked. "I'll check on that. Would you like to go inside and see Shelia's talking bird?"

"Yes, but I can't stay very long. I want to thank you for letting Shelia go to the park with us."

"Mother, look at Shelia's pretty bird," said Danny excitedly. "Her bird can talk!"

"Shelia, your bird looks like it might be a parrot."

"It is a parrot, Mrs. Miller. Fee gee, say hello to Mrs. Miller."

"Hello!"

"Say Polly wants a cracker."

"Polly wants a cracker," said Fee gee. "Cracker! Cracker!"

"Shelia, you have a very pretty bird," said Beth. "How long have you had Fee gee?"

"We've had my bird for over three years now."

"Mr. Johnson, we do have to leave now. Shelia, we sure did enjoy your company at the park."

"Thank you, Mrs. Miller. Danny, I really did have a great time!"

"I did, too. I hope to see you very soon." Randy and Shelia were standing on their porch as Beth drove out of their driveway.

"What's with that little grin on your face?" Randy asked. "You act as though you've got something on your mind."

"Daddy, did you get a good look at Mrs. Miller?"

"Of course I did, Shelia. What's your point?"

"Well, for one thing she's about the sweetest, nicest, best-looking woman I've seen since my mother died."

"If you've got something to say------just say it," Randy remarked.

"I was just thinking that Mrs. Miller would make someone a great wife one of these days. Daddy, what do you think about that?"

"Shelia, Mrs. Miller is still mourning the death of her husband."

"I know that, Daddy, but she won't be mourning forever. If I were you, I would try to be there for her when her mourning stops. Daddy, do you get my meaning?"

"Yes, I suppose I do."

Chapter 7

Summer vacation seemed rather short to Danny Miller and many of his friends. He was in his second week of school. He and Shelia Johnson had become very good friends. Beth has been back working at Madison Electronics for nearly two and a half months now. She has been sleeping somewhat better for the last two or three weeks. She's still very concerned that the man she saw in the park will try to carry out his threat one day. Sheriff Alan Hick's provided personnel surveillance of her house for two weeks after Beth received her threatening letter. Beth places her pistol near her bed each night before she goes to sleep. She's determined to protect herself and her son from her husband's killer. She and Danny visits her husband's grave about twice each month. Beth is far more independent now than she thought she would be following John's death. She has a very good job with Madison Electronics. Also, her money from the sale of her grocery business has been safely invested in a variety of safe money markets, per advice of her C.P.A.

Detective Johnson was very disappointed that there were no hidden cameras at the city park the day Beth had a letter placed inside her car. The very next day he talked with several people at the park to see if they recognized the tall slender man that Beth referred to. No one seemed to know who the man was. John Miller's murder still remains unsolved. The envelope and letter was checked for finger prints, but whoever wrote the letter must have been wearing gloves of some sort. Randy Johnson is very concerned with Mrs. Miller's welfare, and that of her son. He's convinced that the person who wrote her that letter is dead serious in his threats. He wishes he could do more to protect her and Danny from John Miller's killer.

Alone and very depressed, Harry Spears has spent the last three days, and part of those nights at Glen Bernie Rest Home with his cancer stricken mother. The Spears' family doctor has told him that his unconscious mother could die at any moment with her incurable disease. "Mr. Spears, why don't you go home and get some restful sleep?" Doris Thigpen asked. "I'm the head nurse on this floor and I'll be working here until eight o'clock tomorrow morning. I promise to give you a call if your mother's condition changes."

"I am very tired," said Mr. Spears, "I'll go home on your promise to call if her situation deteriorates."

"Very good, you have my promise. Mr. Spears, your mother has told me that you don't have any brothers or sisters?"

"That's correct, I'm her only offspring. When she dies I'll be all alone in this world, except for my cat."

"Mr. Spears, you're a good looking man. Why don't you find yourself a nice lady and then get married? There are plenty of good women out there looking for someone to love and to be a good wife to their husband."

"I wish it were that easy to find a good woman that would be interested in me," said Mr. Spears. "I made enough money when I was younger to retire early, but I don't know how to socialize like some men do. I don't drink, gamble or go dancing like other men do, so how can I meet a nice lady?"

"Mr. Spears, whoever said you would meet some nice lady at a bar or someone that was a boozer? Do you have a computer at home?"

"Yes, I have two computers."

"That's it!" Doris sounded. "Get on one of the dating websites and key in the type of woman you're looking for. I guarantee that you'll get a response from someone. Plan a date for the two of you, and if you don't like her-----back to the drawing board."

"You seem to know a great deal about that sort of thing."

"Mr. Spears, I should know a thing or two. I was married for eighteen years until he was killed in a car accident. All I have to love now is Twinkles."

"Who is Twinkles?" Mr. Spears asked.

"Twinkles is my cat."

"What species of cat is Twinkles?"

"Mr. Spears, I have no idea what kind she is. I was driving home one day from work and I saw this pitiful looking cat beside the highway. I stopped my car, picked up the cat, and then I took her to my house."

"I love cats as well," Mr. Spears remarked. "I have a Persian cat named Thomas."

"I'll bet your cat is very pretty," said Doris, her smiling.

"You look very lovely when you smile, Mrs. Thigpen, or should I call you Miss Thigpen?"

"Miss will do just fine. You say I look lovely when I smile?"

"Yes, by all means you do. Miss Thigpen, I really don't know how to ask you this, but-------."

"But what, Mr. Spears, what would you like to ask me?"

Mr. Spears' face turned a little pinkish. "Well, I was just wondering about something."

"It would help me a tiny bit if you were to tell me what you're wondering about?" Doris remarked, curiously.

"Okay, I'll go ahead and say it. Would you consider going with me to dinner one evening?"

"Mr. Spears, are you asking me for a date?"

"Yes, I suppose I am. Would you consider what I just asked you to do?"

"Mr. Spears, I've already considered it!"

"I guess your answer will be no," he remarked, sadly.

"No, you're wrong. My answer is, yes. Mr. Spears, I hate to tell you this, but the doctor has told me that your mother will probably not last through the night. I think we should wait a few days before we have our date."

"I appreciate you telling me the news concerning my mother. I hate very much seeing her suffer like she's doing."

"In cases like this, death is not such a bad thing," Miss Thigpen remarked.

"I agree with you. My mother has suffered enough."

"Mr. Spears, you seem to be smiling about something."

"It's just that I'm so excited about our upcoming dinner date," said Mr. Spears, excitedly.

"May I ask you a personal question?"

"Sure, Miss Thigpen, go right ahead."

"What made you decide to ask me for a date?"

"Because you're such a very pretty lady, and you've been so nice and friendly towards me."

"I appreciate you saying those kind words, Mr. Spears."

Mrs. Spears died the next night just before midnight. Harry was at her bedside when she breathed her last breath. With tears in his eyes, he placed his hand against his mother's face. Doris Thigpen's heart was touched by the sadness exhibited on Mr. Spears' face. She placed her hand on his shoulders and said, "Mr. Spears, you might not want me to say this, but your mother is much better off now than she was yesterday. She was terminally ill and experiencing a great deal of pain and suffering."

"I know that, Miss Thigpen, I'm relieved that her pain and suffering has come to an end. I'm glad that I've already taken care of my mother's funeral arrangements at Nicholson Funeral Home. My mother asked me about three weeks ago to give you something after she passed on."

"Mr. Spears, why would your mother want to give me something?"

"She said that you had been extremely nice to her while she's been sick. Mother told me something else, but I don't think I should tell you what she said."

"Why not tell me, you've got my curiosity up."

"Well, she didn't say too much concerning you, just three words."

"Three words," Miss Thigpen questioned.

"My mother pointed toward you and said, 'She's the one.'"

"What do you suppose she meant by those three words, Mr. Spears?"

"Mother thought that you would make me a------well, I'm not totally sure what she meant. Anyway, Mother wanted you to have her beautiful necklace that she thought so much of. I would like to give it to you after my mother's funeral. Goodness, I don't even know where you live."

"I live in town at 301 Chestnut Street. Your mother was a very sweet lady. I became quite fond of her while she was here."

"I still hope you and I can go on a dinner date sometime after my mother's funeral," Mr. Spears commented."

"I don't see why we can't. Will it be okay to call you by your first name?"

"Of course you can. My first name is Harry. May I call you by your first name?"

"Yes, I would appreciate you doing that. It's obvious what my first name is because it's on my name tag. Your mother told me a lot of good things about you while she was well enough to talk."

"She did?"

"Yes, she certainly did," said Doris. "She said that you were a very warm hearted, intelligent man that deserved someone to share his life with."

"I hope she didn't tell you about my bad side," Harry said, jokingly.

"Your mother told me that you didn't have a bad side. I got to know her pretty well during the last two months she's been here."

Mrs. Spear's funeral was held on the third day of her death at Nicholson Funeral Home. About eighty people attended her funeral, including Beth Miller, Danny Miller, Sheriff Alan Hicks, Detective Randy Johnson and Doris Thigpen. Before the services started, Harry Spears sat alone on the front row. His head was lowered as though he was grieving. Doris Thigpen got up from her seat; she walked down the aisle and then she took a seat next to Harry. She placed her hand on his. As pitiful as any grown man can be, he whispered to Doris, "Thank you for not leaving me alone on this bench."

Later that day, Mrs. Spears was buried at Cedar Oaks Cemetery next to her deceased husband, Benjamin Spears. After the service ended at the grave site, Beth and Danny Miller walked up to Harry Spears and each of them hugged his neck. "Mr. Spears, I'm very sorry for your loss, but from what I've heard about your mother-----she's in a much better place now."

"Mrs. Miller, I do appreciate you saying those kind words. Danny, if you would come over to my house one day next week, I've got a surprise for you. It's something that I'm going to give you."

"What is it?" Danny asked, enthusiastically.

"If I told you what it was now then it wouldn't be a surprise, would it?" Mr. Spears remarked, him smiling. Doris Thigpen walked over to where Harry, Beth, and Danny were standing. A smile overshadowed Mr. Spears' face. "Mrs. Miller, I want you to meet a good friend of mine. She's a registered nurse and her name is Doris Thigpen."

"Hello, my name is Beth Miller, and this handsome boy beside me is my son, Danny."

"Mrs. Miller, I'm very glad to meet you and your son. I was Mrs. Spears' nurse before she died."

"I happen to be Mr. Spears' next door neighbor," said Beth. "He's a widower and he lives alone except for a roommate named Thomas."

"I've heard that he has a Persian cat. I have a cat as well. My cat's name is Twinkles."

Three days later, Harry Spears drove to his mother's house. As his mother's sole survivor, he has the heart-breaking task of going through her personal things. He took down a shoe box from her bedroom closet. Inside the box was a poem that he had written to her when he was only twelve years old. The poem was entitled, My Mother. It read, 'Even though I'm young I know what I want to say, you're the greatest mother each and every day, when I get grown I know what I want to do, to marry a nice lady just like you, my sincere poem I want you to keep, forever and always until your final sleep.' Tears slid down Mr. Spears' face, him realizing that his mother had kept his poem for all those years. Going through his mother's belongings was the hardest thing that he had ever done. After removing his mother's necklace from her jewelry box, Mr. Spears decided to come back later and finish going through his mother's possessions.

Harry Spears drove into Doris Thigpen's driveway at six o'clock that evening. Harry was very excited as he exited his car with six long-stemmed roses in his hand. This would be his first date since his wife was buried. Nervously, he rang Doris Thigpen's doorbell.

Doris opened her front door. "Harry Spears, you look very handsome in your dark suit and tie."

"Thank you. You look gorgeous in that blue dress!"

"Thank you. I bought it yesterday for this special occasion. Please----come inside. I see you have some pretty roses in your hand."

"I bought them especially for you." He handed the roses to Doris. "The florist I went to only had six long-stemmed roses left. I wanted to get you an even dozen; instead I got what roses they had."

"That was very sweet of you to bring me flowers. Have a seat while I find a vase to put these flowers in. Would you care for a cup of coffee before we go out?"

"If it won't be any trouble," Harry answered.

"It won't be any trouble at all. How do you like your coffee?"

"Just black-----please."

Doris came back a few minutes later with two cups of coffee. She handed him a cup. They sat silent on her couch for several seconds. Finally, Harry reached his hand inside his coat pocket and withdrew his mother's necklace. He handed it to Doris. "This is what my mother wanted you to have."

Doris's eyes opened wide as she took the necklace. "My goodness, it's beautiful! Harry, I really appreciate you giving me this fine looking necklace."

"It was what my mother wanted me to do. Why don't you put it on?"

"You mean-----now?" Doris asked.

"Yes, the necklace will compliment your good looks with its' ruby-red medallion." Doris placed the necklace on her neck. "My goodness, Doris-------I want you to go look in your mirror and see how well you look," Harry remarked, smiling.

She walked over to a wall mirror. "It does look good on me. I'm very grateful that your mother chose to give it to me. You told me yesterday that you had a special place for us to go today. This evening will be our very first date. I'm so excited! Have you decided where we'll be going?"

"If okay with you, I thought we would go to Radisson's Steak House," Harry answered.

"Oh, that's a very good choice, but it's very expensive to eat there."

"Doris, I want you to have the time of your life tonight, if that's possible. I've already reserved a table for us, including a bottle of champagne."

"I thought you never drank alcohol," Doris remarked.

"Well, I don't generally drink alcohol. On the other hand, I don't generally go on a date with a beautiful woman," Harry stated, him smiling.

'Well, I declare-----you do say the nicest things. Well, I guess I'm ready to go, if you are."

"You did something one day that I won't ever forget, no matter how long I live."

"What was that?" Doris asked, very concerned about the statement.

"It was at my mother's funeral. I was sitting on the front row all alone, extremely sad and very depressed. You came and sat down beside me; you even held my hand. Doris, I know I shouldn't say this, but I felt something in my heart that I hadn't experienced since my wife died. I don't know how to explain it, but I felt like you belonged beside me that mournful day. I guess what I'm trying to say is that I love you. Oh my goodness, I shouldn't have said that on our very first date." Tears were visible in his eyes; he held his head downward in an apologetic manner.

"Harry Spears, you just spoke your true feelings concerning me," said Doris. "I'm glad you did because I'm in love with you."

"You are?" Harry voiced, surprisingly. He placed his arms around Doris. "I'm so happy that I don't know what to do!" Without saying another word, Harry leaned forward; he kissed Doris passionately on her lips.

"My goodness, Harry, we'd better get to that steakhouse before you get any more riled up!"

"You mean you didn't like my kissing you."

"Yes, I enjoyed that kiss a great deal, but a woman can only take so much kissing before she comes unraveled. Maybe a glass of that chilled champaign will cool you down a couple notches. Heck fire, I believe I'll drink a glass or two!"

Harry and Doris arrived at Radisson's Steak House fifteen minutes later. They were escorted to their reserved table. They had only been sitting down for a few minutes before their waiter brought them a bottle of champagne embedded into a container of ice.

"I've never been to this restaurant before," said Doris. "I always thought it was too expensive for my budget. Have you eaten here before?"

"Yes, but it was never the same as it will be today."

"Why is that?" Doris asked, concerned about his statement.

"I've never been here with a pretty lady before."

"I appreciate that compliment. How come you and your wife never had any children?"

"We wanted to have children, but my wife couldn't have any. Dr. Michael Long tried everything he could to make my wife fertile, but nothing ever worked. Did you and your husband have any children?"

"Unfortunately, my husband never wanted any children. It took me years to understand why he didn't want any children. I found out after years of marriage that he had been going with other women while he was married to me. Just prior to his death, I found out that he was having an affair with my best friend."

"What happened?" Harry asked.

"I was planning to file for a divorce, but he was killed in a car accident before I had an opportunity to do that. I've had little trust for a man until I met you. You strike me as being an honorable, faithful man that wouldn't cheat on your wife."

"You're right about that, Doris. Not once did I ever cheat on my wife. In fact, I never thought about cheating on her. If you and I were to ever get together, I would never cheat on you either!"

"Harry, the music is playing, would you care to dance?" Doris asked.

"I'm not a very good dancer, but I certainly wouldn't turn down an offer from you."

As they slow danced to the music, Harry whispered in Doris' ear, "I'm very, very happy when I'm around you."

"I feel the same way as you," Doris responded. "I hope that I'm the woman that you have been looking for."

"After this dance, do you know what I would like to do?" Harry asked.

"No, but I hope it's for us to order our steaks."

Harry let out a big grin. "That's exactly what I wanted to do, and perhaps------start sipping on some of that chilled champaign."

"Your mother said you would be a lot of fun once you got to know me. Let's go back to our seats."

Harry and Doris ordered their food a few minutes later. Harry was on his second glass of champaign; Doris was still on her first glass. "Have you ever done much traveling?" Doris asked.

"Not really, but I sure would like to."

"Well, why don't you get into your car and head off somewhere one of these days?"

"I'll keep that in mind. Wouldn't it be nice if you could travel around with me?"

"That might not be such a good idea for a man and woman to travel together unless they're married," Doris remarked.

"Why don't you and I get married?" Harry asked, seriously.

"Goodness, what would people say? Because of your mother, we've only known each other for a couple months, and this is our very first date!"

"Doris Thigpen, I know what I want! I'm in love with you and I don't care what people will think or say. Right here at this table-----right here and now-----I'm asking you to be my wife! I've got plenty of money and I promise to be a good husband to you for as long as I live!" Tears slid down Harry's face as he waited for her response. He placed his hand on top of hers. "Please----Doris, will you be my wife?"

People sitting at three nearby tables waited anxiously for Doris to say something. All of a sudden people in the restaurant were banging on their tables and chanting, 'Please Doris, marry the guy!' Doris lowered her head for a few seconds. The chanting continued. Finally, with tears in her eyes, Doris answered, "Yes, I will marry you!" Harry got up from his chair; he placed his arms around Doris and then he kissed her on her lips. They hardly noticed the thunderous applause they were getting as they embraced each other with hugs and kisses. "Harry, I believe we had better order another bottle of champaign. Better still, maybe we should order more ice for the bottle we already have."

"Doris Thigpen, I sure like the way you think! When do you think we can get married?"

"How soon would you like to get married?" Doris asked.

"I would like for us to get married very soon, but I'll leave that up to you."

"I'm so excited I can hardly think! I could plan for our wedding to be in about thirty days or so. Harry, would that be okay with you?"

"That would be fine with me. Doris, I'm going to make you very, very happy. Before I forget it, how do you like to fish?"

"I love to fish. I even bait my own hook." Doris said, her smiling.

"Have you ever played golf?" Harry asked.

"I should say I have. I've got my own golf clubs."

"My, oh, my-----we'll have a wonderful time traveling, fishing and playing golf," Harry remarked, him smiling.

"Wait just a minute, Harry. I've still got a job. I may not be able to get off from work as much as you would like for me to."

"Let me ask you this, do you still look forward to getting up early and working late, day after day?"

"Of course I don't like to do that."

"Well then-----after we're married you can quit your job forever. I'll take care of all your needs. You won't have a worry in the world. Doris, how does that sound to you?"

"It sounds great!" Doris replied, excitedly. "I'm looking forward to becoming your wife!"

Chapter 8

Thirty-three days later on a chilly Sunday afternoon, Harry and Doris became man and wife. Dr. Emanuel Dorset, Doris' pastor, officiated their wedding at Holy Trinity Methodist Church. For Harry and Doris, it seemed to be the happiest time of their lives. Approximately, eighty individuals attended their wedding. Some of the attendees were Doris' relatives and her friends, many others were friends of Harry Spears. Until now, Harry never realized that so many people even knew about him. Tears came into Beth Miller's eyes when the preacher pronounced them husband and wife. She recalled what Harry Spears' mother's last wish was------that he find himself a good woman to love and look after her son. Danny handed his mother a tissue to dry her eyes.

Also, in attendance was Randy Johnson and his daughter Shelia, Sheriff Alan Hicks, Henry and Delores Miller, and George and Dora Eason.

Harry and Doris were given a big round of applause as they exited the church. People were lined up on both sides of the sidewalk with their tiny bags of rice. All at once, they dashed toward Harry Spears car. Rice rained down on them as the crowd cheered them on. Once inside the car, they both waved at the excited crowd as they drove away. Harry Spears car had shaving cream smeared all over the top of the car, with toilet paper dangling in the air.

Randy and Shelia Johnson walked to where Beth and Danny Miller were standing.

"Beth, that was a beautiful wedding," Randy commented.

"Yes, it certainly was. I just wish that Mrs. Edna Spears could have been here to see her son get married. That very thought was on my mind during the ceremony."

"Shelia, you look pretty today."

"Thank you, Danny. You look quite handsome yourself. Don't he, Daddy?"

"Yes, sweetheart, Danny does look handsome. Do you know why he is so handsome?"

"Why is that?" Shelia asked.

"Because his mother is so doggone good looking."

"Randy, that was a very nice compliment-----thank you," Beth answered with a broad smile.

"Mother, I was wondering where Mr. Spears and his new bride will be going on their honeymoon."

"I don't think you should be that inquisitive concerning that sort of thing," Beth answered.

"I know where they're going," Shelia remarked.

"How in the world would you know that?" Randy asked, curiously.

"I heard a lady say where they're going. They will be spending the next several days at the beach."

"Well, anytime you want to know something------just ask a teenager," commented Randy, him smiling.

Harry and his new bride were on their way to the beach. This would be Doris's first opportunity to see her husband's beach house that was located on the sound side of Emerald Isle. For several days, this would be their honeymoon retreat. Harry had told her already that the beach house looked exactly like the one that he was presently living in.

They had been on the road for thirty minutes. Harry turned toward Doris. He said, "You have made me a very happy man."

"Well, you've made me a very happy woman. I can't remember all the lonely nights that I laid in bed wondering if this day would ever come."

"It's hard to believe that you went as long as you did without marrying someone," Harry commented.

"Why do you say that?"

"Well, for one thing------you're a very pretty lady. I'm surprised that men weren't pestering you for a date."

"There were some that did do exactly that, but I'm a Christian lady and I knew exactly what those men were interested in. What about you, Harry? I'm sure there were some women very interested in you since you've got so much money and all."

"As a matter of fact, I had one woman to call my home phone number. She said she would come to my house and sleep with me all night if I paid her seven hundred dollars."

"My goodness, what was your answer?"

"I would be ashamed to tell you what my answer was."

"Harry, after all------we are married now. You don't have to keep any secrets from me," said Doris.

"Are you sure you want me to tell you what I told her?"

"Yes, I'm quite sure."

"Okay, I'm going to tell you, but you've got to promise me that you won't laugh."

"You've got my promise."

"I said to her, why should I pay you a dime when I've got two good hands that are quite functional? The woman hung up the phone immediately. Doris, you're smiling.

You told me that you wouldn't laugh."

"I didn't say I wouldn't smile." They both started laughing.

They arrived at their cabin an hour later. After Harry opened the cabin door, he turned on the interior lights inside the cabin. "Doris, have a seat and I'll go bring in our luggage."

"Don't you want me to help with the luggage?" Doris asked.

"No, I want you to look in the phone directory and select a good seafood place for us to eat. While you do that, I'll bring in our luggage."

Doris selected Monty's Seafood Shack for their evening meal. That seafood restaurant was only a mile and a half from their cabin. Doris ordered flounder, baked potato and coleslaw. Harry ordered a large bowl of steamed oysters, baked potato and coleslaw. They each ordered sweet tea."

"Doris, don't you like oysters?" Harry asked.

"No, I never eat those things. They're too slimy for me. You don't seem to enjoy eating those oysters, yourself!"

"To tell you the truth, Doris------I don't particularly like oysters myself."

"Well, why didn't you order something else, like shrimp or fish?"

"I was just wondering if it's true what they say about oysters when a man eats them."

"Oh, I see what you're getting at," Doris remarked, her smiling. "Harry Spears, if you've been telling me the truth that you haven't had a woman since your wife died, then you certainly won't need any oysters to get you going. I can promise you that!"

Harry and Doris arrived back at the cabin an hour later. Harry went into one bathroom to shower and shave. Doris went into another bathroom to shower and to get ready for bed.

Harry was the first one to lie down on their honeymoon bed. All he had on was a pair of jockey underwear. A few minutes later, Doris appeared in the dimly lighted room with nothing on but a see through nightgown. Harry looked straight at her curvaceous body as she neared the bed.

"Doris, you were exactly right at the restaurant. I didn't need to eat those darn oysters. I'm about as primed as a man can possibly get." He slipped off his shorts; she dropped her nightgown to the floor. For several seconds they stared at each others' nakedness. All was quiet as Doris lay against her husband's naked body.

It was six months ago today that John Miller was shot down like an animal. The sheriff's department had exhausted all their leads, but they still hadn't found John's killer. Today, Sheriff Alan Hicks and several of his deputies are in the process of discussing the six months anniversary of John Miller's death. Included in the group is Detective Randy Johnson. "The reason I have assembled you men together this morning is to let you know that I and my department will never quit trying to locate John Miller's murderer. According to Detective Johnson, Mr. Miller's murderer is the same individual that tried to break into Beth Miller's house. We've got blood samples from that weirdo because Mrs. Miller shot his ear off when she shot through her door. The reason we know that is because sometime later the killer was at the city park. According to Mrs. Miller the suspect kept looking toward her from different places in the park. He left a threatening letter inside her car stating that she had shot off one of his ears. That man has vowed that he would do terrible things to her before he shot off her ear, and then he would kill her. He didn't stop there; he promised her that he was going to kill her twelve year old child as well. After all this time I'm surprised that he hasn't tried to carry out his threats. He indicated on the letter that she wouldn't know the day, week, month or year that her life would end, but it would end when she least expected it to happen. Are there any questions before I continue?"

"Sheriff Hicks, if Mrs. Miller saw the man in the park, why can't she describe what he looked like?" Deputy Wally Benson asked.

"He never got close enough for her to see exactly what he looked like. He was wearing sun glasses and a hat during the time he was observing Mrs. Miller. She did give us some pertinent information. According to her, he's Caucasian, tall and slender. Mrs. Miller's life and her son's life may very well depend on whether we catch this killer or not. Detective Johnson, don't you have something to say concerning this case?"

"Yes Sheriff, I do have something to say. I have read that letter more than a dozen times. The murderer indicates that Mrs. Miller would know who he is if she knew his name. That indicates to me that sometime during her life she met someone, or someone met her that liked her a great deal. Apparently, Mrs. Miller wasn't interested in him for whatever reason. My theory is this; either it was someone she knew while attending high school or college. Somewhere or sometime this individual was perhaps rejected in some way by Beth Miller. If my theory is correct, I need to jog her memory so we can start getting a list of individuals that we need to talk with. I have no idea why this individual hasn't tried a second time to break into her house."

"Detective Johnson, I have a good idea why he hasn't tried again," Deputy Warren Gooding remarked.

"Ok, Deputy, what is your theory on that?".

"He doesn't want to lose his other ear!" Everyone in the room burst into laughter.

"Detective Johnson, have you ever considered that this guy never did get his ear shot off?" Deputy Barney Eason asked."

"There's no doubt that Mrs. Miller's bullet struck him somewhere because of the blood on the porch and also blood on the shoe left in her yard. It would be very easy to spot a man walking around with one ear. Furthermore, right after the attempted break in we checked every hospital within fifty miles of her house to see if someone came in with a missing ear. We never found anyone that had gone to the hospital for that kind of treatment."

"You've both made very strong points," Sheriff Hicks responded. "However, my honest to goodness opinion is this------unless he's already incarcerated somewhere, he'll carry out his threat in due time. We've got to do everything we can to prevent that potential tragedy. Detective Johnson, I want you to talk with Mrs. Miller this weekend. I'll be praying that she can come up with some potential names."

After Detective Johnson came out of the meeting he wasted no time calling Madison Electronics. He asked the receptionist if he could speak briefly with Mrs. Beth Miller. Within a few seconds, Beth was on the phone. "Hello," she said.

"Mrs. Miller, I'm Detective Johnson, I was wondering if you would be available sometime Saturday to talk with me. It's concerning the letter that was placed inside your car at the park."

"Yes, I'll have time to discuss that matter with you on Saturday. The only other thing I'll be doing is planning Danny's upcoming birthday which is three days from now."

"I've got to do the same thing for Shelia in about thirty-five days from now. It's hard to believe that our children will soon be thirteen years old. Mrs. Miller, had you rather for me to come in the morning or afternoon?"

"How about coming at two o'clock? By then I will have finished with Danny's birthday invitations."

"Will I be getting an invitation?"

"Detective, you know darn well that you and Shelia will be getting an invitation." She said, smiling.

It was Saturday morning, Beth and Danny had just finished eating their breakfast. Still sitting at the breakfast table, Danny turned toward his mother and said, "Mother, I hope you haven't forgotten what happens in three days from now," Danny remarked, overly concerned.

"No, sweetheart, I haven't forgotten about your birthday. What would you like to have?"

"I guess maybe a smart phone or something like that. Most of all, I want you to invite Shelia to my birthday party."

"Danny, you seem to like her a great deal."

"Mother, she's about the prettiest thing I've ever seen, except for you, of course. She told me something that I promised not to tell you."

"What did she tell you to not tell me?" Beth inquired.

"Mother, I gave her my promise that I wouldn't tell you what she said."

"Okay, I won't have you to break your promise."

"There's just one thing!"

"Okay, Danny, what one thing are you talking about?"

"I want to tell you what she said, but that promise-------!"

"Well, I don't have to know what she said."

"I'm not sure about that, Mother. You probably need to know what Shelia said concerning you."

"Danny Miller, promise or no promise, you tell me this instant what Shelia said concerning me!" Beth voiced, loudly.

"Okay Mother, I'll tell you what she said, but you don't have to get hostile with me."

"I'm sorry for scolding at you the way I did, but you kept on teasing me about what Shelia said concerning me. Now for the last time, what did she say concerning me?"

"You're going to be floored when I tell you what she said," Danny commented, him smiling.

"For goodness sakes, Danny-------just tell me what she said!"

"Okay, here it goes. Her father likes you a great deal."

"What do you mean-----likes me a great deal?"

"According to Shelia, Mr. Johnson says nice things about you all the time. Okay, I'm going to let the real cat out of the bag right here and now!"

"Danny Miller, you're talking in circles! What cat are you talking about?"

"Okay, I'll never forgive myself for saying this, but here goes! One night about a week ago, Mr. Johnson asked Shelia how she would like for you to be her mother. Shelia told him that she would love to have you for her mother." Beth's mouth opened up; she seemed startled hearing what Danny had just said. "Mother, there's more to the story, should I continue?"

"Yes. I want to hear the rest of it."

"Well, it seems that Shelia asked her father why he hasn't shown more interest in you, or asked you out on a date. Do you want to know what his answer was?"

"Tell me everything, Danny." Beth answered, tearfully.

"Mr. Johnson told Shelia that he wanted you to have ample time to mourn your husband's death before he attempted to court you in anyway. Guess what Shelia told him."

"Just go ahead and tell me."

"She told her father that it had been six months or so since your husband was killed, and that if he waited any longer it might be too late."

"Too late for what, Danny?" Beth asked, curiously.

"I guess she meant that if he waited too long you might be interested in someone else. Mother, did I do the right thing by telling you what Shelia told me? Mother, where are you going?"

"I'm going to my bedroom for a few minutes. Will you place the dirty towels into the washer for me?" Beth hurried toward her bedroom. She closed her door and then she sat down on her bed. She could no longer control her emotions; tears streamed down her face. Danny walked to her bedroom door. He stood there silently listening to his mother cry.

"Mother, are you okay?" Danny asked, tearfully.

"Yes sweetheart, I'm fine," she answered, wiping away her tears. "I asked you to put the dirty towels in the washer. I'll be out in a few minutes." Danny did what his mother asked him to do. A few minutes later Beth picked up a picture of her husband; she held it lovingly against her face. It was at that very moment that she came to terms with his death. She realized that she couldn't mourn his death forever. Her husband was gone and he would never come back to her. Beth had known for over a month that her feelings for Randy Johnson were more than just casual. Beth walked out of her bedroom a few minutes later. Danny stood, tearfully, in the hallway as she walked to him with open arms. "I love you, Danny. I love you more than anything in this world!" She hugged him, and then she kissed him on his cheek. "Let's you and I go into the living room and have ourselves a good old fashion talk."

As they walked along, Danny said, "Mother, I'm sorry I upset you the way I did."

"It wasn't you that upset me. At some point in my life I had to have that crying spell that you just overheard. I'm just glad that I got it out of my system. Now, sit down on the couch and listen very carefully at what I'm going to tell you. As you well know, I loved your father as much as any wife can love their husband. Danny, your father's memory will always be a part of me, but my memory of him is all I have, or will ever have."

"Mother, what in the world are you saying?"

"Sweetheart, your father left us with precious memories of the things we did together and how we loved each other. Your father is gone; our memories of him is all we have. We can love and cherish those memories for as long as we live, but we've got to move forward with our lives."

"Mother, I surely do miss my daddy."

"I know you do, and so do I. The memory of your father will always be in our hearts. No man will ever replace your father."

"Does all this mean that you may start courting Mr. Johnson?"

"Danny, I haven't said a thing about courting Mr. Johnson! Remembering that no man will ever take your father's place, how would you feel if someday he and I were to start dating? Would that make you jealous?"

"Mother, all in the world I've ever wanted is for you to be happy."

Beth leaned over and gave her son a big hug. "Danny, I love you so much!"

"Uh oh, there you go again-----tearing up. I've told you that it makes me sad when you cry."

"Well then, I'll just have to make it a practice to not cry when you're around." Beth smiled.

Chapter 9

Randy Johnson drove into Beth Miller's yard at two o'clock that afternoon. Beth noticed him through her window when he walked onto her porch. By the time he rang the doorbell, she opened her front door. "Mrs. Miller, I appreciate you taking the time to talk with me today."

"Please come inside." He followed Beth into her living room. "May I get you a cup of coffee?" Beth asked.

"That would be nice. Have you noticed the weather today?"

"Yes, I stepped out on my porch a little while ago. It's rather breezy out there."

"Where's Danny this afternoon?" Randy asked "He's spending the night with John's parents. Mr. Miller, Danny's grandparent is taking him to play golf tomorrow morning. Mr. Miller and his wife, Delores picked him up this morning.

"I didn't know that Danny played golf."

"According to Mr. Miller, Danny has the ability, initiative, and drive to be a great golfer."

"That's a mighty fine boy you've got, Mrs. Miller. If I were to have a son I would want him to be just like Danny."

"That's mighty nice of you to say that. By the same token, if I ever had a daughter I would want her to be just like Shelia."

"Mrs. Miller, I've wanted to ask you something for awhile now."

"What would you like to ask me?"

"Do you suppose we could refer to each other using just our first names?" Randy asked, hesitatingly.

"I don't see why not." They each stared toward each other for a few seconds. "Detective------oops, I mean Randy, what will we be discussing today? Oh goodness, I forgot to get your coffee! I'll be right back!" Beth returned a couple minutes later with each of them a cup of coffee."

"Beth, you know it seems a little awkward calling you by your first name, but it does have a rather soothing sound when I say it."

"I see you have a sheet of paper in your hand," Beth commented.

"Yes, as you can see-----it's the letter that was placed inside your car when you were having a picnic with Danny and Shelia at the park. Beth, whether you realize it or not, you probably know who your husband's killer is."

"What are you saying?" Beth asked, confused.

"The reason I'm here today is to try to jog your memory. I've got to find that killer before he attempts to carry out his threat! It would make me very, very sad if something were to happen to you. Anyway, the killer is giving you tell tale clues throughout that letter as to who he is."

"He is?"

"Yes. I firmly believe that the killer is someone that you met or knew a long time ago. It could have been while you were in high school or when you were in college. It was someone that you strongly rejected. It may have been because you wouldn't date him or something that you said to him. Let's take the first clue in his letter. He said, 'Titter tatter, your head I'm going to splatter. Think real hard, did you ever know an individual that quite often used poetry when he tried to make a point. Remember, this could be someone from your high school days or when you were in college. Try real hard to remember."

Beth closed her eyes momentarily, her thoughts went back in time as she tried to decipher whether she had ever met someone like that. "I remember one guy that quite often used a form of poetry when he tried to describe something, but I'm sure he's no killer. He was in one of my classes during my last year of college."

"Did he ever ask you for a date?"

"Yes, he asked me several times, but I always said no. I thought he was some kind of weirdo, him talking in poetic riddles."

"You did great on our very first tell tale clue," said Randy. "Can you remember his name?"

"Let me think-----yes, I believe his name was Vernon Madison." Randy quickly wrote his name down.

"What was the name of your college?"

"Bridgeport Business College or B.B.C."

"My next question will be the most important one of all. Was Vernon a tall man or short man?"

"He was tall, kind of slender."

"Look at the letter," said Randy, "the killer used rhyming words again toward the bottom part of the letter. He said, 'I'll give you a tiny clue as to who I am. My name could be George, Ralph, or even Sam, but you could care less and wouldn't give a damn.' Vernon Madison could very well be our killer!"

"Randy, I'm not sure about that. He didn't act like any killer that I've ever heard about."

"If you had been a detective as long as I have, you'd know right away that you can't look at a person and know what they're capable of. I'm going to check Vernon Madison out real good."

"Randy, my son told me some things this morning that I was totally unaware of," Beth remarked.

"What kind of things did he tell you?"

"Well, it was more like what Shelia had told him. He didn't want to tell me, but I kept nudging him to divulge the secret that Shelia had shared with him."

"Beth, I'm pretty sure I know what was said to your son. If it's what I think it is-----it's absolutely true." Randy's eyes watered up slightly. "I can't help it if I'm in love with you, but I've never attempted to cross the line while you were in mourning!"

"No you haven't, you've been a perfect gentleman," Beth responded. "I admire you for that."

"I'm a very lonely man, but because of my love and memory of my wife Doris, I haven't tried to date anyone. I'm sure it's the same thing with you concerning your husband; our memory of them is all we have left. Night after night, for the last several months, I have driven by your house hoping that I could keep you and Danny safe from your husband's killer. You're the only woman that has touched my heart since my wife died. My only wish is that you felt the way about me as I do you" Tears came into Beth's eyes. "Now look what I've done; I'm sorry for upsetting you."

"Randy, I do have feelings for you," said Beth, wiping away her tears. "I've been aware of my feelings toward you for over a month."

"I can't tell you how glad I am to hear you say that!" Randy responded, smiling. He placed his hand on hers. "Are you comfortable with my hand on yours?"

"Yes, I don't mind." Beth answered. She placed her other hand on top of his hand.

Silently, they looked toward each other for a few seconds. All at once, Randy moved closer to Beth. As though a passionate urge had taken over his body, he placed his arms around Beth's neck. She reciprocated by leaning closer to him. "Would you be mad if I kissed you on your lips?" He whispered in her ear.

"Is that what you want to do?" Beth asked, seriously.

"Yes, more than anything!"

"Then you have my permission." Randy, tenderly, placed his hands against Beth's face. As though Cupid had shot an arrow through his heart, he kissed her as passionately as he knew how.

"Beth Miller, I love you very much." Again, he held her close to him.

"Randy, what do you think our kids will say when they find out that we're in love with each other?"

"Shelia will be very joyful hearing the news! What about Danny? Do you think he will be happy knowing that you have a man in your life now?"

"We'll just have to wait and see what his thoughts are concerning our relationship. I know one thing!"

"What's that?" Randy asked.

"His crush on your daughter is about as big as my utility barn."

"That's a pretty big crush," Randy commented, him smiling.

"Yes, it certainly is," said Beth, as she hugged his neck tightly.

Henry Miller and Danny were on the twelfth hole at the Shady Oaks Country Club. It was a par three hole; Mr. Miller was holding a nine iron. "Danny, watch me closely as I go through my swing. When you tee off I want you to do exactly like I'm about to do. Danny, are you watching me?"

"Yes Grandpa, I'm watching you closely."

Mr. Miller took one last look at the flag pole; his arms came down swiftly, hitting the ball high in the air. They both watched as the ball came downward and into a water hazard.

"Is that what you want me to do, Grandpa?" Danny smiled. "I don't know whether I can make my ball make a big splash like that."

"Oh, my goodness," Mr. Miller mumbled. "I'll never be able to live this down."

Danny took a full swing with a six iron; the ball landed about eight feet from the flag pole. "Did you say something, Grandpa?"

"Not really. I was just mumbling to myself. Danny, how good are you about keeping secrets?"

"I believe I'm pretty good at keeping secrets. Why do you ask?"

"Well, maybe too much talk shouldn't get out about my twelve year old grandchild beating me on the golf course."

"Grandpa, I won't say a word about your last five holes, or was it the last six holes?"

"Smarty pants!" Mr. Miller mumbled.

"Grandpa, will it be okay if I drive the golf cart?"

"I don't see why not. Just don't run into any pine trees on the way."

"No sir, I won't hit any trees like you did when you backed into that oak tree after our first tee shot. Do you remember backing into that tree when we were in the woods looking for your lost ball?"

"It should be against the law to go golfing with a twelve year old, especially if he's your grandson," Henry muttered. "Danny, I wouldn't mention that little accident when we get back to the clubhouse. Anyway, I don't think I did much damage to the golf cart."

"Grandpa, how many golf balls have you lost so far?" Danny asked, him smiling.

"Smarty pants-----I've only lost four balls, but you can't count two of them."

"Why is that?" Danny asked.

"Two of them went into the water. Since I couldn't retrieve them from the water they shouldn't count as lost balls," George remarked, him smiling.

"Grandpa, what kind of work did you do before you retired?"

"I was a sales manager for a large manufacturing company. Why do you ask?"

"Well, I don't know what I want to do when I grow up."

"You'll figure that out when you get older," Henry remarked. "How is my daughter in-law getting along these days?"

"Mother is doing much better now. Grandpa, I believe she likes a man that she knows."

"What man are you talking about?"

"His name is Randy Johnson. He's a detective with the sheriff's department. He's the one that has been investigating my daddy's murder. Grandpa, he's got the prettiest daughter that I've ever seen. She's about my age and I sure do like her a lot!"

"Well, it's been six months or longer since John's death. It's time for Beth to move on with her life. Danny, how well do you like this guy?"

"Grandpa, I already know that no man will ever be able to fill my daddy's shoes, but more than anything------I want my mother to be happy. Mr. Johnson is a very nice man. I believe Mother likes him a lot. There is just one tiny problem."

"What problem are you talking about?"

"Wouldn't Shelia become my sister if Mother ever married Mr. Johnson? How could I still be sweet on her if she were my sister?"

"She still wouldn't be any kin to you, except by marriage. In that case you would have to decide which you rather have-------a girlfriend or a sister. Do you understand what I just said?"

"Not really, but we had better tee off because there's two golf carts waiting behind us."

Sheriff Alan Hicks and his staff were busy checking out information that Detective Randy Johnson had provided them concerning Vernon Madison. Some deputies were assigned to contact prisons and jails to see if they had him locked up anywhere. Detective Johnson discovered that seven men in the eastern part of his state were named Vernon Madison. He intended to contact each of those men in person; he would be looking to see if the men were tall, slender or whether they had a missing ear. Randy's intention was to start checking on those men the following morning.

At 6:45 the next morning, Randy's phone rang. He picked up the phone to learn that it was Sheriff Alan Hicks that had called him. "Randy, don't come into the office this morning. I want you to go to Central Prison in Raleigh. They have an inmate there named Vernon Madison. Coincidental, he's tall and sort of skinny."

"Thank you, Sheriff Hicks. I'll be on my way there in about thirty minutes."

"Daddy, can you drop me off at school this morning?" Shelia asked. "Mrs. Barnes has a doctor appointment this morning and won't be able to take me."

"What about this afternoon?" Randy asked.

"Don't worry; she'll bring me home this afternoon. Daddy, I shouldn't have, but I told Danny how you felt about his mother."

"Sweetheart, I'm very glad you did. His mother knows now how I feel about her. In fact, we go on our first date this weekend."

"That's wonderful, Daddy. You be real nice to Mrs. Miller! What does Danny think about the situation concerning you and his mother?"

"Sweetheart, I'm not sure that Danny knows that we are about to start dating. If he doesn't, he'll know very soon. I know one thing."

"What's that?"

"He surely does like you."

"Gee Daddy----that's old news. Danny has liked me for a long time."

Randy arrived at Central Prison two hours later. After identifying himself, he was permitted to go inside the prison to the Warden's office. Warden Jake Beasley stood up when he came into his office. "Are you Detective Randy Johnson?" Warden Beasley asked.

"Yes sir."

"Sheriff Alan Hicks called me earlier and said that you would be here this morning. Please, have a seat. I've got a fresh pot of coffee. Would you care for a cup?"

"I believe I will," Randy responded.

Warden Beasley poured coffee into two cups. He handed Randy one of the cups. "I understand from Sheriff Hicks that you're trying to solve a homicide that happened in your county."

"That's correct. We're particularly interested in one of your inmates. His name is Vernon Madison."

Warden Beasley looked up Vernon Madison's file very quickly using his computer. "Detective Johnson, step over here to my computer and you'll be able to see about anything you want to pertaining to Vernon Madison, including a police photograph of him. He's six foot, three inches tall, slender built and he's been incarcerated here for the last three months. He was convicted of stabbing two men at a bar. He received a sentence of three to five years in prison. Do you need any more information on him?"

"Warden I need two things. I need to ask Mr. Madison some questions. I, also, need a blood sample from him. I brought a blood sample for the State Bureau of Investigation to check against his blood sample. If it matches, Vernon Madison is our murderer."

"I can arrange for you to talk with Mr. Madison today, but a blood sample from him will require a court order. Getting the court order from Judge Judith Mc Cory won't be a problem, but it might take some time to get it. I'll place your blood sample in our secured lock box for safekeeping. I'll make sure that the S.B.I gets the blood sample that you brought, along with Mr. Madison's blood sample. I'll do what I can to expedite their testing." Warden Beasley picked up his phone. "Joe, bring Vernon Madison to room A. There's a county detective here to ask him some questions."

"Detective Johnson, you be on guard at all times while you talk to this nut case. I believe he's got some screws loose in his head. There will be two guards in that room, but take my word for it------ watch yourself at all times. How is my old friend, Sheriff Alan Hicks?"

"He's doing just fine, especially if we can solve the murder case that I'm on."

"Okay, follow me; we'll go to room A where Mr. Madison will be waiting," said Warden Beasley.

Once inside room A, Randy Johnson took a seat across the table from Vernon Madison. The warden headed back toward his office, leaving two guards in the room with Randy and the inmate. Vernon Madison looked toward Randy and asked, "Who in the hell are you?"

"Mr. Madison, it's not important who I am!" Randy voiced, sternly. "In this particular case, you're the only one important for what I'm searching for."

"You're not making sense!" Vernon snapped back. "What are you searching for?"

"The truth, Mr. Madison, I'm searching for the truth on something that I'm deeply concerned with. For starters, how did you get that bad looking scar on the right side of your face? It looks as though a bullet may have plowed across it."

"I got caught up in some barbed wire fence," Vernon answered, him smiling.

"I've done some checking on your school background, Mr. Madison. You're a college dropout, but at one time you attended Bridgeport Business College. That's the same college that Beth Eason attended. That was her name until she later married a man named John Miller. Do you remember a woman named Beth Eason, Mr. Madison?"

"Yes, I remember her very well! She thought she was too good to socialize with me! I asked her for a date one time, and she said 'You've got to be kidding me; you act like some kind of nut!' That woman needed to have her head bashed in!"

Extreme anger permeated throughout Randy's body when he said that, but he was intent on keeping his cool. "Mr. Madison, it's been brought to my attention that you may have robbed and killed her husband one night in his grocery store. Is that a possibility?"

Vernon Madison leaned forward; he closed his eyes partially and said, "Things do happen in the darkness of night, especially when the deed is accomplished out of sight. Look all you may, but on that subject that's all I'm going to say. Talk to me as long as you want, if all day. I'll listen attentively, but the absolute truth, I'll never say."

"Very poetic, Mr. Madison," Randy commented. "You're to be congratulated for your poetic skills."

"I should?"

"Of course, you should be congratulated. In fact, I thought you did a rather outstanding job writing that letter to Beth Miller."

"What in the hell are you talking about?" Vernon asked.

"I'm talking about the letter you placed inside her car one day when she was at the city park."

"I don't know what you're talking about."

"You probably don't know how you got that scar on your face either!" Randy said, sternly. "Well, I know how you got it!. Beth Miller shot through her door when you tried to break into her house. You ran off leaving blood stains on her porch; you lost one of your bloodied shoes when you crawled over her hedging. Make no mistake about it, Mr. Madison; you're going to be charged with John Miller's murder! Guards, get this murdering lunatic out of my sight!"

Detective Johnson walked into sheriff's office at four o'clock that evening. "I didn't expect to see you until tomorrow morning," commented Sheriff Hick's. "What did you find out?"

"Sheriff, I would bet my last dollar that Vernon Madison is John Miller's killer! Also, I believe he's the one that tried to break into Mrs. Beth Miller's house. In fact, he's got some kind of wound on his face. It could very well be from a bullet fired from her gun."

"Did you turn our blood samples over to the proper authorities?" Sheriff Hicks asked.

"I did what you asked me to do. I gave the samples to Warden Beasley for safe keeping. He's going to get a court order from a judge authorizing the prison's medical unit to draw some blood from Vernon Madison. The warden will then turn both sets of samples over to the S.B.I.'s crime lab."

"I hope it doesn't take a long time to get those results," said Sheriff Hicks. "I'll see what I can do to rush up the process."

Chapter 10

Two days later, Beth and Danny Miller were sitting in their living room. "Danny, are you very excited today?" Beth asked. "It's your birthday! We've got to be at the Oakdale Country Club by 1:30 today. Your party is scheduled for two o'clock. What's the matter? You don't seem happy today."

"Mother, will you do me a favor?" Danny asked, sadly.

"I will if I can, sweetheart. I wish you would tell me what's bothering you."

"I want you to take me to Cedar Oaks Cemetery."

"I'll take you to the cemetery, but why do you want to visit your father's grave today-----on your birthday?"

"Mother, can you think of a better time for a child to visit their daddy's grave?" Danny asked, seriously.

Beth parked her car at Cedar Oaks Cemetery a few minutes later. "Do you want me to walk with you to your father's grave?"

"I want you to do one more favor for me."

"What is the favor now?"

"I want you to drive to the convenience store about two miles down the road and get us a drink. I want a Pepsi Cola, and you can get whatever you want."

"Danny, we've got soft drinks at home!"

"Mother, please-------don't you understand--------I want to be alone when I talk to my daddy!" Danny said, tearfully.

"Yes, sweetheart, I understand now what you want me to do. I'll be back in a little while." Beth drove out of the cemetery parking lot.

In deep thought, Danny walked to his father's grave. Tears slid down his face as he placed his hand on his father's tombstone. Overcome by sadness, he dropped to his knees. For a brief period his thoughts went back in time when his father took him fishing, hunting, and to other places. Danny wiped his watery eyes; he said, "Daddy, I'm thirteen years old today. I wish you could be here for my birthday party, but I know you can't. I miss you more than anything in this world. I wish you were here for Mother and me. I know that it's not your fault that you can't be here. I want you to know that Mother loves you more than I could ever say. Her memory of you will be in her heart for as long as she lives. I just wanted you to know that. My reason for coming here today is to tell you that Mother has found someone else to share her love with. Daddy, he's a very nice man. Please give me a sign that it's okay with you. Please, let me know that you won't be upset!" With his eyes closed tightly, Danny commenced crying. After about fifteen seconds he heard a bird singing in a nearby bush. He had never heard a bird making such melodic sounds until now. Danny stood up, and that's when he saw the unusual colored bird. He wondered why the little bird didn't fly away, him being only a few feet from the bird. He moved a few feet away from his father's grave; he wanted to see what the little bird would do. To his amazement, the bird flew directly to John Miller's tombstone. Hearing someone drive into the cemetery parking lot, Danny turned around to see his mother sitting in her car. He turned back around; he pointed for his mother to see the bird perched on his daddy's tombstone. The bird flew away a few seconds later. With a big smile displayed on his face, Danny walked to his mother's car.

"I saw the little bird on your father's tombstone. I wonder what made it fly there. Danny, did you accomplish whatever you wanted to do at your father's grave?"

"Yes Mother, I believe that little bird told me everything I wanted to know."

"Are you telling me that bird can talk?" Beth asked, jokingly.

"Yes, in a manner of speaking, I believe it can. Let's go home and get ready for my birthday party."

Beth Miller spared no expense for Danny's thirteenth birthday party. She had reserved the Oakdale Country Club. She agreed to pay Mickey Phelps, a disc Jockey, to play music during the birthday celebration. Beth and Danny arrived at the club at 1:30 that afternoon; she wanted to make sure that Missy Holladay, a local caterer, had all her suggested food on a table. Beth seemed satisfied as she looked over the array of food that Missy had placed onto the large table. There were chips, dips, four kinds of cheeses, nuts, rollout ham and turkey pieces, chicken wings, variety of pizzas and plenty of sodas, tea and lemonade.

"Mrs. Miller, how does everything look?" Missy asked.

"You've done a splendid job. I'm very pleased with everything."

The club room was nearly full by 2:15 that afternoon. All of Danny's grandparents were present. Harry and Doris Spears were at the party. Sheriff Alan Hicks and his wife were present. Several employees from Madison Electronics attended Danny's birthday party. There were many other friends, acquaintances and nearby neighbors that were attendance.

All at once, Danny spotted Shelia Johnson walking into the room with her father. His eyes beamed with joy! He hurried to meet his very good friend. "Hello, Danny," said Shelia. "It looks like you're in for a fine time today."

"Thank you very much. Gee-----you sure look nice today in your blue dress. Isn't that right, Mr. Johnson?"

"Yes, she certainly does. Shelia, how about going over and talk with Mrs. Beth Miller for a couple of minutes. I need to chat with our birthday boy for a little bit."

After Shelia walked off, Mr. Johnson placed his hand on Danny's shoulder. "Is something wrong?" Danny asked, inquisitively.

"I'm not sure, but I can't wait any longer to ask you a question. Darn, it's quite difficult for me to ask you this, but I've got to know how you feel about something." For a few seconds it looked to Danny as though Mr. Johnson was trying to figure what to say to him. "Well, let me go about it another way," Mr. Johnson mumbled. "Well, maybe this is not a good time to ask you what I had on my mind."

"Mr. Johnson its' okay with me, and its' okay with my daddy for you to spend time with my mother."

Randy Johnson's mouth open wide; he was flabbergasted at Danny's remark. A large smile overshadowed his face as he watched Danny heading toward his mother and Shelia. "What a smart boy!" Randy mumbled.

Henry Miller stood up on a chair. "Ladies and gentlemen, boys and girls-----please let me have your attention for just a minute or two." The room became quiet. "As most of you know, Danny Miller is my grandson. We're gathered here today to celebrate a momentous time in this boy's life. Today my wonderful grandson has become a teenager!" Everyone commenced clapping their hands. "The other thing I wanted to mention is this----if you haven't already started eating some of the delicious food you see on the back table, please feel free to do so whenever you choose to. Now, let's all give Disc Jockey, Mickey Phelps a round of applause for the music and his participation in Danny Miller's birthday party." Henry stepped down from the chair.

Randy walked over to where Beth was standing. "Beth, it looks like your son is having a great time."

"I believe he is. If you don't mind me asking, what were you and he discussing a few minutes ago?"

"In the short of it, he's okay with my spending time with you. I was very surprised to hear him say that."

"Randy, the most important thing in Danny's life right now is my happiness. He's reached the full realization that his wonderful father is gone forever. He has treasured memories of his father that he will keep until the day he dies. I have those same kinds of memories of my husband, but I need more than just memories. Do you understand what I'm saying, Randy?"

"Yes, I fully understand. Beth, in no way will I ever try to be a substitute for John Miller because there is no way that I could fill his shoes. I just hope you'll give me the opportunity to show my love and affection to you. I hope you haven't changed your mind concerning our date."

"I haven't changed my mind. You know, I was just thinking about something."

"What were you thinking?" Randy asked, curiously.

"It would be nice to have Shelia's birthday party at this same location when she becomes a teenager.

"That's a great idea! I'll keep that thought in my mind.".

Danny saw his grandparents, George and Dora Eason sitting down next to a friend of theirs.

"Grandpa, Grandma, I want you to meet a special friend of mine. Her name is Shelia Johnson."

"Well, there's one thing for sure, Danny boy----------your special friend is a very beautiful young girl," Mr. Eason remarked.

"Thank you sir," Shelia replied.

"She looks about your age, Danny."

"That's right, Grandma; I'm only about a month older than she is."

"Danny, are you still keeping our little secret concerning the weeded-side of my pond?" George Eason asked, him smiling.

"I sure am, grandpa."

Mickey Phelps took the microphone about a half hour later and said, "Ladies and gentlemen, please let me have your attention." Everyone quieted down to hear what Mickey was about to say. "How many of you here today would like to see our birthday boy, Mr. Danny Miller dance with that charming and very beautiful young girl he's been walking around with since he's been here." When he said that, the crowd commenced shouting, 'Yes Danny! Yes Danny!' They clapped their hands, stomped their feet, and yelled out, 'You can do it, Danny! You can do it!'"

Mickey started a song entitled, 'Thinking of You' by Katy Perry. Nervously, Danny took Shelia by her hand and escorted her to the dance floor. Beth looked at their magnificent performance with teary eyes. Randy Johnson couldn't have been more proud of his daughter. The crowd gave Danny and Shelia a standing ovation as they clapped and voiced praises concerning their performance.

Almost two hours later, everyone gathered around the table containing Danny's birthday cake, as well as a stack of birthday presents. Beth Miller waited patiently for everyone to get situated before she lit the thirteen candles on her son's birthday cake. Danny was sitting at the end of the table, next to the cake. Shelia was standing directly behind him.

"First of all, I want to thank each and every one that's here today," said Beth. "No matter how many children a family may have----each of their children only gets to be a teenager just once. My only regret is that his father couldn't be here for his son's thirteenth birthday." Beth picked up her lighter. "Okay folks, soon as I light these thirteen candles let's all sing happy birthday to Danny." Beth hurriedly lit all thirteen candles. With one big breath, Danny blew them all out. He had a big grin on his face as everyone sang happy birthday to him.

Missy Holliday did the honors of cutting the large birthday cake into smaller pieces. Danny was the first one to be given a piece of the cake. Afterwards, Beth Miller helped Missy hand out the slices of cake.

Shelia, very excited, was the first one to hand Danny her present. He wasted no time tearing away the colorful wrapping from the small box. His eyes beamed with joy as he held up a three-bladed, Old Henry pocket knife. Shelia was overjoyed by Danny's enthusiastic acceptance of her gift.

It took Danny a little over thirty minutes to open all his presents. He didn't tell anyone, but the gift he liked the most was from his mother. Her gift wasn't even wrapped. She just handed him a picture of a blue-colored, Polaris ATV 4-wheeler that would be waiting for him when he got home. His grandparents, Henry and Delores Miller gave him three pairs of pants and three short-sleeved shirts. Danny's other grandparents, George and Dora Eason gave him a new rod and reel along with a large tackle box filled with an assortment of fresh water lures, hooks, sinkers and corks. Randy Johnson's present was two specially made helmets for ATV riders. They were the same color as his ATV.

"Mr. Johnson, did you drive your truck today?" Danny asked.

"Yes, as a matter of fact I did."

"When you leave here, would you mind taking all these presents to my house?"

"No, I wouldn't mind at all." Randy walked toward Beth as she stood next to her mother and father. Shelia remained next to Danny.

"Mother, Father, I would like for you to meet a very special friend of mine," said Beth. "Randy Johnson, these are my parents, George and Dora Eason."

Randy extended his hand to each of them. "I'm very pleased to meet you. Beth has told me so many good things about you both."

"Danny tells me that you're a detective with the sheriff's department," George Eason commented.

"That's right, sir."

"I hope and pray that someday we'll find out who killed Beth's husband," Dora remarked.

"We're working very hard on that case, Mrs. Eason. I won't stop looking for the killer until this case is solved."

"Randy, my father likes to fish in fresh water."

"Mr. Eason, are you a real good fisherman?"

"I guess I am, Randy, especially when the fish are very hungry and close to my hook."

"Daddy, Randy likes to fish, also." Beth commented.

"Well, you need to bring him to our house one weekend so he and I can fish in my pond. Randy, do you like to freshwater fish or fish in the ocean?"

"Mr. Eason, my preference is freshwater fishing. Are there any large bass in your pond?"

I've caught some bass that weighed up to seven pounds, but mostly the bass weigh about three or four pounds." Mr. Eason turned toward his daughter. "Beth, come give your daddy and mother a big hug because we need to get on the road toward home. I'll make sure we say good bye to our grandson."

"It was a pleasure meeting you both." said Randy. "I hope to see you again soon."

"It was nice meeting you as well," said George. "Beth, this man meets our approval."

"Thank you, Father----and you too, Mother." Beth hugged each of their necks.

George and Dora headed out of the building.

"Danny, you sure did have a nice birthday party," said Shelia, with a big smile.

"It sure was! I had no idea that I would get this many gifts. I want your birthday party to be just as good. Shelia, you may not like me anymore after I tell you what I did."

"What did you do, Danny?" She asked, curiously.

"I broke my promise to you. I told my mother what you said concerning how much your daddy likes my mother. I'm very sorry for doing that!"

"Well, I'm not sorry at all!" Shelia snapped back. "I'm glad you told your mother what I said to you."

"You are? Why?" Danny asked, confused.

"I like your mother a great deal. I hope my father and your mother will eventually wind up living together."

"You mean------marry each other?"

"Yes, Danny, wouldn't that be wonderful!" Shelia smiled.

"Shelia, I like your daddy very much, but that might pose a problem for you and me!" Danny remarked, moving his head back and forth.

"What are you talking, about? What kind of problem would it create?"

"Well, for one thing------if they were to marry each other, you and I would become brother and sister, wouldn't we?"

"In a manner of speaking, I suppose we would be."

"Well, Shelia, if we were to become brother and sister it wouldn't be the same as it is now."

"What do you mean, Danny?"

"It's quite simple; I like you a great deal right now, but if you were my sister I would have to like you in a different way. You know, I wouldn't have this little tingling inside my body whenever I'm around you."

"What kind of tingling do you have, Danny?" Shelia asked, seriously.

"Well, it's hard to explain. I guess the tingling starts in my heart when I'm around you. I guess you could say it's like my floating on a cloud when I'm in your presence."

"Danny, since you put it that way, we could still like each other like we do now."

"We could?"

"We wouldn't be a drop of kin if for some reason my daddy and your mother were to ever marry each other."

"Shelia, I hadn't thought of that, but you're right. I'm glad you came up with that."

"I'm glad, too. Danny, I want to keep that tingling inside of you for a long, long time. Also, it would be a good idea for you to keep that floating feeling whenever you're around me."

"Shelia, not only are you pretty, but you're also very smart," said Danny.

Chapter 11

Two weeks had passed since Danny Miller's birthday. He thoroughly enjoyed riding his 4-wheeler in his mother's yard, but he needed more space to ride it. George Eason, Danny's grandfather promised yesterday that he would come get him and his 4-wheeler Saturday morning so he could ride it on his farm. Mr. Eason would be bringing a small utility trailer when he came.

Randy Johnson had just finished shaving and showering when his house phone rang. He hurried to the phone to see who was calling him at eight o'clock in the morning. He picked up the phone and said, "Hello."

"Randy, I need for you to get to my office right away," said Sheriff Alan Hicks.

"What's the matter?" Randy inquired.

"I'm not going to discuss what I've got to say on the telephone. Come directly to my office!"

Randy wasted no time getting to Sheriff Hick's office. He wondered what the urgency was all about. "Sheriff, I got here as quick as I could," said Randy. "You seemed very concerned about something when you called me a little while ago."

"Yes, I suppose you could say I was very concerned. Do you see that folder lying on my desk?"

"Yes, I see the folder," Randy remarked.

"Well, it's from the S.B.I.'s Crime Lab in Raleigh. It's got the results of those blood samples you left with Warden Beasley."

"Do you remember what I told you, Sheriff Hicks?" Randy asked. "I told you all along that Vernon Madison was our killer."

"Open the folder and read its contents," said Sheriff Hicks.

Randy did as the sheriff requested. He opened the folder; he began reading the report from the S.B.I.'s Crime Lab. "I can't believe this!" Randy voiced, loudly. "It says in the report that the blood samples were not even a close match. Well, maybe he wasn't the one that tried to break into Beth's house, but it doesn't mean that he's not John Miller's killer."

Sheriff Hicks opened his desk drawer; he took out an envelope and handed it to Randy. "I received this from Warden Beasley yesterday; read what he wrote in the letter." He handed the envelope to Randy. Randy's mouth opened wide as he proceeded to read the letter.

"Sheriff, I don't understand how this can be!" Randy remarked. "It says in this letter that Vernon

Madison was in a Kentucky jail the night of John Miller's murder. How could I have been so wrong pertaining to this case? All the evidence pointed to Vernon Madison!"

"Don't feel like you're the Lone Ranger," said Sheriff Hicks. "I thought Vernon Madison was our murderer as well. Randy, you know what this means, don't you?"

"I know exactly what it means! It means that Beth Miller and her son's life is still in danger. Sheriff, whatever it takes, we've got to keep Beth and her son safe from a dangerous killer!"

"That makes a couple times you've said Beth, instead of Mrs. Miller. Randy, is there something going on between you and Mrs. Miller?" Sheriff Hicks asked.

"To tell you the truth, I'm in love with Beth Miller. Don't get me wrong, I waited patiently until her time of mourning was over before I made a move toward her. That's the honest truth, Sheriff."

"I believe what you're telling me, Randy. Anyway, it's really none of my business since she's not married anymore. You brought up a very good point about her life being in danger. I tell you something else; there's a man out there somewhere that's missing part of his ear. You and I discounted that possibility whenever we focused our attention on Vernon Madison."

"Sheriff, I don't understand how he could have gotten his ear shot off without him going to a clinic or hospital. We checked on that possibility and found nothing."

"There's no way that individual would have gone to a hospital or clinic if he was wanted by the law or he had a criminal record," Sheriff Hicks remarked. "If in fact he did get his ear shot off, he just used whatever home remedies he had available to tend to his wound."

"I've got to let Beth know that Vernon Madison is not the one that killed her husband or the one that tried to break into her house. I know she will be very upset after I tell her this news."

"When will you tell her?" Sheriff Hicks asked.

"I'll tell her this evening after she gets home from work."

When Beth Miller pulled into her driveway that evening, she saw Randy Johnson talking with Danny as he sat on his 4-wheeler. They both walked toward Beth's car as she exited her vehicle.

"Mother, do you have anything that I need to take inside for you?"

"Yes, I've got some groceries in the trunk of my car. Hello, Randy."

"Hi Beth, how was your day at the office?"

"It certainly was a busy one today. Where's Shelia?"

"She's home. Why did you ask?"

"I thought you and she might want to come eat dinner with us tonight."

"Beth, I would love to have dinner with you and Danny tonight, but I wouldn't want to put you to a lot of extra trouble."

"Believe me, it won't be any trouble at all. I stopped at a Chinese Restaurant on the way home and I bought a variety of food. Drive to your house and get Shelia while I put these groceries away. You should be back here in a few minutes."

"Well, there's one thing about it----I love Chinese food," said Randy, smiling.

"In that case you'd better hurry along before our food gets cold."

Randy was back to Beth's house in a matter of minutes, along with Shelia.

"Mrs. Miller, I understand we're having Chinese food for dinner."

"Yes Shelia, we certainly are. Do you like Chinese food?"

"Oh yes, I really do. Where is Danny?'

"I think he's putting his 4-wheeler in our shed. He doesn't want it out in the weather when he's not riding on it."

"Beth, I would be more than happy to help you prepare your table, or whatever else I can do to help you."

"That won't be necessary, Randy. Just take a seat while I get things organized. Shelia, how about going outside and see what's holding Danny up."

"Okay, Mrs. Miller." Shelia hurried outside; she noticed that Beth's shed door was open. When she got to the shed, she saw Danny wiping debris from his 4-wheeler.

"What are you doing?"

"Hello, I didn't know you were here, Shelia. To answer your question, I was wiping dust and bits of grass off my ride."

"Your mother said for you to come inside so everyone can eat. Guess what Danny; my father and I are having dinner with you and your mother."

"That's great! Wouldn't it be nice if we could all be living together?"

"I've been thinking about that. If you were around me all the time you may not like me as much. I wouldn't like that at all," said Shelia, sadly.

"That's crazy! I'll always like you, no matter what! There's something that you don't realize about me."

"Can't you tell me what it is?"

"I don't think I can-------I would be too ashamed to ask you to do it."

"Danny Miller, what exactly do you have on your mind?"

"Do you promise not to laugh when I tell you what it is?"

"I promise!"

"Shelia, I've always wanted to kiss you on your lips," said Danny, he feeling embarrassed.

"You mean now-----right now!"

"Would it be alright with you, if I kissed you now?"

"Go ahead and kiss me; there's no one looking." Danny placed his arms around Shelia, and then he kissed her gently on her lips. "Did you like kissing me?"

"Wow! I don't think we should do this again for a good while," Danny answered.

"Why is that? Didn't you enjoy kissing me?"

"Shelia, that's the problem. I enjoyed it so much it woke up my stimulator."

"I didn't know you had a stimulator."

"You would have to be a boy to understand my meaning."

"I'm not a boy, but I do understand what you were referring to."

"You do?" Danny asked, very embarrassed. "I think we had better head for the kitchen."

Everyone gathered at the dinner table to eat some Chinese food. "Shelia, how is your food?" Beth asked.

"It's delicious, Mrs. Miller. Thank you kindly for inviting my father and me over for dinner."

"You're very welcome. Randy, you look like you've got something on your mind."

"I do have something on my mind that's of great concern to me. Shelia, after you and Danny are through eating I'd appreciate you two going into the living room and watch television. I need to talk with Beth for a few minutes." A few minutes later, Danny and Shelia retired to the living room.

After the kids left the kitchen, Beth looked toward Randy and asked, "Why have you got that very concerned look on your face?"

"I've got some very bad news!"

"Randy, whatever it is------it can't be all that bad."

"Yes, it certainly can be! Vernon Madison is not the one that killed your husband."

"He's not? I thought you told me that he was John's killer!"

"That's exactly what I said, but he can't be your husband's killer because he was in jail in another state when the murder occurred."

"What about the person that tried to break into my house?" Beth asked, very confused.

"I'm sorry to say that it wasn't Vernon Madison that tried to break into your house. The S.B.I. Crime Lab said the blood samples did not match Vernon's blood."

"What does all this mean?" Beth asked, deeply concerned.

"It means that whoever left that letter in your car is still out there somewhere. It, also, means that you probably did shoot off his ear. Beth, that's the reason I came over here today in the first place. I'm very concerned about your safety, and the safety of your son. I don't know what I would do if you were harmed in any way," he said, seriously. "Beth, I love you very, very much."

"After all this time, why hasn't that man tried to break into my house, or tried to harm me somehow?"

"I can't answer that, but his threatening letter indicates that he will try to harm you sooner or later, unless he's in jail or dead."

"Randy, this might not mean anything, but there was this other guy that went to the same college that I went to. He used to pal around with Vernon Madison. Well, one day at college I was walking down the hall when this guy hit my backside with his hand. I turned around and slapped him as hard as I could. He, immediately, called me some very dirty names. It happened that one of my college professors saw what he did to me, and heard him call me those ugly names. Well, one thing led to another, and finally this guy was kicked out of college. After all these years, do you suppose this could be the person that killed my husband, and tried to break into my house?"

"Do you remember this guy's name?"

"Let me think------it's on the tip of my tongue; goodness gracious, what was his name? I got it! I got it! His name was Gordon Ray Stallings."

"Beth, could Gordon Stallings be the same man you saw in the park?"

"I can't be sure since it's been a long time since I was in college. Anyway, that man in the park was too far away for me to know what he looked like. He was wearing a hat and a pair of sun glasses."

"Let me ask you this; was Gordon Stallings a short man or tall man?"

"The best I remember, he was about the same height as Vernon Madison."

"I'll check this guy out very good before I'm through with him," said Randy, smiling.

"If this is the murderer, why has he waited so long to carry out his threats?" Beth asked.

"Well, we don't know whether he's the guy or not, but let's suppose he is the guy we're looking for. It could be that after he was thrown out of college he continued to fail at one thing to another until his resentment toward you became so great that he lost all his control. Whoever the killer------he's one smart cookie. He laid the groundwork for Vernon Madison and, or Harry Spears to be blamed for your husband's murder. Scholastically speaking, how was Gordon Stallings IQ in college."

"He was extremely smart in class," Beth answered. "He didn't get along with his classmates at all, except for Vernon Madison. Gordon had a mean streak in him a mile wide. One day he placed two thumb tacks in Professor Mark Shiver's chair. Professor Shiver noticed the tacks before he sat down. He asked the class if anyone saw who the culprit was that placed those tacks in his chair. I raised my hand; I told him that Gordon placed those tacks in his chair. Gordon was ordered to go see the college counselor concerning his vicious act. On the way out of the room, Gordon pointed his finger toward me."

"Beth, on another subject, do you have plans for this weekend?" Randy asked.

"No, why do you ask?"

"I would like very much for you and I to spend some time together. Would you like to do that?"

"Yes, that would be nice. Danny's grandfather is coming Saturday morning to take him and his four-wheeler to his house for the weekend."

"Shelia is staying with my aunt over the weekend," said Randy. "How would you like to spend the weekend at the beach with me?"

"You mean-----just you and me?" Beth asked.

"Yep, just the two of us."

"I'm not sure about that, Randy."

"Beth, you have my absolute word that I'll be a gentleman while we're there. We could get a cabin on the beach and watch the waves as they roll in. While we're there, you'll have your own bedroom and bathroom. I could get a cabin not very far from Wellington's Seafood House. Have you ever heard of that place?"

"Yes, I certainly have. I've been told they make wonderful crab cakes there. Alright Randy, we can leave for the beach right after Mr. Miller picks up Danny."

"You'll never regret going on this trip," said Randy. "You have my solemn promise on that."

"Speaking of promises, Shelia's birthday will be here soon. Have you made arrangements for her birthday party?"

"I most certainly have," Randy replied. "I took your advice and rented the same room at Oakdale Country Club that you did for Danny's birthday. Not only that, I contracted with Missy Holliday to cater the food, and Mickey Phelps to provide the music. Now, do I get a compliment from you or not?"

"Yes, you do," Beth responded. "I'll ask you like you asked me. Will Danny and I be on Shelia's invitation list?"

"Are you kidding me? You and Danny are at the top of my invitation list." Randy smiled.

By eight o'clock Saturday morning, Beth and Danny had already eaten their breakfast. George Eason, Danny's grandfather was due to arrive at their house an hour later. Danny was very excited that he would be able to ride his 4-wheeler on his grandfather's farm.

"Mother, what are you going to do while I'm gone?"

"Randy asked me if I would go to the beach with him this weekend. He said Shelia is staying with her aunt today and tomorrow." Beth noticed that Danny had a puzzled look on his face. "Danny, if you're not comfortable with my going with him, I don't have to go. I've got plenty to do at home to keep me busy over the weekend."

"Mother, I want you to go. You deserve to have some time to yourself."

"Danny, are you really sure about that? I saw that look on your face when I mentioned about going to the beach with Randy."

"Mother, I wasn't thinking about you going to the beach. I was just thinking how lonely I would be if something ever happened to you. You're all I've got in the whole world!" Tears came into Danny's eyes.

Beth placed her arms around her son."

As he had promised, George Eason drove into Beth's yard at nine o'clock that morning. He had his utility trailer hooked to his vehicle. Beth and Danny were standing on their porch when he exited his vehicle. "Hello, Grandpa!"

"Hi, Danny, and a very good morning to my lovely daughter. Is there anymore coffee in your coffee pot?"

"Yes, Daddy, the coffee pot is half full. Come inside and I'll pour you a cup."

The three were sitting at the kitchen table while Mr. Eason drank his coffee. "Beth, how are you and your detective friend getting along these days?"

"We're getting along just fine. Randy is a very good man, and a perfect gentleman in all respects."

"Beth, I liked that man the first time I saw him at Danny's birthday party."

"Tell me the truth------since John was killed, do you think I've waited long enough before getting involved with another man?"

"That can only be answered by you. You're my daughter and I know you loved John with all your heart and soul. John is gone; he'll never come back. At some point in your life you'll have to go on living, not just for yourself, but for Danny as well. Beth, if in a round-about way if you're asking for my permission for you to start dating--------you don't need to. Whatever decision you make in that regard, I'll be with you all the way."

Beth got up; she hugged her father. "I want you to know that I love you and mother very, very much."

"Grandpa, Mother is tearing up again."

"That's okay, Danny------I know they're happy tears. One of these days you'll be able to decipher when tears are sad ones or happy ones. Now, before we go I want you to go give your mother a great big hug."

Danny hugged his mother. "Are you sure you'll be okay?"

"Yes, I'll be just fine. I want you and your granddaddy to have a fine time out on his farm. There is one tiny little thing that I need to mention."

"What is that?" Danny asked.

"Stay out of that bull pen!"

"Goodness Mother, you don't have to yell!"

"Danny, we'll load up your ride in a few minutes. At home, I've got a five gallon tank of gas for you to use in your 4-wheeler. My crops have been cultivated so you can ride all over the farm. You can even ride inside my stand of timber."

"Grandpa, how big is your woods?" Danny asked, curiously.

"There's about two-hundred and fifty acres of woodland on my property. I'll show you where the woods' path is. Beth, are you sure you wouldn't want to go home with us?"

"Not this time. I've got plans for this weekend."

Danny and his grandfather left Beth's house about fifteen minutes later. As they were riding along, Danny turned toward his grandfather and asked, "Do you ever have a dream that you can't understand?"

"Yes, I suppose I do. In fact, I hardly understand any of my dreams. Why do you ask?"

"I had a dream last night that I totally don't understand."

"Well, would you like to talk about it?"

"My dream involved my daddy."

"Well son, dreaming about a love one is a normal occurrence. I've had several dreams concerning your daddy."

"Grandpa, this was a very sad dream that I had. When I woke up, I was crying in bed."

"Well, maybe you had better tell me about your dream."

"In my dream, I saw Daddy standing in our living room as my mother kissed Randy Johnson. Grandpa, my daddy just stood there smiling as though he was okay with them kissing each other. He didn't seem to be sad or upset about what they were doing. I don't understand why he didn't get mad or upset about that sort of thing!"

"I believe I can straighten you out concerning your dream. As you well know, your father loved your mother as much as any husband can love their wife. Danny, the reason that your father was smiling inside your dream was because he wants your mother to be happy for the rest of her life. Now what kind of life would she have if all she ever did was to worry and concern herself with nothing but

John's death? She would certainly grow old before her time. Your mother will probably get married again one of these days>"

"Grandpa-----"

"Yes, Danny."

"I feel a lot better now that you've explained why Daddy was smiling in my dream."

"Well, now----I'm very glad to hear that. One other thing, are you going to let me ride on your 4-wheeler when we get to my house?"

"You bet I am!" Danny said, him grinning. "Grandpa, are you suggesting to me that you've never ridden on a 4-wheeler?"

"Well, yes I have. My pickup truck, tractor, golf cart, go-cart, automobile and several more things I own have four wheels," he answering, smiling.

"Grandpa, you know what I mean! Have you ever ridden on anything that looks like my 4-wheeler?"

"As a matter of fact, Danny------I have. I've ridden quite a bit on my go cart, but I'm looking forward to riding some on your 4-wheeler."

Chapter 12.

Randy Johnson and Beth Miller left Beth's house at 11:30 that morning. They were headed toward the beach, about an hour and half drive. Beth remained rather quite for the first few miles of their trip. "Is something wrong?" Randy asked.

"I hope not. I was wondering if Gordon Ray Stallings is the one that killed John and tried to break into my house."

"Beth, I can assure you of one thing! After we get home this weekend I'm going to check that guy out very good. If he is your husband's killer, I'll get him!"

"What concerns me is why he hasn't tried to come back to my house," Beth remarked.

"There could be a multitude of reasons for him not coming back. As I've told you before, he may not want to lose his other ear." Randy smiled. "If it's okay with you, we'll stop at Wellington's Seafood House before we go to the cabin I rented for the weekend."

"That will be fine. I'm looking forward to eating a crab cake there. Besides, I didn't eat very much breakfast this morning. Did you bring swimming trucks."

"I most certainly did! I'm hopeful that you brought something to swim in."

"To tell you the truth, I don't have any swimwear."

"That's no problem. There's a clothing store across from Wellington's where we can get you something to wear. Beth, I want us to have an enjoyable time this weekend. In fact, I'm so excited that I can hardly control myself!"

"Well, I hope you can do something about your control problem," said Beth, her smiling.

"You know darn well what I'm talking about!" Randy shot back. "I've already given you my word that I'll be a perfect gentleman on this trip."

Wellington's Seafood House was packed when Randy and Beth arrived. They took a number and then they waited patiently on the seats provided for waiting customers. Their number was called fifteen minutes later. After they were seated, a waitress took their orders. Randy ordered a seafood combination; Beth ordered flounder, crab cake and a small salad. They both ordered sweet tea. "Beth, how do you like this place?" Randy asked.

"It's very nice. I particularly like the pictures on the wall that represent events or places near or on the ocean. Look at the one to your left------it shows a high wave crashing over the bow of a ship. My goodness, I wouldn't want to be on a boat when that happens!"

"Don't tell me you're afraid of the ocean?"

"I wasn't until I saw the movie, Jaws."

"That was just an old movie," Randy remarked.

"That's true, but it reminded me of things that could be just under the surface of the water, things waiting to take a bite out of me. I'll go into the ocean, but I'm not about to go in depths more than three or four feet."

"After we get through eating, we'll get you a swimsuit. Once we're in the water, I'll keep those water varmints from taking a hunk out of you, I promise."

"What if it's a five-thousand pound shark that has his eyes on me?"

"In that case------it's every man for himself!" Randy laughed. "Doggone Beth, wasn't that funny?"

"Do you see me laughing?"

"Okay, I was just funning you a little. The truth is-----I wouldn't run away if a five-thousand pound shark was about to gobble you up."

"In that case, you're either lying or you're a plain idiot. You'll have to decide which. A five-thousand pound shark will make anyone retreat to safety. I'm sorry; I didn't mean what I said. The truth is-----I believe you would do almost anything to protect me from harm."

"That is the absolute truth, Beth. It seems that I get more in love with you each passing day. I never thought that I could ever love anyone like I did my wife, but you have proved me wrong. I don't think my life would ever be the same without you."

"I feel the same way toward you," replied Beth. The waitress brought them their food. "My crab cake looks delicious. Randy, are you sure you can eat all that seafood?"

"Well, there's one thing for sure-----I'm going to give it a good try."

By 4:15 that evening, Danny Miller had ridden his four-wheeler all over the cleared land on his grandfather's farm. His grandmother had told him to be home by 6:00 that evening for dinner. Not realizing what time it was, he decided to drive into his grandfather's woods. There was a nice path leading into the woods, but the path kept getting more narrow as he drove farther and farther into the forest. Finally, after Danny was deep inside the woods he came to the end of the path. The undergrowth was thick on both sides of the path, too thick to drive his four-wheeler any farther into the woods. For a couple minutes he watched a squirrel climb up and down a long leaf pine. Far deeper in the woods, he heard the whimpering, mournful, sounds of a dog in distress. Danny kept turning his head from side to side, trying to determine the location the sounds were coming from. Determined to find the dog and see what his problem was, Danny removed his helmet; he laid it on the seat of his 4-wheeler. Without regard to snakes, bears, or even bobcats that he may come in contact, Danny pushed his way forward thru thick underbrush. The dog kept making the same pitiful sounds as Danny hurried toward him. His grandfather had told him earlier that day that a small creek was located deep inside his woods. What his grandfather didn't tell Danny was that Mr. Ben Cross, another farmer, owned three-hundred acres of woods joining his grandfather's property.

At 5:45 that evening, Dora Miller said, "George, it's almost six o'clock. Danny should be back here by now. Do you suppose something happened to him?"

"Well, I remember you telling him to be back here by six o'clock."

"That's all well and good, but Danny left his watch inside the bathroom where he washed his hands. How will he know when it's six o'clock?" Dora asked,

"Dora, you're a worry wart," said George. "That boy is thirteen years old. When I was his age I explored my father's woods all during the year without ever getting lost."

"I guess you did, your father didn't own but twelve acres of woodland."

"You've got a point, Dora. Now I'm beginning to worry. If Danny is not back here by 6:15 I'm going into the woods and look for him."

"If he's not back here by then you'll need some help to look for him! Dora snapped, excitedly.

There was no sign of Danny at 6:20 that evening. George and Dora Eason were frantic from worry. "George, it will soon be dark! My goodness, where is that child?" Dora asked, tearfully. "Why in the world didn't you tell Danny to stay out of your woods with that machine he's riding? What if he ran into a tree or something?"

"Please----Dora! I'm worried sick concerning Danny's whereabouts! I shouldn't have to be concerned with you on the verge of a nervous breakdown! I'll get one of my tenants, maybe Mr. Buddy Collier and his two sons to help me find Danny. Dora, please don't worry! I promise you I will find our grandson before I come out of my woods!"

"Should we call Beth and let her know what's going on?"

"Absolutely not, our poor daughter deserves to have an enjoyable weekend at the beach! Anyway, she's an hour and a half from here; how could she possibly be any help to us when we upset her with this news. Enough talking, I'm going to get Mr. Collier and his boys right now!"

"Aren't you forgetting something?" Dora asked.

"What did I forget?"

"A flashlight and your coat. It's not summer any longer; it will get a little chilly during the night."

"That's why I married you, Dora-----to keep me from forgetting things."

At eight o'clock that night, Randy and Beth were sitting on a couch inside their cabin. Randy reached over and placed his hand on Beth's hand. He said, "I hope you had a good time today."

"Yes, I had a very good time. I appreciate you buying my swimsuit that I had on at the beach. I was a little nervous when I first put it on."

"Why were you nervous?"

"I didn't know how you would view me in that swimsuit."

"Beth, you looked wonderful in that blue bathing suit."

"Are you just saying that?"

"I'm telling you the honest truth, Beth. My eyes almost popped out of my head when I saw how gorgeous you looked. As far as I'm concerned, you would look good wearing burlap with a straw hat sitting on your head."

"You've got to be kidding me," Beth remarked, blushing.

"I got so irritated today that I wanted to punch a man in his nose!"

"Why were you so irritated?" Beth asked.

"That tall guy with his cruddy looking mustache was gawking at you like he owned you. I started to ask him if he had a problem or something. That guy doesn't know how close he came to being socked in his jaw."

"I saw that jerk gazing at me," said Beth. "Him gazing at me didn't bother me one bit. All women, especially nice looking women, are gazed at all the time. Randy, you can't go around socking someone for eye-balling a woman, even if it's your woman. Women are used to that sort of thing."

"Okay, since you put it that way. How did you enjoy your seafood dinner at Wellington's today?"

"I enjoyed so much that I would like to eat there tomorrow before we head home."

Randy edged a little closer to Beth. He looked downward for a few seconds; he didn't say a word. "What's wrong, Randy?" Beth asked. "What are you thinking about?"

He looked up. "I was just thinking about how much I love you. It would break my heart if something ever came between us."

"Randy, there's no reason for you to be concerned about something coming between us. I'm deeply in love with you. You're everything in a man that I could ever want. You're good, kind, gentle and a wonderful father to your daughter. I'm just happy that we're together." She leaned forward and kissed him on his lips. Randy placed his arms around her neck; he then kissed her passionately on her lips. "Randy, there are five bedrooms in this cabin, which one do you want to sleep in?"

"Goodness, that's a hard question to answer." He smiled.

"All you have to do is pick a number from one to five," Beth commented. "I prefer number two bedroom. That leaves you four to choose from; which will it be when we decide to go to bed?"

"Beth Miller, you drive a hard bargain!"

"Why is that?"

"It makes no difference which of those rooms I sleep in because I don't think I'll be doing much sleeping."

"Why is that?"

"Goodness, you'd have to be a man to understand that."

George Eason, Buddy Collier and his two sons, George and Vern had been searching the woods for nearly two hours for Danny Miller. They found his four-wheeler an hour ago at the end of the woods path. Again and again they shouted for Danny to answer their call, but there was no answer. "Danny! Danny! Can you hear me?" George yelled.

"Mr. Eason, hold up a minute!" Mr. Collier spoke. "I thought I heard something." They all perked their ears and listened for any kind of sound. "There it is, again, Mr. Eason! Did you hear it?"

"Yes, I heard something way off. What do you think it was?"

"Mr. Eason, I know what was making that sound," said Vern Collier.

"What was it?"

"It's a dog making a whimpering, mournful sound like there's something wrong with him. I believe the sound is coming from near Trent Creek. I'll bet anything that poor dog has got himself or herself caught in one of Junior Wiggins' steel traps. I've heard Junior say that he fur traps on Trent Creek. I don't believe that dog is more than a hundred yards from the George Harris Bridge."

"Vern, we're looking for Mr. Eason's grandchild; we're not looking for a dog." Buddy Collier spoke.

"Daddy, I believe Vern just told us where Danny went. When he came into the woods, I'm sure he heard that dog making those sounds," said George. "Another thing, it was still daylight when Danny came into the woods. He could have easily made his way to that dog."

"Okay Vern, you lead the way toward the sounds of that dog!" George voiced. "We need to hurry; I feel like something bad has happened to my grandson."

Using their flashlights, they walked toward the occasional sound of a whimpering dog fast as the trees and heavy underbrush would allow. The sounds from the dog got louder as they neared the creek. Finally, they reached the creek's edge. "Oh, my God!" yelled Mr. Eason. "Buddy, shine your light toward the base of this oak tree!" Henry dropped to his knees beside his grandson. A half-grown, Labrador Retriever was lying next to him. "Son, can you talk?" Danny could only make mumbling sounds. "What in the world has happened to my grandson?" George sounded, tearfully.

"Mr. Eason, Danny has been snake-bitten by a rattlesnake," said Vern. "The snake is lying about twelve feet from where Danny is. The snake is dead. I guess Danny killed it with that limb lying on the ground."

"My Lord, we're so far into the woods!" Henry remarked. "We've got a long ways to go before we can get him out of here! We've got to get him to a hospital soon as possible!"

"Mr. Eason, the way out is not as far as you think," said Vern. "About a hundred yards downstream from here is the George Harris Bridge. My brother and I can carry Danny out of here. It looks like that poor dog was caught in a trap. I guess Danny freed him and shortly after that he came in contact with that snake."

Henry took out his cell phone and called 911. He told the dispatcher that he needed an ambulance or helicopter at the George Harris Bridge. He said his grandson had been bitten by a rattlesnake and he was unable to talk. Henry told the dispatcher that they would have his grandson at the bridge quickly as possible.

Vern and George led the way with Danny as they headed downstream through the woods. George Eason noticed the nearly half-starved dog trying to hobble along on his swollen foot. George lifted the dog up; he was determined to bring him out of the woods. Following the others, he occasionally patted the dog on his head. George was thankful that the dog had led them to his grandson.

An ambulance was waiting at the George Harris Bridge when George and the others finally exited the woods. Danny was immediately placed inside the ambulance; emergency treatment for his snake bite began. "Mr. Eason, you can ride in the ambulance with your grandson," Mr. Collier advised. "My boys and I will walk home. It will be a pleasure walking down this highway after going through your woods. By the way, we'll carry this dog to my house and do what we can for him."

"I can't thank you and your boys enough," said George. "I really appreciate what you've done for me. I won't ever forget it."

George Eason asked one of the emergency crew which hospital they were going to take Danny. They informed him that Gaylord Medical Center, eight miles away, was the best place to take a snake-bitten individual. Extremely reluctant, George took out his cell phone and dialed Beth Miller's number.

"Beth! Beth! Wake up, sweetheart!" Randy voiced.

"What's wrong? What's the matter?" Beth asked, rubbing her eyes.

"You left your cell phone in the living room last night when you went to bed. From my bedroom, I heard it when it went off. Anyway, you need to talk to your father."

Beth took the phone. She listened as her father told her that Danny had been bitten by a poisonous snake, and that he was at the Gaylord Medical Center. He informed her that his condition was serious. Beth told him that she would be on her way there as quickly as she could get dressed.

"Randy, we've got to go! Danny has been bitten by a poisonous snake! He's at Gaylord Medical Center! I'll get dressed as quickly as I can; you do the same! I want to leave here right away"

They were packed and in Randy's car fifteen minutes later. Beth was in tears as they drove away from their cabin. "I'm sorry for spoiling your weekend," She said, tearfully.

"You didn't spoil my weekend. As long as I'm with you it doesn't matter where we're at."

"I'm worried to death about my son!" Beth commenced crying. "I don't know what I would do if something happens to him! Daddy indicated that he was in a bad way!"

Randy and Beth arrived at Gaylord Medical Center an hour and thirty-five minutes later. George and Dora were sitting in the emergency room when Randy and Beth walked inside.

"Beth, I'm very sorry that I had to call you in the middle of the night, but I knew you would want to be here," said George.

"Daddy, how is Danny?" Beth asked, tearfully.

"From what the doctor told me, he's stable, but he's not out of the woods-----so to speak."

"When can I see my son?"

"The nurse said Dr. William Ivey will talk with us soon as he can concerning Danny's condition."

Dora stood up. "Beth, please have a seat and try not to worry. Danny is a strong boy. I'm sure he's going to be alright."

"Mr. Eason, if you don't mind-----would you tell Beth and me what happened to Danny?" Randy asked.

"Danny rode his four-wheeler down a woods path into my stand of timber. The path goes a long ways in the woods, but it does end. Apparently, when Danny got to the end of the path, he heard a dog making mournful sounds. Not able to drive his four-wheeler any farther, he elected to search for the dog on foot. To make a long story short, we found Danny lying near an oak tree, not more than ten yards from Trent Creek that runs through my woods. A nearly starved dog was lying beside Danny when we found him. It looks as though Danny freed the dog from a steel trap that he was in. Shortly after that he was bitten by a rattlesnake. We never would have found Danny in the dark if it hadn't been for that dog making those whimpering sounds."

"Daddy, where is that dog now?" Beth asked, tearfully.

"One of my tenants, Mr. Buddy Collier and his two sons took the dog home with them to doctor his foot and nourish him back to health. It's a pretty Labrador retriever. When Danny gets well, he might want to keep the animal that saved his life."

A few minutes later, a nurse opened the waiting room door. She said, "I understand that Danny Miller's mother is in the room."

Beth stood up quickly. She was extremely alarmed at what the nurse was about to say. "My name is Beth Miller; I'm Danny's mother!"

"Follow me, Mrs. Miller. I'll take you to your son." Beth followed the nurse out of the room, and down the hallway toward the intensive care unit.

Dora Eason stood up. "I wonder what's going on with Danny," she remarked, being visibly upset."

"Dora, please quit worrying," George said. "I don't want you having a heart attack or something even worse."

"May I get either or both of you something to drink?" Randy asked.

"That would be nice of you," said George. "See if you can get Dora and me some coffee this time of morning."

Randy returned about fifteen minutes later with two cups of coffee. "Mrs. Eason, this coffee is very hot. Please be careful when you drink it."

"That's very kind of you, Randy. I can understand why Beth likes you so well. She's such a good woman and a wonderful mother."

"I whole heartedly agree with you, Mrs. Eason. Since my wife died, Beth Miller is the only woman that I've been interested in. She's a very decent, God-fearing woman that I hope to marry one of these days."

"How would Shelia feel about you marrying Beth?"

"Mrs. Eason, Shelia would be absolutely thrilled!"

"Where is that beautiful daughter of yours?" Dora asked.

"She spent the weekend with my aunt. She'll be back home by four o'clock this evening."

Beth came back into the waiting room thirty minutes later. Everyone stood up, waiting anxiously to hear what she had found out. "I saw Danny------- and thank God he's conscious now," she said tearfully. "Dr. Samuel Bernstein, a doctor that specializes in snake-bite victims, said that Danny wouldn't have lasted much longer if he hadn't had the emergency treatment by the Emergency Management Technicians."

"Beth, does that mean my grandchild will be okay?" Dora asked, sniffing back her tears.

"Yes, the doctor said that Danny is not expected to die, but he will have to remain hospitalized for at least overnight. When he gets home, he'll have to take medicine for several days. My goodness, his whole leg is swollen. I'm very thankful that he will be okay."

Randy placed his arms around her. "I want you to know that I've been sitting here silently praying that Danny will be alright."

"I appreciate you doing that," Beth responded.

"Beth, how soon before we all can visit Danny?" George asked.

"Dr. Bernstein said it would be about thirty minutes. A nurse will come let us know when it's time. "Randy, will you go to your car and get my suitcase? I'm staying with my son tonight."

Randy returned a few minutes later with Beth's suitcase in his hand. It was a short time later that a nurse came into the waiting room. The nurse informed Beth and the others that they could visit with Danny.

Beth was the first one to walk into Danny's room. The others walked quietly behind her. Danny looked up and saw his mother in tears. "Please don't cry, Mother," he whispered softly. She knelt down and hugged his neck. "Grandpa, how did anyone find me at the creek?"

"Son, we wouldn't have found you if it hadn't been for a dog that kept making whimpering sounds. That's how we were able to find you."

"Grandpa, that dog was caught in a trap and he was nearly starved. I had to get him free. A snake bit me when I went after a splint for the dog's leg. I picked up a limb and killed that darn thing! I realized that I would soon be in a bad way, being snake-bitten in the middle of woods, with darkness closing in on me. The pain started off like needles sticking in my leg. Shortly after that, I felt this intense burning sensation. It felt like a blow torch against my leg. Anyway, after freeing the dog, I was thankful that the dog wanted to keep me company. A little while later my body began acting funny so I sat down by a tree. The dog hobbled over to me and laid down."

"Danny, what were your thoughts during that particular time?" George asked.

"Well, I had already determined that I was going to die." Tears came into his eyes. "I remember saying something about that."

"Danny, what did you say?" Beth asked, tearfully.

"Just before I passed out, I said, 'Daddy, I'll be seeing you shortly'. Grandma, I just figured that it was time for me to die." Beth hurried out of the room in tears. Randy followed after her.

"You knew it was getting late when you parked your 4-wheeler at the end of the woods path. What in the world possessed you to go searching for a dog and it nearly night?" George asked.

"Grandpa, I asked myself that same question while I kept going toward the sound of that dog. I really don't know what made me do it. It was something that I just had to do. The pitiful sounds of a dog in distress gave me no choice; I had to keep going forward until I found out why the dog was making those sounds."

Randy and Beth came back into Danny's room. Tears were visible in Beth's eyes.

Dora took hold of Danny's hand. She said, "Son, we're all very grateful that you're alive after that awful ordeal in the woods."

"Mother, Grandmother, I'm okay. You two don't have to cry anymore."

"We're all very relieved that you'll be home in a day or so."

"Thank you, Mr. Johnson. Wait a minute-----I thought you and Mother were at the beach!"

"When we heard what had happened to you-----we were out of that cabin in a flash!" Randy answered. "I'm surprised I didn't get about three speeding tickets."

"Grandma, please don't cry anymore!"

"Danny, I was very worried about you!" said Dora. "You're our only grandson, and we love you so much!" She placed her arms around him.

"Grandpa, I still don't know how you managed to find me in the middle of the woods, in total darkness."

"That Labrador Retriever kept on making those sounds you mentioned. It was as though he was trying to let someone know where you were. Mr. Collier and his two boys helped me with your rescue. Danny, there's no doubt about it, that dog helped save your life."

"Where's that dog now, Grandpa?"

"He's at Mr. Collier's house. He wanted to treat his foot and give him some well deserved food."

"Do you suppose I can keep him as my pet?" Danny asked, him looking toward his mother.

"I tell you what, Danny. If Beth doesn't mind I'll try to get up with the owner and see if he will sell the dog to me. If he will, I'll give the dog to you. Another thing, I'll have your 4-wheeler brought out of the woods sometime today."

Danny rose up in bed a little. "Mother, may I keep the dog?" Danny asked, pitifully.

"You certainly can, sweetheart! If he becomes yours, what will you name him?"

"I'll name him, Lucky."

"Son, that's a pretty name, but why that particular name." George asked.

"Because of that dog, I'm lucky to be alive."

Chapter 13

Danny was back in school four days later. Kids at his school were eager for him to tell about his unyielding effort to save a dog from certain death. His classmate, Charlie Gibbs asked to see his swollen leg and the puncture wounds on his right leg. Shelia Johnson was thankful that Danny lived through his ordeal.

George Eason found out that the Labrador retriever belonged to Jake Benton. Mr. Benton lived within a half mile of where Trent Creek ran underneath the George Harris Bridge. At first, Mr. Benton was not inclined to sell the dog to Mr. Eason. However, after he heard the full story concerning Mr. Eason's grandson and his harrowing experience in the woods, Mr. Benton gave the dog to Danny.

Beth contracted with a small fencing crew to install a sizeable fence in her backyard. This would ensure Lucky's safety from the busy road that ran in front of her house. Mr. Jake Benton donated a large dog box for Danny's dog. Mr. Benton's only request was for Danny to take very good care of his dog.

The bond between Danny and Lucky was very strong. He fed and watered his dog when needed. On one occasion, Danny sat in front of Lucky's dog box; he talked to the dog as though he was a person. He told Lucky how thankful he was for him saving his life.

Several days had passed since Danny Miller's ordeal in his grandfather's woods. Randy Johnson had worked tirelessly trying to figure out where he could find Gordon Ray Stallings. He visited Bridgeport Business College, the college campus where Gordon attended school, but his trail ended there. He and the sheriff's department checked with every law enforcement agency within sixty miles to see if they had a record for Gordon Ray Stallings, but they came up empty. Except for the college he attended, it was though Gordon Ray Stallings never existed. Sheriff Alan Hicks had two bulletins put out over the air waves. One was asking if anyone had seen or knew of a man that was missing one of his ears, or part of an ear. The other bulletin was asking the public if anyone knew someone named Gordon Ray Stallings. Three days passed, not one single response did the sheriff's office receive.

Beth and Danny Miller had just finished eating breakfast. Danny volunteered to do the dishes while his mother did some house cleaning and other household chores. Danny smiled as he looked out the kitchen window at his dog playing with a rubber ball. A little while earlier, he had taken

Lucky's food out to him and placed it in his pan. His love for Lucky became stronger and stronger as the days passed on.

Except for the fang marks still left on his leg, Danny was well from his snake bite. The memory of his helpless ordeal in his grandfather's woods kept haunting him. He hated to tell his mother that he sometimes had nightmares concerning that predicament he was in. One night he had the worst nightmare of all. He dreamed that he had just freed the trapped dog. He knew the dog's leg needed a splint, so he walked a little ways from the creek to find a small piece of wood. Unexpectedly, a giant snake grabbed his leg and commenced turning him inside the snake's coils. The coil kept getting tighter and tighter until it was difficult for him to breathe. In his dream, he managed to utter two words, 'help me'. The dog that he had just rescued hobbled over to the snake; he kept biting the snake until it became uncoiled from around Danny. It was then that Danny watched the enormous snake bite the dog's head, and then dragged him off thru the underbrush.

"What are you thinking about, Danny?" Beth asked. "You've got a worried look on your face."

"I was just thinking about a dream I had three nights ago."

"Will you tell me about it?"

"Mother, are you sure you want to hear about my nightmarish dream?"

"Yes, please tell me what you were dreaming about!" Danny explained the entire dream to his mother. Beth shuddered at the very thought of being squeezed to death by a large snake. "How often do you have those kinds of dreams?"

"A lot more times than I want to talk about. Sometimes my nightmares have something to do with my daddy."

"Tell me about your last nightmare involving your father."

"Let me think------oh, I remember what my nightmare was about. It was in the middle of summer. Daddy and I were fishing in this large river somewhere. It was a very hot day in the middle of summer. We hadn't caught any fish in the last hour. Daddy asked me if I wanted to jump out of the boat and swim a little to cool off. I took one look at the flow of the water and I told him I wasn't interested in getting into that river. Without any further conversation, Daddy took off his shirt and shoes. He placed his wallet, keys and a few other things he had in his pocket in the bottom of the boat. Daddy knew the boat anchor would keep the boat in place while he went for a swim. Anyway, Daddy jumped into the water. Almost immediately he determined that the current was too strong for him to get back to the boat. The current was taking him downstream. He yelled out, 'Danny, pull up the anchor and come get me!' I hurried to the front of the boat; with all my might I tried to pull up the anchor, but it wouldn't budge. Again and again I pulled on the anchor, but it wouldn't come up. When I looked back toward Daddy he was way down the river. All at once I looked horrified as I saw the dorsal fin of a shark moving toward Daddy. It was at this moment that I rolled off the bed. That's when I realized that it was only a dream. I stayed awake the rest of the night, fearful that I might start dreaming again."

Beth sat silent for a few seconds after hearing about her son's nightmare. Tears slid down her face. "You may have to see a doctor if you keep having these kinds of nightmares."

"I don't believe a doctor can do anything about people having dreams," said Danny.

"Well, hopefully you'll soon quit having those kinds of dreams," Beth remarked.

Danny was washing dishes a few minutes later. For a few seconds he stood at the sink holding a dish in his hand. "What's the matter?" Beth asked.

"I was just thinking."

"Well, while you're thinking----shouldn't you turn off the water? The sink is about to run over."

"Mother, I'm sorry. You sure look nice this morning."

"Well, thank you very much. Compliments like that are always welcome in this house. How are you and Shelia doing these days?'

"I guess we're doing okay."

"What do you mean-----doing okay? Have you two had some kind of disagreement?"

"No, Mother, nothing like that," said Danny. "It's just that----oh heck, I don't know."

"I don't understand you, Danny. There was a time that you thought she was the prettiest girl in the whole world!"

"I still do think she's pretty, but------."

"But-------what Danny, I think I'll give Shelia a call myself!" Beth reached for her phone.

"Mother, please don't call her! Please------!" Danny begged.

"Has she started liking someone else?"

He nodded his head, affirming what she just said. "Okay, I'll tell you. I believe she likes Tommy Lewis better than she likes me."

"Who is Tommy Lewis?" Beth asked.

"He's a new kid that just started at our school. Tommy is in a couple of Shelia's classes. He hangs around Shelia as if he owns her. Shelia should tell him to get lost or something, but she doesn't! She seems to like him when he's around her. It makes me sad when I see that."

"You poor boy," said Beth. "It seems that my teenage boy has got the love sick blues."

"Mother, it hurts me inside when I think about her liking someone else."

"Danny, take my word for it------that feeling you have will pass on. I remember when I was about your age. There was a boy named Jamie Henderson that I had a king sized crush on. Just like you're experiencing now, my heart seemed to flutter whenever I was around him. Well, one day I happened to be on the playground watching the school's cheerleaders do their practice routines. I happened to look toward the corner of the school building and there I saw Jamie kissing Florence Davis on her lips. That fluttering feeling that I sometimes felt went away forever. From that point on I hardly spoke to Jamie Henderson."

"Mother, was Florence Davis a good looking girl?" Danny asked, him smiling.

"Well-------yes, she looked okay, but she wasn't a beauty queen."

"In that case why would Jamie want to kiss her?"

"I was told that a lot of boys kissed Florence Davis at one time or another. I'll have to wait until you get older before I explain why they would kiss her."

"Mother, I know about the birds and the bees. What you just said to me in a round-about way is that Florence Davis **was** easy-pickings for the boys. Am I getting warm?"

"Danny, you sure know how to get right to the point," said Beth, slightly embarrassed.

"Mother, I was looking forward to attending Shelia's birthday party today, but I'm worried that she might invite Tommy Lewis. Do you think she'll like the necklace that we bought for her?"

"I'm sure she will. It's a very pretty necklace."

"Tommy Lewis had better not give her a necklace!" Danny remarked. "I don't know why that guy had to come here in the first place!"

"Danny Miller, I want you to stop talking like that this very minute!" Beth demanded. "I've never seen you like this before! What in the world has come over you these last few days? Do you suppose you've still got some snake venom inside your body?"

"I'm sorry, Mother. What time are we supposed to be at Shelia's party?"

"We'll try to be there about 3:30 this afternoon."

This morning was a momentous occasion for Shelia Johnson. Today was her thirteenth birthday. She had finally become a teenager. Randy and Shelia were sitting at their breakfast table. Shelia had prepared, eggs, bacon and toast for breakfast. Randy looked across the table toward his daughter with a big smile and said, "Happy birthday, Shelia!"

"Thank you, Daddy."

"I was wondering what you wanted for your birthday."

"Daddy, do you really want to know what I want for my birthday?" Shelia asked, excitedly.

"Yes, I really do want to know."

"More than anything, I want you to marry Danny Miller's mother!"

"Shelia, I would be more than glad to accomplish your wish, but Beth Miller would have a lot to say about something like that."

"Have you asked her to marry you?"

"Well, no------something like that takes time. Asking someone to marry you is a very delicate ordeal. Rejection can come quick if a person's timing is off. I'm waiting for the right moment to pop the question."

"Daddy, if you wait around too long you might miss the right moment to pop the question to her."

"Shelia, I love Beth Miller a great deal. I want very much to marry her, but why is my marrying her so important to you?"

"Daddy, I'm a girl; I need a mother that I can talk freely with, someone to help me select the right clothing, teach me how to cook, sew and things like that."

"Shelia, I've done the best I know for you," Randy commented, sadly.

"As far as I'm concerned you're the best father that has ever lived, but you're not a woman! A young girl like me needs a woman in her life. Daddy, you need to get on the ball if you ever expect to nail Mrs. Miller down."

"What size nails do I use in order to do that?" Randy asked, him smiling.

"You know what I mean, Daddy."

"Shelia, there is one small problem in my marrying Beth Miller."

"What problem are you talking about?"

"When and if I were to marry Beth Miller, we would all be living in the same house. You would have to make up your mind whether you wanted a boyfriend or a brother. You and Danny living in the same house, day after day, might affect yours' and his relationship."

"Daddy, I've thought about that a lot. If we all start living together in the same house, we'll just have to see how everything works out. What time are we to suppose to be at Oakdale Country Club today?"

"We need to be there at three o'clock this evening. You're going to have a wonderful birthday party. I've arranged for everything to be just like it was for Danny's birthday party."

"Will we have music at my party?" Shelia asked.

"Absolutely, we'll have music! Mickey Phelps, the same disc jockey that played music at Danny's birthday party will be there. Missy Holliday will be our caterer. There is one other thing that I forgot to mention."

"What other thing are you talking about?" Shelia asked.

"Do you know a boy by the name of Tommy Lewis?"

"Yes, Tommy goes to the same school as me. In fact, he's in two of my classes. When did you see him?"

"I saw him yesterday at Sutton's grocery store. He was with his mother and sister. Tommy asked me if it would be okay if he could come to your birthday party. With his mother and sister standing there listening, what was I suppose to say."

"Did you ask him to come?"

"Yes Shelia, I told him that he would be welcome at your birthday party."

"Tommy acts like I'm his girlfriend or something each time he's around me. Danny doesn't like Tommy very much. Daddy, I'm afraid there might be trouble if Danny sees Tommy flirting with me as he always does."

"Is Danny that jealous of you?"

"I'm afraid he is. He was ready to punch one boy out for staring at me."

"I wouldn't worry about it too much, Sweetheart. It's your birthday; those boys won't start anything while you're celebrating becoming a teenager."

Randy and Shelia arrived at Oakdale Country Club at 3:00 that afternoon. Mickey Phelps was already playing music when they walked inside the building. Missy Holliday had a wide variety of food laid out on a long table. Beth and Danny were already sitting at a table when Randy and Shelia came into the banquet room. Danny stood up when he saw Randy and Shelia headed toward them. "Hi Danny," said Shelia. "Mrs. Miller, I hope you're saving two seats for Daddy and me."

"Yes Shelia, I certainly am. Please have a seat, you too Randy." He took a seat next to Beth. "Shelia, it looks like you're going to have a large crowd at your birthday party. I want to wish you a very happy birthday."

"Thank you, Mrs. Miller. Danny, I'm finally a teenager just like you."

"Happy birthday, Shelia. Mr. Johnson, your daughter seems to get prettier and prettier as she gets older."

"Did you hear that, Daddy? I told you how complimentary Danny is toward me."

"Randy, have you found out anything about Gordon Ray Stallings?" Beth asked.

"No, but I'll never quit looking until I find him. I'll do all I can to keep you safe."

"Mrs. Miller, do you have any idea how much my daddy likes you?"

"Shelia, why in the world would you make a comment like that?" Randy asked, slightly embarrassed.

"That's okay, Randy. Shelia, I know how much your father likes me. I like him very much as well. Are you very excited about becoming a teenager?"

"Yes, ma' am. Danny, you seem to be awful quiet this afternoon. Are you going to dance with me like you did at your birthday party?"

"If you want me to."

"Shelia, I guess you and I should go around and meet some of your friends. It looks like we're going to have a nice turnout for your party. Beth, be sure and save our seats."

"I'll do that, Randy."

Beth noticed Danny's expression change. All of a sudden he seemed angered by something. "What's the matter?" Beth asked.

"Mother, look toward the doorway. It's Tommy Lewis and his mother." Danny stood up. "Look at that clown hugging Shelia's neck! I should go over there and straightened him out!"

"Danny Miller, you sit down right this minute!" Beth demanded. "It's Shelia's birthday. Tommy might just be wishing her a happy birthday."

"He don't have to put his paws on her to do that! It makes me mad to see him flirting with my girlfriend!"

"I want to straighten you out right now, Danny Miller; you don't own Shelia Johnson! She's not a pair of shoes that you can claim as your own! Jealousy is one of the worst things that can happen between a boy and a girl, or a man and a woman. Son, I love you and I want you to be happy. Sooner or later, Shelia will become disinterested in you if you become too over bearing with your jealousy. From where I'm sitting, Shelia is just trying to be nice and friendly to Tommy and his mother."

A few minutes later, Shelia brought Tommy and his mother over to meet Beth and Danny.

"Mrs. Miller, I want you to meet Mrs. Sharon Lewis and her son, Tommy."

Beth stood up. "I'm very pleased to meet each of you."

"Hello, Danny boy," said Tommy. "Mrs. Miller, I see you have eight chairs at your table. Do you mind if we sit with you and Danny?"

"Not at all, Tommy. Please----you and your mother can take a seat next to Danny. I'm saving the seats next to me for Shelia and her father."

"Shelia, you can sit next to me, if you want to," Tommy commented, him smiling.

Danny took in a deep breath of air when Tommy made that comment. "Well, I've got to go back and mingle with the crowd." Shelia remarked. "I'll be back in a little while."

Tommy stood up. "Hold on, Shelia------I'll go with you!"

Danny gritted his teeth. Shelia quickly realized that trouble was about to break out. "That's okay, Tommy, you should stay here with your mother. I won't be long. I just need to go around and thank everyone for attending my birthday party."

"Shelia, don't forget what I asked you at the door," Tommy commented. "I want to dance with you when you come back."

"Hey Tommy, let's you and I go get us something to drink," said Danny.

"Sure, let's go." Tommy followed Danny toward the beverage bar. When they got to the bar, Danny kept walking toward a room down a hallway. "Where in the world are we going?" Tommy followed Danny into a room. Danny closed the door behind him. "Danny, what is going on?"

"You numbskull, I'll tell you what's going on!" He grabbed Tommy by each of his shirt collars. "You listen and you listen well, Shelia Johnson is my girlfriend and I'll black both your eyes if you continue with her the way you've been doing!" Danny balled up his fist; he held it in front of Tommy's face. "I won't tell you again------leave my girlfriend alone!"

Tommy backed off a few feet from Danny. "You're crazy as a loon! You don't own Shelia Johnson!"

"What is going on in here?" Mr. Frederick Mills asked. "What are you two boys up to?"

"Sir, who are you?" Tommy asked.

"I'm the custodian of Oakdale Country Club. It looks as if you two were about to fight each other. Take my advice and get back to that young lady's birthday party." Danny and Tommy left the room. They went back to where they were sitting.

"I thought you two went after something to drink," Beth commented. Neither of the boys made a comment concerning something to drink.

A few minutes later, Sheriff Alan Hicks walked up to Beth's table. "Hello Sheriff, how have you been doing?" Beth asked.

"I've been doing just fine."

"Sheriff, the lady sitting across from me is Mrs. Sharon Lewis, and the boy sitting next to her is her son, Tommy."

"I'm very pleased to meet you, Mrs. Lewis, as well as your son. I came over here to borrow these two boys for a few minutes. I need them to help me move a couple tables around."

"They'll be happy to help you, Sheriff," Mrs. Lewis commented. "Tommy, you go help Sheriff Hicks."

Danny got up right away; he had a hunch that the custodian had told him about his and Tommy's confrontation. The boys followed the sheriff into the same room that they were in a few minutes ago. Sheriff Hicks closed the door behind him. "Danny Miller, why were you and Tommy in this same room a little while ago. The custodian told me that it appeared to him that you and Tommy were about to fight each other."

"Sheriff, it was Danny's fault!" Tommy answered. "He fooled me into this room, and then he threatened to black my eyes if I didn't stay away from Shelia Johnson."

"Is that true, Danny?" Sheriff Hicks asked.

"Yes sir, he's telling the truth, but he won't leave my girlfriend alone. Shelia is my girlfriend, not his."

"I'm going to tell you both something right now! If either one of you starts something at Shelia's birthday party------I'm going to take both of you to jail! Is that understood by both of you?"

"Sheriff Hicks, I promise not to start anything," Danny commented.

"What about you, Tommy?"

"I never started anything in the first place. It was all Danny's doing."

"Shelia Johnson deserves to have a peaceful and enjoyable birthday party," said Sheriff Hicks. "I fully intend for that to happen. Danny, I've got news for you------if Shelia Johnson likes this boy, well------there's not one darn thing you can do about it. That girl is only thirteen years old today. By the time she's eighteen she'll most likely have had several boyfriends. I want each of you to shake hands right now." They looked at each other for a few seconds. "I don't want to repeat what I just said!" They shook hands with each other. "Now, you two boys go back to your table and behave yourselves."

Fifteen minutes later, Randy Johnson stood on a chair and said, "Ladies and gentlemen, boys and girls, please let me have your attention." Everyone quieted down. "As most of you know, Shelia Johnson is my daughter. Today is a wonderful time for Shelia because today she became a teenager!" Everyone clapped their hands. "Thank you for that applause. There's food on the table, and Mickey Phelps is playing some great songs. You can start eating whenever you care to. Shelia and I want you to have a great time at her thirteenth birthday party."

Mickey Phelps picked up his microphone. "Ladies and gentlemen, let's all clap our hands to entice our birthday girl to dance with a person of her choice."

No sooner than Mickey laid down the mike, Tommy Lewis stood up; he hurried to where Shelia was standing with her father and Sheriff Allen Hicks. She looked dumbfounded when Tommy took her hand. "I'll dance with you, Shelia." Before she could say anything, Mickey Phelps picked up his microphone and asked the crowd to give Shelia and her young friend a round of applause. Everyone in the room was clapping their hands, except for Danny Miller and his mother. Danny's eyes almost bulged from their sockets as he observed Tommy leading Shelia to the dance floor. He wanted to get up and punch Tommy Lewis, but he remembered what Sheriff Hicks said.

"Look at them, folks-----they're dancing as though they've been rehearsing for weeks," said

Mickey. After the song finished, Tommy led Shelia off the dance floor. She looked toward Danny as they walked toward his table. He sat silent, his head lowered; tears emerged in the corner of his eyes.

"You two looked great on the dance floor!" Mrs. Lewis commented. "Danny, can you dance like my son?"

"Yes, Mrs. Lewis, Danny dances very well," Beth answered, avoiding comments from her son.

Suddenly, Danny got up. He walked over to where Mark Langford was standing with his mother. Mark was a classmate and a good friend of Danny. "I couldn't believe my eyes when I saw Shelia dancing with Tommy Lewis," Mark commented. "Danny, what's happened between you and Shelia?"

"Mrs. Langford, how are you doing these days?"

"I'm doing fine, Danny. Like Mark, I'm curious as to why you weren't dancing with Shelia, instead of that boy."

"Well, Mrs. Langford, I guess that boy likes Shelia same as me. It will be up to her to choose which one she likes best. Has Mr. Langford been fishing lately?"

"Yes, he went last week somewhere and caught a variety of fresh water fish; the cooler was almost full of fish and ice."

"Tell Mr. Langford that Mark and I would like to go fishing with him sometime."

"I'll do that, Danny."

"Well, I guess I had better go back to my table," said Danny. "I'm very glad to see both of you here today."

Danny walked over to the beverage table and got himself a soft drink. He looked toward his table; he saw Tommy Lewis smiling and sitting next to Shelia. For Danny, that was the last straw. He looked around the room until he saw a girl that he recognized. Her name was Becky Howard; she attended the same school as Danny and Shelia. He hurried toward Becky as she stood next to her mother. "Hello, Becky."

"Danny, I thought you would be the one sitting next to Shelia, not Tommy Lewis. Mother, this is Danny Miller-----the boy that I've told you about quite often."

"I'm pleased to meet you, Danny."

"Thank you very much, Mrs. Howard. Becky, would you care to dance with me?"

"What will Shelia think about me dancing with you?"

"I'm sure it won't be a problem," Danny answered. "How old are you?" He asked, as they headed toward the dance floor.

"I'll be fourteen in twenty one days."

"Will your boyfriend be mad with me if I dance with you?"

"Danny, I don't have a boyfriend."

"Well now-------we'll have to do something about that, won't we?" Danny and Becky commenced dancing to a song sung by the Brothers Four entitled, 'Beautiful Brown Eyes'. As they were dancing, Becky whispered to Danny, "Have you noticed that I have brown eyes?"

"Of course I did, that was the first thing I noticed about you." Becky moved her head a little closer to Danny's as they danced to the music."

With a stern expression, Shelia's fingers were tapping against the table, her observing Danny and Becky holding each other on the dance floor. "Tommy, look how happy that girl seems on the dance floor with Mrs. Miller's son," said Mrs. Lewis. "That looks like a match made in Heaven." Shelia got up from the table. She walked hurriedly toward the women's bathroom.

Beth Miller followed behind her. Shelia was in tears when Beth entered the bathroom. "Shelia, why are you crying? Today is your birthday, Sweetheart. Please-----don't be upset because Danny was dancing with that girl. I'm sure he was just trying to prove something with you and Tommy Lewis." "Mrs. Miller, it hurt my feelings when I saw Becky wrapped around Danny the way she was! Danny should have known that it would upset me if he danced with Becky."

"Shelia, in all fairness-----how do you think Danny felt when you were on the dance floor with Tommy Lewis? Please -------you're a teenager now! You're above this petty jealousy that seems to be driving you and Danny apart! I've already told him the same thing! I think the world of you, Shelia. I just want you to be happy. Let's go back to our table; I want you to forget all this foolishness."

"Thank you, Mrs. Miller for being such a good friend to me. You're absolutely right; Danny and I have acted foolish. All I'm going to think about now is enjoying my birthday celebration."

Beth placed her arms around Shelia. "You and I talking things out is all it took to straighten everything out," Beth commented.

"You're absolutely right, Mrs. Miller. You just said the very same thing I told my father this morning. I told him that I needed a mother to help me decide things as I get older."

"You told him that," Beth inquired. "What was his response?"

"Mrs. Miller, I believe you know what he told me concerning you."

Shelia mingled with the crowd for the next thirty minutes. She tried her best to avoid any kind of confrontation between Danny and Tommy. Beth acted as though nothing was wrong when she took her seat across from Mrs. Sharon Lewis. Danny remained quiet as his mother tried her best to be sociable with the Lewis family.

Randy Johnson stood in a chair at 6:30 that evening. "Ladies and gentlemen, please give me your attention! Thank you. First of all, before I forget it-----I want to thank everyone for coming to my daughter's birthday celebration. I want everyone to gather around the table at the back of the room. My daughter is already sitting next to that big birthday cake. She's prepared to blow out all those candles." Randy stepped down from the chair. Beth lit all thirteen candles. Shelia blew out all the candles with one breath of air. Everyone started singing Happy Birthday to Shelia."

Shelia stood up like an adult and said, "Thank you all for making my thirteenth birthday the most memorable of all. Goodness, I never expected to get so many presents!" Tommy Lewis was the first one to hand her his present. "Open it up girl," said Tommy, "see what I got for you."

Shelia opened his present to find a necklace inside. It was similar to the one that Danny had purchased for her. "It's nice, thank you Tommy."

Shelia continued opening presents for the next thirty-five minutes. She kept wondering why she hadn't found Danny's present. After opening all her presents that were on the table, Danny handed her his present. With much sadness, he held his head downward as she removed the wrapping around his present. "Danny, your present is beautiful!" She jumped up; she hugged Danny's neck as if it was the most beautiful present in the world.

"Shelia, my present looks almost like his! I didn't get a hug!"

"Tommy, I appreciate your gift a great deal, but Danny's present has a different meaning to me."

"Why is that?".

"You should know by now, Danny is my boyfriend." Danny's mouth opened wide. All at once a big smile appeared on his face. Tommy looked downward, as though he had been outfoxed by Danny Miller.

Danny walked a few feet away from Shelia. Beth went to where he was standing. She noticed the tears in his eyes. Danny tried to keep his mother from seeing his face. He wiped away his tears with his hand. "Danny, what's wrong?"

"There's nothing wrong, Mother. I'm just overwhelmed with happiness. Also, I realize that I have been a jealous fool. I'm ashamed of the way I acted tonight. I'll tell you about it when we get home. From now on I'm going to listen to your advice."

"Beth, is something wrong with Danny?" Randy asked.

"Not at all, he's very happy that Shelia likes the necklace that he gave her. You know, Randy-----we've got two wonderful children that any parent would be proud of."

"Beth, I really like that one word you just used."

"What word was that?"

"The word 'we've.' Randy smiled.

Chapter 14

The following Saturday, Danny and Beth were sitting at their dinner table. He noticed that his mother hadn't eaten any food on their table. "Why aren't you eating anything?" Danny asked.

"Randy and I are going out for dinner this evening. Is that okay with you?"

"Mother, you don't have to get my permission to go on a date."

"I know that, but I was trying to be nice about it. Why don't you give Shelia a call this evening? I'm sure she would like to talk with you for awhile."

"I'll do that. Two real good Western movies will be on tonight. I guess I'll be watching them when they come on."

"When I leave this evening, you make real sure that all the doors and windows remain closed. I don't want to be worrying about someone opening one of our doors and walking inside our house."

"I promise I will keep every door and window secured. Mother, has Mr. Johnson popped the question to you yet?"

"That question could mean anything! Could you be a little more meaningful with your question?"

"Okay, has he asked you to marry him?"

"My goodness, no------why would you ask me a question like that?" Beth asked, curiously.

"Well, he better get on the ball! Sooner or later you're going to run into Mr. Right! That will mean curtains for Mr. Johnson!"

"Danny, I've never heard you talk like this before! What has come over you?"

"I guess you could blame it on my being a teenager. What time is Mr. Johnson coming over?"

"He's picking me up at 7:00 this evening. I need to start getting dressed. By the way, didn't I hear you having a dream last night?"

"No, it wasn't a dream, it was a darn nightmare!"

"If it was that bad, please tell me about it."

"I thought you had to get dressed for your date."

"Danny, please-----tell me about your nightmare!" Beth pleaded.

"Most of my nightmares all start at the same place. They all take place where Lucky was caught in that trap. In this nightmare I waded a little ways in Trent Creek to undo the trap on the dog's foot. All of a sudden the sand under my feet started going down. I realized very fast that I was in quicksand. The more I tried to move the tighter the sand got around my feet. I tried to holler, but words wouldn't come out of my mouth. I kept going down, down, until the only thing out of the water was my neck and head! It was then that this grizzly bear came through the thicket; he walked right up to the edge of the water within three yards of my head."

"My God, Danny-----what did you do?" Beth asked, her hands trembling.

"I rolled off my bed! That's why I have a little knot on my forehead."

"For goodness sakes, you do have a little knot!" Beth remarked, placing her hand against his forehead. "If you continue to have nightmares like the one you just told me about, I might need to take you to a doctor."

"Mother, I've told you before------I'm not going to one of those head-shrinking doctors!"

"Danny, I'm talking about a doctor of psychology."

"Those kind of doctors are all the same. They act a little weird to me. I've seen them on television with their little note pads. In fact, one patient was lying on a couch talking his head off while the doctor was sound asleep."

"Danny, that was television," said Beth. "Anyway, I've got to get dressed before Randy shows up."

"Mother, where are you and Randy going tonight?"

"I really don't know; he didn't say where we were going. He just said it would be a big surprise."

"Uh oh!" Danny mumbled.

"What was that 'uh oh' all about?" Beth asked, inquisitively.

"This is the night!".

"Danny Miller, what in the world are you talking about?"

"He's going to pop the question to you tonight. I sure would like to be a fly on the wall when he gets up enough nerve to ask you to marry him," said Danny, smiling.

"I've heard enough!" Beth remarked. "I'm going to get dressed!"

Randy rang Beth's doorbell at seven o'clock that evening. Danny opened the door. He said, "Mr. Johnson, you look real nice in your new suit and tie. Please come inside."

"Thank you very much, Danny. How have you been lately?"

"I've been doing okay. Did you see Lucky when you drove up?"

"I sure did. It looked like he was having a great time splashing around in that small kiddy-sized pool. I know one thing-----he sure looks a lot better since he's put on some weight."

"My dog loves the water. When I go to my grandparent's house again I'm going to take Lucky so he can swim in Grandpa's pond. Where is Shelia this evening?

"She's at home; one of her girlfriends is spending the night with her."

A couple minutes later, Beth walked into the living room. "You're one fine looking woman!" Randy commented.

"Thank you very much for saying so. You look rather handsome, yourself. I guess I'm ready to go if you are."

"Mr. Johnson, don't I have a pretty mother?".

"Danny, she's pretty and beautiful."

"I can see already that this is going to be an interesting night for you two," Danny commented, him nodding his head up and down." Still smiling, he went to his room.

"Randy, you'll have to excuse my son," said Beth. "Sometimes he comes up with off the wall stuff."

"Beth, your son is a teenager now. Teenagers are prone to come up with all kinds of sayings."

"I'll be right back," said Beth, "I've got to give my son a big hug before I leave." She went to Danny's room door; she tapped lightly on his door. "Danny, it's your mother, open your door!" A few seconds passed, and then Danny opened his door. "Why are you in your room?"

"I was just resting a little," he answered.

"Are you sure you're alright?"

"Yes, Mother, I'm fine! Now you and Mr. Johnson go have a good time somewhere."

"Well, give your mother a big hug."

Danny hugged her tightly around her waist. "I love you, Mother."

"I love you as well." She kissed him on his cheek. Tears emerged from Danny's eyes, him observing his mother as she walked down their hallway.

Randy and Beth were about three miles from her house when she remarked, "Danny appeared to be upset when I left my house a few minutes ago."

"What do you mean?" Randy inquired.

"To be honest with you, it seemed as though he was about to cry. I wonder why."

"I have no idea why he would be upset," Randy commented. "About the only thing he asked me was concerning Shelia. He asked me where she was this evening. I told him that one of her girlfriends was spending the night with her."

"Danny still thinks Shelia likes Tommy Lewis a great deal. He's very concerned about that."

"Beth, Shelia is not interested in Tommy Lewis!"

"Danny told me that she's with him quite a bit at school."

"On the contrary, Tommy Lewis just won't give up on Shelia. He still acts like he's going to be her boyfriend. The reason she spends so much time with Tommy Lewis at school is because he keeps following her from one place to the other. Shelia doesn't want to be rude to Tommy because she's a very good friend with his sister, Toni Lynn."

"Sister, I didn't know he even had a sister," Beth commented. "I didn't see Toni Lynn at Shelia's birthday party."

"That's because she was out of town with her father. Shelia already knew that Toni Lynn couldn't be at her birthday party, so she brought Shelia a gift before they left town. Beth, my daughter talks about Danny all the time. Nothing has changed between those two."

"I'm certainly glad to hear that," Beth replied. "I know Danny will be very excited to hear the news!"

"Whoa, you mean Danny thought Shelia liked Tommy as her boyfriend?"

"I'm afraid so, Randy. He's been rather despondent every since Tommy Lewis appeared at his school. Make no mistake about it; Danny is crazy about your daughter! I can hardly wait to tell him that Shelia is not interested in Tommy Lewis."

"Beth, I thought Shelia made it quite clear on her birthday that Danny was her boyfriend."

"I did too, but since Shelia has been spending so much time at school with Tommy------well, you know what I mean."

"Shelia thinks the sun rises and sets with Danny. You and I are in love with each other. Our children are in love with each other. Whoa, that didn't sound like it did when I said you and I are in love!"

"It's okay, I know what you meant," said Beth.

"You haven't asked me where we're going this evening."

"That's because I trust your good judgment. However, it would be nice to know where we're going since it would eliminate any supposition on my part."

"Okay, I'll tell you. I'm going to take you someplace you probably have never been. We're going to Caesar's Palace Steak House on West Darby Road."

"Well, you're right about one thing," Beth commented, "I've never been in that place. I've heard that if you ask how much something cost at Caesar's, then you can't afford to eat there."

"I'll admit Caesar's is not a cheap place to dine, but the atmosphere in there is magnificent for special occasions," Randy responded, him smiling.

Their reserved seating was near two palm trees. Directly in front of them was a beautiful pool of water; an underwater light enhanced the brilliance of the colorful fish swimming back and forth. For several seconds, Beth stood in front of her table admiring the magnificent scenery on the walls and ceiling of the spacious restaurant.

"Beth, now you know why this is not a cheap place to dine," said Randy. "How do you like it?"

"It's a beautiful place. I had no idea that this restaurant would like this inside. Look to your left! They've got a little train moving along the wall with a squirrel as the conductor. Each of the little cars is filled with a variety of nuts. I think that's so cute."

Randy and Beth sat down at their table. "Do you hear that music?" Randy asked.

"Yes, I hear it. You mean they've got a dance floor here?"

"Not only do they have a dance floor, but a live band will be playing here starting at eight o'clock this evening. I've been practicing a few dance steps."

"Who have you been dancing with?"

"Not who, but what-----," Randy answered, grinning.

"If not who, then what?" Beth inquired.

"Don't laugh, but I've been practicing with a broom."

"Who was the better dancer, you or the broom?"

"I asked you not to laugh. Anyway, you and I are going to have a wonderful time tonight. It's going to be a very special night for me because I'm going to tell you how much I love you. I'll let you be the judge whether my broom improved my dancing performance."

The waiter brought a bottle of chilled champagne and sat it on Randy and Beth's table.

Beth picked up a price list lying on the table. "Randy, that bottle of champagne sells for nearly fifty-dollars! Goodness, I was wondering how they were able to afford everything they've got in here."

"Beth, I just want you to enjoy yourself this evening. I know you don't normally drink alcohol, but tonight is a very special occasion. It would please me a great deal if you would help me drink some of this expensive champagne while we sit here and talk to each other."

"I'll try to drink some if it means that much to you." Randy opened the bottle; he filled Beth's glass with the bubbly fluid. Afterwards, he poured some into his glass. With their glasses raised----- they toasted each other. "Wow, this doesn't taste like I thought it would," Beth remarked. "I thought champagne would taste sweet. This has a more flat taste to it."

"Don't you like it?" Randy asked.

"It's okay. I imagine the more you drink-----the better it gets. You've got a silly looking grin on your face. What's with that?"

"I was noticing your expression when you drank some of your champagne. It was as though you were drinking some bad tasting medicine or something."

"Did I grimace that bad?" Beth asked.

"No, I was only kidding."

The band started playing music at eight o'clock that evening. "Are you ready to see if my broom taught me anything?" Randy asked, him smiling.

"Yes, I'm anxious to see how well a broom-trained dancer does on the dance floor." Randy and Beth danced to three songs before going back to their table.

"How well did I do?" Randy asked.

"You did very well. I had no idea that you could dance like you did. I don't believe that you learned your dancing skills from a broom."

"You're right about that. I was just kidding you about the broom. My wife taught me how to dance. She and I danced quite often on Saturday nights. Did you and John ever go dancing?"

"Yes, quite often before Danny was born. We never went dancing too much after that."

"Beth, tell me about John. I know already that he was a great husband and a wonderful father."

"John was a people person. He seemed to like everyone that he came in contact with. I never heard him say a curse word or an ugly word. He, especially, enjoyed helping people overcome their difficulties. He would bring me flowers on special occasions. Also, he spent a great deal of time with Danny. Why are you interested in knowing about John?"

"As I said before, I can never fit into John Miller's shoes, and I should never try to. I want you to love me as I am. However, there are certain things that I can do that are similar to what he did. For example, I can bring you flowers on special occasions. I could spend a great deal of time with your son. Goodness, I'm getting mushy again; let's go back to the dance floor before I ruin the whole evening for us."

"Randy, you're not ruining our evening! I enjoy you saying nice things to me."

"Do you hear that love song the band is playing?" Randy asked. "That's one of my favorite songs. Please-----dance with me!" He held Beth's hand as they headed for the dance floor. Randy placed his arms around her waist; he held his face against hers as they commenced dancing. He whispered softly, "I never thought I could love another woman as I love you."

After the song ended, Randy and Beth went back to their table. The waiter came and took their order. Beth ordered a t-bone steak, baked potato and a small salad. Randy ordered prime rib, mushrooms and green beans. They each ordered sweetened tea.

"Randy, I know our dinner is going to be very costly," Beth mentioned. "I wouldn't mind one bit helping pay for it."

"Don't be silly, Beth Miller! This is my treat tonight. I told you this was going to be a very special evening for both of us."

"I've told you about my husband, how about telling me about your wife," Beth commented.

"I met Doris during my senior year in college," Randy answered, "she was a very beautiful woman, weighing about one-hundred and fifteen pounds. She had blonde hair and blue eyes. Beth, I swear she reminds me a great deal of you."

"How is that?" Beth asked. "I don't have blonde hair or blue eyes."

"I'm not talking about things like that. I'm referring to her moods, disposition, beauty and her love and affection of children. You and she were quite a bit alike in many regards. Beth, I'm not asking you to be like Doris was. I love you just as you are. I can't help that you have similar qualities as she had. Let's you and I go back to the dance floor before I say too much. This is one night that I don't want to mess things up."

Chapter 15

Danny watched one western movie and part of another one before falling asleep on the living room couch. He was awakened at 9:55 that night by his dog barking. Lucky continued to bark as Danny slipped his shoes on; he hurried out of his house. He was anxious to see why Lucky was making so much noise. Standing fifteen yards from the dog fence, he could clearly see his dog due to the overhead solar light. "What's the matter, Lucky? Did you see a cat or something?" Danny asked. The dog kept jumping against the fence and barking very loud. "Lucky, you quit that barking! You're going to wake up Mr. Spears and the rest of our neighbors! I'll go get you something to eat; that should quiet you down." Danny wasted little time getting back inside his house. He went into the kitchen and opened a can of dog food. He hurried back outside; Lucky kept on barking as Danny empty the dog food into his metal dish. "Doggone it, Lucky; you've got to quit your barking!"

"Is something the matter, Danny?" Mr. Spears asked, him standing on his porch.

"No sir, everything is fine. My dog seems to have a barking problem tonight."

"His barking is no problem to me. I just wanted to make sure you're alright."

"Thank you, sir. You're the best neighbor anyone could have," said Danny. "I'll take Lucky inside the house for a little while. Maybe that will quiet him down." Lucky took off running soon as Danny opened the fence gate. Danny raced after him until they reached the front porch. After the front door was open, Lucky ran to a spare bedroom door and commenced barking. Immediately, Danny knew something was wrong. He hurried down the hall, and then into his mother's bedroom. Danny locked the bedroom door; he commenced searching for his mother's pistol. He finally found the gun in one of her dresser drawers. It was underneath one of his mother's sweaters. Nervously, he sat on the bed with the safety turned off the pistol. Lucky continued to bark and jump against the spare bedroom door.

Danny felt inside his trousers for his cell phone, but then he remembered leaving it on the couch. Five minutes passed; Lucky was still barking and jumping against the door. All of a sudden Danny heard a gun go off. He heard his dog make a couple whimpering sounds, and then everything became quiet. A few seconds later, Danny heard the other bedroom door slam back against the wall. Tears streamed down Danny's cheeks as he held the pistol toward the bedroom door.

"Boy, come out of there!" A voice sounded. "If you don't step out here, I'm going to break the door down!"

Danny was at the point of panic. "Who------who are you?" Danny cried out.

"Open this damn door and you'll find out!"

"I'm not going to open my door! You go away and leave me alone!"

"I didn't leave your daddy alone! What makes you think I'm going to leave you alone? In fact, I'm going to kill you and your damn mother! That wretched bitch shot my ear off and I'm going to fix her good when she gets here**!"**

"Why did you shoot my daddy?"

"Open your door and I'll tell you."

"You can forget about me opening this door, you murdering rascal! If you think I'm going to let you harm me or my mother you're crazier than I think!" Danny wiped away his tears. With the pistol in his hand, he became less afraid as time passed on.

"You rotten little twerp, I just killed your ugly dog! I'll give you five seconds to open your door, and then I'm going to kick it down! Do you hear me----boy?"

"Okay, Mr. Bad Guy-------start kicking my door down!" Danny yelled, him standing eight feet from the door with the pistol raised.

With a mighty kick, Gordon Ray Stallings kicked the door open. Danny fired his mother's gun three times. Gordon fell inside the bedroom. For a couple minutes, Danny just stood there gazing at the man with one ear. All at once, Gordon tried to raise himself up. "You low-down, sneaking rascal," Gordon yelled, "You shot me three times in my stomach! You're as sneaky as your stringy-head mother! If it's the last thing I ever do-----I'm going to kill you!"

"You had better stay on that floor!" Danny insisted. "You're never leaving this house alive! You murdering butcher, you killed my daddy! Why did you do it? Why?" Danny cried.

"I wanted to get even with your mother, you little twerp! She's the reason that I got kicked out of college! She thought she was too good for me! Soon as I pull myself up from here I'm going to wring your little scrawny neck! Why are you still standing there pointing that pistol toward me?"

"I'm going to kill you! That's why I'm holding this pistol toward you. You'll never get another chance to hurt my mother. Shooting my dog was a very bad thing you did! You don't know this, but that dog saved my life a while back." Danny wiped his watery eyes.

"Boy, I want to kill you so bad that it lessons my pain while I'm trying to get up."

"Go ahead, try to stand up!" Danny insisted. "When you do get up I'm going to shoot you some more!"

"Boy, are you crazy or something? Normal people don't shoot someone down like a cur dog!"

"You're right, Mister------right now I'm just like you. You shot my daddy in his back and I'm going to shoot you until you're dead!"

"We'll see who does the shooting-------you good-for-nothing kid!" Gordon yelled. He started crawling toward his pistol that was lying no more than a few feet from him. "Gun or no gun------- I'm going to kill you if it's the last thing I ever do!"

"Stop or I'm going to shoot!" Danny cried out. Gordon stopped crawling; he turned his head toward Danny's pistol. Danny reached for a picture frame sitting on a small table. He walked closer to Gordon; he held the picture frame so that he could get a good look at the photograph inside. "Do you recognize this man?"

"Yes, I see him. That was your ugly father that I shot and killed!"

Still holding his father's photograph in his left hand, Danny cried out, "I'm sorry, Mister, I can't afford for you to come back someday and kill my mother."

"What are you going to do?" Gordon asked.

"What someone should have done a long time ago."

Gordon lunged for his pistol that was between him and Danny. Danny fired three bullets; two into his forehead and one in his throat. Danny's pistol dropped to the floor as he observed Gordon's body lying motionless on the blood-soaked carpet. As if he was in a daze, Danny walked out of the room. He saw Lucky lying dead in the hallway. He dropped to his knees beside his dog. Danny closed his eyes as he rubbed his hand against his dog's head. His tears fell freely on the hallway flooring.

"Oh, my God, Danny what happened here?" Mr. Spears asked, nervously. "I heard some shots and I came running over here."

Danny pointed to his mother's bedroom. With tear-filled eyes, he turned toward Mr. Spears. "The man in my mother's bedroom is the one that killed my daddy. He killed my dog, too! He broke my door down and I shot him! I shot him, Mr. Spears! He killed my daddy and I'm glad he's dead!" Danny cried.

Randy and Beth were on the dance floor at Caesar's Palace when Randy's cell phone vibrated. "That darn phone, I thought I turned it off."

"Answer the phone, Randy, it might be an important call," Beth suggested. They were still standing on the dance floor when he answered the call.

"Hold on a minute; I can't hear you very well where I am." Randy and Beth walked off the dance floor to a quieter area. "Okay, I can hear you now," said Randy. Beth noticed Randy's expression change quickly as he listened on his phone. Finally, Randy placed his phone inside his jacket. He just stood there with a blank look on his face.

"What is the matter?" Beth asked, extremely alarmed.

"That was Sheriff Alan Hicks on the phone. We need to get back to your house as quickly as we can."

"What's wrong, Randy? Is Danny okay? Don't you hide any information concerning my son from me?" Beth cried out.

"Danny is fine, Beth! I promise you he's okay! It's just that------!"

"Just that-----what?" Beth asked, tearfully.

"Okay, I guess I might as well tell you now. You'll find out anyway in a few minutes. Gordon Ray Stallings got inside your house somehow. He shot and killed Danny's dog!"

"Oh, my God! Oh, my God! What about Danny?" Beth screamed out.

"Danny shot and killed Gordon Stallings after he broke your bedroom door down. He had threatened to kill Danny. Your son didn't intend for Gordon to kill him. Danny fired several bullets into Stallings. There's something else, he was missing a good part of his right ear. Beth, do you suppose we'll ever be able to go on a date without something happening?" After sniffing back her tears, she gave him a faint smile.

When Randy and Beth returned home they saw a lot of people behind yellow tape that encircled her yard. Sheriff Deputies and police were checking the grounds for any kind of evidence. Randy and Beth were stopped briefly by a young policeman when they tried to enter Beth's yard. After showing the cop his badge and credentials, they were allowed through. As they entered Beth's house, she saw her son sitting in their hallway holding his dog's head in his lap. She stood there, momentarily, realizing the grief and pain that her son must be feeling. Randy gently placed his hand on Beth's shoulder; they walked slowly toward her grieving son. Beth dropped on her knees beside Danny and his dog. Without uttering a single word, Danny placed his arms around his mother. They embraced each other for a few seconds, and then Beth said, "Danny, please come with me to the living room so we won't be in the way of these deputies.

"Mother, my dog is dead!"

"I know that, son. Please------get up and go with me to the living room. Lucky will be okay right where he is for now."

"Your mother is right, the law will be busy in here for a couple hours or so. Beth, it looks like I'm back on duty."

"I understand, Randy. Danny and I will be in our living room if you or anyone else needs us for anything."

"Danny, I know you're very upset about everything that has happened here tonight," Randy remarked. "However, sooner or later you will need to talk with me or Sheriff Hicks concerning the events that occurred here tonight. Do you think you'll feel like talking about it in a little while?"

"Yes sir, I can talk about it." Beth held Danny's hand as they walked toward their living room.

An ambulance crew removed Gordon Stallings body from Beth's house two hours later. Shortly after that, Sheriff Hicks and Detective Randy Johnson came into Beth's living room.

"Danny, you're a very brave boy to save your life the way you did," said Sheriff Hicks. "I know this will be hard on you, but could you tell us exactly what happened here tonight."

"Please Danny------while it's fresh in your mind!" Detective Johnson remarked.

"Do you feel like talking, Danny?" Beth asked.

"I'll tell you everything." Danny answered, sniffing back his tears. Sheriff Hicks turned on his recorder. "After my mother and Randy left my house, I decided to watch a movie. After that I fell asleep watching another movie. I was awakened by my dog barking. I sat up on the couch a few seconds thinking that Lucky had seen a cat or something. My dog kept on with his barking. Finally, I went outside to see what was wrong. I didn't see a cat or anyone that would cause my dog to bark. He was jumping against my fence like he needed to get out. Anyway, I decided to go back into my house and get Lucky some dog food. The dog food didn't stop him from barking. About this time Mr. Spears came onto his porch and asked me if everything was alright. I said sure, but Lucky kept on with his barking. I figured the best thing to do was to open the gate and take Lucky inside our house for a little while. My dog ran past me and onto our front door. He pawed and jumped against our front door until I opened it. Lucky ran straight to one of our spare bedrooms. Again, he jumped and pawed against the door as if he knew someone was hiding inside."

"What did you do then?" Sheriff Hicks asked.

"I figured right then and there that someone was in that spare room. I ran until I got inside my mother's room. After locking the door, I started looking for my mother's pistol. After finding it, I sat on her bed until I heard a shot ring out. I knew at that moment that my dog was dead."

"How did you know the dog was dead?" Detective Johnson asked.

"Well, as soon as that shot was fired Lucky made a couple whimpering sounds and then he didn't bark anymore."

"Go ahead, Danny," said Detective Johnson, "I'll try not to ask another stupid question."

"I heard the spare bedroom door swing open real hard after that shot was fired. That man tried to get me to open my door, but I said absolutely not. He kept saying threatening things to me."

"What kind of threats, Danny?" Sheriff Hicks asked.

"Well, he said he was going to kill me. That man said he was the one that shot my daddy. He said some bad things concerning my mother. He said he was going to fix her good for shooting off his ear. He called her an ugly name that I can't repeat. The last thing he said to me was, 'I'm going to kill you soon as I kick this door down'. I knew he was serious; I stood up directly in front of the door, and when the door flung open I pulled the trigger on mother's gun. I shot him three times. The man fell directly in front of me. I backed back a couple of steps because the man was still alive. He was still cursing and threatening to kill me. I told him not to pick up his pistol, but he reached for it anyway. That's when I shot him three more times. Mother, I guess my dog saved my life twice before he was finally killed-----one time in the woods and another time in my own house. Lucky let me know that someone was in my house." Danny burst into tears. Beth placed her arms around her son.

Sheriff Hicks stood up. He turned off his recording machine. He extended his hand to Danny. "Son, you've accomplished what my whole department has been unable to do. You single-handedly took down a vicious, murdering scoundrel that deserved to die. I've been told how much you loved your dog, Lucky. My department will not even attempt to replace Lucky because Lucky cannot be replaced. However, with your mother's permission and with your permission I promise you that I will look far and wide until I find another dog that will look a great deal like Lucky."

"That's very kind of you, Sheriff Hicks," Beth responded. "Danny, is that okay with you?"

"I appreciate the offer, but I don't want another dog," said Danny, tearfully. "No other dog in the world could ever replace Lucky."

"Beth, there's no way you can sleep in this house until some things are taken care of," said Randy. "You may not want to do this, but I've got two extra bedrooms in my house. Both of the bedrooms have private bathrooms. You and Danny are welcome to stay there for as long as necessary. It might take a cleaning crew and a repairman a day or so to get your house back in order."

"I really do appreciate your offer, but I don't want to leave my home. Danny can sleep in his own bed and I can sleep in one of our spare bedrooms. Tomorrow, I'll buy some new carpet for my bedroom. I'll hire someone to replace my door."

"That won't be necessary," Randy commented. "I'm off tomorrow; I'll be glad to install a new door to your bedroom."

"Mr. Johnson, will you take Lucky outside and lay him next to his dog pen?" Danny asked, tearfully.

"I certainly will, Danny. Sometime tomorrow morning, you and I will give Lucky a proper burial."

"Mother, it makes me sad that I named my dog Lucky."

"Why Danny, why would you say something like that?" Beth asked.

"Because Lucky was about the most unlucky dog I've ever heard about."

"Danny, you can look at it another way," Randy commented. "There's no doubt about it, your dog was instrumental in saving your life on two different occasions. I believe he was very lucky to be able to do that."

Mr. Harry Spears walked into the living room. "Mrs. Miller, one of the officers outside was nice enough to let me come inside for a couple of minutes. Is there anything I can do to help you or Danny?"

Danny got up; he placed his arms around Mr. Spears' waist. Tears emerged from Mr. Spears eyes. "Danny, I'm so thankful that you and your mother are alright." Mr. Spears turned toward Beth and said, "I'm not trying to be presumptuous, but you and Danny are welcome to come to my house until things get settled here."

"Mr. Spears, we sincerely appreciate the offer, but we're going to stay here. I appreciate your kindness."

"Well, I'll go now. I promised the officer that I wouldn't stay but a minute or two."

"Bye, Mr. Spears," said Danny.

"That is one good-hearted man," Beth commented.

"I'm going to take Lucky outside. After that I need to get back with Sheriff Hicks and the other crew. Beth, is there anything else that I can do for you or Danny?" Randy asked.

"I don't think so. I'm going into the kitchen and make myself a pot of coffee. I don't believe Danny or I will be doing any sleeping before daylight."

At four o'clock that morning, Beth and Danny were sitting on the living room couch. Everyone was gone except for them. Beth was drinking on her second cup of coffee. "Danny, are you okay?" Beth asked. "You haven't said a word in the last fifteen minutes."

"Why would I be okay, Mother? My daddy is dead, my dog is dead, I'm now a murderer, and my girlfriend has got a new boyfriend."

"You're wrong, Danny, you're no murderer! You did what you had to in order to stay alive! Another thing, Shelia doesn't have a new boyfriend."

"Mother, I've got eyes! I've seen how she is when she's around Tommy Lewis!"

"Randy told me that Tommy is not Shelia's boyfriend. She's trying to be nice to him because she is a good friend of his family."

"You mean that------he's not----"

"No, Danny, he's not Shelia's boyfriend. That girl still likes you as much as she ever did."

A brief smile appeared on Danny's face. He mumbled, "Well, I'll be doggone!"

Chapter 16

Randy Johnson was back at Beth's house at nine o'clock that morning. Beth and Danny were in their living room when Randy knocked on the front door. Beth unlocked her door. "I hope I didn't come too early this morning to replace your bedroom door," said Randy.

"You're not too early at all, but I haven't bought my new door yet."

"I took the liberty of buying you one from Starnes Building and Supply Store. It's in the back of my truck. It's exactly like the one you had in your bedroom. If you don't like it, I can take it back to the store."

"That was very thoughtful of you, Randy; I'll pay you for the door. How much was it?"

"Please-------Beth, let me do something for you without you thinking you have to pay me!"

"I appreciate what you did, Randy. That was very thoughtful of you. I'll get Danny to help you bring the door inside."

Randy was standing beside his truck when Danny walked outside. "Good morning, Mr. Johnson."

"Good morning, Danny. Let's you and I carry this door inside your house. How would you like to help me put the door up? I've got all the tools we'll need on the front seat of my truck."

"I'll do all I can to help you."

"Well, that's all anyone can do," Randy remarked.

Randy and Danny had removed the old door and re-hung the new door by 10:45 that morning. Beth came by to see their handiwork as they inserted the last screw in a door hinge. "How do you like our work?" Randy asked, him smiling.

"You and Danny did a fantastic job. At least I can close the door now so I won't have to look at that blood-soaked carpet! Randy, would you care for a cup of coffee?"

"Yes, I believe I would. After drinking my coffee, I'm going to help Danny bury his dog. I need to be home before noon because I promised Shelia that I would take her to Abernathy's for lunch. Beth, have you ever eaten at Abernathy's restaurant?"

"No, but I've heard that it's a good place to eat."

"Would you and Danny care to join us?"

"I appreciate the invite, but Danny's grandparents will be here around noon. Mother called me the first thing this morning to let me know they were coming."

After Randy had finished drinking his coffee, he and Danny went outside to the dog pen. Randy noticed tears in Danny's eyes as he looked down at his dog lying motionless on the ground. "Danny, I tell you what-----if you'll get me a shovel out of your shed, I'll dig the hole. All you'll have to do is pick the spot where you want your dog buried."

A few minutes later, Randy gently placed Lucky into the hole he had dug. Danny turned his head away as Randy commenced shoveling dirt into the grave. Immense grief permeated throughout Danny's body, him keenly aware that Lucky had saved his life on two different occasions. No longer could he hold his emotions, he dropped to his knees and commenced crying. For the first time in his life, Randy Johnson was lost for words.

Randy helped Danny up after he finished crying. Danny wiped away his tears; he found a brick and placed it next to his dog's grave. He planned to get a more suitable marker soon as he could.

George and Dora Miller drove into Beth's yard at noon. Dora exited the car, and then she hurried into Beth's house. George Eason got out of his car, but he didn't go inside the house right away. In deep thought, he commenced walking in Beth's yard. That's when he saw Danny standing near his dog pen. With immense sadness, he walked up to Danny and said, "Son, I see you've buried your dog over by that brick."

"Yes sir. Mr. Randy Johnson is the one that actually buried Lucky. All I did was watch.

"Grandpa, Gordon Stallings was the same man that killed my daddy! He wanted to kill me, and my mother! Grandpa, I shot him with my mother's gun!"

"I know you did, Danny. It's been on the news all morning." George placed his arms around his grandson. "I'm so thankful that you were able defend yourself. How is your mother doing? I know she had to be very upset when she found out that you had shot and killed someone in your house."

"Mother is doing okay. She's just thankful that I didn't get hurt or even worse. Grandpa, I wish I had never named my dog Lucky."

"I guess I can understand that, Danny. However, I think that name was appropriate since you happened to come along and free him from that steel trap. He certainly would have died had you not rescued him. That means your dog was very lucky to have a friend like you. Son, I want to ask you something? How do you feel about shooting the man that killed your father?"

"I don't understand what you mean, Grandpa."

"Well, let me put it another way. Psychologically speaking, does the shooting dwell on your mind most of the time? The reason I'm asking is because you're so young; one day you might need some sort of counseling concerning the matter."

"Grandpa, I don't need any counseling; I'm glad I shot that man! He killed my daddy; he shot my dog, and he wanted to kill me and my mother! I wish I could kill him again!"

"Son, I hate to hear you say that you would like to kill him again! That doesn't sound like the Danny Miller that I know. It was well enough for you to kill him when you thought your life was in jeopardy. If I had been in your shoes-----I would have done exactly the same thing. I realize that you're still upset about the whole thing, but I surely wouldn't be saying that I would love to kill him again. From what I've heard, you emptied your gun toward him when he broke open your mother's door. That being true, you're not to be blamed for taking his life. It wasn't like you wounded him or something like that. I tell you what, let's you and I go to your house and see what your mother and grandmother are doing."

As they started walking back towards the house, Danny spoke, "Grandpa, am I a killer?"

"Danny, why would you even ask a question like that?" George asked. "Heavens no, you're not a killer! I can't believe you would ask a question like that!"

"The reason I asked the question is because I don't feel sorry for what I did. I promised my daddy after he was dead that I would kill the man that shot him in his back. I was hoping to do just that! I didn't know that I would ever get the chance to do it."

"Danny, stop right there, I want you to listen to me, and listen well! Don't ever repeat to anyone what you just said to me!"

"Why do you say that, Grandpa?"

"Talking like that can get you into a lot of legal problems with the law. Just don't ever say things like that again!"

Dora and Beth were in the living room when George and Danny came inside. "George, did you tell Danny what you caught out of your pond yesterday?" Dora asked.

"What did you catch, Grandpa?"

"Son, I caught an eight pound, four-ounce bass using a yellow Jitterbug. That's only half my story. Later, when I walked down to the far end of my pond, I saw a bass near the top of the water that was even bigger than the one I caught. Danny boy, I decided not to even try to catch him. I said right then and there, I'll save that big boy for my grandson to catch."

"Grandpa, what did you do with the fish you caught?".

"Well, we ate part of him yesterday in a fish stew. The rest of that fish is in our refrigerator."

"Danny, I'm very glad that horrible man didn't hurt you!" Dora remarked. "I nearly had a heart attack when I heard what happened on the morning news. Right away your granddaddy told me to get ready to go see Beth and Danny."

"Grandpa, is my 4-wheeler okay?"

"Of course it is, I've got it under one of my barn shelters. I was in such a rush to get over here today that I didn't even think about bringing it with me."

"I rather you leave my ride at your house. There's hardly anywhere here to ride it. You've got big fields and a large wood's that I can ride in."

"Are you sure you want to go back into my woods?' George asked, smiling.

"Yes sir, I'm sure; this time I won't go looking for anything that sounds like it's in some kind of trouble."

The following day, Sheriff Alan Hicks and Detective Randy Johnson were on their way to see Dr. Rodney McGuire, the County Coroner. "Sheriff, did Dr. McGuire say why he needed for us to come to his office?" Randy asked.

"He said that something didn't add up concerning how Gordon Ray Stallings was killed."

"What is there to understand?" Randy asked. "Gordon Stallings broke down his mother's door where Danny was hiding; fearful for his life, Danny fired his gun to stop him."

Fifteen minutes later, Sheriff Hicks and Detective Johnson walked into the coroner's office. Lorraine Day, receptionist, told them that Dr. McGuire was in his laboratory, second room down the hall. Dr. McGuire was sitting at his desk when they walked inside the laboratory. "We came as soon as we could." Sheriff Hicks spoke. "You seemed a bit disturbed when you and I were talking on the phone earlier today."

"I want you both to come with me into the next room," Dr. McGuire said. They followed the doctor into the refrigeration room. Actually, the room is not refrigerated, but it contains refrigerated compartments where dead bodies are kept until final disposition. Dr. McGuire pulled out one of the compartments that contained Gordon Stallings body. The doctor pulled back the thin sheet that covered the body. "I want you both to look at the six bullet wounds on this man's body."

"Well, there are three entry wounds in his stomach in close proximity of each other," Detective Johnson commented. "There are two bullet wounds in his head, and one in his neck. "Danny said that he shot Stallings when he broke down the bedroom door."

"All that sound plausible until you look at Stallings x-ray," said Dr. McGuire. "Come over here and take a good look at the x-ray hanging on the lighted wall. The stomach wounds would not have killed Gordon Stallings right away. Yes, I'm sure he would have died in an hour or so, but those wounds are not what killed him. Particularly notice that the stomach wounds are horizontal wounds. Each of those bullets went straight into his body."

"Dr. McGuire, what are you getting at?" Sheriff Hicks asked.

"I'm glad you asked. Now look at the other x-ray of his head and neck wounds. What do you see?"

"Each of those wounds seems to go in a downward angle," Sheriff Hicks remarked.

"Exactly!" Dr. McGuire responded. "I've been doing this kind of work for twenty-nine years. I've seen about every kind of murder victim that you can imagine. I'm troubled by my prognosis of this case. There is something wrong with the boy's account of what actually happened. You're not going to like what my theory is concerning this killing."

"Well, Dr. McGuire, what is your theory?" Sheriff Hicks asked.

"I believe that Gordon Stallings did break open Mrs. Miller's door. In fact, I believe that her son did shoot him when he appeared in the doorway. In all probability, he shot at the biggest part of his body which would have been his chest or stomach area. I believe Stallings fell to the floor mortally wounded, but not dead. Initially, I believe that the Miller boy only fired the pistol three times. Now I want each of you to take a good look at the head and neck wounds on Mr. Stallings. The head wounds are within two inches of each other. Believe it or not, there was gun powder residue on Stallings's face and neck. That means whoever fired those three bullets had to be closer than when he was shot in his stomach area. The reason I can say that is because there was no gun powder residue on his shirt."

"For goodness sakes, Dr. McGuire, what are you trying to tell us?" Randy asked.

"It's my theory that Gordon Stallings was still alive after being shot in his stomach. For whatever reason, the boy or someone else walked a little closer before firing three more shots into his head and neck. Most likely-----it was the boy doing the shooting because the bullets were fired from the same gun."

"Dr. McGuire, I appreciate you giving us your prognosis of the case," said Sheriff Hicks. "We'll check everything out right away. Come on, Randy-----we'll go back to the office."

When they got into Sheriff Hicks car, Randy looked toward the sheriff. "No matter what happened, Sheriff Hicks, Gordon Ray Stallings went inside Beth Miller's house to kill her and her son," Randy voiced. "He killed Danny's dog, and then he tried to kill him!"

"I understand what you're saying, Randy but this does shed a different light on the subject. If Gordon Stallings was lying on the floor mortally wounded, why would Danny want to shoot him three more times?"

"Sheriff, I'll look into the case," Randy commented. "I'll find out if Danny was telling the truth."

"I'm afraid you can't do that. You're too involved with Mrs. Miller and her son. I'll have to assign Detective Marcus Hendrix to the case."

"Sheriff, please don't do that! You know how Marcus works! He takes great pleasure in finding people guilty each and every time he gets a chance!"

"Randy, that's his job," said Sheriff Hicks. "I'm not at all sure that he takes pleasure in finding someone guilty. For now, you'll have to stay away from Beth Miller and her son."

"What on earth are you saying? I'm about to ask Beth Miller to marry me! How am I going to stay away from her?"

"I just don't want you to be around either one of them while we're determining whether Danny Miller committed murder or not!"

"Sheriff, we've been friends for a very long time, but I will not give up seeing the only woman I've loved since my wife died. She means more to me than my job does!"

"If that's the case-------you'll have to turn in your badge when we get to my office. I'll place you on administrative leave until this investigation is over. Randy, I'm sorry to do this, but the law is the law! There is absolutely no way that you could do this investigation in an unbiased way. I know it and you darn well know it!"

"Sheriff Hicks, you know damn well that Danny Miller shot Gordon Stallings to save his own life!"

"Comments like that are why you won't be investigating this case, Randy. I can only go by what the coroner told us. I hope to God that you're right about Danny! I just need to know if that boy shot Gordon three more times while he was mortally wounded. If he did, that would bring on a whole different set of circumstances. When we get to my office, I want you to leave your badge and gun with me. Randy, you're a very good detective; I don't want to lose you. You'll get your badge and gun back after Marcus finishes his investigation. Did you understand what I just said, Randy?"

"Yes--------I understand, but Danny Miller better not be labeled as a murderer during this pending investigation. If he does-----you can forget about me coming back to the sheriff's office! Gordon Ray Stallings killed his father and his dog! He went to Beth Miller's house to kill her and Danny! Gordon Ray Stallings, that son-of-a-bitch needed killing-----no matter how Danny managed to do it!"

When they got back to the court house, Randy placed his gun and badge on Sheriff Hick's desk. He stood there a few seconds as he gazed at his sheriff's badge. "Go home, Randy. I don't want to fire you today," said Sheriff Hicks. "I understand how you feel about Beth Miller and her son. You're getting all upset for nothing. We don't know why that boy shot Gordon Ray Stallings three more times while he was, presumably, on the floor. I'm sure there's a perfectly good explanation as to why he did that." Without saying another word, Randy left the sheriff's office.

Beth got home from work at 5:20 that evening. She had barely gotten to her front door when Randy pulled into her driveway. Beth waited on her porch as Randy walked hurriedly toward her. "Randy, is something wrong? You've got a very worried look on your face."

"Beth, I need to go inside; I need to talk with Danny before another detective comes here to do the same."

"What's wrong?" Beth asked, very concerned.

"I'll tell you inside," Randy remarked. "Please------let's go inside before it's too late!" They went inside Beth's house, and then onto her living room. Danny was sitting on the couch.

"Hello, Mr. Johnson."

"Hello, Danny."

"Randy, before it's too late for what?" Beth asked, curiously.

"Please have a seat and I'll tell you all about it. Danny, will you do me a great big favor and go outside for a few minutes? I've got some very important things to discuss with your mother."

"Sure, I will, Mr. Johnson. Mother, today is the day!" Danny remarked, him smiling.

After Danny had left the room, Randy held his head downward for a few seconds. Beth placed her hand on his. She asked, "What's wrong? I've never seen you so upset!"

"The sheriff and that damn coroner made me so mad that I've probably lost my job.

Detective Marcus Hendrix will be here at any time to question Danny about Gordon Ray Stallings killing."

"Danny shot that murdering scoundrel in self-defense!"

"I know that, Beth. However, the coroner sees it another way. He thinks that Danny shot Stallings three times when he broke down the door. I've seen the x-rays myself and the bullet wounds. It does appear that he was shot three more times when he was on the floor. I've been taken off the case. I'm not even supposed to be here! I wanted to talk with Danny before Detective Hendrix interrogates him.

Beth, I love you and Danny more than I can even explain! I can't be here whenever Marcus talks with Danny. I don't want that glory-seeking fool to upset the only boy that I've ever wanted to be my son!"

"What do you want me to do?" Beth asked, nervously.

"Have Danny come back in here and tell us what happened when Stallings broke down your door."

Beth walked hurriedly to her front door; she opened it and saw Danny standing underneath his basketball goal with a ball in his hands. She told him to lay down his ball, and then come inside the house. Thinking he was about to hear some exciting news, Danny rushed toward the house.

"Mother, is the news what I think it is?" Danny asked, him smiling.

"Come inside, Randy wants to ask you some questions," Beth answered.

Once inside, Danny sat down on the couch in front of Randy and Beth. "You wanted to ask me some questions?"

"Yes, I do. First of all-----it's vitally important that you tell me exactly what happened the night that Gordon Ray Stallings was killed. From what I understand, you determined that someone was hiding in one of your mother's spare bedrooms. The reason you came to that conclusion was because Lucky was barking and jumping against that bedroom door. You immediately ran into your mother's bedroom and locked the door behind you. Next, you searched until you found your mother's pistol. Am I right so far?"

"Yes sir, that's precisely what happened," Danny answered. "Mr. Johnson, why do you need to know all these things?"

"I'll get to that in a few minutes. Why didn't you use your cell phone and call for help?"

"After reaching for my cell phone in my trousers, I realized that I had left it on our couch."

"Tell me what happened from here on."

"I heard a gun go off inside our hallway."

"What then?" Randy asked.

"Lucky made a couple whimpering sounds and that was it, except for someone messing with my doorknob. It was then that I heard a man's voice yell out, 'Boy come out of there! If you don't come out I'm going to break the door down!' I was so scared that my hands were trembling and my legs felt weak. I was afraid for my life so I held that pistol straight toward the doorway."

"You're doing very well, Danny," Randy commented. "Keep going, tell me everything."

"I remember asking him who he was. He used a curse word when he told me that he was not going to leave me alone. He said he was the one that killed my daddy and that he was going to kill me and my mother. It seems that he was very angry toward my mother for her causing him to get booted out of college. The next thing I knew----he busted the door open. I fired Mother's gun toward him three times."

"Danny, how do you know that you fired three times or several times?" Randy asked.

"That man yelled out that I shot him three times in his stomach."

"Was Gordon Ray Stallings still alive after you shot him?"

"Yes, he was still alive! He was cursing and threatening to shoot me when he got up. Am I in big trouble for shooting Gordon Ray Stallings?" Danny asked, nervously.

"It all depends on what happened after you shot him three times."

"Mr. Johnson, he fell to the floor after I shot him the first time." All that time he was getting closer and closer to his pistol that was laying on the floor in front of me.

"Oh, my goodness!" Beth mumbled. Tears started sliding down her face.

"Is that when you shot him three more times?" Randy asked.

"I didn't shoot him then. He said when he got up he was going to wring my scrawny little neck. He told me that I was as sneaky as my stringy-head mother. That's when he tried to get up. I told him not to get up or I would shoot him again." I told him that he shot my daddy and that I was going to shoot him some more, if he got up." In tears, Beth got up and walked toward the kitchen.

"Is that when you finally killed him?" Randy asked.

"No sir. I didn't actually shoot him until he reached for his pistol that was lying about a foot from his hand."

Randy grabbed Danny around his neck! He gave him a loving hug! "Beth! Beth, come in here!" Randy cried out. "Danny didn't commit murder! He shot Gordon Stallings in self-defense!"

"Danny is not in any trouble?" Beth asked, tearfully.

"Absolutely not! I'm proud of you, boy!" Randy stated. He hugged Danny's neck again. "There's just one thing that Danny needs to tell Detective Marcus Hendrix. After Stallings fell to the floor, he reached for his pistol. At that point----Danny emptied his gun toward him. Danny, don't for one second mention anything that you were planning to kill Stallings before he left that room. Please-----don't do that! I'm so happy that I don't know what to do!" Randy broke down in tears.

Beth placed her arms around Randy's neck. "I'm very thankful that you came here before that other detective had an opportunity to question Danny."

"Mr. Johnson, now you see why we need you as part of our family," Danny commented. He hugged Randy's neck. He whispered in Randy's ear, "Ask her now before it's too late."

All at once, Randy dropped to his knees in front of Beth; he held each of her hands. His eyes were watery as he looked toward her. "Beth, I love you very, very much. I'm asking you to marry me. I very much want to be your husband. Please say you will marry me."

"Mother, what are you waiting for?" Danny asked. "You know darn well that you love Mr. Johnson!"

"Yes, Randy, I'll marry you," Beth responded, excitedly. Danny was all smiles while observing his mother and Randy kissing each other.

Chapter 17

The following evening was a very special occasion for Randy, Shelia, Beth and Danny. They were all at Chico's Italian Restaurant celebrating Randy's and Beth's upcoming wedding in thirty-two days. Danny and Shelia were very excited about their parents marrying each other.

"Danny, I've always wanted myself a son like you," said Randy. "I guess now my hopes and dreams will come true."

"Mr. Johnson, after you and my mother are married, where will we live?"

"Your mother and I will have to work that out, Danny. Whatever she recommends will be okay with me. We might even sell both our houses and then move into a larger one. It's all up to Beth as to what she would want us to do."

"That's not true, Danny," Beth remarked. "Randy and I will always work together on major decisions."

"Danny, has Detective Marcus Hendrix been by your house yet?"

"He's supposed to be at my house tomorrow morning at 10:00."

"Don't forget what I told you when he starts asking you questions."

"I won't forget. Mr. Johnson, since yesterday I've been worrying about something."

"Well Danny, what seems to be worrying you?"

"After you and Mother are married, can Shelia still be my girlfriend?"

"Well, I don't see why not. However, you may eventually just want her as your sister. The bond between a brother and sister is probably tighter than a boyfriend/girlfriend relationship."

"That may be true," Danny responded, "but for now I rather that she be my girlfriend. Shelia, do you agree with me on that?"

"Yes, I certainly do!"

"Randy, what in thunder are we going to do about these two love birds?" Beth asked.

"I'm confident that everything will work out okay between them."

"Mr. Johnson, Mother knows already that I have terrible nightmares quite often. I had a very bad nightmare last night. I told her about it early this morning."

"What was your nightmare about?" Randy asked.

"In my dream I was alone at Cedar Oaks Cemetery. The sun was about to set. All of a sudden I noticed the dirt and grass moving in front of Daddy's grave. There came a rumbling sound from beneath the grave. I was so scared that I couldn't move! Dirt and grass kept moving upward as though something was trying to come out of the ground. I tried to run, but my feet wouldn't move! It was then that it happened!"

"Danny, what happened?" Shelia asked, inquisitively. She shuddered at the very thought of what he was about to say.

"Two decayed looking hands stuck up from the soil. The fingers were moving back and forth. For several seconds I thought it was my daddy coming up from the ground. I felt like I was about to have a heart attack when a body rose up from the ground. That thing-------half submerged into the ground looked toward me with fiery red eyes! Mr. Johnson, it was Gordon Ray Stallings! He said that whenever I least expected it, he was coming to my house and kill me and my mother!"

"Oh, my God-----Danny, why didn't you wake up?" Shelia asked, her hands trembling.

"I did wake up after that thing opened its mouth and spewed some green sticky stuff all over me. I tried as hard as I could to get that sticky stuff off me but I couldn't. I let out a scream and that's when I awoke on the floor."

"When I heard Danny screaming, I rushed into his bedroom," said Beth. "He had just awaken and was trying desperately to untangle himself from his bed covering."

"That was a terrible dream!" Shelia voiced. "Daddy, can't you do something for Danny so he won't have those kind of dreams?"

"I don't know what I can do, Sweetheart, but we'll surely try to do something for Danny to eliminate his nightmarish dreams. Danny, I never see your 4-wheeler when I go to your house."

"I keep it at my grandfather's farm. He's got plenty of land for me to ride it on. In fact, I'll be at the farm this weekend. Grandpa has got me a five-gallon can of gas waiting for me under his barn shelter."

"Is riding your 4-wheeler a lot of fun, Danny?" Shelia asked.

"It sure is! How would you like to ride with me at Grandpa's farm?"

"I would love to do that! I've never visited a real farm. Daddy, would it be okay for me to go to Mr. Eason's farm?"

"Shelia, I don't know about that."

"Oh, fizzle sticks," Shelia mumbled, visibly disappointed.

"Randy, I'm taking Danny to Daddy's farm Saturday morning. I'll pick him up Sunday evening. Mrs. Dora Miller would be extremely thrilled to have Shelia visit her over the weekend. She's got several bedrooms in her house. Two of her guest bedrooms have their own bathrooms, including shower and tub. After all, Shelia and Danny will soon be living under the same roof. I wish you would consider letting her go with us Saturday morning."

"Shelia, you can go, but I want you to be extremely careful while riding on that 4-wheeler. Danny, I'm holding you responsible for ensuring Shelia's safety while she's at the farm."

"Mr. Johnson, I promise I will look after her!"

Sheriff Alan Hicks phoned Randy Johnson the next day at two o'clock. The sheriff asked him to come to his office. Randy entered his office thirty minutes later. "You wanted to see me, Sheriff Hicks?"

Without saying a word, Sheriff Hicks handed Randy his badge and gun. "We've cleared up that matter concerning Danny Miller. It appears that the boy shot and killed Gordon Ray Stallings in self defense. It all happened like the coroner stipulated. Stallings burst through the door; Danny shot him three times. Stallings fell to the floor, but he was still alive. At some point, he tried to pick up his pistol. At close range, Danny fired three more rounds into him. The boy had no other choice, but to kill him. Randy, I'm very glad that it turned out the way it did." He extended his hand to Randy. "I'm glad to have you back with us."

"Sheriff, I'm sorry for getting upset like I did."

"I understood your feelings toward Beth Miller and her son. How are things going between you and her?"

"They're going great! I've asked her to marry me. She has agreed to do just that! I'm one of the happiest people in the world!"

"I'm glad for you and her, as well as the two kids involved. Randy, we've got another murder on our hands. This time it involved two elderly people that lived at 342 Melton Wood Road. Someone robbed and killed them two nights ago. Detective Marcus Hendrix is already working on the case. I've told him, you being more experienced than he, that you will head up the investigation, but you two will be working together. I want you to get with him so he can fill you in on all the details. Do you have any questions?"

"No sir. I'm just happy to be back working."

"Randy, there is just one tiny thing that I need to ask you."

"What is that, Sheriff?"

"Am I being invited to the wedding?"

"Yes, you certainly are------provided that is."

"Provided what?" Sheriff Hicks asked.

"Provided you bring along your fine looking wife," Randy remarked, him smiling.

Randy and Shelia were invited to have dinner with Beth and Danny the following evening. Beth had stopped at her favorite Chinese restaurant on her way home. She bought an assortment of food for their dinner. The only thing she had to prepare was some sweetened tea. "Okay, everyone, let's sit down and enjoy this delicious Chinese food," said Beth.

"Mrs. Miller, I've already told my friends that my daddy is marrying the prettiest woman in our county."

"That was very sweet of you, Shelia. Now you can go back and tell your friends that I'm marrying the sweetest, most-handsome man in our county." Beth smiled.

"Gee Daddy; did you hear what Mrs. Miller just said?"

"I sure did, Sweetheart. My future wife says the nicest things about everyone."

"Randy, have you talked with Sheriff Alan Hicks concerning your job?" Beth asked.

"Yes, I talked with him yesterday. He took me off administrative leave yesterday. I'm working with Detective Marcus Hendrix on another murder case."

"Mr. Johnson, where did this happen?" Danny asked.

"The murder occurred at 342 Melton Wood Road. The murdered man and woman were Johnny Rodgers and Mildred Rodgers. Mr. Rodgers was eight-seven; Mrs. Rodgers was eight-two years old."

"How were they killed?"

"Danny, we're eating dinner!" Beth sounded. "You can ask Randy anything you wish when we retire to our living room."

"Mrs. Miller, my father has a surprise for you."

"Shelia, why did you want to say a thing like that?" Randy asked. "Beth, you'll have to overlook my daughter at times."

"Why is that?" Beth asked.

"It appears that she can't keep a secret for very long," Randy answered, blushing.

After dinner, Beth, Danny, Randy and Shelia went into the living room. "That was very delicious food we had for dinner. I was very hungry when I came here, but not any longer," Randy remarked.

"Mr. Johnson, how were the elderly couple killed?" Danny asked.

"They were lying in their bed when someone fired two bullets into each of their heads. A .38 caliber pistol was used to commit the murders."

"Do you suppose you'll ever determine who the killer was?" Beth asked.

"I'm fairly certain that we will," Randy replied. "Whoever committed the murders had to be someone who was kin to them or at least knew them."

"How do you know that?" Beth asked.

"First of all, the house wasn't broken into. Secondly, their neighbors said that Mr. and Mrs. Rodgers always kept their front and back door locked. That indicates to me that someone had a key to their house."

"Shelia, I've got some new games on my computer. Would you like to see them?" Danny asked.

"Yes, I certainly would." They both walked to Danny's bedroom where his computer was located.

Beth and Randy were still in the living room. "Randy, you've got a silly grin on your face," Beth sounded. "What in the world are you up to?"

"I want you to go out with me somewhere tomorrow evening. It will be Friday, so it shouldn't interfere with your work. This time I hope we won't get interrupted."

"Where do you want us to go?"

"We could go to the Sagebrush Inn on Delmar Street? I've been there once and it seemed to be a very nice place to eat and talk. However, they do serve liquor and beer there. I know you don't drink, nor do I. I like the fact that they have private tables in that restaurant."

"What time should I be ready to leave home?" Beth asked.

"I'll pick you up at seven o'clock. We won't be out too late because you've got to leave early Saturday morning for your trip to your parents' house. Shelia is already packed for the weekend. I hope she and Danny have a great time at his grandfather's farm. I'm a little nervous about her being away from home for the weekend, but I'm confident that Danny will look after her."

"Yes, he will certainly do that!" Beth answered.

"What time should I bring her to your house Saturday morning?"

"You don't have to bring her at all," Beth remarked. "I'll be going in that general direction anyway. Tell Shelia to be ready by 9:15 Saturday morning."

Randy, placed his hand gently against Beth's face. "I feel like I'm the luckiest man in the whole world."

"Why do you feel like that?"

"Since my wife died, you're everything I've ever wanted in a woman. I don't think I could ever live with myself if something caused you to not love me." He placed his face against Beth's. I know I've told you several times already, but I'm going to tell you again. I love you more than I could ever say." Randy kissed Beth on her lips. "Each time I kiss you-----it gets better and better."

"Randy, there's something that I've been wondering about."

"What could that be?" He asked, seriously.

"I'm madly in love with you, but I don't know a great deal about you."

"Beth, what is there to know about me?"

"Well, where were you raised? How many of your relatives will be attending our wedding."

"I'll answer all those questions for you. I was raised in Knoxville, Tennessee. My wife and I attended Brentwood Business College. Well, she wasn't my wife while we were in school, but we married shortly after graduation. She was from here, so we decided to buy a house here. Both my parents are dead. They were killed in a hit and run accident. I had no brothers or sisters. I've only got one aunt, my mother's sister that will be attending our wedding. Her name is Mable Lang. She and her husband never did have any children. Her husband died three years ago. Did I answer all your questions?"

"Did the authorities ever get the hit and run driver?" Beth asked.

"Yes, they finally got the man that killed my parents. "Believe it or not, it was nine days before my marriage when they were killed." Tears came into Randy's eyes.

"I'm very sorry that you lost your parents in such a needless way." In tears, Beth commented.

"Anyway-----in a solemn voice, Randy spoke, "the man that killed my parents was named Elmer Golf. He was fifty-one years old. At the time of the accident, Elmer was drunk, driving an old dump truck without a proper driver's license and his tags were expired."

"Good grief!" What did the law do to that man?" Beth inquired, curiously.

"A tip was called into the Sheriff's office that Elmer Golf was the hit and run driver that killed my parents. Soon afterwards, two squad cars came to an abrupt halt in Elmer's yard. Four deputy sheriffs' walked onto Elmer's porch. One deputy knocked on the door, but there was no answer. The deputy knocked again, and then again. It was obvious someone was in the house because the deputies heard footsteps inside the house. All of a sudden, Elmer opened his front door, him pointing a shotgun at the officers. Not taking any chances, two of the deputies fired their pistols point-blank into Elmer's body. He was killed instantly."

"My goodness! Now, what do you need to know about me?" Beth asked.

"I don't need to know one single thing, except that you love me."

Beth leaned over; she kissed him passionately on his lips. "Does that answer your question?" She asked.

"I believe it does!"

Randy arrived at Beth's house at 6:45 the following evening. Danny answered the doorbell. "Hello, Mr. Johnson, where are you two going tonight?"

"I'm taking your mother to the Sagebrush Inn. This will be a very important night for both of us."

"Please come inside. My mother will be in the living room shortly."

"Danny, what will you do tonight while we're at the Sagebrush Inn?"

"I'll be getting my things together for my trip tomorrow. Is Shelia excited about going to the farm over the weekend?"

"Yes, she seems very excited about being with you on your granddaddy's farm." Randy answered. "Danny, this is her first trip like this! I trust that you will look after her."

"Mr. Johnson, I would protect Shelia with my very own life."

"Well son, no one could ask for more than that. My goodness, Danny-----look at your beautiful mother walking into the living room."

"Well, you look very handsome yourself. Danny, when the washing machine stops I want you to place the clothes in the dryer, and don't forget to turn the dryer on. Randy, I guess I'm ready to go."

"Mother, haven't you forgotten something?"

"I certainly have not! You know I don't go off without giving you my goodbye hug." Beth placed her arms around her son. She whispered, "I love you, Danny."

"I love you, too." Danny turned toward Randy. "Mr. Johnson, how are you doing on your murder case?"

"Which one are you referring to? I'm working on two at the present time."

"I'm talking about the one where two elderly people were shot on their bed."

"We've got a suspect in that case, but no arrests have been made. Well, I guess we had better go. Why don't you give Shelia a call? That way you and she can discuss your plans for tomorrow."

"Thanks, Mr. Johnson, I'll do that right away," Danny answered.

Randy and Beth arrived at the Sagebrush Inn at 7:20 that evening. There were plenty tables available since it was still early in the evening. Randy asked the hostess for a table with some degree of privacy. She led them to a more secluded location in the restaurant.

"This table is across from the bar, but you can have more privacy here," said the hostess. "Your waitress will be here directly."

"Well, what do you think about this place?"

"It's very nice, Randy. What kind of food does the Sagebrush Inn specialize in?"

"They have a wide variety of food on their menu. They've got steaks, lobster, grilled salmon, pork, Italian foods, and a wide array of American foods." Their waitress came and took their beverage orders. Soft background music was playing throughout the restaurant, except for the bar area. Two large screen televisions were tuned to sports channels for the bar patrons. Basketball was on one television and football was on the other one.

"How come you happened to choose this particular restaurant for us?" Beth asked.

"You mean------you don't like it?"

"Of course, I like it. I was just curious as to how you selected this particular restaurant instead of some other one."

"Well, I'll tell you why, since you've asked me. I've only been here one time before now. I saw a man and a woman sitting at a table a little ways from ours. At one point the guy, with tears in his eyes, got down on his knees and begged the woman to marry him. She just sat there with a blank look on her face. Other people in the restaurant started chanting 'Please marry the guy! Please marry the guy!' I had tears in my eyes when she finally got up and placed her arms around his neck. He kissed her two or three times. Finally, as excited as one can be, he yelled out, "I'm getting married! Did everyone hear me? I'm getting married in a few days!" In fact, the waitress wouldn't even let them pay for their meal. She told the couple that their meal was on the house."

Beth's eyes watered up, her hearing the story. "Randy, I really appreciate you bringing me to this restaurant. I could see in your face how much that couple affected you." Randy reached inside his jacket and withdrew a small box. He handed it to Beth.

Her eyes lit up as she held the tiny box in her hand.

"Go ahead----open it up," said Randy.

Beth opened the box. Her mouth opened wide as she gazed at the beautiful engagement ring. "Randy, it's beautiful!"

"Put it on your finger."

She slipped it on her ring finger. "It fits! Randy, it looks so expensive!"

"Not for you-----it isn't! Beth, I've already proposed to you at your house, but I would like to do it again, right here----right now." He reached across the table and placed his hands on hers. "Beth Miller, the very fact that I'm so deeply in love with you, will you please marry me?"

"Yes, I will marry you." Randy got up; he placed his arms around Beth. He kissed her passionately on her lips. "Randy, do you think you'll have any more of those kisses on our wedding night?" She asked, smiling.

"Beth, sweetheart-------that was just a primer kiss. The real kisses will commence on our wedding night. That's one night that I've been looking forward to."

Chapter 18

Beth, Danny and Shelia were on their way to George Eason's and Dora Miller's farm by 9:30 the next morning. Danny and Shelia were in the backseat of Beth's car. "Mrs. Miller, I've never visited a farm before," said Shelia. "Does Mr. Miller have cows, horses, chickens and things like that?"

"He surely does, Shelia. He, also, has ducks, goats, and turkeys."

"Danny, do you suppose we could ride Mr. Miller's horses?"

"Sure, we can. Shelia, you're going to have the time of your life at the farm. There's so much you can do there that you'll never want to leave."

"I'm so excited I can hardly control myself!" Shelia stated.

Detectives Marcus Hendrix and Randy Johnson pulled into Zachary Jones driveway at 9:45 that morning. Zachary and his wife Felicia lived at 343 Melton Wood Road, about three-hundred yards from Mr. and Mrs. Johnny Rodgers house. The Jones's were middle-aged, black people. They had one grown son that worked in a small town about a hundred miles away. Zachary worked as a janitor at Wellington Mills, a shirt manufacturing plant. Mrs. Josephine Knox, a retired school teacher and widower told the sheriff's office that she saw Zachary Jones in Johnny Rodger's backyard the day of the murder. Mrs. Knox lives in a house on the same side of the road as where Johnny Rodger's house is located. According to Mrs. Knox, Zachary seemed to be sneaking around Johnny Rodgers house the day of the murder.

Zachary was standing on his porch when the two detectives exited their car. "Are you Mr. Zachary Jones?" Detective Johnson asked.

"Yes, that's my name."

"Mr. Jones, my name is Detective Randy Johnson and my partner's name is Marcus Hendrix. We're investigating the murders of Johnny and Mildred Rodgers. Did you know Mr. Johnny Rodgers and his wife very well?"

"I knew them very well. My wife and I were very upset when we heard that they had been killed. Mr. Johnny was always good to me and my wife. Mrs. Mildred was very good to us, as well. I hope they get whoever killed them. They never deserved to die the way they did!"

"Mr. Jones, it has come to our attention that you were at their house the day they were murdered," Detective Johnson remarked.

"That's true, but I didn't kill them. They weren't my kin, but I loved those two old people. Mr. Johnny is the one that helped me get my job at the shirt manufacturing plant. Mrs. Mildred is the one that helped my wife, Felicia get her job at Draper's Dry Cleaning Service. No sir, I would never do anything to harm those two nice people."

"Why were you at Mr. Rodgers' house the day of the murder?" Detective Hendrix asked.

"Mr. Johnny told me that I could come to his house and pick some pears off his tree. When I went to his house, I forgot to take my bucket with me. After I got there I happened to see a five-gallon bucket sitting not too far from the tree. I knew Mr. Johnny wouldn't mind my using his bucket, so I picked it up. I was surprised to see a Smith & Wesson .38 caliber pistol underneath the bucket. At that time I didn't know that Mr. Johnny and his wife had already been killed. I picked up the pistol and brought it home. I never did get any pears that day. Felicia told me later that the pistol I found could very well be the murder weapon. She advised me to turn it into the law, but I was afraid to do that. I didn't want to go to jail for something I didn't do."

"Mr. Jones, where is that pistol now?" Detective Johnson asked.

"It's on the top shelf in my closet."

"Do we have your permission to go inside and retrieve that gun?"

"Yes sir, I'll go with you and show you where it is." Detective Johnson went to his car and got some latex gloves. Afterwards, the two detectives followed Zachary inside his house.

"I told you that you should have turned that gun into the law," said Felicia. "I'm going to tell you lawmen something------my husband didn't kill Mr. and Mrs. Rodgers! Zachary wouldn't even kill a fox that was in the edge of our yard!"

"Mrs. Jones, we've never said that your husband killed anyone," Detective Hendrix commented. "We just want the gun that he told us about." Detective Johnson reached on top of the closet shelf and retrieved the gun using the hand with the latex glove.

"Detective Johnson, I swear to you that everything happened the way I said it did!" Zachary remarked. "My fingerprints are on the gun because I picked it up, but I'll swear on a stack of Bibles that I didn't kill my best friends in the whole world! I would never have picked that gun up if I had known that Mr. Rodgers and his wife were lying dead inside their house! Are you taking me to Jail?"

"Yes, we certainly are!"

"Wait just a minute, Marcus; we're not taking Mr. Jones to jail at this time."

"Randy, are you crazy? This man was at their house the very day that those folks were killed. He's even admitted to having the murder weapon!"

"How do you know that it's the murder weapon?" Detective Johnson asked. "Mr. Jones, tell me this------did Johnny Rodgers and his wife have any children?"

"Yes sir, they had one adopted boy. From what I understand they adopted him when he was fifteen years old. By now, Mr. Alex Rodgers should be forty years old or more."

"We're going to take this gun with us, Mr. Jones. I want your word that you won't leave the county you're living in without letting us know," said Detective Johnson. Randy handed him his card.

"Sir, I'm not going anywhere. Those old folks were nice people. I'll never forget how good they were to us."

Detectives Johnson and Hendrix drove out of Zachary Jones' driveway a few minutes later.

"Randy, I believe you're making a mistake not arresting that man for murder."

"Marcus, do you honestly believe that he would turn over a pistol that he found at the Rodgers home if he was guilty of murder? Do you?"

"Well------when you put it like that------I guess he wouldn't."

George and Dora Eason were sitting on their porch swing when Beth drove into their yard. They stood up as Beth and the children got out of her car. "Shelia, you remember my grandpa and my grandma. You're going to like them a lot!" Danny remarked. All three of them hurried toward the porch. "Grandpa, Grandma, look who I brought with me?" Danny sounded, excitedly. "You remember her----she's Mr. Randy Johnson's daughter. Her name is Shelia."

"Of course, we remember that beautiful girl!" Dora remarked. "You're very welcomed to our home, Shelia."

"Grandma, she's never been on a real, honest-to-goodness farm before," Danny remarked, smiling. "She's going to stay here the whole weekend! I'm going to show her all your animals and other things you have here on the farm!"

"Shelia, don't forget to ride on Danny's 4-wheeler while you're here," George remarked. "Beth, Dora told me about your upcoming marriage." George commented. I'm as happy as I can be about you marrying Mr. Johnson. Henry Miller called yesterday to see how I thought about you getting married soon. I told Henry that you should get married again and get on with your life. He agreed with me, wholeheartedly. Shelia, what do you think about your father marrying Beth?"

"Mr. Eason, I'm very happy that Daddy has found someone that he loves and adores. I'm excited that Mrs. Miller will soon be my mother."

"Well child, come here and give your grandma-to-be a big hug," said Dora. Shelia gave Dora a hug, and then she kissed her on her face.

"Dora, that's not fair at all," said George. "Grandfather's need a hug once in awhile." Shelia gave George a loving hug."

"Shelia, we're looking forward to you becoming our grandchild." Dora responded. "For Heaven sakes, I forgot to invite you all into the house! I'll cook breakfast for everyone. Beth, how was your drive here?"

"It was a good drive. For some reason there wasn't a great deal of traffic on the road. Mother, after I eat I'll need to head toward home. I've got a lot of things to do before my wedding."

"I can surely relate to that. What time tomorrow evening will you be back to get Danny and Shelia?"

"I should be here by six o'clock in the evening."

Everyone waved bye as Beth drove out of her parents' driveway. Afterwards, Dora Miller turned toward Shelia and remarked, "We're delighted that you're spending the weekend with us. There's a lot for you to see here, if you've never been to a farm before. We've got horses, chickens, turkeys, cows, goats, pigs, bee hives and a few cats here and there. What would you like to see first?"

"Mrs. Miller, I'm so excited about all this that I can hardly be still," Shelia answered, excitedly. I thought I saw some bunny rabbits in a cage when we drove into your yard."

"You certainly did!" Dora answered. "I forgot about George's rabbits. He only keeps twelve or so at the time. When they get more than that, he gives them away to friends and neighbors."

"Danny, will you take me to the rabbit pen before we start exploring everything else here?"

Danny and Shelia walked to the rabbit pen that was located near a utility barn. "Look Danny, that mother rabbit has some little babies! Oh, my goodness, they're so cute! How in the world did all that rabbit hair get in there for the babies to lie in?"

"The mother rabbit used her teeth to pull off her own fur to make bedding for her young."

"Oh my, wouldn't that hurt?" Shelia asked.

"I guess you would have to ask the rabbit about that." He answered, him smiling.

"Don't be silly! Anyway, what kind of rabbits are these?"

"The rabbits in this cage are Dutch rabbits. They don't get very large."

"What about the rabbits in this other cage?" Shelia asked.

"These are New Zealand rabbits. They get much larger than the Dutch rabbits do. Look how pretty their white fur is."

"Danny, I love it here! I wish we could spend a whole week on the farm. How will I be able to see everything in two days?" Shelia asked.

"Maybe you can come again sometime. Do you want to see the rest of the animals now, or had you rather go sightseeing with me on my 4-wheeler?"

"I want to do it all!" She answered, excitedly.

"I don't believe we can do it all at the same time," Danny remarked. "Let's go for a ride on my 4-wheeler and later today I'll show you the rest of Grandpa's animals."

"Okay, but be sure to let me see all the other animals."

After Danny told his grandparents that they were going for a ride on his 4-wheeler, they took off across an open field. When they neared the woods line, Shelia asked, "Danny, why are all those wooden boxes lined up near that flower garden?"

"Those are Grandpa's bee hives. We won't get too close to them. I got too close one time and I got stung twice before I could get away from those bees."

"Why has he got bee hives?"

"Grandpa takes out the honey at certain times of the year. Do you recall that fruit jar sitting on the kitchen table?"

"You mean that syrupy-looking stuff?" Shelia asked.

"Yes, that was honey. You should have tried some of it" Danny stopped his 4-wheeler at an opening in the woods. "Do you see that woods path leading into the woods?"

"Yes, I see it."

"That's the path I went into the day that I got bitten by a poisonous snake. When I see this path it reminds me how close I came to losing my life. It, also, brings back memories of my dog, Lucky."

"Danny, I'm very glad that you didn't die," Shelia voiced. "I'm sorry that your dog was shot and killed. By the way, are we going into the woods on your 4-wheeler? If we are, just remember this-----I'm not putting my feet on the ground at all. I might not live if I get bitten by a poisonous snake!"

"We won't go into the woods today, but we may do that tomorrow. Have you ever been to a haunted house?" Danny asked.

"No. Why do you ask?"

"How would you like to drive by Mr. George Wellington's haunted house?"

"Who is he, and why is the house haunted?"

"Grandpa took me near there one time. He said that Mr. George Wellington was picking huckleberries in Vine Swamp a very long time ago. While he was in there he got bitten by a rabid animal."

"What animal bit him?" Shelia asked, curiously.

"No one ever found out whether it was a fox, raccoon, or dog. Anyway, after being bitten, Mr. Wellington got lost in the woods for several days. He eventually became raving mad with rabies. No one knows how he got out of the woods, but he finally got back to his house. He picked up a hatchet from his wood shed, and then entered his house."

"Danny, please don't tell me that he used the hatchet on his own flesh and blood!" Shelia remarked.

"I'm sorry, but that's exactly what he did. He killed them all while they were in bed."

"That is awful! What happened to him?"

"He died from the rabies he had. No one has ever lived in that place since the tragedy occurred. People say that house is haunted. We could ride by there just so you could see the house."

"Yes, I would like to see the house, but I'm not going inside that place!" Shelia remarked.

Danny powered up his 4-wheeler; they commenced riding across the field in a direction that would eventually take them to the haunted house. Shelia held her arms around his body as they rode over rough terrain. "Guess what Shirley Smith said about you several days ago," Shelia commented.

"What did she say?"

"She said that she would like to kiss you square on your lips."

"You heard Shirley say that?" Danny asked, as they crossed over into another field.

"No, I sure didn't hear her say that! If I had-----I would have slapped her!"

"Well, how did you hear about what she said?"

"Patricia Wells told me about it."

"Did you ever say anything to Shirley about what she said?"

"Yes, I only said four words to her."

"What were the four words?" Danny asked.

"Only in your dreams."

"Shelia, we've got to ride on a highway for a very short distance. We'll have to pass by Mr. Bynum Long's country grocery store on the way to the haunted house. Would you care for something to drink? I'm getting a bit thirsty."

"I'll have something to drink if you do. Do you suppose he'll have a diet Dr. Pepper in his store?"

"Yes, he certainly will. How are you doing with your helmet?"

"It's a little too big for me, but I'm managing okay," Shelia answered.

"Your father bought both these helmets for my birthday."

"Danny, do you still have the knife I bought for you on your birthday?"

"I've got it right here in my front pocket. Shelia, you can't imagine how thrilled I am that you're with me today. It's going to be a special weekend for me."

"You're very sweet, Danny. Quite often I'm confused concerning you."

"How is that?" He asked.

"We'll be living in the same house after our parents are married. I guess at that point I'll have to make up my mind whether to have you as my boyfriend or my brother."

"That's not fair, Shelia! I like you way too much to just be your brother! At least let me be your boyfriend as long as you can. On second thought, that sounds so stupid for me to say that. How would I ever be able to kiss you on your lips if I ever thought that you might become my sister! Do me a favor and not mention this sister stuff to me for a long while." Danny shuddered at the very thought of kissing a sister on her lips.

"Did you say something, Danny? I thought I heard you whispering about something."

"I didn't say a thing. Okay, that's Mr. Long's grocery store ahead of us. We'll stop there long enough to get something to drink."

Danny parked his 4-wheeler in Mr. Long's parking lot. He and Shelia walked inside the country store. "Danny Miller, it's good to see you again," said Mr. Long. "Who in the world is this pretty young lady with you?"

"Mr. Long, her name is Shelia Johnson. She's one of my best friends in the whole world! We would like to buy two diet Dr. Peppers. One for me and one for Shelia."

Mr. Long handed the drinks to Danny and Shelia. Being thirsty, they commenced drinking their sodas. "Is she any kin to you, Danny?"

"No sir, she's no kin at all at the present time."

"Let me get this straight----she's no kin to you now, but she may very well be kin to you later. Did I get that right?"

"Yes sir. You see------her father is going to marry my mother in a few more days. At that point she could become my sister."

Mr. Long scratched his head. He asked, "What is Shelia to you now, your girlfriend?" Mr. Long asked, smiling.

"You hit the nail on the head, Mr. Long. She's about the prettiest thing I've ever seen."

"You're right about that, Danny Boy! Where are you two headed?"

"I'm going to take her by the haunted house down the road."

"You must be referring to the two story house owned by the late George Wellington."

"Yes sir, that's the one. My grandpa showed it to me not long ago."

"You and your grandpa didn't go inside that old house, did you?" Mr. Long asked.

"No sir, we were on horseback when Grandpa showed me the house."

"Let me give you two a piece of advice-----do not go inside that Wellington house! Joe Nelson, a customer of mine came here several years ago to get a carton of milk. He told me that he was going to stop by that place on his way home. He was never heard of again. His old Chrysler was sitting in the Wellington yard, but until this day-------Joe has never been found."

"Are you afraid of that place," Mr. Long?

"Your question should be-----would you go inside that house? My short answer, Heavens no! Everyone living around here thinks there is evil lurking inside that house. One night I drove by that place on my way to see my brother, Ezra. Unless I'm crazy or something, I thought I saw the figure of someone in a lighted room upstairs. The figure seemed too small for an adult. Perhaps it was the form of a small child. Anyway, you couldn't pay me enough to go into that house!"

"Mr. Long, we're not going into that house; we're just riding by there to see it."

"Elmer Smith lives on this very road, about a half mile past the Wellington house. I don't know whether he was telling me the truth or not, but he told me something unbelievable about that house."

"Mr. Long, what did he tell you?" Danny asked.

"According to Elmer, he was feeling pretty good one Saturday morning. Purely for exercise, he decided to walk to my store, and then walk back to his home. When he walked in front of that house he stopped. He told me this after he stopped, 'First of all, I don't know why I stopped in front of that house, but I did. It was something inside me that caused me to turn toward it. After doing so, I had this longing to go inside the house. It was as though I was being mentally enticed to go into the Wellington yard. It was like a magnet pulling me toward where I didn't want to go. Momentarily, I closed my eyes as I started walking toward the Wellington yard. All at once-------with all my will power, I turned and ran straight down the road as fast as I could. Several seconds later, I realized that I was back to my normal self. That eerie feeling that I experienced in front of that house was gone.' Again, I don't know if Elmer was telling me the truth, but he acted like it was true. In fact, he wouldn't even walk back in front of the Wellington house. He got Larry Crenshaw to drive him home from the store."

"We appreciate you telling us about the Wellington House," said Danny. "We've got to be on our way before it gets too late in the day."

"Thanks for stopping by, Danny----and you too, young lady."

Danny and Shelia were on their way toward the haunted house a couple minutes later. Shelia seemed a bit nervous concerning that place. "Danny, I'm not going into the Wellington yard or the Wellington house!" Shelia stated, nervously.

"Oh, we won't go in there. We'll just look at the place from the road. We'll be there in three more minutes."

A very short time later, Danny stopped his 4-wheeler on the opposite of the road from the house, which was located about eighty yards from the 4-wheeler. Shelia trembled as she looked at the lifeless appearance of the unpainted, two-story house. The undergrowth and weeds surrounding the house made it look even more ghostly.

"Shelia, what do you think about this old house?"

"I wouldn't go into that house for all the money in the world!" Shelia said, shivering. "It looks like ghosts might live there!"

"Danny, what are you looking at?"

"I'm looking at that pear tree. That thing is loaded down with big pears."

"If there were any there I wouldn't eat a pear that was grown in that yard!" Shelia vowed.

"I'll go get you one----if you'll eat it."

"I believe you're seeing things. There's not any pears on that tree! Danny, let's go back to your granddaddy's house. Please----I feel like something wants me to go into that house!"

"Are you joshing me?" Danny asked. "Those are the biggest pears I've ever seen!"

"Danny, there are no pears on that tree! Let's get out of here!" Trembling, Shelia cried out again, "Danny, something is wrong with that house! Please---------let's go!"

Danny turned his 4-wheeler around; they headed back down the road toward Mr. Jones' store. "Shelia, are you okay?"

"Tell me the truth; were you joshing me about seeing pears on that barren tree?"

"That tree was loaded down with big pears. Didn't you see them?" Danny asked.

"I didn't see a single pear on that old tree. You must have been seeing things."

"Shelia, I swear I saw pears on that tree!"

"I hate to tell you this, but that tree was as barren as a telephone pole," Shelia commented. "Danny, I'm glad you brought me to that old house, but I'll never visit that place again. I can't explain it, but it was like an overpowering force enticing me to go into that yard. I believe it affected you as well, causing you to see something that wasn't there."

"It sure did look like there were pears on that tree," Danny commented.

"Would you have gone into that yard if I hadn't been with you?"

"Do you want me to tell you the absolute truth about that?" Danny asked.

"Yes, I do. Did you want a pear bad enough to go into the Wellington yard to get it?"

"I don't believe I did, but like you------something kept reminding me of that pear tree. I believe, at that particular time, that I would have gone after a pear. I'm like you; I don't think I'll ever go back to that place. Do you like riding horses?"

"I've never ridden a horse," answered Shelia.

"We'll change that situation tomorrow when you ride on grandpa's horses. There are several more places that I'm going to take you today on my 4-wheeler. After that, we'll go back to my grandparents and eat a hearty lunch."

"Danny, I want to see the rest of the farm animals before we go home tomorrow."

"That won't be a problem. I'll show you all of them after we eat breakfast tomorrow morning. Shelia, what do you think of grandpa's farm?"

"I think it's wonderful to live on a lot of land out in the country. I love animals a great deal. Danny, do you suppose I might be able to hold one of those newborn bunnies?"

"I'll make sure you do that tomorrow morning. Well, we just turned onto one of my grandpa's fields. We'll be back near his house in a few minutes. Are you getting tired of riding?"

"Well, since you mentioned it, I could use a little break from your 4-wheeler when we get back to the house."

"There is one thing that we could do before we get back to my grandparents house." Danny suggested.

"What's that?"

"I could stop my 4-wheeler long enough to kiss you."

"Are you sure you want to?" Shelia asked.

"Does a bunny hop? Does a dog bark? Does a fish swim? Does a -----?"

"Stop that!" Shelia sounded. "I get the picture."

Danny slowed his 4-wheeler down until it stopped moving. He got off his 4-wheeler, and then turned toward Shelia. "I've wanted to kiss you for the last thirty minutes," said Danny. He took off his helmet and laid it on his seat. She took off her helmet. Danny placed his hands against her shoulders.

"There's just one thing before you kiss me."

"What thing are you talking about?" Danny remarked, seemingly confused about her comment.

"Will you be kissing me as your girlfriend or your soon-to-be sister?"

"Shelia, why in tar nation did you have to bring that up? I was ready to pucker up and kiss you like my lips belonged on yours! Now I don't know what I should do! Darn it, I'm not so sure our parents should marry each other since we'll have this girlfriend/boyfriend, sister/brother situation." Danny picked up his helmet; he threw it against the ground in disgust. Shelia got off his 4-wheeler when she saw tears in Danny's eyes.

She placed her arms around his neck. "Danny, whether you're my boyfriend or my brother I will always love you."

"Shelia, for now I only know you as my girlfriend. That brother business will have to come later, much later!"

"Do you still want to kiss me?" Shelia asked.

"Yes, I do want to kiss you, but it won't ever be like it was before all this brother stuff came into play." He placed his arms around her, and then kissed her gently on her lips.

"What's the matter?" Shelia asked. "You're not kissing me like you used to."

"All this brother business didn't use to come up just before I kissed you."

"Well, you only gave me a peck on my lips! If you're still my boyfriend you'll have to do better than that." With a smile on his face, Danny squeezed tightly around Shelia's waist; he kissed her passionately for several seconds. "Wow, that's the boyfriend that I used to know!" Shelia remarked. "I don't think I can handle another kiss like that at the moment."

"Why not?"

"I may tell you someday----why not," Shelia smiled.

Danny and Shelia rode into his grandfather's yard a few minutes later. George Eason was feeding his horses. "Shelia, Grandpa is in the barn; would you like to go see his horses?"

"Yes, very much so!" They hurried into the horse barn.

"Did you kids have a great time on the 4-wheeler?"

"We sure did, Grandpa! I took Shelia all over your fields. I took her by Mr. Long's store to get us some drinks."

"Danny, don't tell me that you took Shelia to the Wellington house?"

"I did Grandpa, but we didn't go into the yard. We stayed on the side of the highway for just a few minutes before leaving the place. Grandpa, was there something wrong with us going there?"

"What you did was okay, but stay away from that place!"

"I will stay away from there, but tell me this------what's wrong with that place? I saw a pear tree loaded down with great big pears. I had a good mind to go pick me a couple."

"I drove by there yesterday and I didn't see a single pear on that tree," Henry remarked.

"Grandpa, you must need glasses or something! Shelia was on the back of my 4-wheeler; she saw all those pears on that tree, didn't you Shelia?"

"No, I didn't see any pears. Danny, I told you then that you must be seeing things. That tree was as barren as it could get!"

"Grandpa, I know I'm not crazy! I saw that tree loaded down with pears!"

"Danny, take my word for it-----there were no pears on that tree! For whatever reason, it looked to you as though the tree was filled with pears."

"Mr. Miller, what's wrong with that Wellington house?" Shelia asked.

"I really don't know, but a lot of unexplained things have happened there."

"Mr. Miller, you've got three very pretty horses. Do they have names?"

"Of course, they have names. From stall one thru stall three their names are Silver, Lady and Gertrude."

"Gertrude, Mr. Miller. Why that name?" Shelia asked.

"I named her after one of my teachers," he laughed.

"Danny, you promised me that I could hold one of the baby bunnies when we got back here."

"Grandpa, will you go riding with us tomorrow?" Danny asked. "Shelia has never ridden on a horse."

"Yes, providing that you help me feed all my animals after we eat."

"I'll be glad to do that."

"You two come to the house in about an hour. Dora will have our lunch cooked by then?" George advised.

Chapter 19

At six o'clock that evening, Harry and Doris Spears were at Beth Miller's house. Beth had invited them over for dinner. They were all sitting in the living room talking about various things. "Mrs. Spears, I've never seen such a change in your husband," Beth remarked. "He's always been friendly and nice, but until he married you he seemed rather sad at times."

"Harry just needed a woman in his life," Doris answered. "To tell you the truth Mrs. Miller, I needed a man in my life, as well. I've never been happier than I am now. Harry has been so good to me since we've been married. He's asked me several times to quit my job. I told him that I would consider doing just that."

"Mrs. Miller, I told Doris that she didn't have to work ever again," Harry commented.

"Maybe her working is not such a bad thing, Mr. Spears," said Beth. "Not that you may need it, but it gives a break for each of you. Sometimes too much togetherness is not always a good thing. By the way, Randy Johnson, my fiancé will start up my grill in about thirty minutes. I've got some beautiful looking t-bone steaks that I bought from Radcliff's Butcher Shop."

"Mrs. Miller, how are your wedding plans coming along?" Doris asked.

"Believe it or not, I've finished with everything except for buying my wedding dress. I've sent out all the invitations, selected the site for the wedding, made arrangements for the reception, and obtained Mrs. Amanda Phillips as my wedding director. My own pastor will conduct the wedding ceremony."

"How excited are you about getting married?" Mr. Spears asked.

"After John's death, I thought I could never get this excited about getting married again. Randy Johnson is a wonderful man; I love him very much. I've always wanted a daughter, and I'll have one after marrying Randy. You both have seen his daughter, Shelia. She's beautiful, intelligent and she thinks a great deal of me."

"Where is Randy, Mrs. Miller?" Mr. Spears asked.

"He and another detective have been working on a murder case the entire day. He promised me he would be here by 6:20 this evening."

"Who got murdered?" Mr. Spears asked.

"An elderly couple was killed while they were sleeping in their bed. I believe Randy said that their last name was Rodgers. They lived out on Melton Wood Road."

"Wait just a minute!" Mr. Spears sounded, seemingly shocked. "Was their names Johnny and Mildred Rodgers?"

"Yes, that's exactly who they were! Did you happen to know them, Mr. Spears?"

"Yes, I certainly did! I'm very sorry to hear that they got killed," Mr. Spears commented. "They were two very nice people. In fact, I've been to their house. I'll bet that sorry, good-for-nothing son killed them both!"

"Mr. Spears, you say that the Rodgers had a son?" Beth asked.

"I believe he was an adopted son. Mr. Rodgers told me that they adopted him when he was about fifteen years old. I believe his name is Alex. He must be in his forties by now."

Beth's doorbell rang. She answered the door. "I told you I would be here by 6:20 this evening," said Randy.

"Come inside, we've got a discussion going on that I'm sure you'll be interested in." Mr. Spears stood up as they entered the living room. "Randy, you already know my good friends, Mr. Spears and his wife Doris."

"Yes, I certainly do." Randy shook hands with each of them. "Beth, are you ready for me to grill our steaks?"

"Not right now. Randy, we were just talking about Mr. and Mrs. Rodgers that were murdered recently. I just found out that Mr. Spears knew both of them. Listen at what he has to say about them."

Mr. Spears spoke, "Well, it all started about three months ago when I saw an advertisement in the newspaper for a shotgun for sale. It didn't interest me until I noticed that the gun for sale was an Oak Leaf brand shotgun. I knew right away that those type guns were manufactured in 1913 by a company in New York, named The Hunter Arms Company. The reason I knew this is because my father used to own one year's ago. For several years in a row at Thanksgiving, Daddy would win a turkey with that shotgun. It had a long, 32 inch barrel, and was fully choked. Anyway, my parents were away from home one day. While they were gone someone broke into their house and stole my father's shotgun. To make a long-story short, I called the number in the advertisement. A very nice sounding man answered his phone. He said his name was Johnny Rodgers. I asked him if he still had the gun for sale. He said that he did. I told him that I would be at his house that very day to buy his shotgun. He gave me his address, which was somewhere on Melton Wood Road. I can't remember the number now. Mr. Rodgers and his wife, Mildred were sitting in a porch swing when I drove into their yard. They both graciously invited me into their house. In fact, Mrs. Rodgers asked me if I cared for something to drink. In the meantime, Mr. Rodger's went into his bedroom to get the Oak Leaf shotgun. He brought it into the living room and handed it to me. Almost instantly, I recognized that the letter 'S' was engraved on the barrel. The 'S' stood for specialty. Thoughts raced through my mind that this might well be my father's gun. However, there were many of these guns manufactured in 1913. I could never be sure that this exact gun belonged to my father. I asked Mr. Rodger's why he would sell a gun like this. He said that he actually didn't need the money. About that time, his adopted son came into the house. He said, 'Old man, somebody told me that you were trying to sell that gun I gave you years ago! Well, you're not going to sell that gun to this man or anyone else!' That's when Mrs. Rodgers stood up and said, 'Just a minute, Alex! You gave this gun to Johnny! It's his to do whatever he wants to! You need to go back to your house if you've come here to cause trouble.' By this time I was ready to get out of the Rodger's home, but I was afraid their son was going to hurt them or something. He appeared to be drinking, and he seemed awful angry."

"What happened after that, Mr. Spears?" Randy asked.

"Their son, Alex, pointed his finger toward Mr. Rodgers and threatened him."

"What was the threat?"

"I remember what he said quite well. He said, 'If you sell that damn gun you'll live to regret it! I went to a lot of trouble to get that gun and you had better not sell it!' Almost staggering, Alex walked toward the front door; he slammed it shut on his way out. I looked toward Mrs. Rodgers; that poor woman had tears in her eyes. She said, 'Now you know why my husband needs to get rid of that gun.' Mr. Rodgers, as heartbroken as a man can get, looked toward me and said, 'The biggest mistake of our life is the day we adopted Alex! We've tried our best to turn him around, but nothing has ever worked concerning him. He has just about put us in the poor house with his doping, drinking and gambling. He seems to get meaner and meaner as he gets older. Mr. Spears, I apologize for his behavior.' I told him that Alex's behavior wasn't his or his wife's fault. Mr. Rodger's insisted that I take the gun with me. I paid him twice as much as he had advertised for the gun."

"Mr. Spears, unwittingly, you may have helped us solve a murder case. I'll go have a talk with Alex Rodgers the first thing on Monday morning. Beth, I'm going to light up the grill."

"Mr. Johnson, is there anything I can help you do?" Mr. Spears asked.

"Certainly, you can go out on the patio and keep me company."

All was quiet at George Eason's house at midnight. Shelia was asleep in one of the spare bedrooms. Danny was asleep in a bedroom across the hall from her. Danny and Shelia had a very busy day riding on the 4-wheeler, visiting the haunted house, and seeing all the animals on Mr. Eason's farm. Danny had even taken Shelia to Brutus's pen, the bull that almost killed him.

At 1:15 that morning, Danny started dreaming about the George Wellington house. In his dream, he was visiting with Mr. Wellington's children of his own age, Fred 13, Mary 12, and Oscar 15. Danny was all smiles as he and the other three picked pears off the pear tree. Mrs. Wellington was sitting in a chair on her front porch. She had tears in her eyes because her husband had been missing for days. A little while later, Danny walked to the porch and asked Mrs. Wellington if she wanted one of the pears he had picked from her tree. She smiled and then said, 'No thank you.'"

Very little was said at the dinner table. Danny noticed in particular that they didn't have electric lights inside their house. They only had kerosene lamps and candles for lighting. In his dream, he thought that was rather unusual. Danny never got frightened until they were in bed. He was on a cot next to Oscar. Fred was sleeping in another bedroom. Mary was sleeping in her own bed down the hall. Danny realized that Oscar was sound asleep because he was snoring. Danny was about to fall asleep when he heard someone walking up the stairs. For the first time, he became scared; he pulled his covering up to his mouth. The next thing he saw was a man holding a kerosene lamp in one hand and a hatchet in the other one. Danny tried to scream, but the words wouldn't come out. He watched in horror as the man swung the hatchet downward, again and again into Oscar's body. Blood spattered over on Danny while the man viciously attacked Oscar. Almost to the point of a heart attack, Danny watched the man go out of the doorway, and then down the hallway toward Mary's room. Danny managed to slip out of bed; he tiptoed down the stairway until he reached the front door. It was then that he heard footsteps coming hurriedly down the stairs. Danny reached for the doorknob, but it was locked. He commenced yelling, 'Get away! Get away from me!' Shelia rushed into Danny's room; she turned on the overhead light. "Danny, Danny Miller, wake up! Wake up, please!" Shelia cried out.

Danny rose up in bed; he was covered with sweat. "Shelia, what are you doing in here?"

"You were hollering out for someone to get away from you."

George and Dora came to Danny's room. "Danny, we heard you screaming! Were you having another one of your dreams?" Dora asked.

"Grandma, I was having the worst dream of all," he said, tearfully. "It was about that awful haunted house! Grandpa, in my dream I saw Mr. Wellington kill one of his boys with a hatchet! I was in a bed right next to him when it happened." Danny was shivering all over. Dora placed his covering around his back. "Oscar's blood spattered all over me! I got out of bed and hurried down the stairs! I wanted to get out of that place! When I tried to open the front door it wouldn't open. Mr. Wellington came after me with a hatchet in his hand! That's all I remember because, thank goodness, Shelia awakened me from that terrible nightmare. I'll never go back to sleep again!"

"Shelia, why don't you go back to bed and get your rest," Dora commented. "You do the same, George. Danny and I will go to the kitchen and have some hot chocolate until he feels like going back to bed again. Come with me, Danny. You shouldn't go right back to bed for a while. I'll not have you dreaming that horrible dream again."

Shelia was out of bed two hours before Danny got up. He didn't go back to sleep until three o'clock in the morning. Shelia was looking at two new born goats when Danny walked outside.

"Grandma wanted to know if you wanted some more breakfast," Danny commented.

"Tell Mrs. Eason that I don't care for anything else. I ate over an hour ago. Danny, did you dream anymore after you went back to bed?"

"Thank goodness I didn't! Shelia, I think something is the matter with me!"

"Why do you say that?"

"I keep having these awful dreams. I've got to the point that I'm afraid to go to sleep at night."

"Danny, I believe everyone has a nightmare or two during their lifetime," Shelia answered.

"For Heaven's sakes, I've had that many inside three weeks! I wish there was some way I could quit having these nightmares!"

"Have you prayed to God and told him about your problem?"

"I guess I haven't, Shelia."

"When you go to bed tonight-------explain to God what your problem is. God can fix anything."

"Grandpa is going on a trail ride with us after I eat some breakfast. He's already fed the horses, and the other animals. I should have gotten up and helped him."

"You didn't have to help him this morning because I did. I fed Silver, Lady and Gertrude all by myself-------that is, with Mr. Miller's instructions." Shelia smiled. "Also, I helped feed the chickens, ducks, goats, rabbits, cows and even old Brutus. Danny, that old bull looked as gentle as a kitten."

"Believe me, that old bull is not gentle! The reason he didn't paw at the ground when you were standing outside his pen is because you're a girl. Had I been there----that old fool would have been snorting, and pawing at the ground. Brutus doesn't like me at all!"

"Why doesn't he like you?" Shelia asked.

"I have no idea why he doesn't like me, unless he's still sore about me shooting him in the butt with my paint ball gun."

"How many times did you shoot Brutus?"

"I only shot him four times. He had two red marks, a blue one and a yellow mark on his butt. Do you think that's why he chased me out of his pen?"

"I would certainly think so. Did your grandfather ever find out that you shot his prized bull?"

"I'm afraid he did. After Grandpa saw Brutus's butt he came straight to me."

"Did he whip you for shooting Brutus?"

"No, he did not. However, when he found out that I shot his bull------he asked me three words?"

"What were the words?"

"Where's that gun? Those were the three words. I brought my paintball gun to him. Without saying a single word, Grandpa smashed my gun against the horse barn about three times. I looked down on the ground; my paint gun was in four pieces. You want believe what Grandpa did next. He came to me and hugged my neck. He pointed toward the broken pieces of my paint ball gun. He never got angry at all, but he did say six words."

"Okay, what were those six words?" Shelia asked.

"A valuable lesson you just learned. Grandpa patted me on the back, and then he walked away. I picked up the pieces of my paint ball gun and threw them into a trash can. That was a very valuable lesson that I learned that day. Well, I'm going inside and eat a little something. Do you want to go inside with me?"

"I think I'll go back to the chicken pen. A mother hen is hatching out some little chicks. Guess what, that mother hen pecked my hand when I tried to take one of her baby chicks out to look at it. Danny, I'm very glad that I was invited to spend the weekend with you and your grandparents. They're so nice that I could stay here forever. I'll be proud to call them as you do, Grandma and Grandpa after our parents are married. After we get through riding the horses, I want to ride some more on your 4-wheeler. You could take me to their pond, and then we could go down that woods path on a nature tour. Just one thing-----as I told you yesterday, I'm not putting my feet on the ground while we're in the woods. Snakes and I don't get along very well!"

———

Randy Johnson decided he wouldn't wait until Monday to go question Alex Rodgers.

He drove to Marcus Hendrix house to see if he wanted to ride with him. Marcus answered his doorbell. "Randy. Don't tell me that you're working on a murder case on the Lord's Day."

"I guess I am. How would you like to ride with me to see a possible murder suspect?" Randy asked.

"Which murder are we talking about?"

"Mr. and Mrs. Rodgers murder. Get your gun and badge. I'll wait for you in my car." Marcus got into Randy's car a few minutes later. "We're going to a small apartment at 301 East Ream Street," said Randy. "That's where Alex Rodgers lives."

"Who is that?" Marcus asked.

"He's the adopted son of Johnny and Mildred Rodgers. He might, also, be their killer."

"Why do you think that?" Marcus asked.

"You'll find out when we get there------providing that he's home."

Randy drove into the driveway at 301 East Ream Street. There was an older model car sitting in the driveway. Randy and Marcus got out of their vehicle; they walked cautiously toward the front porch. Randy rang the doorbell. A few seconds later a man opened the front door. He smelled like a whiskey brewer; he was unshaven and barefooted. "Yeah, what do you guys want?" Alex asked.

"Is your name Alex Rodgers?" Randy asked.

"That's right, what's it too you? What do you guys mean------coming here in the middle of the morning?" He staggered backwards, and then he regained his position against the door.

"Mr. Rodgers, my name is Detective Randy Johnson; my partner's name is Detective Marcus Hendrix. We've come here to ask you a few questions concerning your parent's death."

"I was home asleep when they were killed."

"Mr. Rodgers, how do you know when they were killed?" Detective Hendrix asked.

"Well, I------Oh hell, I guess I don't know when they were killed, but it wasn't me that killed them!"

"We've never said that you killed them," Randy remarked. "If you don't mind, we would like to go inside and ask you a few questions. Maybe you can help point us in the right direction. It's a known fact that someone killed your parents. We just need your help in determining who killed them."

"Well, in that case-----come inside." Randy and Marcus followed Alex inside his house. They noticed several empty liquor bottles, some on the floor----others on small end tables. The room had an unpleasant odor, probably coming from three bags of trash, located close to the kitchen entrance.

Randy and Marcus took seats in the living room. Randy sat down next to a pile of wrinkled clothes that had been washed and dried. "You guys will have to overlook my messy house. I haven't been doing much cleaning these days. However, that situation is going to change very soon. I'm going to buy myself a new house."

"Mr. Rodgers, where do you work?" Marcus asked.

"I'm between jobs at the present time."

"Where did you work?" Randy asked.

"I worked at Maynard Lumber Company about three months ago," Alex answered. "Since then, I've been drawing unemployment. I pretty much know who killed my parents, if you want to know!"

"Mr. Rodgers, that's why we came here," Marcus remarked. "We were hoping that you could shed some light on your parent's murders. Who do you think may be their murderer?"

"I was at my parent's house the day before they were killed. Zachary Jones came to their house and asked my father if he could get a five gallon bucket of pears for his wife to make into preserves. My father told him that it would be okay for him to do that. Zachary said he would come back the following day to get the pears."

"Mr. Rodgers, you heard him say that he needed a five gallon bucket of pears for his wife to make into preserves?" Randy asked.

"That's what he said," Alex answered, lighting up a cigarette.

"Mr. Rodgers, you've been a lot of help to us," said Randy. "I appreciate you talking with us today. Marcus, it's Sunday; let's go home."

After Randy and Marcus had driven out of Alex Rodgers yard, Marcus remarked, "I'll bet three months pay that Alex Rodgers planted that pistol underneath that five gallon bucket in easy view of that pear tree. When results come back from ballistics, Alex's fingerprints will be on that gun, as well as Zachary Jones fingerprints."

"There's no way that Alex would have placed the pistol underneath that bucket without wiping it clean," Randy remarked. "Tomorrow, I want you to compile a list of life insurance companies to see if Alex Rodgers has an insurance policy on his parent's death."

Chapter 20

Danny, Shelia, and George Eason were sitting at the kitchen table. Dora had just finished cooking a big lunch for everyone. George had done what he had promised Danny he would do; he took Shelia and Danny on a trail ride across his fields and that of his neighbors' field. Danny rode Silver during their trail ride. Shelia had a nice ride on the horse named Lady. As usual, George rode his favorite horse, Gertrude. "Mrs. Eason, might I help you place the food on the table?" Shelia asked.

"Yes, you certainly may. Did you hear that, George? We've got a very smart female grandchild that will soon join us." Shelia got up and helped Mrs. Eason place the food on the table.

"What's the matter, Grandpa?" Danny asked. "I see you moving your head back and forth."

"I was just thinking how fortunate we will be when we have two grandchildren to love and spend time with. What are you two going to do this afternoon before Beth comes to take you home?"

"Grandpa, Shelia wants to go fish in your pond for a little while. After that, she wants to go on a scenic ride down your woods path. Actually, she wants to see where I got off my 4-wheeler when I went after the dog. Could we borrow a couple of your fishing poles?"

"Yes, you certainly can. They're under the barn shelter where they always are. Shelia, I want you to be careful around my fishing pond. Be sure to stay on the side that gets mowed quite often. I nearly stepped on a poisonous snake the last time I went to the pond."

"That settles it," Shelia commented, "I no longer want to go fishing! I rather go for a ride on the 4-wheeler. Mrs. Eason, when I go back outside, may I hold a couple of those baby chicks?"

"Sure you can, but the mother hen may peck your hand when you try to do that."

"I've already been pecked by that hen. This time I'll let Danny get the little chicks for me," Shelia smiled.

George broke out in a big smile. "Danny, now you know how the cliché got started concerning men that were hen pecked." Everyone commenced laughing, except for Danny.

Twenty minutes later, Danny and Shelia were on the 4-wheeler heading toward the woods path that Shelia wanted to travel on. When they entered the woods, Shelia asked Danny to drive slow so she could enjoy the scenery, and perhaps see an animal or bird. About two minutes later, Danny stopped his 4-wheeler. He turned off its engine. Without saying a word, he pointed toward a large oak tree about sixty yards away. Shelia looked in that direction for a few seconds before she saw what

Danny was pointing at. A big smile appeared on her face while observing a large raccoon sitting on a tree limb. "Danny, what is that thing?" Shelia whispered.

"It's a raccoon. I'll bet you don't see what's on the limb below the raccoon."

"No, what do you see?" Shelia asked.

"Look toward the end of the limb. You'll be able see four little baby raccoons moving back and forth."

"Oh, my goodness, I see them now! Those little things are so cute. What keeps them from falling off that limb?"

"Raccoons, for the most part are tree dwellers." Danny answered. "That's how they protect themselves from predators, such as owls, hawks and even bobcats. Let's move on down the path; we'll drive very slowly so you can see other kinds of animals, and perhaps a bird or two."

They had only traveled about a fifty yards when Danny stopped his 4-wheeler again. He hurriedly turned off its engine. "Shelia, don't be afraid, but there's a rattlesnake ahead of us. I'm going to lean to one side so you can see the snake. Don't worry; the snake is twenty-feet in front of us." Nervously, Shelia looked at the big snake coiled up in a striking position. "A snake just like that one is what bit me at that e creek."

"Danny, that thing looks so big!" Shelia commented, her shivering at the very thought of being bitten by a poisonous snake. "How will you get around that thing?"

"That's no problem, I'll just go out of the path a little ways, and then I'll turn back into the path. Otherwise, I could just pick up a limb and kill the snake."

"No! No, Danny! Please don't do that! I don't want you bitten again!" Shelia remarked, tearfully.

"Okay, we'll drive through the woods a little ways, and then we'll be back on the woods path."

"Danny, I know one thing------this has been a very eventful ride so far."

Shortly, they were back on the woods path again. Danny was driving his 4-wheeler very slow so they wouldn't scare all the animals and birds away. All of a sudden, Danny stopped again; he turned off the engine. He pointed to a Dogwood tree ahead of them. The tree was next to the woods path; a large bird was feeding on clusters of red seed that was on the tree. "What kind of bird is that?" Shelia whispered.

"You're looking at a very rare sight, indeed," answered Danny, him smiling. "Notice how big that bird is. That bird is big as a crow. His feathers are mostly black, but look at his head? My goodness, look at that red head of his. Those red feathers look like they're being blown backwards from the wind."

"Again, what kind of bird is that?" Shelia asked.

"That's a Pileated Woodpecker. It's the very first one that I've ever seen alive. I sure do wish I had my camera!"

"I've got my cell phone. Will that work?"

"Yes, please take a picture of the bird before it fly's away. I want to show the bird's picture to Grandpa and Grandma." Shelia held her cell phone toward the bird; she snapped the camera three times to get at least one good image. The bird flew out of the Dogwood tree, disappearing inside the woods."

"Danny, how did you know what kind of woodpecker it was?" Shelia asked.

"I was looking up birds on the internet one day when I happened to see a list of woodpeckers. Until I saw it on the internet, I never knew that a woodpecker got as big as the one we just saw. It also mentioned something about an Ivory Billed Woodpecker that may be extinct. If it still exists, it would be the biggest one in the world."

A few minutes later, Danny stopped his 4-wheeler at the end of the path. "Is this where you heard the dog making a noise?" Shelia asked.

"Yes. Do you see that broken little twig to your right?"

"Yes, I see it."

"That's the direction I went when I left my 4-wheeler where it is now."

"Danny, since it was getting late in the day, what made you go farther into the woods?"

"Shelia, if you were here and heard the pitiful sound coming from that dog, you may have done the same thing."

"Wrong! Wrong, and wrong again! In the first place------I wouldn't be in this woods all by myself. Didn't you even think about your mother and grandparents as you went strolling through the woods late in the day?"

"I guess I didn't, Shelia. It was a feeling inside me that caused me to go searching for that dog in distress. Would you have missed me had I not come out alive?"

Tears came into Shelia's eyes. "Why on earth did you ask me that stupid question? Danny, I can't believe you just asked me that!"

"Please, Shelia-----don't cry! I'm sorry I asked you that foolish question. Please-----don't be angry with me!" Danny placed his arms around her neck. He used a tissue from his pocket to wipe away her tears. "I'm going to turn around and let you kick me in my butt for saying that!"

"I don't want to kick you."

"Okay, I'll let you break both my little fingers." Danny said, smiling.

"You're such a nut. Shelia answered. "I don't want to break your fingers either."

"Okay, we'll settle this once and for all," Danny remarked. "Either you break both my little fingers or let me kiss you on your pretty lips. Now, which of those choices do you choose?"

"You're telling me that I have to choose one over the other," Shelia answered.

"Yep, one or the other!"

"Okay, I've made my choice."

Danny puckered up his lips, and then leaned forward. "Danny, go pick up that pine limb over by that tree."

"Why do you want that old limb for?".

"I'll need it to break your fingers," Shelia broke into laughter.

"You silly girl, you had me going for a moment. Now, how about my juicy kiss?"

"On one condition!" Shelia answered.

"I can't believe it, I'm only a teenager and I'm already getting bribed by a pretty girl. Okay, what is your condition?"

"That you let me drive your 4-wheeler out of these woods."

"Shelia, you drive a hard bargain, but a kiss from you is worth the sacrifice." He placed his arms around her neck. For several seconds he stared into her light-blue eyes.

"Danny, what are you waiting for?" Shelia asked.

"I was just thinking how pretty you are." He leaned forward and kissed her tenderly on her lips. He pulled back for a couple seconds, and then he kissed her again.

"Danny, what's the matter? You look like you've got something on your mind."

"I do have something on my mind. That's why we need to head out of here right now. I'm going to start up my 4-wheeler. After that, I'll sit behind you so you can drive us out of here. My mother should be at Grandpa's house in a little while. I do hope you've had a good time today."

"I really didn't have a good time!' Shelia remarked, with a frown on her face.

"You didn't?" Danny asked, very confused at her remark.

"That's true. I had a great time today, and yesterday," she smiled. "Okay, tell me when I'm doing something wrong."

"Shelia, it's hard to do anything wrong with my 4-wheeler because it's got automatic gear shifting."

"How about that tree ahead of us, if I hit it, wouldn't that be wrong?"

"You've got a good point there. Just drive slowly and stay on the woods path."

Danny and Shelia were standing in front of a rabbit pen when Beth drove into George Eason's driveway. They both hurried toward her car. Danny opened the car door for his mother. "Why didn't Daddy ride with you?" Shelia asked.

"Sweetheart, he's been working on a murder case the entire weekend. He was at my house just before I left to come here. He told me to give you a kiss for him." Beth leaned over and gave Shelia a big hug, and then she kissed her on her cheek. "Okay Danny, it's your turn for a hug." She hugged and kissed him.

"Mrs. Miller, I've had a great time this weekend!"

"I'm very glad that you did. You'll have to tell me all about it on our way home."

"Mother, we can't go home until we have dinner with Grandma and Grandpa," Danny remarked.

"I know that, but we can't stay very long after dinner. Let's go inside and visit with your grandparents." Danny led the way. Shelia held Beth's hand as they stepped up on the porch. Beth and Shelia followed Danny into the living room.

"Look who's here, Grandpa?" Danny commented.

"Beth, it's good to see my lovely daughter. Dora has cooked up a big dinner for us. She even baked a chocolate and a lemon pie."

Dora walked into the living room. "Beth, you got here just in the nick of time. Dinner is ready for us to eat. Why didn't your handsome fiancé come with you?"

"Mrs. Miller, he's been working the entire weekend on a murder case. He told me that he would come with me the very next time I come here."

"Dora, can we eat now? I'm about starved."

"George, you're always about starved." She smiled.

Beth drove her car out of her parents' driveway at 6:45 that evening. Danny and Shelia were sitting in the backseat of the car. "Mother, how did you like Grandma's chocolate pie?"

"It was very good, but I liked the lemon pie the best. Shelia, tell me about your weekend."

"Mrs. Miller, I had so much fun I hardly know where to begin. Just being on the farm was a wonderful experience. When you were a young girl, did you ever hold a baby rabbit in your hands?"

"Yes, I certainly did. In fact, my uncle had over a hundred rabbits of all types and colors."

"I sure do like your parents. I can hardly wait until I can call them grandma and grandpa. Your daddy let Danny and I ride his horses. My horse was named Lady. It was a pleasure riding her because she was very gentle. Also, I fed the chickens, cows, horses, goats and I even helped Mr. Eason feed his rabbits. He's such a very nice person. His wife is just as nice. Danny even showed me the Wellington house."

"Danny, why did you take Shelia to that awful place?" Beth asked, sternly.

"Mother, we didn't go into the yard or the house. I showed it to her from across the road."

"You should know better than to go there! I've heard most of my life that the Wellington house is haunted!"

"Mother, you won't ever have to worry about me going there again!"

"Why is that?"

"Let me ask you this, have you ever noticed the pear tree in the Wellington yard?"

"Yes, I've seen the tree that you're referring to."

"Mother, I swear I saw that tree loaded down with pears, but Shelia said it was totally barren of fruit. Grandpa told me that I was just seeing things when I thought fruit was on that tree."

"Danny, that sort of thing is what I'm talking about. No sane person would even venture into that yard! Anyway, what else did you see or do, Shelia?"

"We did a lot of riding on Danny's 4-wheeler. Oh, we did see a rattlesnake, raccoon, and one of the prettiest birds I have ever seen! Mrs. Miller, when we get to my house I'll show you that bird on my cell phone. Danny, what kind of woodpecker did you say that it was?"

"It was a Pileated Woodpecker. Mother, that bird was as big as a crow."

"Mrs. Miller, yours and Daddy's wedding is coming up soon. Have you and he discussed where we're going to live?" Shelia asked.

"We talked a little bit about that yesterday, but no final agreement has been reached. Where would you like for us to live?"

"It doesn't really make any difference to me, as long as we all live together."

"What about you, Danny? Which house would you like for us to live in?"

"Well, I've thought about that quite a bit. I think we should sell both houses and move into a two-story house."

"Do you know where a two-story house is located?" Shelia asked.

"I sure do. It's an old fashioned house, and it's already air conditioned."

"Who owns the house?" Beth asked.

"It's owned by an old fellow by the name of George Wellington." Danny burst into laughter.

"Danny, that's not funny at all!" Shelia snapped back at him.

Randy Johnson was standing on his porch when Beth drove into his driveway. He walked hurriedly toward Beth's car. Shelia quickly exited the car; she hurried to her father and then placed her arms around his waist. "Did you miss me a great deal?" Shelia asked.

"I most certainly did!" Randy kissed Shelia on her cheek. "Did my baby have a good time at Mr. Eason's farm?"

"Daddy, I had the best time of my life! It was wonderful there! They had horses, rabbits, goats, chickens, cows and a very big bull named Brutus!"

"I want all of you to step inside my house because I've got two gallons of home-made ice cream in my freezer," said Randy. "I bought it this afternoon from Mrs. Wendy Gallagher's Ice Cream Shop."

All four of them were sitting at the kitchen table a few minutes later. "Danny, you seem to be enjoying this ice cream."

"Mr. Johnson, this is the best ice cream that I've ever had! I believe I'll have a second helping."

"Danny, another helping will be your third one," Beth commented.

"Beth, let the boy eat; there's plenty more in the container."

"You hear that, Mother, Mr. Johnson is a man of wisdom."

"Daddy, I can hardly wait until you go to Mr. Eason' farm," said Shelia, excitedly. "He's got all kinds of farming equipment and other stuff. Oh, I forgot to tell you! I got pecked by a chicken!"

"Did it hurt?" Randy asked.

"No, it didn't hurt at all. It mostly startled me when I tried to grab a little chick from beneath her."

"Well, no wonder the chicken pecked you. She thought you were trying to steal one of her offspring," Randy smiled.

"Daddy, just wait until you taste some of Mrs. Dora Eason's cooking? She knows how to cook anything!"

"Shelia, what was the most exciting thing that you did while you were at the farm?"

"I can't just name one thing, Daddy. Everything we did was exciting. Oh, guess what, we saw a bird that I've never seen before. Danny, tell Daddy what kind of woodpecker that was."

"It was a Pileated Woodpecker."

"I've got a picture of the bird on my cell phone," said Shelia. She showed Beth and her father an image of the woodpecker. "I'll bet neither one of you have ever seen a bird like this one."

"You're right about that," Randy commented. "Where did you see this bird?"

"He was in a dogwood tree feeding on red berries." Danny answered.

Beth and Danny remained at Randy's house for a few more minutes. At Beth's car, Randy hugged and kissed her. "Danny, I want to thank you for making my daughter's weekend a very memorable one," said Randy. "Beth, each passing day I'm getting more excited about our wedding!"

"I am as well. How are you coming on your murder investigation?"

"I'll know a lot more after tomorrow or the next day," Randy answered. "We're checking for evidence against our main suspect now. Do you have any plans for tomorrow evening?"

"No, I don't think so."

"Would you and Danny have dinner with Shelia and me tomorrow evening? Before you say anything------I've got six great old big t-bone steaks in my refrigerator just waiting to be grilled."

"Why have you got six steaks, instead of four?"

"I took the liberty of asking your neighbors, Mr. and Mrs. Spears to join us for dinner."

"That was very sweet of you to do that. What time should Danny and I be here?"

"Would 6:30 in the evening be okay?"

"Yes, that will be fine." Beth answered.

"Danny, I'll see you at school tomorrow."

"I'm looking forward to it, Shelia."

Randy and Shelia waved bye as Beth drove out of their driveway.

Chapter 21

Detectives Randy Johnson and Marcus Hendrix were in Sheriff Hick's office the next day at ten o'clock. It was determined that only Zachary Jones fingerprints were on the pistol that he had given to the detectives. Ballistics had determined that the same pistol was the one used to kill Johnny Rodgers and his wife Mildred. "Randy, I don't think you have any other choice than to arrest Zachary Jones for the Rodgers murders," said Sheriff Hicks. "He had the gun and he was at Mr. Rodgers house the day of the murders."

"Sherriff, I would bet money that Mr. Jones didn't have anything to do with those murders!" Randy responded.

"Why on earth would you say that?" Sheriff Hicks asked.

"Mr. Jones wouldn't have turned that pistol over to us if he was the murderer. We'll go arrest him if you say so, but I don't want it to wind up like it was with Mr. Harry Spears or Vernon Madison. This time I want to be sure who the killer is before we arrest someone. Marcus, how are you coming along on the assignment I gave you?"

"I got several faxes off my printer before I came here. I was in such a hurry that I didn't get a chance to read any of them." Detective Hendrix took the copies of paper out of his briefcase and laid them on Sheriff Hick's desk.

"Randy, what assignment was Marcus working on?" Sheriff Hicks asked.

"It's my belief that Alex Rodgers is the one that killed his step parents. I asked Marcus to contact insurance companies to see if Alex had any life insurance on Johnny and Mildred Rodgers. Alex Rodgers was about as close to his step parents as I would be to a dead skunk."

"Well, that sounds like a well thought out plan," Sheriff Hicks remarked. "Marcus, divide up those insurance replies amongst us. We'll find out very quickly whether Alex had any life insurance on his step parents."

Three minutes later, Sheriff Hicks said, "I believe I've got something! It says here on this insurance form that Alex Spencer Rodgers has two-hundred and fifty-thousand dollars of life insurance on Johnny Edward Rodgers. Wait a minute-----wait just a minute here, here it is------it seems that Mr. Alex Spencer Rodgers has another two-hundred and fifty-thousand dollars of life insurance on Mildred Darlene Rodgers. There's something else that looks quite interesting."

"What do you see, Sheriff Hicks?" Randy asked.

"It appears that Alex Rodgers signed up for this insurance a little over two years ago. It looks like it was ten days over the two-year waiting period. That would seem rather convenient for Alex, since that length of time wouldn't affect him collecting the insurance money. I think I'll put a hold on him collecting any money until we have determined that he's not the killer."

Randy stood up and said, "I thought it might be something like this! Sheriff Hicks, I believe Alex wiped the pistol clean and then he placed a five-gallon bucket in easy sight of that pear tree. He placed the pistol underneath the bucket. He already heard Zachary Jones say that he was going to pick a five-gallon bucket of pears that day. Mr. Johnny Rodgers had already given Zachary permission to get the pears. Alex figured that Zachary would use that bucket to get his pears. He, also, thought that Zachary would keep the pistol since he didn't know that someone had been killed with it. He's a shrewd customer, but he's not shrewd enough to get away with killing his own step parents."

"You men have done a good job coming up with this information so fast. Hold off on arresting Mr. Jones until you've had an opportunity to further investigate Alex Rodgers. If in fact he's guilty, it won't be easy getting him to confess to the murders. Using the serial number on the 38 caliber Smith & Wesson that you got from Zachary Jones, did either of you determine where that gun was originally sold?"

"Yes, we certainly did, Sheriff Hicks," said Randy. "A man named Julian Anderson bought that pistol from Johnson's Gun Shop twelve months ago. Mr. Anderson died of natural causes three months later. Johnson's Gun Shop is not more than twenty miles from where we are."

"If in fact Alex did place the gun under the bucket, how did he get it from Julian Anderson?" Sheriff Hicks asked.

"That's the question that we need answered," Marcus commented. "Sheriff, we could go see Mr. Anderson's wife and see if she can shed some light on that subject."

"Do you know where Mrs. Anderson lives?" Sheriff Hicks asked.

"Yes sir, she lives within ten miles of here. Randy and I have her address."

"Well, maybe that would be a good place to start. However, I doubt seriously whether she would know anything about her husband's gun."

"We'll go to her house right after lunch," Randy commented. "After that, we'll drive to Alex Rodger's house. His house is littered with whiskey bottles, some full and some empty. I don't believe he can afford to buy all that liquor on unemployment money, especially after paying house rent, utilities, insurance payments and groceries. I wouldn't be surprised if he isn't using his step parent's credit cards."

"When you do go to his house I want you both to be very careful and observant. If he was mean enough to kill the very people that took him in, fed him and furnished him a place to stay------he wouldn't think twice about killing either one or both of you."

Randy and Marcus drove to Patricia Anderson's house at 1:30 that afternoon. Mrs. Anderson was watering some flowers as they exited their car. Mrs. Anderson turned off the water as the men walked toward her. "I'm Detective Randy Johnson and my partner is Detective Marcus Hendrix; are you Mrs. Patricia Anderson?"

"Yes, that's my name. How may I help you?"

"Mrs. Anderson, we're investigating a double murder which has nothing to do with you or your deceased husband. Before Mr. Anderson died, he owned a .38 caliber Smith & Wesson pistol. It seems that was the gun used to commit those murders. We were wondering who your husband may have sold that gun to."

"I know the gun you're talking about. Julian taught me how to shoot it within a week after he bought it from Johnson's Gun Shop. In fact, I was with him when he bought it. My husband, bless his soul, died within three months after he purchased that gun."

"So you kept the gun after your husband passed away," Detective Johnson commented.

"It was my intention to keep it, but one day I drove to see my sister, Irene Davenport. I was gone most of the day, but when I returned home I saw this vehicle driving out of my driveway. I didn't think too much about it until three days later when I looked for my pistol inside my closet. The pistol was gone, and so were two of my credit cards. I guess it was about three weeks ago when this happened."

"Mrs. Anderson, did you contact the authorities?" Detective Hendrix asked.

"No, I sure didn't, after realizing I probably didn't lock my front door the day I went to my sister's house. I did cancel the credit cards that were stolen from me."

"Mrs. Anderson, can you remember what that car looked like?" Detective Johnson asked. "I mean can you remember the color, make, model, or whether it looked new or old?"

"It was an older car, light-blue in color and it had a cracked window on the driver's side." Randy was busy writing down her description of the car in question.

"Mrs. Anderson, you have been a great deal of help to us," Detective Johnson remarked. "If everything works out okay, how would you like to get that gun back?"

"I wouldn't want it back, my knowing that it had killed two people. Dispose of the gun after all the legal activity has been completed. I would feel better knowing that the murder weapon had been destroyed."

"Mrs. Anderson was a very nice lady," said Marcus, as they headed toward Alex Rodgers house.

"Yes, she certainly was," Randy answered. "I sensed that she was still grieving over her husband. "Maybe one day she'll find herself another man that will love her and help fill the void in her life. For a long time I was in her shoes. It's ironic that it took a murder for me to find the right woman for me. What about you, Marcus? You're a middle age, single man. Why haven't you found yourself a good woman to love and share your life with?"

"I just haven't found the right woman like you have."

"Marcus, we just left a woman about your age. She's very attractive and all alone in that big old house. Perhaps you might need to go back to her house in the near future to express your gratitude for her helpful assistance in this murder investigation. I did notice that she seemed interested in you."

"You're crazy, Randy Johnson! That woman wouldn't be interested in me!"

"Well, there's one thing for sure-------you'll never know unless you go back to her house."

"I wouldn't know what to say to her. She may already have someone that she's interested in!"

"Marcus, do you think Mrs. Anderson was a good looking woman?"

"Yes, of course I do!"

"Do you think she would be the type of woman that you would be interested in?"

"Well-----yes, I believe so."

"I recommend that you go back to her house tomorrow. Tell her whatever you can to get her attention. Take your camera and ask her if you can take some pictures of her beautiful flower garden. Just be nice and carry on a conversation with her. Women, in general, are very smart. She'll know right away that you have some interest in her. You'll know very soon whether she shows some interest in you. She might invite you into her house for tea or coffee, and that's a very good sign."

"What if she invites me into her house for milk and cookies?" Marcus asked, smiling.

"In that case, go ahead and purchase an engagement ring," Randy commented. "I hope Alex Rodgers is home today. I can't be at his house too long today. I've got a dinner party scheduled for 6:30 this evening. I'm having Beth, Danny and Mr. and Mrs. Harry Spears over for dinner. I'm cooking big t-bone steaks on my grill this evening."

"Why did you have to mention the term 'big t-bone steaks' since I'm not invited for dinner?"

"Well, I could stop by the butcher store and pick up another t-bone steak," Randy remarked.

"I was just kidding. My parents are coming over to my house this evening. I might just do what you said concerning Mrs. Anderson. The more I think about her, the prettier she seems to get."

"Who knows, Marcus-----you might be just the guy she's been waiting for. Anyway, it's worth giving it a try. Well, we're at Alex Rodgers driveway. He might be home since I see a car parked at the side of his house."

"Randy, take a good look at that car," Marcus advised. "It's an older model car, and it's light-blue in color."

"Marcus, you're absolutely right! When we get up there we'll see if the vehicle has a cracked window on the driver's side." Randy stopped his car in front of Alex's front porch; when they exited their car, they looked toward the light-blue car. They both saw the cracked window on the driver's side of the car. When they got on the porch, Randy knocked on the door. They both heard footsteps inside the house, but no one answered the front door. Randy knocked on the door again; still there was no answer. "Alex Rodgers, you open this damn door or I'm going back to the office and get a search warrant to search your house!" Randy yelled out. "If you think I'm joking you'll be badly mistaken! Now, open this door! We need to talk with you!"

Finally, Alex opened his front door. "I thought someone was here to rob me; that's why I didn't open my door any quicker."

"Alex Rodgers, we're here to arrest you for stealing a gun out of Patricia Anderson's house about three weeks ago," Detective Johnson remarked.

"Are you crazy? I don't even know a woman named Patricia Anderson! Which house am I accused of stealing a gun from?"

"Mr. Rodgers, we've uncovered a great deal of information about you since the last time we were here," Randy commented.

"I don't have to say anything to you cops!"

"That may be so for now, but sooner or later we're going to find out about that gun you stole," Marcus commented.

"Put your hands behind your back!" Detective Johnson demanded. Alex did as he was asked. Detective Johnson quickly snapped the handcuffs on him. "Detective Hendrix, read him his rights."

"I can't believe you guys are arresting me for something that I didn't do." The two detectives remained quiet as Detective Johnson drove toward the county jail.

After Alex Rodgers was processed into the county jail, Randy and Marcus went to the sheriff's office. "How did it go with Mrs. Anderson?" Sheriff Hicks asked.

"She positively identified Alex Rodger's car as the one that was at her house the day her pistol was stolen," Randy answered. "Mrs. Anderson went to her sister's house the day that her pistol was taken. That would be about three weeks ago. Anyway, when she returned home she saw an older model car, light-blue in color and with a cracked window on the driver's side. That car was leaving her driveway as Mrs. Anderson was coming into her driveway. Alex Rodgers car fits the exact description that Mrs. Anderson gave us. There's no doubt in my mind that Alex Rodgers stole that gun so he could kill his step parents."

"I'm inclined to agree with you that he did kill both of them," said Sheriff Hicks. "Proving that he did may pose a big problem."

"There's something else, Sheriff Hicks. We arrested Alex Rodgers for unlawfully entering a dwelling without proper authorization and for stealing a handgun. We didn't mention a thing about him being the primary suspect in a double murder. I thought a couple days in lockup would make it much easier when we interrogate him concerning his step parent's murders."

"You had better be able to prove that he committed those murders rather quickly because a first year law student could get him out of jail on the charges you have filed against him," Sheriff Hicks remarked. "He could say his car was stolen on the day Mrs. Anderson said her gun was taken from her house. If I were you and Marcus, I would be right back here tomorrow morning doing a tough guy/nice guy routine on him. He just might slip up before he even realizes it. That will be your best bet; the present charges against him won't hold up at all when his lawyer gets here. He'll be out of jail and gone to where you may never find him."

Beth and Danny arrived at Randy Johnson's house at 6:15 that evening. Beth wanted to see if there was anything she could do to help Randy prepare for their steak dinner. Shelia answered the doorbell. "Hello Mrs. Miller, you too Danny------please come inside. Daddy is doing something in the backyard." Beth and Danny followed Shelia into the living room.

"Shelia, do you suppose there is anything I can do to help your father with the dinner?" Beth asked.

"We'll ask him when he comes into the house. That was very thoughtful for you to ask. Danny, why are you so quiet this evening? Have you had any bad dreams lately?"

"I was wondering where we'll be staying after Mother and Mr. Johnson gets married. The last bad dream I had was when you and I were at Grandpa's. That was one of the very worst dreams I've had. I hope I don't have any more dreams."

Randy walked into the room. "Beth, I'm delighted that you and Danny are having dinner with us tonight. Mr. Harry Spears and his wife will be here shortly. We're going to have a great dinner together!"

"Mr. Johnson, did you spray yourself with the garden hose?" Danny asked.

"No, but I did get a little wet fixing a water pipe in my backyard. That darn thing had been leaking for two or three days. I made up my mind to fix it once and for all." He walked over to Beth; he gave her a hug and a kiss. "There's just ten more days before our wedding. I'm very excited!"

"So am I," Beth answered. "Everything has been taken care of except for buying my wedding dress. I'm going to buy it this coming Wednesday."

"Mr. Johnson, I've been wondering-------where will we stay after you and Mother get married?" Danny asked.

"We'll discuss that very thing tonight after dinner."

"Randy, what can I do to help you prepare for dinner?" Beth asked.

"I would like for you to entertain Mr. and Mrs. Spears while I'm grilling our steaks. We're having t-bone steaks, salads, and large baked potatoes for dinner. I've got six kinds of dressing for our salads."

The doorbell rang five minutes later. Randy answered his door. "Mr. and Mrs. Spears, I'm delighted that you're joining us for dinner; please come inside. Beth Miller and her son are already inside." They followed Randy into the living room. "Beth, I'm sure you're well acquainted with these two nice people."

With a big smile on her face, Beth hugged each of their necks. "Yes, indeed I am. These are two of the nicest people that I know. Mr. Spears, since you married this nice lady, I haven't seen you a time without a smile on your face."

"Doris has been a wonderful wife to me, Mrs. Miller. She and I are totally compatible and we enjoy doing things and going places together. I'm very happy being married to her."

"By the same token, Harry Spears is the kind of man I wanted to spend the rest of my life with," Doris remarked.

"If everyone will excuse me, I'll go outside and cook our t-bone steaks," Randy commented.

A few minutes later, Mr. Spears said, "If everyone doesn't mind, I'll go outside and see how Randy is coming along with our steaks."

The aromatic smell of freshly cooked meat was already in the air when Harry Spears stepped out on the porch. "I came to see how you were doing."

"Mr. Spears, these steaks are coming along just fine. How do you and your wife like your steaks cooked?"

"Doris likes hers well done. I like mine about medium well done. I haven't mentioned to Mrs. Miller the main reason that Doris and I are here. I sure hope she doesn't get upset when she finds out what you and I have been talking about."

"Trust me, Mr. Spears; I really believe Beth and Danny will really like my idea."

After everyone had finished their meal, they retired to the living room. "Mr. Johnson, you're to be congratulated for such a fine meal," Mrs. Spears commented. "My steak and baked potato were perfect, and so was that delicious salad I had. I believe you had available about every kind of dressing that a grocery store sells. It was very nice of you to invite us for dinner."

"She's absolutely right," Mr. Spears responded. "Everything was just perfect!"

"Mr. Spears, there's a rumor going on that I might be losing my favorite neighbors. I hope it isn't true that you and your wife will be moving to the beach. Until now, I've been very hesitant to inquire about the rumor."

"Beth, that rumor is correct," Randy answered. "Mr. Spears, if you don't mind I'll try to explain to my future bride why we're all together this evening. Beth, I don't want you to be angry with me for what I'm about to say. The very minute that I heard about Mr. Spears and his wife moving to the beach, I gave Mr. Spears a call. I asked him if he was going to sell that big house he lives in. He told me that he was going to sell it. I asked him if I could come over and see the house. He told me that would be just fine. When I got to his house, I was amazed at everything that I saw inside. He's got six bedrooms, four and a half bathrooms. The enormous sized master bedroom has two bathrooms, his/hers. Beth, you've been inside his house several times, so you know how it looks. I'm being asked all the time by Shelia and Danny about where we're going to live. You don't have to make up your mind this evening, but would you consider us buying their house. We could put both our houses on the market, and then pay Mr. Spears the price he's asking for his house."

"Mr. Spears, when are you and your wife moving?" Beth asked.

"We're moving at the end of this week. I own a home on the sound side of the beach. The movers will take most of our things to the beach in four days from now. Doris is retiring from her work in two more days."

"Randy, I love their house, but this is such a shock to me right now. If they do agree to sell us their house, how would we be able to pay for it before we sell our houses?"

"Mrs. Miller, I've already told Mr. Johnson that I wouldn't expect any money from either of you until you and he have sold your houses. You're one of my very dearest friends, and I really am not in a hurry for payment of my house. If you want my house-----you can get it. I can't think of anyone that I rather have living there."

"Beth, I've got twenty-five thousand dollars that I would be willing to pay toward the purchase of their house right now. Mr. Spears just said that we could pay the remainder after we sell our houses," Randy remarked.

"Mother, please say yes!" Danny begged. "Mr. Spears has a swimming pool, Koi fish pond, and a tennis court in his backyard. He's, also, got a three-car garage, and two large storage buildings.

"Mrs. Miller, it will be your decision, but Daddy really does like that house," Shelia commented.

"Mrs. Spears, you must like the beach a great deal," said Beth.

"I love the beach, Mrs. Miller. I've often dreamed about living on or near the beach."

"Mr. Spears, won't you even miss your beautiful home?" Beth asked.

"I really don't see why. You see-----I used the same house plans for my beach property as I did for my present house. The only difference will be that I won't have a tennis court and a Koi fish pond. However, I will miss my friends here very much. Doris and I will drive back here whenever we have to urge to visit everyone again."

"Harry, let's you and I go home so Mr. Johnson and Mrs. Miller can discuss what their plans are concerning your house. Mr. Johnson, thank you very much for our wonderful dinner," Mrs. Spears commented. "Shelia, Danny, it was very good seeing you this evening. I hope you both much happiness as time goes on."

Danny and Shelia gave Mrs. Spears a big hug. After that, they gave Mr. Spears a hug. "Mr. Spears, could Shelia and I go to the beach and visit with you and Mrs. Spears sometime?" Danny asked.

"You certainly can! In fact, I'll be expecting to see all of you at my beach house before too much longer."

After Mr. and Mrs. Spears left Randy's house, Beth sat silent on the couch as though she was worried about something. Randy asked Shelia and Danny if they would go to another room to play games or watch television. Afterwards, Randy placed his arms around Beth's neck. "Beth, are you mad with me for doing what I did concerning Mr. Spears house? If you are, I'm very sorry for not including you in my plans. Sweetheart, I wanted everything to be a big surprise for you. Oh, my goodness------you've got tears in your eyes! Beth, please forgive me! I love you very, very much, and it hurts me terribly to see you sad!

"Randy, I'm not mad with you. The shock of knowing that Mr. Spears and his wife are moving makes me very sad."

"What about their house, Beth-----do you like the idea of us acquiring that big house?"

"Yes Randy, I've often wished that I owned that big house. Since you're paying twenty-five thousand dollars down on the house, I'll pay a matching amount. That way after our houses are sold, we'll have already paid fifty-thousand dollars toward the purchase of our new home." Randy wiped a tear from his eye as he leaned toward Beth. He kissed her twice on her lips. "Why the sad look?" Beth asked.

"I've been very worried that you might be mad with me concerning my plans for our new home. Thank goodness you're not! Beth, tell me something-----why did Mr. Spears have such a large house built since he and his previous wife never had any children?"

"Mr. Spears thought that they were going to have several children, but that never happened. Randy, there is just one small thing."

"What's that?"

"Don't ever plan major decisions again without involving me with the planning!"

"I promise I won't ever do that again!"

Chapter 22.

At 9:30 the following morning, Detectives Randy Johnson and Marcus Hendrix were already inside the interrogation room when Alex Rodgers was brought in for questioning. "My lawyer will be here this afternoon!" Alex said, loudly. "I'm thinking about suing each one of you!"

"You sit your ass down in a chair right now!" Detective Johnson sounded. "You will definitely need a lawyer when we're through with you today."

"Detective Johnson, let's try not to be too rough on Mr. Rodgers," said Detective Hendrix. "After all, he has been rather cooperative with us."

"You had better listen to your buddy," responded Alex, "I may not sue him, but I'm going to fix you good!"

Detective Johnson stood up, "I'm going to bash your head in if you say one more threatening word to me!"

"Mr. Rodgers, excuse us for a moment," said Detective Hendrix, "I need to talk with my partner outside. I want to see if I can calm him down a little." They both stepped out of the room for a couple minutes. "Randy, you're doing great. I'm going back in for about ten minutes. After that, I want you to come back in. I'm hoping I can get him to slip up somewhere during the interrogation."

"That will be fine. I'll be observing you and him through the one way window". Detective Johnson had no intention of leaving that window until he got the sign from his partner to come back in.

Detective Hendrix went back inside the interrogation room. "I told my partner to stay outside until he cooled off a bit."

"I'm glad you did. He was about to get on my nerves."

"Mr. Rodgers, there is one little bit of evidence that needs to be cleared up."

"What evidence is that?"

"It's about the Smith & Wesson pistol that we got from Zachary Jones. It definitely had Mr. Jones fingerprints on the gun. Also, it had your fingerprint on the gun as well. How could that be since you never touched the gun?" Alex seemed to be in shock that he had left a fingerprint on the gun. "Mr. Rodgers, did you understand my question? I'm sure there's a logical explanation as to why that is."

"Are you absolutely sure it was my fingerprint on that gun?"

"Oh, definitely so, it was checked for authenticity several times. There's no doubt about it being your fingerprint. Now, with that evidence and an eye witness that saw you and your car leaving the house where the gun was stolen-------well, you see my point. I'm afraid people will start believing that you used that same gun to kill your step parents. You certainly wouldn't want people to start thinking that, would you?"

"Okay! Okay, I did take the gun, but I didn't kill my step parents! I admit that I stole the gun! I thought I wiped away all my fingerprints. Wait a minute, where did they find my fingerprint?"

"Believe it or not, you left your fingerprint on the butt of the gun. I guess you forgot to wipe it there."

"How could I have been so stupid?" Alex mumbled. "Anyway, I certainly didn't kill my step parents!" Detective Johnson came back into the room.

"Have you cooled off a little?" Detective Hendrix asked his partner.

"I'm okay now. I've been at the vending machine. Would you believe that darn thing now requires a dollar and fifty cents for a soft drink? What have you found out since I've been gone?"

"Mr. Rodgers has admitted to stealing the Smith & Wesson gun from Mrs. Anderson's house, but he said that he didn't kill his step parents. I'm inclined to believe that he didn't kill them, unless he can't tell us why he wanted to steal that gun, or why he wanted to remove his fingerprints from the murder weapon. Detective Johnson, let's you and I step outside for about five minutes so Mr. Rodgers can gather his thoughts concerning those two matters that I just mentioned."

"I need a cigarette," Alex stated. "Do either of you have a cigarette on you?"

Detective Hendrix pulled out a small drawer from the table. He picked up a pack of cigarettes. "Is this your brand?"

"They're fine. I'll smoke anything at the present time. Would you happen to have a light?" Alex asked.

"I carry a lighter with me all the time," said Detective Hendrix. "You never know when one of my friends might need a light." After lighting Alex's cigarette, the detectives left the room.

"Marcus, you were outstanding in there!" Detective Johnson said. "I'm surprised that Alex fell for that lie you told about his fingerprint being on the gun. You know darn well that his fingerprint wasn't on that gun."

"Well, he didn't know that, but that did get him to admit stealing the gun," said Detective Hendrix. By the way, since when did our vending machine start charging a buck and a half for a soft drink?"

"I was kidding about that," Detective Johnson answered. "I didn't want Mr. Rodgers thinking I was listening in on yours and his conversation. I believe you've got him on the ropes right now."

"I believe you're right, Randy. Until a few minutes ago we couldn't prove that he actually stole that pistol from Mrs. Anderson's house. We'll both question him now rather hurriedly. We won't give him much time to think about his answers."

The detectives returned to the interrogation room. "Mr. Rodgers, we're going to ask you a few questions, and we want straight forward answers," Detective Johnson remarked. "The first one is this, why did you steal that gun from Mrs. Anderson's house. Were you planning to kill someone with it?"

"Okay, I'll be honest with you," said Alex, "I happened to see her drive out of her driveway as I passed her house. I stopped down the road about a half mile away; I started wondering if she had anything worth stealing inside her house. I turned my car around, and then I drove back to her house. I knocked on the door, but no one came to answer it. That's when I picked the lock to get inside. All I was going to steal was some jewelry and maybe a few dollars, but I saw the pistol inside one of her desk drawers. I got the pistol and quickly left the house. I drove out of her driveway before anyone could see me."

"I believe you're telling us a fib about the whole thing!" Detective Johnson voiced. "First of all, Mrs. Anderson saw you coming out of her driveway in the late afternoon, not the morning. Also, her pistol was not kept in a bureau drawer; you got it from inside her clothes closet. In her clothes closet was some jewelry and at least fifty dollars in plain sight. You went there purposely to find a handgun so you could shoot your step parents!"

"You're wrong! I didn't kill them!"

"Let me ask you this, Mr. Rodgers-------have you ever owned an Oak Leaf shotgun?" Detective Johnson asked.

"Why are you asking me that? What has a shotgun to do with someone being killed with a pistol?"

"You once told your step parents that you went to a lot of trouble to get that gun," said Detective Hendrix. "What did you mean by that? In other words, what trouble did you go through in order to get the shotgun? We've been told that you stole that shotgun."

"You all are getting me all confused about everything! It's hard to think when I'm being asked one question after another."

"You stole that shotgun from a man with the last name of Spears," Detective Hendrix remarked. "We, also, know that you threatened your step parents life when they were about to sell the gun to the owner's son. You threatened to kill them, Mr. Rodgers! We have someone that will testify in court that you threatened to kill them in his presence! Things are closing in on you, Mr. Rodgers. They're closing fast!"

"You guys are fishing for straws! You can't prove I killed somebody!"

"I wouldn't be too sure of that, Mr. Rodgers," Detective Johnson sounded. "We know about the two-hundred and fifty thousand dollars of life insurance that you took out on each of your step parents. You took out the life insurance a little over two years ago; ten days over to be exact! You planned the eventual murder of your step parents over two years ago!"

"It was Zachary Jones that killed my step parents, I tell you! He had the murder weapon in his possession, not me!"

"You thought you were being pretty smart when you placed the murder weapon underneath that five-gallon bucket," Detective Johnson commented. "You knew good and well that Zachary Jones would use that bucket to gather pears for his wife. You're not getting one dime of that life insurance money because the names on the insurance forms are forged by you. Johnny and Mildred Rodgers wouldn't sign for you to get a penny from their deaths! The only thing you're going to get is a death sentence when you face twelve jurors in a court of law. However, there is one way around a death sentence."

"What are you talking about?" Alex asked.

"Well, for starters------we've got enough evidence against you to ensure a speedy trial and a death sentence for you. If, however, you admit that you killed your step parents I'm sure that we can convince the District Attorney to spare you from a death sentence. You better make up your mind quickly because when we walk out of here with all the evidence we have against you-----the offer no longer exists. You'll be strapped down on a hard table while you're observing someone ready a needle with something that will drain you of life! Your mind will be in a whirlwind realizing that you only have less than two minutes to live!"

"Okay! Okay! I'll confess! I killed my step parents! I don't want to be strapped down on a table and have poison pumped into my veins! I'll tell you everything! Just don't let them kill me the way you just described!"

"Everything that was said in this room has been recorded," Detective Johnson remarked. "We'll do all we can to prevent you from being executed." Alex Rodgers seemed totally confused, him shaking his head back and forth in total disbelief as a guard took him back to his cell.

The detectives were all smiles as they walked out of the room. They hurried into Sheriff Hick's office.

"That was the most brilliant interrogation I've ever seen!" Sheriff Hicks remarked. "I watched the whole thing on my television screen in my office. You two solved a robbery and a double murder in one sitting in the interrogation room. I want you both to know that I'm very proud of you both. Another thing, I'll remember this when our promotion cycle comes around again! I'm so doggone pleased with you that I'm going to let both of you off for the remainder of the day and tomorrow as well. Of course, that's only if another murder doesn't occur during that time."

Randy and Marcus walked outside of the building. "Well, I'm going to see a real estate agent today," said Randy. "Marcus, what are you going to do for the rest of the day?"

"The first thing I'm going to do is go see Mrs. Patricia Anderson. The more I think about that woman the more I like her."

"What are you going to tell her?"

"Randy, I don't have the slightest clue as to what I might say to her."

"Well, you could start off by telling her that the information she gave us helped solve a double murder."

"Yes, I could tell her that," Marcus commented. "At least that will give me an opening. Do you have any other suggestions as to what I can say to her?"

"I'm no expert on these kind of matters, but you might tell her that she has a beautiful flower garden, and that you would like very much to see it again. Marcus, you'll be able to determine right off if she's interested in you. The main suggestion I'll give you is this------just be yourself and don't pretend to be someone that you're not. Women can readily sense when a man is faking who he really is."

Marcus Hendrix had never been as nervous as he was forty-five minutes later as he turned into Patricia Anderson's driveway. He started one time to back out of her driveway before she saw him there. He had two different forces urging at the same time. One was telling him to drive away very quickly; the other one was telling him to ring Patricia's doorbell. He took in a deep breath of air and then he exhaled. With a great deal of apprehension, Marcus exited his car. Nervously, he rang Mrs. Anderson's doorbell. Hearing someone walking toward the door made him feel even more nervous. The door opened and Marcus saw Patricia Anderson standing in her doorway. "Yes, may I help you?" She asked.

"Mrs. Anderson, I'm Detective Marcus Hendrix."

"Yes, I remember you. You came here with another detective. Please come inside my house."

Marcus felt a little relieved since he had overcome the first obstacle of getting into her home. She led him to her living room. "Please have a seat." She sat down across from him. "I guess you're back here to ask me some more questions about my late husband's gun."

"Not really. I came back here to tell you that you helped us solve a double murder."

"My goodness, how on earth did I accomplish that?" She asked, her smiling.

"You gave us accurate description of the car that you saw drive out of your driveway the day your gun was stolen. The owner of that car is in our jail right now charged with robbery and murder."

"Well, I'm very pleased to hear that. Is there something else I can do for you?"

"Yes, Mrs. Anderson, there surely is! You've got a magnificent flower garden and I was wondering if you would mind my seeing it again."

"Oh, Heavens no-----I would be happy to show you all of flowers. I didn't realize that you were a lover of flowers. We can go out through my back entrance." Marcus followed her until they were in her backyard.

"Mrs. Anderson, I have never seen so many beautiful rose bushes in my life," Randy commented. "You must have every variety of rose bushes that exist in your flower garden."

"Oh no, there are lots of varieties that I don't have."

"Do all these rose bushes have names?"

"Yes, of course they do. In my yard I have floribunda, hybrid tea, grandiflora, ballerina and care free wonder rose bushes."

"Nothing is prettier than a beautiful flower, except perhaps a beautiful woman like you."

"My gracious, I'm very flattered that you would say that about me," Mrs. Anderson remarked.

"To tell you the truth, I told my partner that you were a very beautiful lady."

"You told him all that!"

"Yes, I certainly did! Mrs. Anderson, I've never been married in my entire life. I know I shouldn't say this, but I just had to come back today and see you once again. There, I said it! I'll leave before I get run off your property." Marcus turned around with his head lowered; he started walking toward his car."

"Detective Hendrix, wait a minute," Mrs. Anderson remarked. She walked to where Marcus was standing. "How would you like a glass of tea with me inside my kitchen?"

"Mrs. Anderson, I would be greatly thrilled to have tea with you." Marcus followed her to her house, and then onto her kitchen.

"Please have a seat at my kitchen table while I make us some tea," Mrs. Anderson commented." A few minutes later, she poured him and herself some freshly made tea. She took a seat across from him. "Mr. Hendrix, I'm glad you stopped by here today."

"May I ask why?" Marcus asked, curiously.

"I've gone through a long mourning period since my husband passed away. I've hardly had a decent life since then. I have no need to seek employment because my husband left me very well off. I've been spending a great deal of my time tending to my flowers and keeping my house neat and clean. However, being in this house alone all day, day after day, has taken a toll on me. I really need to go places, do things, and get on with my life. Maybe a good place to start with those plans is for you and me to get less formal with names. My name is Patricia. May I call you Marcus?"

"Yes, that would please me very much. Patricia is a beautiful name. Mrs. Anderson, oh, I meant to say Patricia. Would you consider going to dinner with me one evening?"

"Yes, I would be delighted to accompany you on a dinner date."

"Patricia, my heart is beating faster than usual because I'm so thrilled that I hardly know what to do!"

"When would you care for this dinner date to happen?" Patricia asked.

"How about having dinner with me this evening?" Marcus asked, excitedly.

"That is pretty fast, but I' m willing to do that if I have enough time to get dressed. Where do you think we'll be going?"

"If it's okay with you, I'll pick you up at seven o'clock this evening. That should give you ample time to prepare for our dinner date. Patricia, do you have a favorite restaurant that you like to eat at?"

"It really doesn't matter to me where we go, but my favorite place to eat is the Lantern Inn Steakhouse."

"That's exactly where we'll go," said Marcus. "Patricia, I can guarantee that you'll never be sorry for going on a dinner date with me! I'm going now, but I'll be here at seven o'clock this evening. My, oh my, I can hardly wait to tell my partner that I'm going out with one of the prettiest ladies in the entire county!" Marcus shook Patricia's hand before leaving her house.

He turned his radio on as he drove out of her driveway. He felt like he had overcome a monumental task in getting her to go on a dinner date with him. "Man, oh man, I can hardly wait for this evening to arrive!" Marcus mumbled.

As he had promised, Marcus Hendrix was back at Patricia Anderson's house at 7:00 that evening. Patricia answered the doorbell. "My, oh my, you look beautiful, Patricia!" Marcus stated.

"You look exceptionally well yourself, Marcus. Your blue suit is one of my favorite colors. Please come inside." Marcus followed her into her living room. "Please have a seat; I'll be ready to go in two or three minutes. Did you tell your detective friend that you and I were going on a dinner date?"

"Yes, I certainly did! He was as surprised as I was earlier today. He was already aware that I liked you the first minute I saw you. Patricia, I can't tell you how excited I am to just be with you!"

"I wonder why that is?"

"I can't answer that, but I know how my feelings are toward you."

Thirty minutes later, Marcus and Patricia were sitting at a table inside the Lantern Inn Steakhouse. "You selected a very nice place for us to have dinner," said Marcus.

"Thank you. Just wait until you try one of their steaks. I eat here once every week or two and I've never had a bad steak here."

"I know one thing, I like the songs that the Disc jockey is playing," Marcus remarked. "Patricia, do you enjoy dancing?"

"Yes, I enjoy slow dancing very much. I'm not too keen on rock and roll type music."

"Would you dance with me now?"

"It would be my pleasure." Marcus took her hand and they walked gracefully toward the dance floor. He held her left hand in his; he placed his right arm around her waist and they began to dance to the sound of the music. "Marcus Hendrix, you're a very good dancer!"

"I was about to say the same thing about you. I hope you'll give me many more dinner dates in the weeks and months ahead."

"So far, I see no reason why I shouldn't do just that," Patricia answered, smiling.

Chapter 23

It was Thursday evening, Beth and Danny Miller were sitting at their dinner table. Beth had a great deal on her mind since her wedding was only three days away. She and Randy Johnson would be getting married Sunday at four o'clock at Grayson Baptist Church. She had been looking forward to this day for some time. Her wedding rehearsal was scheduled for Saturday evening at five o'clock. "Mother, what are you thinking about?" Danny asked. "You've hardly touched your food."

"I'm sorry, I was just thinking about my wedding."

"You don't look too happy about it."

"You're wrong about that, Danny. I'm looking forward to becoming Randy Johnson's wife, but-----."

"But----what, Mother?"

"I had a dream last night that has been weighing heavy on my mind."

"What kind of dream did you have?"

"I dreamed that your father came to our house last night with twelve long-stemmed roses in his hand. He told me that he loved me very much and that he would always love me. He was about to kiss me, but I suddenly awoke from my dream." Tears came into Beth's eyes.

"I've already told you that Daddy wants you to marry Mr. Johnson! He wants you to have a lot of happiness in your life! You can't back out on Mr. Johnson now! That wouldn't be fair to him, Shelia or me! I'm tired of living in a broken family! I need him in my life-----Shelia as well!"

"Danny, I didn't say I wasn't going to marry Randy. My dream came at an awkward time, especially with me getting married in three more days. I wonder why I had that dream."

"I have dreams all the time, but they're not real. If they were, I would already be dead! I thought you were in love with Mr. Johnson."

"I am. I love him very much. My dream will not have an impact on our getting married."

"For goodness sakes, that dream has already had an impact on you getting married! I believe you're having second thoughts about the whole thing!"

"Danny, that's not true. Anyway, let's talk about something else. Look out the window at Mr. Spears' vacant house. He and Doris are gone now, as well as all their belongings. Mr. Spears gave Randy and me two sets of keys to his house. He left three bags of fish food inside a utility barn. We need to go over and feed his Koi fish."

"Let's go over there now," Danny commented. "Another thing, why can't we start moving our stuff over to our new house?"

"Well, I guess we could," Beth answered. "Let's walk over there and feed the fish. While we're there we can explore the house. In fact, I've never seen inside the house in its entirety."

"Okay, let's go now." As they got up, their doorbell rang. Danny hurried to answer the door.

"Hello Danny," said Mr. Johnson," is your mother at home?"

"Yes sir, she's probably in the living room by now. Please come inside. Shelia, I'm very glad that you came with your father."

"Thank you, Danny. We came over to see our new home. Would you and your mother like to walk across the yard with us?"

"What a coincidence!" Danny responded. "Mother and me were about to go over there. You can help me feed the fish."

"Oh, I would love to do that."

Randy noticed that Beth had tears in her eyes. He placed his arms around her waist. "Beth, is something wrong?"

"I'm fine; just hold me for a little while. Danny and I were about to go see our new home when you rang the doorbell."

"That's why Shelia and I came over. I think we should start taking some things over there before our wedding this Sunday."

"Danny just said the same thing. Let's go over there and see what kind of cleaning might be needed before we take anything over there. Did Mr. Spears accept our fifty thousand dollar deposit on the house?"

"He didn't, but his lawyer did for him. I've got copies of the legal agreement in my desk at home. My realtor has already got a for sale sign in my yard. When will you have your sign put up?" Randy asked.

"It's being put up tomorrow. I happened to get the same realtor as you. Maybe both houses can be sold in a close proximity of each other."

"That sounds very good," Randy commented. "Okay, let's all go over to our new home."

Danny and Shelia fed the fish while Randy and Beth explored the house. "How many fish did you count, Danny?" Shelia asked.

"I've counted them three times and I've gotten a different count each time. My first count was twenty-seven, and then it was twenty-four and my last count was twenty-eight. They move around so much it's hard to count them. Well, that should be enough feed for them today, let's go inside and explore that big house."

"Randy, this big room is the master bedroom," said Beth. "On each side of the room are two large bathrooms. The blue one can be yours and the pink one will be mine. What are you looking at?"

"I'm looking at the area where our bed will be located?"

"Why is that so important to you?"

"Sweetheart, you'd have to be a man to understand why a bed is so important to them. The bedroom will always be my favorite room in the house."

"Randy Johnson, there's a lot more to marriage than sex," Beth responded.

"That's very true, but without it there would be no marriage at all." He smiled.

"I can't believe the man that I'm about to marry is a sex addict."

"Beth, that's not true. I'm a normal man with normal feelings. Not once have I tried to entice you to do something that should only been done after two people are married. Isn't that true?"

"Yes, that's true. I have a great deal of respect for you not trying to have your way with me. In fact, we might not be getting married if you had."

"Why did you have tears in your eyes when I arrived at your house?"

"Randy, I rather not say anything about that. I just want you to know that I love you dearly, and I can hardly wait to become your wife."

Randy placed his arms around her waist, and then kissed her gently on her lips.

"What about this, Shelia-----our parents can't wait until they go on their honeymoon?" Danny smiled.

"Oh, my goodness," Beth sounded. "How long have you kids been standing there?"

"It might not do for us to say."

"Danny Miller, you tell me this instant-----how long have you and Shelia been standing there?" Beth asked, feeling embarrassed.

"Mrs. Miller, we just came upstairs," Shelia remarked. "We've been at the fish pond except for the last few seconds. This must be yours and Daddy's bedroom. Danny, let's go find ourselves a bedroom that we like." They ran down the hallway.

"I was about to have a heart attack thinking they overheard our conversation," Beth commented. "Randy, I'm very pleased that you talked Mr. Spears into letting us acquire this house. After we see everything up here, I want to go downstairs and see the kitchen again. It's so big; I'll have difficulty filling up the cabinets with our kitchenware. From what I've seen so far we won't need to do any prior cleaning before moving our stuff inside. He must have hired a cleaning crew to clean the entire house."

"Mrs. Miller, Danny and I have chosen our bedrooms, but there's still three left," said Shelia. "I had no idea that this house was this big. Would you and Daddy like to see our bedrooms? "Of course, we would. Randy, let's you and I go see the bedrooms that our teenagers have chosen."

Danny and Shelia ran ahead of Beth and Randy. "Okay, this is my room," Shelia remarked, happily. "How do you like it?"

"It's a beautiful room," Randy answered. "I know one thing; you'll have plenty of room in here for your things."

"Mrs. Miller, do you like my room?"

"Sweetheart, it's a gorgeous room! I'm certain that you'll enjoy your time in this room."

"Okay, let's go see Danny's bedroom," Shelia suggested. They walked down the hall to his bedroom.

"Mr. Johnson, how do you and Mother like my bedroom? Look, I've got a large bathroom, same as Shelia.

"It's very nice, Danny," said Mr. Johnson.

"Mother, how do you like my room?"

"You've got yourself a beautiful room, Danny. I love the blue colors and the animal paintings on the wall."

"Mr. Johnson, when will we start living in this house?" Danny asked.

"We'll start living here soon after your mother and I return from our honeymoon."

"Daddy, where are you two going on your honeymoon?"

"Sweetheart, only Beth and I know about that. However, I can tell you that we'll be gone for seven days."

"What if we need to get up with you and Mrs. Miller?"

"Mr. George Eason will know how to contact us."

"Where will I stay for a whole week?" Shelia asked.

"Randy, Shelia could stay with Danny at my father's farm while we're gone." Beth suggested. "They enjoyed her visit when she was there before."

"Please-----Daddy! I love being on their farm! Danny will look after me, won't you Danny?"

"I sure will, Mr. Johnson! I won't let anything happen to her!"

"I suppose that will be okay, but my Aunt Mable was looking forward to Shelia staying with her while we're on our honeymoon."

"Daddy, I don't want to stay with her! There's nothing to do there, except sit in the house all day and watch her sew or crochet!"

"Okay, it's settled-----Danny and Shelia will be at Mr. Eason's farm while we're away." Beth remarked.

All four of them were sitting in Beth's living room an hour later. They had been discussing various things concerning their recently acquired home. Danny raced to the phone when it rang. He picked up the receiver and listened for a several seconds. "Mother, its Mr. Spears on the phone. He wants to talk to you."

Beth hurried to get the phone from Danny. "Hello, is that you, Mr. Spears?"

"Yes, I wanted to tell you something, but first----have you looked into my garage yet?"

"Yes, we all have. You have a new looking bass boat and some archery equipment inside your garage."

"Yes, that's true," Mr. Spears answered. "Mrs. Miller, I'm very sorry to say that I won't be able to attend your wedding Sunday."

"I'm very sorry to hear that, Mr. Spears," Beth answered. "I hope you and your wife are not sick or anything."

"No, neither of us is sick, but we will be out of the country on your wedding day. Mrs. Miller,

Doris and I are going on a six country tour starting tomorrow morning. We both apologize for not attending your wedding, but the opportunity for this trip came up suddenly."

"Mr. Spears, I hope you and your lovely wife have a wonderful time during your travels. How long will you be gone?"

"Almost two months. There are two more reasons that I made this call to you. My wedding gift for you and Mr. Johnson is my new bass boat that's in the garage of your new house."

"Mr. Spears, I couldn't possibly accept such an expensive gift like that!" Beth responded.

"I want you to listen to me, and listen well! Doris and I have already agreed to give you and your future husband that boat. I've already had the title changed into Mr. Randy Johnson's name. It will be yours and his boat. He'll be getting the new title in the mail very soon. Now, the third reason I called is to let you know that there's two sets of archery equipment sitting in the right corner of the garage. There's a set for a male and another set for a female. I want Danny and Shelia to have that archery equipment."

Tears came into Beth's eyes. "Mr. Spears, I really don't know what to say about all this."

"You don't have to say anything. I want you and your family to enjoy those things that I have given you. Beth, no matter where Doris and I travel, you and your family will always be on our minds. Oh, my goodness-----I almost forgot the most important reason that I called. You and Mr. Johnson can use my house at the beach during your honeymoon. There's one of the bedrooms that has never been used. You can't miss it because it's more than a bedroom; it's like a suite, very big, and light-blue in color. Anyway, it's just a thought. My house key will be placed underneath a sizeable rock near my front porch. It won't cost you a dime to spend as much time there as you please."

"I appreciate the offer, Mr. Spears," said Beth. "I'll talk it over with Randy. Thank you from the bottom of my heart for your wedding gift, and for the archery equipment for Danny and Shelia. I hope you have a wonderful time, and don't forget to take a lot of pictures to show us."

Beth had tears in her eyes when she rejoined the others. "Beth, what's wrong?" Randy asked.

"There's nothing wrong. I just got through talking to one of the nicest people that I have ever met."

"What did Mr. Spears have to say that brought you to tears?"

"Randy, that wonderful man has given us his brand new bass boat!"

"My God, he did what?" Randy asked, smiling.

"He's had the boat title changed into your name. We should be getting the new title in the mail in a few days. That's not all he gave us," Beth remarked, looking toward Shelia and Danny. They both stood up. "He has given each of you a complete set of archery equipment."

Danny and Shelia were very excited. "Mother, can Shelia and I take the archery equipment with us when we go to Grandpa's house? Danny asked, enthusiastically.

"I don't see why you can't. Just be sure that you don't shoot any of your grandfather's animals, or one of you."

"Mr. Johnson, now that you and mother have another fishing boat, when will you take Shelia and me fishing?"

"I'll plan to do that shortly after we return from our trip."

"Danny, how about you and Shelia sit on the porch swing for a few minutes," Beth remarked.

"Come on Shelia, they probably want to discuss their honeymoon plans," said Danny, smiling.

Randy waited for the door to close behind Danny and Shelia. "You need to tell me something."

"Yes, but I didn't want to tell you in front of our children. Mr. Spears and his wife are leaving in the morning for a six nation tour. They'll be gone for two months. Mr. Spears said that we could use his house for our honeymoon if we wanted to. I know you've already made plans, but staying at his house won't cost us one penny. Also, it's on the sound side of the beach. It can't be too far from that seafood place where you and I ate that delicious seafood."

"Hello beach, here we come," said Randy, happily. "I'll call the other place tonight and cancel my reservation. I can hardly wait to spend seven days and nights with the woman that I love!"

"I hope our honeymoon will take you down a notch or two," Beth remarked, smiling.

"We'll just have to see about that, won't we?" Randy boasted.

Chapter 24

Danny knocked on his mother's door the following morning at 7:20. "Mother, you need to get up! It's Friday, and you're going to be late for work."

"I'll be right out, Danny." Beth opened her room door. "Starting today, I'm on vacation for three whole weeks. I'll start breakfast in a few minutes. What would you like for breakfast?"

"I want bacon, eggs, rice and toast," Danny answered. "Mother, I want to ask you something."

"Okay, ask me whatever is on your mind."

"Promise me that you won't ever tell anyone what I'm about to ask you."

"I promise. Now what is your question?"

"Can Shelia still be my sister if I've kissed her already on her lips?" He asked, seriously.

"Well, yes and perhaps no------if you continue to kiss her like that you shouldn't consider her to be your sister. However, if you no longer kiss her like that, you and she can act as sister and brother. Danny, what else have you and Shelia been up to?"

"Mother, I swear on my Daddy's grave that we've only kissed each other. I know what you're referring to, and that didn't happen!"

"Okay, I believe you," Beth responded. "Why are you bringing this up now?"

"Well, I'm only thirteen years old now and I've got my whole life ahead of me. To just like one girl for years and years is something to think about. If she was my sister I could love her until the day I die."

"Danny, have you discussed your feelings with Shelia?"

"Not yet, but I probably will do that while we're at Grandpa's farm."

"Mother, do you suppose these feelings I've got is because I'm maturing some?"

"That's a very strong possibility, Danny. I thought you liked Shelia more than you could even describe."

"That's it----exactly. I do love her as much as ever, but in a different way. I really believe I want her as my sister, not my girlfriend. That way she can have other friends besides me. If she has another boyfriend I'll be watching him like a hawk! I would never let some boy slick talk my sister in doing something that she shouldn't do!"

"It will be interesting to see how Shelia feels when you explain all this to her," Beth commented.

At ten o'clock that morning, Beth told Danny that she needed to take care of some business. She told him that she would be back in an hour or so. Beth drove her car out of her driveway, and onto the main road. Before her marriage to Randy Johnson, Beth felt the needed to visit her husband's grave at Cedar Oaks Cemetery.

There was no one else at the cemetery when Beth drove into the parking lot. She sat in her car for several minutes, trying desperately to come up with the right words to say at her husband's gravesite. Finally, she exited her vehicle and then she walked slowly toward John's grave. She held a bouquet of flowers in her hand that she had bought at Mildred's Flower Shop on her way to the cemetery. Beth knelt down beside her husband's grave; she removed the older flowers from the flower pot and then placed the new flowers in it. She placed her hand on her husband's tombstone. "John, I really needed to come here today. As I told you before, I've met a very nice man that loves me a great deal. We're getting married this coming Sunday. Danny told me that you're happy that I have found someone to love and take care of me and your son. I hope Danny is right about that. The man I'm marrying cannot and will not be a replacement for you. No one on this earth could fill your shoes. When we were together, I loved you as much as any woman could love a man, but you're no longer here. I will always love the memories of you and the life we had together. I don't know if it's any comfort to you, but your son killed the man that killed you. Don't worry, it was in self defense. John, I hope one day that you and I can meet again in the afterlife. Until then I will cherish our wonderful memories together." With tears in her eyes, Beth walked toward her car.

Danny was standing on the porch when his mother drove into her driveway. He observed his mother carefully as she opened her car door, and then she walked slowly toward her house.

"Mother, I bet I know where you've been."

"How would you know that?"

"I'll bet you've been to Cedar Oaks Cemetery to square things with my daddy. I've already told you that he doesn't mind you marrying Mr. Johnson. My daddy was not a selfish man."

Beth placed her arms around Danny and said, "Quite often you seem to be much older than your years. Yes, I did drive to Cedar Oaks Cemetery. I felt like I should tell John that I was getting married Sunday. Guess what else I told him."

"Did you tell him that I shot and killed the man that killed him?".

"My goodness, Danny------how could you have known that?" Beth asked, curiously.

"It was just a guess. I didn't really know what you told him."

"I'm beginning to wonder about that." Beth remarked.

George and Dora Eason had just finished eating lunch. After Dora had done the dishes, they both went into their living room. "Dora, I think Beth's upcoming marriage to Randy Johnson is a very good thing, for them and those two kids."

"Yes, I totally agree. I surely did enjoy Shelia's visit with us. She's a very fine young lady. I can't wait until she can appropriately call me grandma. "Our daughter's wedding rehearsal is tomorrow afternoon. I'm glad that she found someone that she loves and he loves her."

"I wonder what Danny thinks about her marrying someone else?"

"He's thrilled that she's marrying Mr. Johnson. Beth told me that herself." Dora answered.

"Did you know that she's selling her house?"

"No George, I didn't know that. Why would she sell that nice house of hers?"

"You were at the grocery store when she called yesterday. She said she and Randy were going to sell their houses so they could buy that big house next to hers."

"You must be talking about Mr. Harry Spears' house," Dora remarked.

"That's the one."

"Where is Mr. Spears moving to?"

"He and his wife have already moved to the beach. Mr. Spears owns a house on the sound side of the beach." George stated. "You would never know it, but that man has a lot of money. I've often wondered why Danny doesn't visit his other grandparents. Do you think he loves them as much as he does us?""

"Heavens yes, George! You would have to be an idiot not to know why he prefers coming here instead of visiting his other grandparents.""

"Dora, are you saying I'm an idiot?"

"I'm not saying that at all. The reason he likes coming here more is because you've got a big farm and lots of animals. Danny loves his daddy's parents a great deal. They live in town and there's nowhere for Danny to roam around. Mr. Henry Miller takes Danny golfing sometimes, but he doesn't care that much for fishing and other outdoor activities. If the situation was reversed and his other grandparents had a big farm------well, you get my point."

"We'll soon acquire a granddaughter, what do you think about that?"

"I'm as thrilled as I can be about that!" Dora answered. "Shelia Johnson is a very pretty girl. I'm looking forward to her visiting us from time to time. I'll teach her how to sew, make quilts and things like that."

"Dora, a teen aged girl wouldn't be interested in doing some of those old timey things!"

"You just wait and see about that! I won't have a granddaughter of mine growing up without knowing how to sew something together!"

"How do you think Shelia and Danny will get along living under the same roof?" George asked.

"They've been brought up in a Christian environment; they'll do just fine."

"You reckon Randy and Beth will have more children?" George asked.

"What kind of question is that? How would I know what goes on in their bedroom?"

"Delores, you're not that old!" George remarked, smiling. "You know exactly what went on in our bedroom!"

"You talking like that, thank goodness no one is here, except for us! You're getting too old to have those kind of thoughts on your mind!"

"That's what you think!" George stated. "I ordered myself some action pills."

"What kind of action pills are you talking about?" Dora asked, inquisitively.

"When we go to bed tonight I'll introduce you to them." He remarked, smiling.

"George Eason, do you mean to tell me that you bought some of them sex pills I've seen advertised on television?"

"They're the ones."

"Do they really work?" She leaned forward with interest.

"I'll demonstrate their effectiveness tonight."

"My goodness, George---------what would our daughter think if she knew we were still doing that kind of stuff?" Dora asked.

"Well, I'm not going to tell her--------are you going to tell her?"

"I certainly am not!" She remarked. "What makes you think those pills will work?"

"I took one two hours ago. I can assure you that they work!"

Today would be a very exciting day for Beth Miller and Randy Johnson; it was Saturday, their wedding rehearsal was scheduled for 5 o'clock this evening. Beth had already packed her suitcases with all the clothes she would need during her honeymoon.

Randy Johnson had done the same with the clothes he would need. Randy cooked bacon, eggs, and rice for his and Shelia's breakfast. As they sat at the breakfast table, Randy noticed that Shelia seemed to have something on her mind. He observed her holding a glass of milk in her hand, but she wasn't drinking any of it. "Shelia, what's wrong? Aren't you glad that I'm getting married tomorrow?"

"I'm very glad that you're marrying Mrs. Miller."

"Well, why the sad expression on your face?"

"I was just thinking about Danny."

"Shelia, what about Danny?"

"Daddy, I still like him very much, but I'm not sure I want to be his girlfriend forever."

"What brought this on?"

"I don't see how we can continue being girlfriend/boyfriend when we're living in the same house. I just want Danny to be my brother. Daddy, is that all bad?"

"No sweetheart, I think that is a good thing that you feel that way. Brothers and sisters can love each other as long as they live. Have you told Danny about how you feel?"

"Not yet, but I will tell him at his granddaddy's farm."

"Tell me the truth, Shelia-----have you started liking some other boy?"

"Well, I like Tommy Lewis more than I used to."

"I thought you couldn't stand to be around that boy!"

"Daddy, Tommy has changed since you've seen him," said Shelia. "He doesn't even act the way he used to."

"Shelia, Danny Miller will black both that boy's eyes when he finds out that you're interested in Tommy Lewis!"

"I don't believe so, not after I have my talk with him," Shelia responded. "What time do we have to be at Grayson Baptist Church today for the wedding rehearsal?"

"Mrs. Amanda Phillips, our wedding director, wants all wedding participants to be at the church by five o'clock today."

"Daddy, will you still love me just as much after you're married as you do now?"

"What a fool question that is! Of course, I'll love you as much! Shelia, you're my daughter, I love you very, very much! Why would you even ask me a question like that?"

"You'll need to love Danny as well."

"That's true. I'll learn to love him just like he was my own son, but I'll still love you just as much as I do now. You see------I've got plenty of love to share with all my family."

"Do you think Mrs. Miller will ever love me like I was her very own daughter?" Shelia asked.

"She already loves you like you were her daughter."

"Daddy, I love Mrs. Miller like she was my own mother."

"That's very good, Sweetheart, we're going to be a very happy family."

At five o'clock that evening, all participants in Beth and Randy's wedding were at Grayson Baptist Church for their wedding rehearsal. Amanda Phillips, wedding director checked off each name to ensure the rehearsal was ready to begin. Mrs. Phillips briefed all participants concerning their places and when they should do certain things. "Ushers, I want you to remember that the groom's parents sit next to the aisle on the second row, to your right as you walk down the aisle. Parents of the bride sit on the second row, to your left. Other relatives can be seated directly behind the grandparents, respective of their kin. Ushers, have you got it straight as to what your functions are?" The ushers acknowledged that they all understood their duties. "Okay everyone, I believe we're ready for a dry run," Mrs. Phillips remarked. "Ushers, please escort family and guests to their rightful seats."

The rehearsal went like clockwork; all wedding participants were right on cue. Mrs. Phillips was exceedingly pleased how everyone did their part in the ceremony. "Mrs. Miller, I couldn't be more proud of everyone for a superb performance. If they do this well tomorrow evening I'll be so delighted!"

"Mrs. Phillips, you are planning to come to our wedding reception tomorrow evening, aren't you?" Beth asked.

"I don't see why I can't."

"Mrs. Miller, I met your parents before the rehearsal started," said Mrs. Phillips, "they seem like such nice people. I can tell you one thing-----they're very excited about you getting married. I believe they're already counting on more grandchildren and you're not even married yet." She laughed.

"Mrs. Phillips, I believe I overheard something about more grandchildren," Randy remarked.

"I was telling your future bride that her parents are very excited about her marrying you. I believe they're already counting on more grandchildren from you two."

"Mrs. Phillips, if it's left up to me we'll certainly make Beth's parents very happy in that regard."

"Don't pay any attention to him, Mrs. Phillips; I'll definitely have something to say about more children."

"Ladies and gentlemen, please give me your attention!" Mrs. Phillips voiced. "Everyone did extraordinary tonight during the rehearsal. I'm proud of each of you for doing your part during the ceremony. Tonight was a practice run, but tomorrow will be the real thing. No one, except us of course, will know or even care about the rehearsal. I'm confident that tomorrows wedding will be done perfectly. We owe Beth and Randy nothing less but our very best during tomorrow's ceremony. The wedding starts promptly at 4:00 tomorrow evening. I want all the wedding participants to be in this church by 3:10. Remember, one late arrival can affect the wedding. I'm looking forward to seeing all of you tomorrow evening."

Beth walked over to her parents. "Daddy, you and Mother can stay at my house tonight."

"Sweetheart, I appreciate the offer, but we've already rented a motel room for the tonight and tomorrow night." George answered. We don't need to be in your house the night before your wedding. You'll have enough on your mind without having to be concerned with us. Besides, I don't often get a chance to be in a motel with a woman." he grinned.

"Beth, your father hasn't changed a bit over the years. I thought when he got old and weary that he would slow down a bit, but he hasn't. He's all the time buying something to keep him young and healthy."

Randy walked over to where Beth and her parents were talking. "Mr. and Mrs. Eason, I'm looking forward to becoming a part of your family."

"We couldn't be more delighted," Dora responded. "Beth, you're marrying a very handsome man."

"Thank you, Mother. Randy is not only handsome, but he's also very sweet and well-mannered. It's ironic that I fell in love with the detective that investigated my husband's murder."

"Randy, did you ever find out who killed Mr. and Mrs. Johnny Rodgers?" George asked.

"Yes sir, we certainly did. Their step son, Alex Rodgers killed them both to collect insurance money."

George and Dora shook their heads in total disbelief that a step son could do that to someone that had clothed and fed him. "What ever happened to Zachary Jones, the man you originally thought was the killer?" George asked.

"It seems that Johnny Rodgers had a Will filed at the courthouse leaving his entire estate to Zachary Jones and his wife. However, if Alex Rodgers hadn't killed his step parents, he would have eventually inherited all their property. There is an irony to the whole thing. Mr. Johnny Rodgers net worth is fifty-thousand dollars more than the insurance that Alex had taken out on them. Alex will spend the rest of his life in prison. Zachary Jones and his family will spend the rest of their life living in Mr. Johnny Rodgers house with a lot of money to go with it."

"Mr. Johnson, someone should tell Alex Rodgers what a fool he was," Dora mentioned.

"I believe he already knows that, Mrs. Eason. It turns out that Mr. and Mrs. Rodgers had a lot of trust and respect for Zachary Jones and his wife."

Danny and Shelia hurried toward Danny's grandparents as they headed toward the door.

"Grandpa, did you and grandma know that Shelia is spending the week with us while Mother and Mr. Johnson are on their honeymoon?"

"Yes, your mother called us yesterday and gave us the good news." George answered. "Shelia, we're very excited that you'll be living with us for several days."

"Thank you, sir. I'm very excited about going back to your farm."

"Danny, won't you and Shelia miss a lot of school during this time?" Dora asked.

"No, Grandma, we're on school break during this time."

George and Delores Eason were eating breakfast at Lou's Diner, located in walking distance of their motel. They were eating buffet style at the nearly packed restaurant. "George, why do you keep smiling so much while you're eating?" Delores asked.

"I was thinking about last night."

"You should be ashamed of yourself-----you and those darn pills! I hardly got any sleep last night. You must have taken a double dose or something. George, what would people think if they knew you were taking those kinds of pills at your age?"

"I'm not going to tell anyone about my pills," George smiled. "I'm fairly sure you're not going to tell anyone."

"Heavens no, I wouldn't be able to look anyone in the face if they knew what we were doing in bed! Don't you think you're too old for such nonsense?"

"I may be too old, but a part of me is still active and raring to go," he laughed.

"Men, you're all alike! You're born with something on your mind and you can't ever get it off until you kick the bucket!"

"Amen to that!" George laughed.

Henry and Delores Miller were sitting at their breakfast table. "Henry, what are you thinking about?" Delores asked. "You look as though you've got something on your mind.

"I was just thinking about our son and how much he loved his family while he was living." Tears came into his eyes.

Delores got up; she placed her arms around his neck. "I miss him too, Henry. I remember telling him one time that he should sell his grocery store and do something else. He said, 'Mother, I enjoy what I'm doing. I wouldn't want to do anything else.'"

"Delores, don't cry. Here, take this napkin and wipe your eyes. I hardly mention anything about

John, but I think about him all the time. He didn't deserve to die the way he did. I'm glad Danny shot that man to death! I would have killed him myself had I known who he was!"

"Henry, I'm surprised that you're talking that way!" Delores commented. "No matter how much you worry yourself about John, he's not coming back! We cherish memories of our son, but life goes on. I want you to quit torturing yourself about John's death. Today is a special day for you and me. Beth is like a daughter to us; it's her wedding day and I'm not going to let anything affect my happiness for the occasion. Henry, have you noticed how much Danny favors his daddy?"

"Yes, I have. He looks a great deal like John."

"There you have it," said Delores. "We've still got an image of our son whenever we look at our grandson. Henry, always look at it that way."

"I had never thought about it like that. No matter how bad things get, you seem to bring out the bright side in all situations. I guess you know that I love you a great deal."

"Yes Henry, I've always known that. There is one other thing."

"What's that?" Henry inquired, his ears perked.

"You need to be with your grandson a lot more than you have been. Danny is thirteen years old now. You need to do something with him besides taking him to a golf course."

"I promise, Delores------I'll start spending more time with Danny."

Chapter 25

Randy Johnson was all smiles as he finished packing his suitcases with clothes and items he wanted to take on his honeymoon. Today was Sunday, his wedding day. Shelia was in her room filling her suitcase with clothes and accessories for her trip to Mr. George Eason's farm.

At Beth Miller's house, everything was very much the same. Beth had already packed her things for her trip, but she was doing a final inspection to determine if she had everything she needed. Danny's suitcase was already packed and ready to go. He had even brought the archery equipment from their new house and placed it inside his room. Danny had made up more than a dozen paper targets so he and Shelia would have something to shoot at with their bow and arrows.

Grayson Baptist Church was over half full by 3:10 that day. A prelude of classical music was being played composed by Franz Shubert, entitled, 'Ave Maria.' Friends and guests were still coming into the church to see Randy Johnson and Beth Miller get married. Amanda Phillips, the wedding director was already speaking to some of the wedding participants that had already arrived.

Sheriff Alan Hicks and his wife were already seated. Sitting next to them was Marcus Hendrix and Patricia Anderson. At least nine of Beth's co-workers, including their spouses and her supervisor were there to see Beth get married. Two deputy sheriffs and their spouses were in attendance.

It looked to Amanda Phillips that it would be an overflowing crowd of people to attend the wedding. She looked at her participant list at 3:30; she was relieved that everyone had shown up.

Wedding music was being played to set the stage for the upcoming wedding.

Beth Miller was already in a private room getting dressed for her wedding. Maid of Honor, Felicia Smith, Beth's co-worker was assisting her with her wedding dress and for anything else Beth needed her for.

Invited guests had already been seated. Randy Johnson, best man and Reverend Jake Stryker entered the room from a side door and took their places at the ceremonial space; they turned toward the guests. Ushers escorted the grooms' parents to the second row, on the right side of the aisle. As practiced the prior day, Amanda Phillips was going to ensure that all other participants were to enter on cue. Mrs. Phillips eagerly checked her watch to see when the processional music would start. At 3:50 Mrs. Dora Eason, Beth's mother was escorted next to the aisle on the left side of the second row. Other close kin were already seated on the third and fourth row, respective of their kin location.

Mable Lang, Randy's Aunt was sitting in the middle of the chapel. She came from thirty miles away to see Randy and Beth get married. She is Randy Johnson's only Aunt. Danny and Shelia were seated next to Mr. and Mrs. Henry Miller, John Miller's parents. Tears were in Dora Eason's eyes as she waited impatiently for her daughter to come walking down the aisle. Tommy Lewis, Toni Lynn, his sister and their mother were in attendance. Tommy had already spied out Shelia sitting beside Danny Miller. Shelia happened to look his way; Tommy gave her a big smile.

At four o'clock the processional music commenced; Mrs. Margie Riggs, music coordinator played a song sung by Henry Purcell, entitled Trumpet Tune. All wedding participants, in their proper sequence, walked down the aisle toward the front of the church.

After they were all standing in their proper positions, the Bridal Chorus echoed throughout the room. Beth Miller and her father appeard at the entrance way of the room. All heads turned toward Beth and her father as they walked slowly down the aisle. Beth looked beautiful in her Sue Wong, Ivory Empire, and Waist-lace Gown. She and her father continued to walk forward until she stood in front of Reverend Stryker.

Reverend Stryker looked toward the guests momentarily. "Ladies and gentlemen, boys and girls, we are gathered here today in the sight of God, and in the face of this company, to join together Randy Johnson and Beth Miller in holy matrimony, which is an honorable estate, instituted by God. Therefore, it is not to be entered inadvisably or lightly, but reverently and soberly. Into this holy estate these two persons present come now to be joined. Who then gives this woman to this man?" Mr. George Eason answered, "Her mother and I." Mr. Eason turned around; he walked back to the second row and took a seat beside his wife.

Danny leaned forward as Reverend Stryker continued with the marriage protocol. Suddenly, he realized the bond between his mother and his father was about to be broken. Tears slid down his face as he listened closely at Reverend Stryker's words. Delores Miller noticed the tears in her grandson's eyes. She handed him a tissue to wipe away his tears, and then she placed her hand on his.

Reverend Stryker continued on with the protocol of the wedding. Occasionally he would read scriptures from the Bible that correlated to marriage and its vows. At the close of the wedding ceremony the minister joins their hands together and said, "Let no man put asunder in as much as Randy and Beth have consented together in holy wedlock, and have witnessed the same before God and this company, having given and pledged binding love and devotion to each the other and having declared same by giving and receiving of a ring, I pronounce you man and wife. Seal the promises you have made with each other with a kiss." Danny and Shelia both stood up as Randy kissed his wife on her lips. Dora Eason closed her eyes in joy. George Eason cleared his throat, trying to contain his emotion. Henry and Delores Miller displayed broad smiles. "Ladies and gentlemen, I present to you Mr. and Mrs. Randy Johnson."

The wedding participants exited the room in the same manner as they had done during their rehearsal. Amanda Phillips, Wedding Director was beaming with joy for a flawless wedding ceremony. She couldn't have been happier as she congratulated the wedding participants.

About fifteen minutes later, everyone that participated in the wedding went back inside the church chapel so photographer, Carrie Wingate could take more pictures.

In the meantime, several individuals were outside doing a real number on Randy Johnson's car. Danny Miller happened to be one of those individuals. Toilet paper was waving in the wind from being stuck to various parts of the car. Shaving cream was smeared over much of the vehicle. The words, 'Just married' was written on the back glass.

Inside, Reverend Stryker called everyone to attention. "Ladies and gentlemen, I've been asked to remind everyone that the reception will be at Oakdale Country Club, six o'clock this evening. There will be food and music at this reception; everyone in attendance of this wedding is invited to attend. Thank you."

Thirty minutes later, mostly everyone was standing outside the church with their tiny bags of rice awaiting Randy and Beth to hurry toward their car through a two row passageway. All of a sudden, hand in hand, the newly married couple appeared on the entrance porch of the church. Randy and Beth were all smiles as they looked toward the cheering crowd. Danny and Shelia were standing near Randy's car. They were both very proud of their parents as they stood together, holding each other's hand. Beth and Randy position themselves for a short rush toward Randy's car. All at once, with their heads lowered they made a dash down through the crowd of well-wishers and rice throwers. They hurriedly opened the car doors and got inside. Beth and Randy were both waving at the crowd of well wishers as they sped away, dragging tin cans and milk cartons behind their car.

It was pre-arranged for Gorge and Dora Eason to take Danny and Shelia to the reception. George walked up to the two teenagers as they continued looking in the direction their parents had gone. "Danny, no matter how you look at it, you've got yourself a sister now," said George. "Shelia, I very much want to be your grandfather. Look over near the porch, Dora is in tears; she's so happy that she's got a granddaughter."

Shelia hurried over to where Mrs. Eason was standing. "Grandmother, please don't cry!"

"Oh, my goodness, Shelia, you called me grandmother!" Tears ran rampant down Dora's face as she hugged Shelia. George and Danny walked to where Dora and Shelia were embracing each other. "George, she called me Grandmother! I'm as happy as a human being can be! I've wanted a granddaughter for all these years, and now I have one!" George stood there; he couldn't have been more pleased knowing how happy his wife was. "Shelia, give your grandfather a big hug because he loves you too."

"Grandfather, lean over so I can give you a big hug!" Shelia remarked. George displayed a broad smile as she hugged his neck.

It was at this very time that Danny realized that Shelia could no longer be his girlfriend. He would have to settle for her being his sister. "What about me, Shelia, don't your brother get a hug?" Danny asked.

Tears came into Shelia's eyes. She, too, realized that the boyfriend/girlfriend relationship that she and Danny had was over for good. "Yes, Danny, my brother will always get a hug from me."

Nearly a hundred people were already inside the ballroom at Oakdale Country Club by 5:45 that evening. There were many more standing outside for one reason or another waiting to come inside. Randy and Beth's caterer, Missy Holliday had prepared a wide array of food that she and her staff had placed on two long tables. A locally known disc jockey, Mickey Phelps was already playing soft, relaxing music as guests continued to come into the ballroom. Henry and Delores Miller were seated at a table near the front of the room. George and Dora Eason were seated two tables across from them. Danny hurried to his grandparents table. Henry and Delores stood up. "Granddaddy, I just want you both to know that I love you both." Danny commented, tearfully.

"Son, we both know that---don't we Delores?"

"Yes, we do, Danny. I just want you to know that we're very happy for you, Shelia, Beth and your new father. From what I've heard, Beth couldn't have chosen a better man for her husband. Now, you give your grandparents a great big hug." Danny did just that.

"Danny, you make sure we get a big hug from our granddaughter before we leave tonight."

"I will, grandma. I sure will! Granddaddy, don't forget to take me golfing sometime."

"The nest time I take you golfing------well, I hope my golf game will be a little better."

"I hope so, too----grandpa." Danny said, smiling. Henry nodded his head back and forth, him thinking about Danny's comment.

Mable Lang was all smiles as she entered the door at Oakdale Country Club. She knew she couldn't stay too long because she didn't like to drive at night. She was determined to stay long enough to see and congratulate Randy and his new wife.

Danny was talking to Marcus Hendrix and his girlfriend, Patricia Anderson. Shelia was envying the large wedding cake that was sitting on a round table. Tommy Lewis spotted Shelia as she looked up and down at the several layer cake. He hurried to where she was standing. "Hello, Shelia," Tommy commented. "You look very pretty in your new dress."

"Thank you for saying that." She smiled. "Where is your mother?"

"She's at a table with my father and sister. Your mother looked very pretty in her wedding dress."

"Thank you, Tommy. Look at this magnificent cake, isn't it beautiful?"

"It's beautiful, but not as beautiful as you are," Tommy commented, blushing. "Do you suppose Danny will be mad for me talking with you? I hate to say it, but I'm a little bit afraid of him. He's a mite dangerous when he gets mad."

"Why should he get mad? I'm free to talk with anyone I want to. Besides, since his mother married my daddy------well, it's more like we're now sister and brother."

"Don't you like Danny anymore?"

"Are you crazy? I love Danny, but more like my brother than a boyfriend!"

"Uh oh, Danny is coming this way," Tommy uttered. "I'll bet he's going to be mad!"

Danny walked up to Tommy and Shelia. "Shelia, Grandpa wanted me to tell you that he had packed your suitcases and mine into the trunk of his car for our trip home tonight. Tommy, isn't this a beautiful little lady?"

Shocked to the core with Danny's candor, Tommy answered, "She's about the prettiest thing that I've ever seen!"

"Tommy, are your parents with you this evening?"

"Yes, they're sitting at a table with my sister."

"Sister, I didn't know you had a sister? Shelia, did you know that Tommy had a sister?"

"Yes. She's a very pretty girl."

"I'll introduce you to my parents and my sister, Toni Lynn," said Tommy. Danny and Shelia followed Tommy to his parent's table. "Mother, Father, Toni Lynn, I would like for you to meet two of my friends, Danny Miller and Shelia Johnson." Tommy's parents stood up. "The big guy is my father, Roland Lewis and the lovely woman is my mother, Margie Lewis. That pretty, blonde-headed, blue-eyed girl sitting at the table is my thirteen year old sister." Danny's eyes opened wide; he was mesmerized by her beauty.

Toni Lynn stood up. She said, "Shelia, it was a beautiful wedding. The very thought of two people united in marriage brought me to tears. Danny, I know you're thrilled to have a new sister."

"Yes, I'm very thrilled. I never knew that Tommy had a sister, especially a very beautiful sister," Danny commented. "Mr. and Mrs. Lewis, it was very nice meeting you. Gosh, Toni Lynn, I hope to see you again real soon."

"Wow!" Toni Lynn mumbled as Danny and Shelia walked toward Henry and Delores Miller.

"What was that, dear?" Mrs. Lewis asked.

"That was one fine looking boy!" Toni Lynn commented. "I hope he'll come back and dance with me sometime tonight."

Danny and Shelia stopped at his grandparents table. "Shelia, I want you to meet our other grandparents, Mr. and Mrs. Henry Miller.

Henry and Delores gathered around Danny and Shelia. Tearfully, Delores hugged Shelia's neck. "Grandmother, please don't cry."

"Henry, she called me grandmother!" She hugged Shelia's neck again.

"Mrs. Miller, I'm very happy that I have two grandmothers now."

"How about a big hug for me, Henry asked."

Shelia hugged Henry's neck. "I'm, also, glad that I have two grandfathers now." She smiled.

"Granddaddy, I guess we had better go see some of my mother and father's guest now, but we'll visit you again before we leave tonight.

"Ok, Danny and thank you for bringing our new granddaughter to our table."

Mickey Phelps picked up his microphone at 6:30 and said, "Ladies and gentlemen, boys and girls please let me have your attention! I just got word that our newlyweds just drove into the parking lot. Please------everyone turn toward the entrance way and be prepared to give our honored guests a thunderous applause!" For a few seconds there was absolute quiet. All at once the door opened and there stood Randy and Beth Johnson. Everyone cheered and clapped their hands as the couple made their way into the room. Mickey immediately played a song by Elvis Presley, named "Such a Night'.

George and Dora Eason stood toward the front line. Beth quickly hugged her mother and father when she got to them. "Mother, I'm so happy!" Beth remarked.

"Your father and I are very happy as well," said Dora. "Randy, we're proud to have you as our son-in-law."

"Thank you very much, Mrs. Eason. I'm very excited to become a part of your family."

Danny and Shelia were standing a little farther away, but Randy and Beth spotted them in the crowd. They hurried to their children. Beth placed her arms around Shelia and Danny at the same time. "I want each of you to know that I love you a great deal."

Tearfully, Randy hugged Shelia and Danny. "For years I have wanted a son and there's no one I rather have for a son than you, Danny. I want to be a father figure to you, but I'll never try to replace your own father. No one can do that, but I will love you as if you were my very own child."

"I appreciate that, Mr. Johnson."

Randy looked around until he spotted his Aunt. "Beth, come this way----I want you to meet my only Aunt."

"Mable Lang saw Randy about the same time he saw her. Displaying a broad smile, she hurried toward him. "Aunt Lang, this is my beautiful wife, Beth."

"Well, Randy------you've got yourself a very lovely wife."

"Thank you, Mrs. Lang for that nice compliment." We're very glad that you came to our wedding. Did you drive here by yourself?"

"Yes I certainly did-----which reminds me that I need to be leaving in a few minutes. I don't like driving very far at night, especially thirty miles."

Randy and Beth took turns hugging his Aunt's neck. "Randy, I want you and Beth to come visit me sometime after your honeymoon."

"You have my promise that we will do just that. Have a safe drive home-----and remember I love you a great deal."

"I know that, Randy------I've always known that. Goodbye and have a wonderful honeymoon. Beth, it was a pleasure meeting you." Mable Lang headed for the front door.

"Your aunt is a very nice lady."

"Yes, she certainly is." Randy commented, smiling.

A few minutes later, Mickey Phelps picked up his microphone. "Ladies and gentlemen, please let me have your attention for just a moment! "Food has been provided by Mr. and Mrs. Randy Johnson for your eating pleasure. Eat, drink, and dance at your will. There is one other thing that I will ask someone to do. Mr. and Mrs. Randy Johnson, please come to the dance floor and dance to a popular tune by Celine Dion named, "Because You Loved Me." Everyone starting clapping their hands to get the newlyweds to the dance floor. With gracious smiles, Randy held Beth's hand as they walked toward the dance floor. Mickey voiced loudly, "Folks, let's give our newlyweds a round of applause as they make their way to the dance floor." Nearly everyone had their eyes turned toward Randy and Beth as they danced gracefully to the sound of the music. Danny hugged Shelia's neck for a couple seconds as they watched their parent's performance. After the song had stopped, Mickey picked up his microphone. "Ladies and gentlemen, it just doesn't get any better than that! Let's give them another round of applause for their dancing skills."

A few minutes later, Tommy Lewis came to Henry Miller's table where Shelia and Danny were sitting. "Grandpa, Grandma, this boy is Tommy Lewis," said Danny.

Henry and Delores shook hands with Tommy. "Son, it's a pleasure meeting you." Henry commented."

"It's my pleasure----indeed." Tommy answered. Nervously, Tommy turned toward Shelia and asked, "Will you dance with me, if it's okay with Danny?"

"Yes, I would be glad to dance with you. Danny, why don't you ask Toni Lynn to dance with you?"

"I know she will, Danny," Tommy remarked. "In fact, she wanted me to ask you if you would dance with her."

Tommy took Shelia by her hand and led her to the dance floor. Henry didn't say anything right off; he kept observing Danny to see how he reacted to Shelia dancing with someone else. Finally, Henry couldn't contain his thoughts any longer. "Danny, is Toni Lynn a pretty girl?"

"Yes sir, she's very pretty!"

"Delores and I would like for you to dance with her, that is-------unless you're afraid to ask her."

"Grandpa, I'm not afraid to ask her to dance with me! In fact, I'll go do it right now!" He walked hurriedly to where Toni Lynn was sitting. Danny looked her square in her eyes and asked, "Would you care to dance with me?"

"Yes! I was hoping you would ask me." Danny took her hand and then led her to the dance floor.

As they were dancing, Toni Lynn said, "Danny, you sure do have a pretty sister."

"Thank you very much. I was just thinking how pretty you are."

"Gee Danny, I appreciate you saying that I'm pretty," Toni Lynn remarked. "You sure are a good dancer."

"My goodness-----so are you."

Mickey Phelps picked up his microphone at 8:15. "Ladies and gentlemen, please let me have your attention once more. Before anyone cuts that beautiful wedding cake, it's my honor and privilege to ask Mrs. Beth Johnson and her father, Mr. George Eason to come to the dance floor.

You know folks, there's an old custom in our country that whenever a father gives away his daughter, well----he's allowed to dance with her one more time." The crowd burst into laughter. George Eason led his daughter toward the dance floor. "Folks, let's give this father and daughter a thunderous applause." People were cheering and clapping their hands. "Mr. Eason and his beautiful daughter will be dancing to a familiar tune entitled, 'Daddy's Little Girl', by Michael Buble." Mickey started the song.

As they commence dancing, Beth noticed tears in her father's eyes. She whispered, "Daddy, I love you very much."

"I know that, sweetheart. I've always known that you loved me and your mother. I just want you to know that we're very proud of you."

"How about that, folks? Let's show our appreciation to Mr. Eason and his daughter for their marvelous performance on the dance floor."

Randy and Beth were busy talking to their guests. They didn't even realize that Shelia and Danny were dancing, but not with each other.

A short while later. George Eason walked up to Beth and Randy and said, "I've got Danny and Shelia's suitcases in my car. We'll be driving home tonight after the cake cutting, and after you two hit the road. I don't care to drive late at night."

"Mr. Eason, watch out for Shelia and Danny; I wouldn't want them to get hurt or anything."

"Randy, Dora and I will take very good care of them."

Mickey Phelps picked up his microphone. "It's time now ladies and gentlemen for the traditional cake cutting. We've got to get this pair of newlyweds on their way to wherever they're going on their honeymoon. Please assemble yourselves near that big, magnificent looking wedding cake. Just remember, after the bride and groom have left, the party still goes on until 10:30 tonight."

Randy and Beth readied themselves near the cake. They both held the long knife blade as it sliced through the cake. They each tasted the cake, and then they gave each other another piece of cake. Danny and Beth were all smiles as Missy Holliday, Delores Miller and Dora Eason helped to pass out slices from the large cake.

Randy and Beth left the ballroom a few minutes later to change their clothes in individual rooms for their trip to the beach. After dressing, they came back into the ballroom to say goodbye to their children, parents, and other well wishers. It took them a few more minutes to say goodbye to everyone, including their children and parents. Randy and Beth waved one more time as they exited the country club.

Standing with his wife, George Eason told Danny and Shelia that it was time to drive home.

After George had driven a few miles toward home, Dora realized that Shelia and Danny were not talkative at all. "Did you young teenagers have a great time at the reception?"

Danny spoke first. "Grandma, I had a great time dancing and being with Toni Lynn Lewis. Did you notice how pretty she was?"

"Well, yes I did," Dora answered. "Her brother is a very good looking boy, isn't he Shelia?"

"He sure is, Grandmother," she answered, smiling. "Isn't that something, a brother and sister liking a brother and his sister?"

"George, did you get all that?" Dora asked, smiling.

"I believe I did. We truly have ourselves two genuine grandchildren now."

Randy and Beth had been on the road for twenty minutes. It would be another hour and fifteen minutes before they reached their destination at the beach. "Mrs. Johnson, you were the prettiest woman in that church today. I'm the happiest person in the whole world."

"I appreciate you saying that, Randy. Did you notice Danny and Shelia tonight?"

"What do you mean?" Randy inquired.

"Danny seemed infatuated with Toni Lynn and Shelia with Toni Lynn's brother, Tommy."

"Yes, I noticed that, but I expected this sort of thing to happen all along."

"You did?"

"Yes. Danny and Shelia are going through a transition period; they're becoming bonded together as brother and sister. I didn't expect it to happen until we all started living under the same roof." Randy reached over and placed his hand in hers. "We're going to have a great life together, you, me and our two kids. Beth, I've got some real good news."

"What news is that?

"Sharon Brooks, my realtor called me at nine o'clock this morning to tell me that someone was buying my house. It's a pretty sure thing because the buyer paid her ten thousand dollars to retain the house until the deed and paper work could be handled by the person's lawyer. She asked me if I could be out of my house within thirty days. I told her that wouldn't be a problem at all."

"That's wonderful news," Beth remarked. "I have some good news myself. My realtor placed a sold sign on my house yesterday. She'll have my money available for me when I return from our honeymoon. She didn't say how long I had before I would have to move, but I imagine it will be about thirty days."

"We'll start the moving process soon as we get back home," Randy commented. "I'm looking forward to living in that big house."

Randy and Beth arrived at Mr. Spears' house at 11:30 that night. As Mr. Spears had said, the key was under a large stone near the entrance to the house. It took Randy and Beth awhile to check out all the other rooms to ensure no one else was inside the house. "Beth, this big bedroom is the large bedroom that Mr. Spears told you that no one had ever used. This will be our bridal suite while we're here. Randy made two trips to the car for their luggage.

An hour later, Randy had taken his shower and was lying naked underneath a thin sheet. Thoughts of passion raced through his mind, him envisioning his wife standing naked inside the nearby shower. He was very anxious for her to come to bed. Finally, he saw her standing in the doorway with nothing on, but a see through night gown. He took in a deep breath, realizing his inner-desires were about to be fulfilled. Beth lay down beside her husband. Randy reached over and turned off the small table lamp.

Printed in the United States
By Bookmasters